Angels do leave footprints

by

Robert J Moon

Dedication

For my supportive inherited family.
For our dear friends and for those who live and give from their hearts.

ISBN 978-0-578-86600-0

Table of Contents

It Begins

Scott had awakened this Saturday morning just as he had every other morning…with a smile. His dishwater blonde hair was tousled "bed-head" partly covering his green eyes. He lightly licked his lips with a gentle "smack", rolled over onto his right side to gaze at his "life partner" (as he called it) lying beside him. He thought Alex to be so handsome. His thick black hair, flawless morning scruff, defined jawline, olive complexion. He thought to himself "how did I get so lucky with such a handsome and kind, loving man?" He reflected how they had met four years ago at the gym.

*****

Scott was on his way out of the Pacific Heights Health Club after his intense workout, steam and shower. After chatting with Rick, the handsome self-admittedly bi-sexual who always flirted with more men than women, he turned and saw him. The guy doing sit-ups with one of those ab-rollers. After a few moments of a quandary about whether he should go say hi or not, battling over if he could handle the rejection, how to introduce himself…he concluded and muttered to himself, "Oh WTF! The worst he could say is no". He pushed himself forward and took twelve steps until he was standing next to him. He looked down watching the sweaty guy grit his teeth as he forced himself up with his eyes tightly closed, then slowly moved down to a lying position. He paused and looked up to see someone standing next to him.
"Hi! My name's Scott. And you are?"
He paused looking up to Scott and let go of the sides of the ab roller and sat up. "Alex" he replied panting while smiling and flashing his

straight white teeth as a few trickles of sweat ran down his temples. His forehead glistened with tiny beads of moisture.
"Nice to meet you. I haven't seen you here in the gym before. Did you recently join?"
"No. I've been coming here for about three months."
"Oh really? Funny…I haven't seen you here before."
"I've seen you. You're always talking to everyone. I was just waiting for you to get to me." He quipped with a tone of friendly sarcasm.
Scott thought to himself, "He's a funny one. Wow." Then asked, "would you like to have lunch tomorrow?" He took a chance.
"Sure!" replied Alex.
"How about noon? We can meet at the corner of Fillmore and Sacramento. I know a great little place. You like Italian?" He knew Vivande Porta Via would be the perfect spot. Exposed brick walls, cozy little wooden tables, white tablecloths, candle votive in glass containers, with tasty California-Italian styled cuisine.
"Great. I'll see you then" replied Alex coolly yet with a warm grin while looking Scott in the eyes. Scott reached out, and they shook hands. A flash. Breath stopped. Heart pounded. Time stopped for a moment. He knew it right then. This was the one. He nodded to Alex with confirmation, smiled, "Okay then" he said. He took a step back then turned to head out. He felt like his world just changed, and not sure why.

He just smiled and started thinking about what he would wear. He promised himself, this was not going to be like his last relationship. Happy start…then the abuse. That was a story of its own. He bounced in his steps as he drifted out on his cloud leaving the gym with an air of hope and anticipation. He tried to hold it back as much as he could, yet he kept smiling.

*****

It was time for lunch with Alex. Scott walked a few blocks from his apartment at Sacramento and Steiner to the corner of Fillmore. He was punctual and smiling as he neared the corner to see Alex was already there sporting khakis, black loafers, a Gap blue button-down shirt, with a black belt. As he closed in, he noticed his hair was perfectly gelled. He stood 5ft 10, a very fit 180 pounds. He

spied a bit of his black chest hair peeking through the two undone buttons of his shirt. He looked into Alex's warm brown eyes.
"Hey!" Scott happily exclaimed. "It's so nice to see you. I'm glad you accepted lunch. There's a place just down the street here, Vivande. It's a cute little Italian restaurant. Would that work for you?"
"Sure," replied Alex. He smiled back. He also wondered why Scott was wearing a double-breasted suit. He very undetectably surveyed Scott up and down and asked "Um…Why are you so dressed up?"
Scott realized he was wearing his light brown Armani suit. He had just bought the Ferragamo brown shoes on sale at Saks Fifth Avenue two weeks ago. "Sorry. I have two vendor meetings later today. I'm in retail and the meetings are a bit formal, so I had to dress the part."
"Vendor meetings?"
"oh...yes. I'll share over lunch."
"Oh. Good. I thought I might have missed something. You kinda look like you're headed for an interview or something," he chuckled nervously.
"Nah. And I am not trying to impress you. I promise." He lied. "By the way…I'm sorry. I didn't ask your last name."
"Galway. Alex Galway. What about yours?"
"Scott Rupert".
"Nice to meet you, Scott Rupert."
"Nice to meet you, Alex Galway. Ready for lunch?"
"Sure. I'm starving. Let's head."

As they headed to their lunch destination, they shared some of each other's history. Alex started talking stating he was Black Irish from Canada. He was in the U.S. on an H1B visa working for a friend of his. He shared mentioned his family and siblings. He had three brothers and a sister. His parents divorced when he was young and they both remarried. He and his brothers and sister stayed with their mom, Karen, and were pretty much raised by their stepdad, Brian. He joked as one of his brothers loved genealogy and obsessively studied their family having discovered the name "Brian" meant "noble, high man" and was derived from the Celtic element 'bre' which means "hill". There was more to it, but he moved the topic to Scott.

As Scott was preparing to share about himself, they arrived at Vivande. It was a quiet day in the restaurant. There were only two available tables occupied of the thirty. Anthony, the restaurant

owner, was just near the door, and greeted Scott with a warm smile, opening his arms.
“Scott! So good to see you again! Welcome back! It’s been a few weeks.” He moved in with his open arms to hug Scott in his bold Italian manner. “And you bring someone with you!" He looked at Alex. "I am Anthony. My wife, Giselle…she’s there behind the counter,” he shared as he moved towards Alex while motioning to his wife to come out. “Giselle! Come out here to see Scott and his friend!” Giselle smiled, removed her latex gloves as she was handling food for a take-out order. She brushed her wispy thick grayish and dark blonde hair back behind her ears and shoulder. She stood five foot six and was of the modest petite build. She donned a cream-colored apron with sunflowers that covered her white button-down shirt and black slacks. As she neared, you could see the light in her bluish-green eyes twinkle with resounding happiness. “Oh, hello! So nice to see you again, Scott,” she stated graciously.
Anthony looked to Alex, “Who are you? What’s your name?”
Alex looked into Anthony’s deep brown smiling eyes. He could see that Anthony was in his 60’s, balding, about his height. He was just shy of his height. His white shirt and black pants seemed to be the matching uniform of the place, only he wore a tie loosely knotted with the top button undone. “Alex”.
Anthony moved in and hugged Alex, as Alex reciprocated. He felt a little surprised, yet comfortable with the warm salutations.
Giselle moved in and hugged them both, kissed them both on each side of their cheeks, “So good to see you.”
“You here for lunch, I see? I give you a nice little table in the corner by the window. Come, come!” He motioned both Scott and Alex towards the table ushering them to their seats. “How about a nice glass of Pinot Grigio?”
Scott looked at Alex and raised his eyebrows inquiring if this was acceptable. “Sure!” replied Alex. “Great!” added Scott. Giselle placed some water glasses on the tables and placed two menus on the table. I’ll be right back. Anthony and Giselle walked away to give the couple a moment.
“Wow. They're so nice,” cited Alex.
“Yeah. I’ve been coming here for a couple of years. Not all the time. I just like the place, and the food is really good.”

“Nice spot.” Alex glanced over the menu and spied what he wanted. “I am in the mood for rigatoni with Bolognese and a small salad.”
“That was fast,” stated Scott as he perused the menu. “I think I’ll have the ravioli and a small salad as well. That was easy,” he commented smiling.
Giselle returned with the generously poured glasses of Pinot Grigio and a small decanter for refreshing the glasses. She took their orders and whisked back to the open kitchen.
Scott and Alex resumed their conversation. Scott shared his being a “military brat” with his father having been in the Air Force. They moved across the country and lived in Germany for a few years. Similar to Alex, he shared his dad, Nicholas was married to Kris, his stepmom, and that his natural mother had died when he was about a year and a half. Scott had two half-brothers and a full brother. The brothers were estranged. Scott added called his parents almost every other week. He was constantly trying to build his relationship with them. They had problems with his coming out being gay. He really wanted to build that bridge and hoped that one day they would grow like so many other parents with gay children.

Their food arrived. They continued talking, laughed at each other’s stories. The next thing they knew and realized, it was just over two hours later, and they had the day yet ahead of them.
“This was a wonderful time,” shared Scott.
“Thank you for such a great lunch,” Alex added. “Do you think we can do this again?” he hoped.
“Absolutely! My shop is just down another block across the street. 'Scott’s Closet'. I am in and out all day,” he joked hoping Alex would catch the pun and that it wasn’t too lame a reference.
“Great!” Maybe I’ll stop by some time?” He missed it.
“Anytime,” Scott replied indicating an open door for Alex.
They hugged and almost kissed, but both thought it too soon. They were tempted but held back.
“See you later at the gym?” asked Scott.
“Absolutely,” replied Alex.
They both turned and walked their opposite ways. Neither noticed, but both looked back at the other separately. Both felt their worlds changed.
Nine months later, they were a couple.

*****

Scott gently raised his hand from beneath the warm comforter, reached over, and lightly tickled Alex's ear. Alex twitched his head and brushed his hand over his ear hoping sleepily for relief. Scott then began to lightly blow into his ear. He wanted attention from his lover. Grinning…Alex opened his sleepy brown eyes, rolled over, pulled Scott's head to his and they began to passionately kiss. This was Scott's idea of the beginning of a perfect day.

Coffee was brewing and its aroma floated through the house while Scott and Alex got dressed and polished for the beautiful June day that lay ahead. Khakis and button-down shirts with loafers seemed to be the theme of the day for them both. However, Alex was always making sure their outfits did not match. He loathed matching outfits. He would go out of his way to make sure matching didn't happen in any way. If Scott wore a blue shirt, Alex would wear a different color plaid shirt. If Scott was wearing black shoes, Alex would opt for a different color. He did not want to be "twins" like some of the other gay couples seem to do. Not that it was bad or wrong, it simply was not Alex's style. He would periodically remind Scott, and make sure to ask whether for the day or to some event or dinner.

"You want to meet me for lunch today?" asked Scott.

"I wish. I have some errands I have to run," replied Alex.

"Why don't we run errands together? We could kind of play around for the day, do some shopping, grab a bite, catch a movie…you know…just hang out."

Alex thought fondly of what Scott was saying. It had been about two months since they had spent a day like that. Their schedules were crazy with activities, events, and the frequency of friends and family visiting with them. And on top of all that, their workloads. It was not that they minded. It simply did not leave much quality time for just the two of them. Alex looked sweetly at Scott, and thoughtfully replied, "You know…I would love to. However, you have to go to the store, and I have some picture development to complete. It's your night to close the shop instead of Troy, and I'm trying to get the next few sets of prints ready for some clients by the end of next week as promised. How about you and I doing our day tomorrow? Sunday. You can have Troy cover the store for you."

"You're right. Great idea," replied Scott. "Tomorrow. It's a date."

*****

Sunday morning arrived. Alex and Scott felt a little giddy preparing for the day they had planned together. They showered, groomed, and dressed as if it were their first date. Scott changed his shirt several times. Alex changed his khakis to shorts, then back to khakis. Finally, he decided on jeans. Once ready, they moved downstairs to their kitchen nook for a light breakfast consisting of coffee, some fruit, English muffins, or whole-wheat toast. Sometimes they would add eggs, but not today. As Alex was sipping his coffee with cream and sugar, Scott quietly asked,
"What's today? I feel like I am forgetting something but not sure what...." sipping his coffee with cream. He had a slightly panicked look in his eyes as he was working to remember something. Alex thought for a moment. He grinned, thinking that they finally had a day to relax together. He was thinking after errands maybe they could watch a movie they could play in the VCR, get caught up on the laundry, and take care of the dishes in the dishwasher. Brandon would handle the rest of the cleaning when he comes Monday. Then cautiously replied,
"*Su-u-unday. June 3rd, 2001...why?*" Suddenly, he paused thinking. Scott nudged his leg, smiled back, and asked,
"I know that you little shit. I mean, what is the *DATE* today? When is your sister supposed to arrive? Didn't she call out-of-the-blue about a couple of weeks ago? You kind of blew it off. I remember you hung up and said '*Right. That's gonna happen*', yet agreed to it." Mimicking Alex's sarcastic tone and mannerisms like he was over it.
"HOLY SHIT!!" resounded from Alex's mouth with such frustration that it made Scott lightly shrink into his chair while clutching his cup of life and making that "*OMIGOD I could totally just die*" scrunched look on his face. "I cannot believe I forgot about my sister visiting! Damn it all!" Panic set in. Alex then started rattling off the things they needed to do. "You know this means we have to go shopping, get the room ready for her, and you know what?!? Screw the rest of the house. Brandon can take care of what's left, tomorrow." He paused. Then a thought came to him. "We also have to get her a gift. I love doing that for her. It's been a while since I've given her something nice. Maybe she'll open up a bit. It's been a while. We can stop by Saks. Then...because I am so

wiped…I just want to spend whatever time we have left, alone with you before she arrives. At home, or if you want, we can go to a movie. Okay? Store…movie?" Scott reached to the back of Alex's head, and lightly rubbed his hair, then ran the back of his fingers down Alex's cheek while looking at his handsome profile with affection.

"Saks, huh? Well okay then. You're disgustingly sweet to her no matter what. I love that about you, among other things," said Scott with affection He then asked, "How come I am the luckiest guy in the world?"

Alex replied, "you know something? I think we both are." Alex picked up Scott's hand and kissed the back of it then lowered it to rest on his thigh. Crisis averted, he thought to himself. They strategized over breakfast and enjoyed each other's company for the following hour.

After finishing their breakfast and chit-chatting about the political events that drove them both crazy, they began the routine of preparing the house for their visitor scheduled to arrive Tuesday. After they picked up the house and finished dishes, they headed to conquer the guest room. They had to change the sheets, fluff the pillows, and noticed the porn left behind from Dave and his friend Jake from Sonoma.

"David And Goliath and the magical Sling" muttered Scott as he read the video cover with great intrigue. He was always amazed how porn companies could twist actual movie and story titles into creative porn plots. He noticed the others underneath. "You've got male," "A few hard men." The titles always made Scott and Alex laugh. This video had the side view image of a sling that held an oiled-up nude muscle god fit for any hot Calvin Klein ad, while another profiled leather accessorized muscular Adonis stood holding up the sling-ed man's feet above his head.

"Hey, Alex. Did you ever hear about the magical sling in the David and Goliath story?" yelled Scott to Alex who was replenishing the towels and paper products in the guest bath.

"Um…I plead the fifth. I had some crazy times at university. You know how us Canadians are," replied Alex jokingly. "Your fifth amendment saves us!" he laughs.

"Gurl! One day you are gonna share a bit more about the stories of your college days," Scott quipped back. Then he added, "I don't

know why Dave always leaves videos behind. Think it's a hint of some kind?" he joked.
"Oh, who knows" he replied waving his hand. "They're always so much fun and ***always*** have the best valley hotel gossip," Alex snickered.

After they finished the basic housework, enough for Brandon to handle the rest Monday, they wrote their grocery list together, checking and cross-checking between them. They always tried to stick to the list to avoid unnecessary items that Alex sometimes seemed to try to throw into the cart. Scott was always focused on the mission at hand when it came to shopping. Alex, on the other hand, enjoyed wandering and perusing the aisles pondering the meal possibilities he could make that week. Procrastination and schedules conflicted with what he hoped to do, versus what reality would afford. He simply wasn't time conscious. They returned home, put away the groceries, and then decided on a movie. It was a classic black and white movie day. "Stage Door" from 1937 with Katherine Hepburn, Ginger Rogers, and Lucille Ball in her early days. Alex and Scott agreed it was one of the greats. They laid on each other on the loveseat in the family room just off the garden while munching on the popcorn Scott made. Afterward, they moved to do some light garden clean-up and swept. At the end of the day, they ordered a pizza from Giorgio's on Clement street. A large pepperoni and mushroom with the crust extra crispy. Sometimes they ordered the large anti-pasta salad…sometimes not. Tonight, the salad was craved by them both. After eating, they sat on the sofa in each other's arms and watched the news. They dozed off, waking around eleven pm. They nudged each other and groggily moved upstairs. After completing their bedtime routine they climbed to bed.
"Thanks for the lovely day, Schmoo," shared Scott complimentarily.
"Same to you, Smoo" replied Alex. He leaned over, kissed him, then snuggled and spooned with Scott as they both fell asleep.

The Arrival

It was Tuesday. Alex's sister, Michelle, arrived from Chicago. When flying in, she was always amazed at the beauty of San Francisco from overhead. She loved how the city seemed to be constructed right on the water. She became even more enamored as her airport shuttle seemed to fly through the 6th Street exit into the city. It seemed as though the shuttle raised as if floating, enabling passengers to survey the magical city and impressive skyline. As they navigated the streets, neighborhoods, and avenues, she soaked in the Victorian and Edwardian-styled homes. She adored the colorful painted ladies with rich histories. She was glad to have refused Scott and Alex's offer to pick her up at the airport. She liked the shuttle. They would interrupt her quiet experience with their stories distracting her from the scenery and views. She also enjoyed taking the shuttle because she also loved how people would start talking amongst each other sharing who they were visiting. Some were returning home and they expressed how much they missed being away from their Emerald City. Scott had teased her in the past to be a *"nosey parker"*. He held a similar flair with people. It was amazing the last time when they met for the first time, they were, as Alex proclaimed *"chatty Cathys."* Usually that was what Scott referenced Alex to be. However, when Scott and Michelle got together…. chit-chat-chat-chitchat. This visit was a little different. She needed these quiet moments on the shuttle before she could tell them her news. It had been a while since they had spoken. The timing of her messaging was on her mind.

Michelle couldn't help noticing a nice-looking man sitting in the row just in front of her to the left.

“Hi. My names’ Michelle,” she smiled as she tapped him on his shoulder.
“Gabriel.” The piercing blue-eyed, unshaven square-jawed man replied turning around to look at her. He ran his manicured hands through his thick brown hair while flashing his perfectly bleached white grin. He quickly surveyed her.
“You live here in San Francisco?” asked Michelle. She tried desperately not to let on how handsome she thought he was and worked to hide her interest. It was his eyes that caught her.
“Yeah. Lived here all my life. It’s paradise, you know. I take it you’re visiting. Slight accent. Midwest?” He turned his body so he could face her a little easier. There was room given no one was next to him.
“Chicago, actually. That was fast. Very good. I’m impressed,” she replied. She was, too. She had lived in Chicago since she had escaped from a moment in her past, which haunts her now and then. She also took French lessons to avoid acquiring that nasal Midwest sound. She was determined given she already had a Canadian accent that would be pronounced when she had a little too much to drink. Adding the “nasal flare” as she called it was something she just didn’t want. She loved it from the midwesterners she knew. She just didn’t want to murk her Canadian influence. French was perfect, given the Quebecoise aspect of her culture.
“Ah. No secret to it really. I have some friends in the “Windy City”, and I spied your paper ticket in your hand,” he winked. “So how long are you visiting for?”
“A few weeks. My brother lives here. I've read so much about this city, and…well…who knows?” she replied with a hint of mystery. He stared out the window and lightly commented on how much he loved watching the fog roll in. They bantered back and forth in a friendly fashion yet with caution. They might never see each other again, so they kept it shallow. Michelle thought Gabriel was nice but could tell there was more to him. For some unknown reason, an alarm bell seemed to go off inside her.

The shuttle began to maneuver through all the street repairs nearing Fillmore just past Pine Street. Gabriel noticed they were nearing his Pacific Heights apartment.
“If you want, I’ll give you my number. Give me a call if you want to go on my dime tour,” he grinned through his offer. He thought he probably would not hear from this black-haired beauty; not that it

mattered. His dime-tour offerings gave him reason to tour the city to remind him of what this small metropolis had to offer.
“You know? That would be great.” She decided to ignore the alarm bells for now. She could always just walk away from him if she became annoyed, or if something seemed amiss. “I’ll be staying with my brother. I don’t want him to feel like he has to entertain me all the time while I’m here.”
“Great! Here's my card. And this is my stop.” The shuttle arrived at his apartment building on the corner of Jackson and Webster streets. The apartment building had a lower brick design and a light olive-toned taupe color painted stucco for the upper two stories with white trim. The traditional bay windows were aligned commanding the exterior focus of this charming apartment building. “See ya later!” he exclaimed as he leaped off the shuttle toward his domain.
Michelle felt a little excited. She reviewed his card. “Gabriel. Time is money.” To the right of the text was a profiled nude muscular man blowing a horn. “Curious,” she thought. Oh well. She was sure it meant something and would find out later. The shuttle made two more stops then reached hers. The shuttle driver confirmed her arrival.
“Your stop, miss. 2610 Sacramento. Need help with your bags?” It was three o’clock and they made good time.
“No. But, thanks though.” She opened the sliding shuttle door and clumsily hopped out. Her black hair flopped over her face while her fake Louis Vuitton fluttered forward while the shoulder strap slid to her elbow nook. “Why did I wear these damn pumps?” she muttered to herself, as she worked to quickly compose herself. She stumbled her way to the back of the blue and gold-colored van, opened the back door eyeing her two bags. A simple black Samsonite roller suitcase and a smaller matching square bag. “Of course, they would be at the bottom of the pile,” she whispered with frustration as she gave each a few heavy yanks freeing them from the other suitcases and bags without everything tumbling out. She sighed with relief as some fell into the vacant gaps. She closed the vehicle’s rear doors, knocked twice on the rear driver's side, waved to the diver in the mirror, and yelled “Thank you!” She turned as she composed the bags, then headed towards the stairs of the bright white with dark blue trim freshly painted 1929 stucco styled home. A beautiful magenta flowered bougainvillea rose from the corner next to the stairs, hugging the house. It was beautifully manicured and pruned

to grow as an accent above and around the garage door. As she began to head up the stairs, she took a deep breath. She looked at the regal mahogany-stained wood door with a horizontal series of three beveled glass windows about a foot and a half high each about 6 inches wide about a foot from the top of the door. "Here we go," she said to herself as she ascended towards the door. She reached the landing at the top of the stairs and pressed the doorbell located left of the door.
"*Bing-Bong. Bing-Bong*".
She waited for her hosts to open the door. She looked around and noticed a little envelope clipped to the mailbox with her name scribbled in blue ink. She pulled the envelope, and opened it to find a key and a little note:
"Hi, Michelle! Can't wait to see you when we get home. Lots to catch up on. Your room is all ready. Up the stairs turn right. It's the room in the front of the house. Help yourself in the kitchen if you're hungry. Just don't eat too much. Dinner is at 7 pm! XOXOXO Scott and Alex"
The note brought a warm light smile to her face. "Thank goodness I can have a little time to settle before the inquisition begins," she whispered to herself. She pulled the key from the envelope and luckily selected the deadbolt lock in which to snugly push it in. With a twist and a light push on the handle, the door gently swung open. She reached back and grabbed her luggage handle and her bag bringing both in behind her before closing the door.

She noticed Scott and Alex had made some cozy decorating choices to their rented home. The wood floors had recently been refinished. There were rich, light, warm architectural tones…cream and taupes with the molding painted stark white throughout. There was a simple beautiful Victorian oak armoire in the entryway with a small side table that housed a candle and a golden alabaster bowl holding different colored alabaster eggs. Next to them, a small vase with some baby purple iris, a few red, white, and yellow roses with a hint of green, and a sprig of eucalyptus. The living room, to the right of the entryway, had a comfy cream-colored thick-twilled styled sofa, an overstuffed ornate wood-trimmed burgundy velvet chair with a Mexican pine coffee table that she would later find concealed an entertaining and eclectic video library collection from view. There was a lovely painted fireplace with an elegantly framed and signed Léonore Fini above it. Hanging above the sofa, were two large pastels of abstract dancers she remembered one of her brothers had sold to Alex several years ago. There were two beautifully detailed small Gerard Brender Brandis prints perfectly positioned in antiqued gold wood frames, one on each side of the pastel dancers. The sofa faced the large sheer covered window bordered by gold-colored drapes and matching valance. Mexican pine coffee tables were on each side of the sofa. She could imagine the Christmas tree by the fireplace near the picture window during the holidays. As she headed towards the cherry wood stairs with the white painted molding, spindles, and the verathaned redwood handrail, she noticed the formal dining room to the left. There was a rectangular bureau against the wall in the room with stark white painted wades coating that was bordered with a generous dish lip atop. A contemporary brushed silver chandelier hung from the middle of the vaulted ceiling. The deco-styled rectangle expandable wood dining table with chairs that picked up the built-in trimmed themes could easily accommodate up to 10 for a sit-down meal. The kitchen was just past the dining room. Michelle decided she would visit there in a little bit. Right now, she needed to get settled. The artwork was impressively hung along the stairs wall covering almost every inch from the bottom of the stair molding to an inch from the ceiling. Student art, Jean Miro, Calder prints, and a few other artists adorned the wall. She carefully maneuvered her bags up the steps to avoid knocking any of the artwork. She was thankful for the gray-beige Berber runner so as not to hear the *'thunking'* of her bag.

Michelle reached her assigned room and immediately felt she was "home." The once rod-ironed bed now had a wood headboard, and a thick Pottery Barn quilt neatly folded on the foot of it covering the lovely off-white thick duvet that hugged a down comforter. There was a rectangular wood chest at the foot of the bed for an added look. The wood floors matched the main floor. There were matching wood shelves and a dresser that caught the glow of the late afternoon sun shining through the floor-length sheers and deep jewel-toned blue-green velvet panels. The afternoon lighting and wood tones enhanced the warm glow of the room. A few pieces of Canadian Inuit artwork hung on the walls. There were small area rugs and runners throughout the upstairs areas that absorbed the sound of her steps. She placed one of her bags on the bed and the other on the chest then began unpacking. As she hung her clothes in the modest hidden closet and loaded the drawers with her "unmentionables," she decided to take a quick shower. She contemplated a catnap before the boys returned home. She thought it might help clear her head. She needed to strategize how to tell them what she needed to. Some things had been kept secret for too long. They were the first of the family she planned to talk about what happened seven years ago. She felt a pit in her stomach and shook it off. She took a deep breath, grabbed her toiletries bag, and then headed for the bathroom just down the hall to shower.

*****

Scott was in his 1928 Fillmore Street shop, Scott's Closet when he happened to glance out the main display window while positioning some of his latest subtle adult toys and candles. He noticed an airport shuttle drive by. He glanced at his Chloe Cow Clover Stornetta watch stainless steel watch he had won at last year's Sonoma Valley wine auction to see it was almost three o'clock. He scurried to the phone next to the cash register and called Alex at his studio.

"Moonscape Studio. This is Alex." Alex had practiced his professionalism for phone calls for months to get this down, just right.

"Hey! It's just me," stated Scott.

"Hi, love. What's up? Having a good day?"

"It's kind of slow today. Just a few gift card sets, but I did manage to sell one of your photos," Scott replied with a smile in his voice.

"That's great! Which one?" asked Alex anxiously.

"The Pasa Robles set."

"How much?"

"Your list price."

"You just made my day, love. Thanks! That set had been sitting there for a few months. I was beginning to think it sucked." Alex was always stressed about his photograph sales. His aspirations were high when it came to his photography. His Executive Producing job for a prominent radio personality at where he nicknamed "KJB" radio had low pay but was heaven to the social and networking connections. The radio station sometimes felt like it was run by either the mafia or the mob. The leader had the ego of 'the godfather' and valued his sycophants. There were also a few others in leadership roles that pushed the talent instead of partnering with

them. The funny thing was, everyone there had love-hate relationships with it all. It kept things interesting, that was for sure. Regardless, his photography was where his true passion laid. Scott was always so supportive of his dreams, and he wanted to be successful at this.
"It takes a team, Schmoo. I have another question for you, though. The real reason for my call is your sister. What time is your sister scheduled to arrive?"
"I'm not sure," Alex answered. "I think her plane was scheduled to land around one-thirty." Alex looked at the Swiss watch Scott gave him for Christmas two years ago and noticed it was around three. "You think she might be at our house about now?"
"I don't know, but I did see one of those airport shuttles just drive by the shop. Did you call Mary by chance? I was able to get hold of Melissa yesterday and she was going to reach out to some of our friends. So far we have about eighteen for tonight." Scott always loved hosting little cocktail events at their house.
"Yes. I spoke with her, and she's bringing a few of the guys, and picking up the wine from BevMo that I ordered," replied Alex.
"Cool. I'll pick up the trays at Molly Stones around the corner. You think she'll be up to a little 'welcome to San Francisco' party?" asked Scott with reserved excitement and added hesitancy.
"I've never known her to not be up for any kind of party. She thrives in petite soirees."
"Great! I can't wait. It's been a little while since we have seen some of our local friends, despite your parents' recent visit."
"I know. It's been a little while since you and I have spent some quality time alone. The weekend was nice, but we were so busy getting everything ready for Michelle's visit." Alex took a breath. "Soon, though! I'm working on a surprise. I should know in a month or so. When Michelle leaves, we are gonna do just that. You and me," Alex shared with a hint of excitement.
"You're my angel, you know that?" Scott stated. "Oh…one other thing. When your sister called and left a message the other night, she seemed a bit cryptic. Something about her looking forward to talking about some things. Any idea what might be going on with her?"
"Not a clue. She was always one to disappear. She has a flair for drama. As you know, she'll call now and then. Nothing consistent. She's also always been a bit introverted and withholding. Not sure

where she gets that from in our family. God! I hope she's not pregnant. It can't be anything about my mom and dad because I just spoke with them the other day and they seemed to be fine. They didn't say anything, except that Michelle didn't seem to be herself lately. They were hoping she might visit them sometime, but you know the history there," Alex shared in his lengthy response. He was also getting antsy. He had some film to develop and really wanted to get some prints completed before ending the day and looked at his watch again.

"Yep. I get it. Oh well. You getting out of the studio soon?" asked Scott.

"I'll leave here around five-thirty or so. I need to finish some more picture development before heading out. You?" Alex asked pointedly.

"I'll get out of here as soon as Troy shows up. He should be here any minute. Bless that queen's heart. It was supposed to be his day off, but he was the only one I could call to close the shop." Scott nervously looked at his watch. Time was gonna be tight to prep for the guests.

"That's a surprise. He usually is always busy with tricks waiting in the wings," joked Alex.

"Well. He said he's in his '*famine mode*' for the moment. He hasn't seen anyone at the gym that interested him that he hadn't already '*done*'. I think he's a little depressed about that. Do you mind if he comes tonight? I forgot to ask him…goofy me."

"Fine with me. I gotta go. The timer is about to go off. See you later. Smooches."

"Love you, too. See you at home. Big kiss," Scott concluded and hung up the phone. Just then, he smelled Eternity cologne waft into the store.

"Hey Girl!" screamed Troy with a big smile on his face. He ran his hand up the right side of the door frame, leaned against it, and positioned his right foot in front of himself while holding the store door open, fingers spread with his right hand, arm fully stretched. His wavy blonde-dyed hair flopped over his left eyes protected by his wire-rimmed oversize glasses. His pink polo-styled Gap shirt was neatly tucked into his denim loose-fit jeans held in place by a worn brown belt. His Converse sneakers needed washing. He batted his big blue eyes at Scott and added, "Troy to the rescue, hon!" and smiled his '*come fuck me*' smile as he called it.

Scott giggled. “Hey, girl! Thanks for coming in! I can’t tell you how much I appreciate it.”
“Girl! Just show your appreciation on my check,” Troy stated and winked. “Baby needs to pay rent, soon. Otherwise, I’m moving in with you!” he joked.
“Don't worry. I will. How about a day’s pay?” suggested Scott. He knew it was expensive in this city, and Troy was also a reliable friend. He was more like family to him and Alex.
“Two days and I will shut my mouth and paint my nails,” Troy replied happily negotiating with his ‘sister’.
“Queen! You're only going to be here a little over three hours. Two days? I don’t think so. One,” countered Scott mirroring Troy’s queening dialogue while giving him ‘the teasing eye and grin’. His tone was clear he was not to be taken advantage of.
“Fine. But remember I am doing ***you*** a favor,” Troy snapped while half-smiling and floating his tall trim frame to the chair behind the register.
“I know. And I am grateful, queen,” Scott affirmed. “If you aren’t busy, how about stopping by the house after you close the shop? We are having some friends over, and in my self-absorbed state, I spaced asking you the other day. Sorry. Can you make it?” asked Scott with a glimmer of hope.
“Sure, girl. Can I bring a date if one happens to jump in from off the street and into my arms?”
“Absolutely. The more the merrier,” Scott replied.

Scott began to gather his things as Troy was getting settled. He updated Troy about the days' sales in case a client came in to ask. He added what the daily sales goal was and where they stood. Scott directed Troy to take care of the stationary paper shipment that arrived and to prep it for their next card project. The two of them had discussed, shared creative card design ideas, and prepared a spot in the loft space that overlooked the main floor of the shop. Troy obliged Scott, and jokingly blew him a kiss, and waved Scott out the door. “Buh-bye. See you later, girl. Go do what you got to do,” Troy murmured. Scott blew Troy a kiss back and headed towards Molly Stones only a few blocks away on California and Steiner.

As Scott was approaching Molly Stones, he saw Gabriel. “Shit,” muttered Scott tersely.
“Hi, handsome. Wanna go tumble?” asked Gabriel jokingly.

“Sorry. I haven’t had my syphilis shot today,” Scott replied sarcastically.
“Well. Aren’t we a little testy today? What’s wrong, handsome?”
“Nothing. I just have some things to do and in kind of a rush,” Scott replied. “How’ve you been?” he asked not really caring.
“Fine. Just got back from visiting my Chicago friends. Now I’m replenishing my supplies,” Gabriel replied smoothly holding up a bottle of recently purchased lube and winked.
“Oh. Welcome back, then. I really have to run. Sorry,” said Scott as he glanced at his watch.
“Oh. Okay. Sorry to keep you. Maybe I’ll see you guys out sometime?” Gabriel asked with a grin and impish glance. “Yeah, Sure. Maybe,” said Scott while maneuvering past him. He usually wasn’t rude, but he was in a rush. Gabriel always ‘rubbed’ him the wrong way.

Scott entered the grocery store searching for Irna. He had spoken with her Sunday when he placed their urgent food orders for their spontaneous gathering welcoming Michelle. Irna stated she would “*see to it, personally*” and would be there with the food trays waiting for him. She never let them down. As he approached the deli counter, he spied her. How could one miss her large brown eyes watching beneath her light blue tinted wire-framed eyeglasses?
“SWEETIE!” blasted from Irna’s bright red lips in her New Jersey tone.
“Hey! How are you?! Thank you so much for saving us, yet again,” responded Scott.
“Fine, darling. I just finished your trays,” said Irna, while snapping her gum. “I’ve been watching for you. Punctual as always,” she winked. Scott blushed.
“You are amazing! I mean it. Really. Thank you! Thank yohank you!" he uttered appreciatively.
“For you, dear, anything,” she responded with warmth while waving her long red manicured nails in front of Scott’s face, then patted his cheeks. Scott was always touched by how Irna seemed to always be so nice to him and Alex without ever really knowing them. They had an unusually close friendship like they had known each other all their lives. Yet, they had only met her a few years ago when she started working at the store. She was the only one at the deli he and Alex would deal with.

"Now darling. Keep these three trays refrigerated. Cantaloupe with prosciutto, dolmas, and hummus with pita and veggies." She brought over four additional trays that seemed to tower over her five-foot-two petite frame and her newly styled and lacquered red-haired wig. "Put these four in the oven on *low* right when you get home. I put extra foil over the lids to keep them warm. I also put something special in the bottom one marked with a smiley face. My own special recipe," she winked again.
"What's in the blue tray?" asked Scott noticing there was an additional fifth tray with their names on it.
"You'll see. I just know you guys will love them," she responded animatedly waving her hands.
"You are a dear. You know that?" reminded Scott affectionately.
"So are you, sweetie," she reciprocated.
"You wanna come over tonight? Meet some of our friends?" asked Scott hoping he was not overstepping any lines of their relationship. "It'll be fun."
"Thank you, dear. Some other time. This old bag of bones wants to get off her feet and watch my JAG, Frasier, Scrubs and NYPD Blue shows tonight. It's been a bitch of a week and it's only Tuesday," she answered smiling as she rolled her eyes then waved her hands again.
Scott chuckled, "Okay then. You're always welcome. You know that, right?"
"Thank you, dear. Have a good time. See you later in the week," she said. As she turned away, Scott noticed that her hair never seemed to move, and snickered through his smile. He remembered her hair was jet black last week, and before that, blonde. They were always the same style. Nevertheless, she was adorable and always seemed to be either very relaxed or just one of those people who were friendly and a bit "out there". He wondered if she was stoned half the time. He blew it off. Regardless, he just loved her for who and how she was. She was her own person.
"Hey, Tony! Delivery! Come help Scott here with his trays. He lives only a couple of blocks away!" yelled Irna to "Tall Tony". He scurried over, from one of the registers after bagging one of the patron's groceries. "Sure, Irna!" He stacked five of the trays in his long arms holding them close to his solid six-foot-six frame.
"I got these. You ready?" he asked looking at Scott.

“Yes. Thanks so much, Tony.” We are just up to the left on Sacramento off Steiner.
“Yep. Let’s go. You lead the way,” Tony stated in his tenor voice. “I don’t like to talk, much, so I hope you don’t mind me being quiet on the way."
“Not a problem,” replied Scott as they headed out. As they walked to Scott’s and Alex's house, Scott pondered about Irna and her story. “Hey Tony…Do you know much about Irna? She doesn’t share much, and we think the world of her. She's kind of a wonderful mystery to us.”
“Nope. I only started there about 4 months ago. She doesn’t tell me much either. She just asks a lot of questions…interested in me…ya know…friends-like. A real nice lady,” Tony replied.
“Hm. Okay.” Scott pondered for a moment, then quickly moved his thoughts back to the evening ahead. He was eagerly anticipating seeing Michelle and some of their friends. He felt some intrigue in the air, and not sure why. They quickly arrived at the house. Scott placed his two trays on the landing and pulled out his house keys and opened the door. “Here we go,” he stated and looked at Tony. Let’s just walk these to the back in the kitchen and place them on the counter. I’ll take it from there.” Tony followed Scott into the kitchen and placed the trays as directed by Scott. Scott pulled a ten-dollar bill from his small Cartier wallet he received from his Account Executive days with the company and handed it to Tony. “Thanks so much, Tony.” Tony folded the bill and shoved it into his front right jeans pocket. “Sure. Thanks! Have a nice evening,” and turned and walked out closing the front door behind him. “I like that. A man of few words.” muttered Scott as he started to manage the trays per Irna’s guidance. As he began to move items around and strategize his actions to prepare for his and Alex’s guests, he heard the shower running upstairs. “She’s here,” he whispered aloud with a smile.

Preparing

"GIRL!" he screamed up the stairs. "You almost done up there?" he exclaimed knowing full well she had her "*lady things*" (as he put it) to do yet. He quickly jogged up the stairs two at a time.
"IS THAT YOU, SCOTT?!" replied Michelle, loudly.
"YEAH! IT'S ME! YOU ALMOST DONE?" he yelled back so that she could hear both through the door and over the water.
"I'LL BE OUT IN A MINUTE!" she stated with confirmation.
"GIRL! I THINK YOU'LL NEED MORE THAN A MINUTE! IT TOOK ME UNTIL I WAS SIXTEEN BEFORE I KNEW," he jokingly quipped.
"YOU'RE SUCH A QUEEN," she yelled affectionately.
"PRINCESS, PLEASE," he happily retorted while playfully snapping his fingers. He then quickly sauntered off to their master bedroom on a mission.

Michelle turned off the water, grabbed an exceptionally large bright thick yellow bath towel from the rack just outside the shower stall, and hurriedly dried off so she could see her host. She had brotherly affection for Scott and was looking forward to talking with him. The one thing she could always count on was his blunt candor. She knew never to ask a question unless she truly needed an honest answer. Scott never held back. She both loved and hated that about him. She wrapped the large bath sheet around her and grabbed another smaller towel to wrap around her head as she stepped out of the bathroom, with her tendrils of hair still lightly dripping.
"Scott?"
"Yo!" he replied from the master bedroom just down the hall. He had just pulled out her gift from a sweater shelf in their small walk-in closet.

“I have been looking forward to seeing you. When is Alex going to be home?” she asked loudly while she began to towel dry her hair in the hallway while she waited for him to appear.
“He should be home around sixish. He's trying to finish developing a set of pictures at the City College studio for some clients,” he replied.
“Oh. Good. Before I get dressed, are we doing anything tonight, or are we staying in? Just so I know how to dress.” Michelle was secretly hoping for a quiet night. She had things to share and needed to warm up to the conversation. She also needed to build up her courage. It had also been a long day of travel. Her flight had also been delayed about three hours and coming from Chicago meant she had a very early start. She was thankful to have booked the direct on United. She was also lucky to snag a complimentary upgrade. A quiet night would be just the thing she needed.
“We’re gonna stay in. Dinners’ around seven,” Scott replied as he emerged from the bedroom with a large gift box in hand. A large red bow adorned the glossy black paper-wrapped treasure. Scott was a master at his bows. “Here, doll.” Scott held out the package towards the towel-wrapped Michelle. She shrieked with joy as she grabbed the box from Scott’s hands, eager to open with excitement and curiosity. She loved getting presents, and especially from Alex. Throughout their childhood, Alex always gave the best presents. They were always so thoughtful. She ran into her cozy room with Scott following enthusiastically two steps behind her.
“Alex and I saw this in the window at Saks and could not resist,” he stated with a little nervousness unsure if she would like the contents. Michelle didn’t seem to be paying much attention to what Scott was saying. She was engrossed in the careful opening of her gift. She undid the ribbon and managed to free the paper surrounding the box without any tears. She lifted the lid of the box and released her prize.
“Love it,” she yelped. She lifted the black slacks with the matching black top that would lightly hug her body showing off her feminine form. “I have always wanted an outfit like this, but never had the guts to buy one. Now I don’t have a reason not to wear something like this. I don’t know what to say,” Michelle added. She was touched as she sat on the bed holding and adoring her new outfit.
“We saw it and knew you would look amazing in it. With that gorgeous black hair, blue eyes, and that flawless skin of yours…Girl! You are gonna turn heads wearing that! Not that you

don't already," complimented Scott as he sat next to her. "Put it on!" he added. "Alex and I squabbled over the sizes, but he won. Dammit. I think he was right, though." He winked at her.
"Is something going on tonight other than dinner at seven?" she asked suspiciously.
"Actually... I want Alex to see you in it when he gets home…" Scott glanced at his watch. "Shit! It's four-twenty. You get dressed," he directed and started to calm himself down. He knew he was giving away that something was planned. "I have to go downstairs…" then the phone rang. He gave her a peck on the cheek then hopped off her bed. He headed into the hallway and ran to the phone in the Master bedroom. Michelle knew something was up and proceeded to finish drying her hair and pulling her "*glamour bag*" she bought at a thrift market that held her brush and other cosmetic goods.
"Hi. This is Scott."
"Hi Scott. Laura. Mer and I can't seem to find the note for the party tonight. Is it at seven or eight tonight?" she asked.
"Seven-ish. The closer to seven, the better. If you come a little earlier, I could use your help," he whispered clandestinely into the phone hoping Michelle could not hear through the nearly closed door.
"Mer is running a little late. We probably won't be there until after seven. Is that okay?" asked Laura.
"That's fine. This is a last-minute thing, so we'll see you when you get here. No stress. We didn't plan this very well. Shame on me and paint my nails green. I am such a mess!" replied Scott jokingly in a hushed tone. "Alex won't get home until around six anyway, so we'll just make do," he added. "If things run a little late, then they run late."
"Great! See you then! We can't wait to see you guys!" said Laura, relieved. She hung up the phone.
Scott hung up and headed down the stairs to the kitchen and storage refrigerator in the garage. He was mumbling to himself about forgetting Irna's instructions on placing the four trays in the oven immediately, and he needed to grab the case of Domaine Chandon and the Mondavi Chardonnay Alex had pulled that morning. He was thankful he had set in the garage refrigerator to chill. He reached the kitchen on his way to the wines when the phone rang again. "This is Scott," he answered hurriedly.

“Hi Scott! This is Ally,” informed the soprano voice with the Australian accent. “I’m just calling to ask if you want me and Jerry to come over a little early to help set up for tonight.”
“How nice of you to offer,” replied Scott appreciatively.
“Absolutely! I could use all the hands available. When can you get here?”
“How about an hour? That would be about five-thirtyish,” she replied.
“Perfect! You’re a gem! Thanks! Gotta go! My balls need heating,” he whispered with humor as he unwrapped some of the trays getting them ready for the oven. He was trying desperately to speak lightly to keep the party a surprise.
“Luv ya!” Ally chuckled and hung up.
Scott hung up feeling less rushed with the extra hands on their way. He began to resign himself to the fates. He placed the four trays in the oven as directed. Two trays of beef and lamb meatballs, a tray of chicken wings with dipping sauce in the middle that he removed to keep cool, and another tray of sausages. After placing them in the oven to warm them, he headed down to retrieve the wines.

*****

After blow-drying and brushing her hair, Michelle laid her new outfit out on the bed and began to get ready for the evening that lay ahead. She was deeply touched by the gift and thought affectionately about her brother Alex, and Scott. She was happy that her brother had found happiness and hoping she too would have something close to what he had. She began to wonder how her news was going to be taken by them, and how exactly she was going to tell them. It had been a few years, and it was something she needed to share. She didn’t want a lecture from anyone about her past. She sat and positioned herself at the small efficient corner vanity in her room and pulled out her makeup. She began to lightly apply her foundation powder. She remembered Scott used to work in the cosmetic industry. He often told her that she didn’t need a heavy foundation with her beautiful skin. She then applied a little smoky colored eye-shadow and black eyeliner. She dabbed a little blush on her highbrow, then pulled her brow pencil to finish off her recently manicured eyebrows. She remembered Scott had shared with her “*every lady uses a brow pencil for that polished look*”. He was correct. It made a difference. The natural-colored lip liner was next, followed by the matching lipstick. After she conservatively applied her blush, she leaned back a little and assessed her work. She looked good. She was not vain but appreciated herself.

She rose from her seat and dressed. The clothes were about perfect. A little snug, but they looked good. She had put on a little weight, but nothing overly noticeable. She moved to her jewelry bag and pulled out a simple elegant silver chain sporting a small diamond Alex had sent to her for Christmas three years ago. She sent him two ties and two shirts that she had bought on sale at the Banana Republic. She always thought his gifts were always better than hers. Nonetheless, they both had similar tastes in styles. Not flaunting yet stylish. She added a thin black belt to her new slacks and pulled out her black Winnie fabric closed-toe casual ankle-strapped pumps. Perfect, she thought, as she checked herself in the mirror when finished. After she considered herself complete, she laid back on the bed for a moment anticipating the evening. She took a breath. Then another. "Let's do this," she mumbled to herself, then got up and headed for the kitchen. On her way, she heard the phone ring again.

*****

Scott had loaded the trays in the oven, brought up the wine glasses, napkins, and placed the bottles of wine just outside the door out back to stay chilled with the evening air. “Princess Palace. This is Scott,” he answered the phone with humor.

“Hi love,” said the male voice.

“Hi baby! You on your way home?” asked Scott to Alex recognizing his voice.

“Sure am! I finished the sets. It’s almost five-thirty. I should be home around six depending on traffic. How are you?” asked Alex with a hint of concern. He knew Scott might start to be feeling a little stressed given this rushed planned event.

“Fine. Just trying to get things ready. Everyone usually arrives a little early, and it’s a school night, so, who knows? We probably should have waited until the weekend. Oy! Why do we do this to ourselves?” Scott replied trying to reclaim his calm.

“Michelle will appreciate it. It will be nice to see everyone, and they won’t stay late, which makes it easy. Don’t worry, smoo. We always

pull it off, and everyone always comments for a week. I love you." Alex stated back to Scott reassuring him. "Did Michelle make it?" he asked.
"Thanks, and yes. She's here. She was here when I got home. She looks great! Don't kill me, but I gave her the outfit we got her," he informed Alex while biting his lip and looking up to heaven with hope. As he mentioned it to Alex, Michelle appeared in the kitchen doorway. "…and WOW!" he stammered into the phone while looking at her appraisingly.
"I wish you would have waited, but you are you, after all. You have no patience, sometimes," chuckled Alex. "Does she like it?"
"She does! And *Gurl*, does she look grand in it!" he replied while looking up and down at Michelle winking, smiling, and nodding towards with approval and affirmation.
"THANK YOU!" she yelled hoping her brother heard.
Alex chuckled heartily on the phone. "Tell her I love her, and I will see you both shortly. Big hug. Let me get outta here so I can get to you quickly. Muwah!"
"Big hug back. Hurry home honey-bunches-of-ohs," replied Scott affectionately. They blew kisses through the phone to each other and hung up. Michelle noticed a certain heartfelt warm look on Scott's face when he spoke with Alex. His eyes showed endearing affection, love, and appreciation for his life partner. She felt a pang of jealousy, and yet she was so happy for the both of them. She stepped a few paces towards Scott, then patted him on the shoulder.
"Still got it, huh?" She said as looked into his deep bright green eyes.
"Yep. Hands down." Then softly sang to her "Fish got to swim, and birds got to fly. I got to love one man till I die. Can't help lovin' that man of mine…". They both giggled and she cupped his cheeks with her hands and gave him a sisterly peck. He then added, "I am really lucky. He's just the most wonderful, supportive, big-hearted, loving guy I have known. I just never thought I would have met someone like him and that he would be so good to me. I pinch myself every day because I keep thinking I am in a dream, and that one day I'm gonna wake up to find it gone. Or maybe it wasn't real. What did I do to deserve such a loving person in my life?" Scott began to shake his head, and added, "Whatever it was, I'm glad. I don't know what I would do without him."

Michelle saw small tears forming in Scott's eyes, and was touched by this genuine show of emotion. She gave him a warm tight hug. "Oh honey…you two saps deserve each other. I hope I have what you have one day." She shifted and tilted her head. "It seems like what you two have is downright nauseating, you know that?" she whispered working to lighten the mood. Scott looked back and giggled again at her.
"I am so glad you're here. You know that?"
Michelle looked up and smiled. "So am I sweetie. So am I." There was a pause. She sniffed. She looked at her watch. "What's that smell?" she asked.
"What smell?" replied Scott sniffing to mimic her. The phone rang. Scott shifted his attention, distracted, and grabbed the phone. "It's your quarter. Make it count. This is Scott," he stated into the phone.
"Scott? Ally. Honey…did you forget to invite Fred and Bitsy?" she asked nervously.
"Shit. Yes. I think Alex may have mentioned it to them, but don't quote me. Did you speak with them?" he asked petrified.
"Yes. When I mentioned this evening, she seemed a bit surprised and was going to run to talk with Fred. Maybe I'm just overreacting. I thought it best to check, just in case," she stated biting her nails.
"Let's salvage this. Can you catch her and let her know you and I spoke, and I feel like crap that I messed up and would love for her to come? Or however, you want to put it. I trust you." Then muttered "shit."
"I'll handle it. Don't stress. I think she will be relieved. Gonna run. See you later." She hung up to save the moment.
"Who was that?" asked Michelle.
"Our friend, Ally. Something about some event at the radio station that Alex is working with her…you know…. radio stuff," he coyly replied.
"You are not a good liar. I heard something about 'coming over.' I have a sneaky suspicion," she said as she then looked up in the air and sniffed. "What is that smell, though?" she asked and moved her glance to the stove.
"Oh…just some stuff I threw together for dinner tonight. It's heating up in the oven," he replied.
Michelle whisked her hand out, moved to the stove, and opened the oven door to resolve the mystery scents. "People are coming over, aren't they?" she casually asked in a slightly singing soprano voice.

“Well…maybe just a couple of people. Do you mind?” he asked with a slight wince and hope in his voice. He had been caught. The surprise was gone.
“No." She lied. She was tired, but this bought her some time. "I don’t mind. Just as long as it’s not a huge group of people. Are Ally and Jerry coming over? I remember having met them last time I flew through here,” she asked surrendering to the evening’s events. "They're really sweet."
“Yes. And Laura, Meredith, Fred, Bitsy, Troy from the store, Brandon, and a few others. Not a big group, I promise,” he shared.
“Okay then. As long as we make time to chat during my visit,” she said. “Well...what can I do to help?” she offered.
“Talk to me while I prep. If you see something you think you can take over, just interrupt. I’ll hand it over and move to something else. We will play it by ear. Cool?” he offered.
“Great!” Let’s do this,” she replied.

They teamed up and organized the needed supplies. They would take turns to poke into the oven to make sure nothing was burning and joke with each other. Scott turned on his CD player with speakers set up through the house. He had some top 40 hits and classics he loved to play when he set up for a party. Some Whitney Houston, Ace of Base, All 4 One, and others played in the background while he and Michelle placed napkins, glasses, plates, flatware, and foodstuffs into easy-to-grab locations. “I saw the sign…” sang Michelle and Scott as they partnered in wine glass positioning. They made a good team. Things quickly landed into place when they heard a familiar voice exclaim from the front door foyer, “HONEY! I’m home!”
Scott threw a blue and white striped kitchen towel over his shoulder and jogged to the entryway to greet his lover. “Hi sweetie!” he expressed as he moved in to wrap his arms around Alex, and then kissed him. He stated, “Welcome home. Your sister…”
Alex interrupted to complete the sentence “is right behind you.” He kissed Scott back, released him, and walked over to his sister. He picked her up while giving her a bear hug. “Hi, sis! It’s so good to see you! It’s been way too long. We have got a lot to catch up on.” said Alex affectionately with a hint of consternation.
“I know,” she replied. Let’s get a glass of wine while we get ready for your guests to arrive,” she added changing the subject while also revealing her knowledge of the hastily planned surprise soiree.

"*He told you,*" Alex said in a low soft accusatory voice. He looked at his lover with one eyebrow lowered and the other raised and smirked. "Can't keep a secret, can you?" he condemningly stated staring with a humorous condescending glance towards his partner.
"No," she replied attempting to protect Scott. "It was the phone ringing, the whispering in the other room on the phone, Ally calling, trays in the oven…I am not stupid, you know," Michelle said smiling.
"You are pardoned," he motioned at Scott placing two fingers on his shoulder. "We didn't plan that very well. Sorry. It was just something we threw together because we were excited about your visit. I am also off, tomorrow. My boss JB has his ride into the station, and his topics are all set up. I got the prints finished for my clients ready for delivery Thursday. Scott is working the first half of the day, so you and I have all morning to ourselves. Is that okay?" shared Alex in his lengthy diatribe to Michelle as he reviewed both of their faces while he reviewed their schedules for approval.
"That was a mouthful! Phew! I'm exhausted from listening to you!" she said in jest. "Sounds great," replied Michelle.
"Thanks, Schmoo," said Scott. "I almost forgot I had half the day tomorrow. I'll double-check with Troy when he gets here to make sure he didn't forget, either," he added.
"You look good by the way," stated Michelle, noticing how fit Alex looked. She thought to herself how the past few years had been good to him. He had obviously been going to the gym with Scott given the appearance of his physique. His boyish looks we now more manly and handsome. She noticed how Khakis seemed to be the uniform for everyone. Scott had on a black shirt, while Alex donned a red polo.
"So do you. You look great, too," replied Alex. "Love that outfit on you!" he winked and smiled at Scott. "I told you," he added looking for affirmation from his lover.
"Yes, you did, and yes, you were right," replied Scott. "Now…can we move from adoring each other for a moment and can we please finish getting the place ready? Guests are going to be here anytime, now." He pulled the blue and white striped kitchen towel off his shoulder, twirled it, and slapped it on Alex's butt. Alex grinned replying "Let me put my stuff down upstairs and I will join you in just a moment. I need to change my shirt and quickly freshen up."

"I've got a better idea!" chimed Scott. "Michelle.... why don't you go upstairs with him? You two should have a few moments together before people arrive. I can do most of what's left here. I have this under control. Oh...wait here for a moment..." Scott scuttled off. Michelle and Alex looked at each other and heard some rustling, a few clinks of glasses...then a "POP!!" of a freed sparkling wine cork from its green bottle prison. A few seconds later, Scott reappeared with three glasses of bubbles. He provided each a glass, and toasted, "Welcome to San Francisco, dahlink! May your visit change your life for the better and bring you two closer. I love you both," and they clinked glasses. "Cheers!" added Alex and Michelle in unison.

"I'll drink to that. I love you both, too" smiled Alex.

"Here! Here! You have no idea how happy I am to be here," commented Michelle. "I am sure this will be a life-changing trip," she coyly added hoping her hosts did not catch her meaning. They didn't.

They sipped the bubbly nectar, then Alex moved to journey his way upstairs with Michelle following him. "Thanks, Scott!" Michelle expressed to Scott with warmth in her tone.

"Anytime," he said and winked back, then moved into the kitchen to finish the food prep while "Stay (I missed you)" by Lisa Loeb played through the house. Michelle caught the song and thought it ironic this played while she followed Alex.

They reached their master bedroom, and Alex turned to Michelle. "I'll be just a moment. Let me just wash my face quickly and freshen."

"Sure," she said.

"oh...would you mind dropping my backpack by the door over there? I'll put it away when I get there. I'll be just a moment," he asked while handing her his black leather backpack.

"No problem. See you in a minute," she accepted the bag and navigated her way to drop it where he directed. "Um..." she turned, interrupting Alex's entry to the master bath. "Are you going to wear that shirt, or can I pick one out for you. You did, after all, pick out my clothes. I would like to return the favor?" she asked with a devious smile.

"I will change my shirt but pick out a few for me to choose from. I haven't seen you for a few years, so I'm not sure what you'll choose," he replied with some hesitancy.

"Don't you trust me?" she asked mischievously.
"Girl. Let's not go down that road right now," he winked back. She gave him a brief glare then dismissed his sarcasm.

Alex ducked into the bathroom, while Michelle went to check out his and Scott's closet. She was dying to see their wardrobe. She spied the partially open sliding closet door. They had painted the walls a noticeably light lavender with white trim and a white ceiling. There were masculine eggplant velvet draped panels that hung in front of two large windows that opened out over the garden with near-transparent sheers beneath them. There was a sliding glass door that opened to a small deck that overlooked their semi-private green coveted oasis retreat from city noises. The bed had a taupe duvet with a subtle embroidered pattern that matched nicely with the hint of lavender in the room. There were matching pillow shams along with decorative pillows on the bed with a brown, taupe textured lap blanket on the end of the bed that added to the warmth of the floors. She noticed a desk and computer in the left-back corner of the large room, with a tall narrow bookshelf next to the desk holding a phone/fax machine, among their computer software books. She quickly distracted herself from the bottle of lotion she noticed next to the clock radio on the nightstand next to the bed and began to review their modest size walk-in closet. Scott's clothes were obviously on the left. She could tell by the pressed shirts arranged by color hanging perfectly on their hangers as if just from the cleaners. Scott also separated his dress shirts from the casual styles. She turned her vision to the right side and began to fumble through Alex's fashion frenzied shirts with no order to them. "He's still got fun taste," she whispered to herself. She pulled out a black Donna Karan long-sleeved shirt, a Prada pink short-sleeved polo, a navy wool sport coat, a light gray sweater vest with deep ruby trim, and a blue long-sleeved shirt. "Let's see what he does with this," she whispered smiling triumphantly at her choices.

Moments later, Alex stepped from the bathroom. "Let's see what we have here," he stated as he began to peruse her selection. "Hell no," he commented pointing at the long sleeve black shirt. "Scott's wearing this, and we are not twins. Let's just be clear. I do not do *twinsies*." He snapped his fingers and picked up the black Donna Karan and hung it back up with his other shirts. "I like the jacket, but not with the vest and blue shirt. That's more Scott. I do like the polo though. Nice job, sis. Safe choices," said Alex with hinted

approval. “You still know me.” He patted her shoulder and ran his hand down her arm showing his appreciation.
“Thanks,” she said as she sat on the bed with her glass of champagne still in hand. “It’s really good to see you. We have so much to catch up on.”
“You can say that again” added Alex. “How’s work? Are you still with that landscaping firm, or have you moved to freelance? Are you seeing anyone? I've left a couple of messages in the past few months. Nothing from you. I have no idea if you are sick, happy, sad, or anything. Then you call out-of-the-blue. ‘Guess what? I’m coming out to visit. Can I stay with you?’ That’s what we get on the machine. All I can conclude is that something’s up. Am I right?” blasted Alex softly in his unexpected rant to Michelle, searching for answers. She was supposed to be his older sister. He seemed to be the one holding the responsibility role, with some frustration.
Michelle looked at him with understanding eyes and a slight wince. “You’re right. I have not been a ‘*good sister*’. I keep a lot to myself. I alienate people,” she tensely admitted with calm staring at her glass of diminishing bubbles. She gulped the final contents of the glass. Alex finished dressing while looking down at her for answers. She then continued. “And yes. Something *IS* up. A lot of things are, actually, at the moment. Things got jumbled and confusing for me in Chicago, and I needed to clear my head. I am trying to simplify my life. Gary, the guy I was seeing…I found out he was screwing around on me with some bimbo from the office next to mine. The apartment building I was living in was sold to converted to condos, which I couldn’t afford…so I am looking for a new place to live. Then to top it off, all my clients just want the same thing over and over. The same trees, same oversized pots with the same flowers…blah blah blah. Boring! I was getting increasingly frustrated with everything. I need a change. You were the one that came to mind who I thought could help me figure out what I am doing wrong all the time. Goddamn it! I need some help, and you know that’s not easy for me to say.” She looked up as Alex was still staring at her. He had finished dressing and was holding his Pasha cologne, not moving. He was looking at her with sad astonishment. “I needed to see you. We used to be so close. I want to get that back. I thought this trip would help us both. It would give me time to sort things out, and get my brother back,” she added softly. Alex

recognized her deep sincerity. She was reaching out. He did not want to let her down.
“Me too. Ever since you left me in L.A., we haven’t been the same,” he said looking at her in her eyes. He lightly sprayed his cologne and walked through the small cloud forcing a small smile on Michelle's face as he did it. He then sat beside her.
“Oh God,” she quietly said. “You were 22. I was 25. Mom and dad were amazed we took off and moved there with no jobs. We just up and left,” she laughed.
“Yes. But we both wanted to do things we could not do where we were in Canada. We did not want to get stuck. My friend at the time, Lee, had a perfect opportunity that led me to where I am now. We both ended up working two jobs to make ends meet in that crappy apartment. Who knew that stoves and refrigerators did not come with most of the places?” Alex reminisced. “Then we met that guy…what was his name?” Alex asked struggling to remember.
“Let’s just call him ‘asshole to the thousandth degree’” replied Michelle coldly.
Alex continued despite being a little surprised at her comment. “I thought things were going well. You two seemed to get along. We were having fun only to find out frustrating L.A. could be. Everyone only wanted to know you if you could do something for them…vogue on the outside, vague on the inside.” He paused. He changed his tone to one of being baffled. "After five months, I come home from a crappy day. Couldn’t wait to talk with you about getting fired. You were gone. No note. You left everything but your clothes…. JAKE! That was his name! JAKE!” Alex said while slapping his palm on his forehead and getting up off the bed. He continued struggling to recall the scene. “He stopped by to say goodbye. I asked if he knew where you were, and he said ‘no’ and that I would not see him again. He was leaving L.A. but didn’t say where. What happened?” Alex asked looking to Michelle for an answer.
“You know…I really don’t want to talk about that right now. Can we talk about it later? I've had a long day. I would just love to have some fun with my brother, and his wonderful guy. This is a bit of a downer to talk about this after I just arrived. Do you mind? Can we talk more about another time and just have some fun tonight?” she asked Alex hopefully. She wasn’t ready to tell him everything just

yet. “I am sure Scott could use some help, and your people should be arriving anytime now,” she added.
“You always wanna talk later. Never now. Always later,” Alex replied with some frustration. He was also trying to be empathetic. He just blasted her, and she had only been in their home for a couple of hours. He changed his tone. “Funny. I told Scott the other day that you would talk when you’re ready, and here I am giving you the inquisition single-handedly. Sorry. Yes. Let’s talk about it later.” He slid on his black squared heavy loafers and finished adjusting his belt.
“Even your leathers match!” Michelle commented with a forced giggle quickly adjusting her attitude. “You fashion queens!” she waved her hand with her empty champagne glass and turned to the door for her exit. She turned back to him, “Thank you, Alex,” she stated softly and started to move into the hallway. Alex grabbed his glass, gulped the tiny sip left. “Love you,” he replied. “C’mon, girl! Let’s get down there and help my man.” He gently pushed her down the hallway following closely behind. “CALVARY’S COMING! …SCOTTY! WE ARE ON OUR WAY!” he yelled down the stairs.

They reached the bottom of the stairs and noticed the dining room. Four large candles of varied heights we lit adding a warm glow to the room. Lemon branches with fragrant flowers and a few lemons still attached surrounded their bases. Plates, flatware, and napkins were strategically placed on the sturdy four-foot-four door darkly stained knotted oak bureau holding a glass door matching case raised about two and a half feet by two thickly “S” shaped carved legs accommodating the 40 plates below. Flatware was neatly organized in small baskets lined with white linen napkins.
“WOW!” Michelle exclaimed complimentarily. “This looks beautiful!”
“Thanks” replied Scott with appreciation. Alex chimed in.
“Scott and I went through paint chips for a solid week before we settled on these colors. Another week moving things around. It’s a start.”
“We make a good team, baby,” Scott added.
“Well. Whatever. Nice job, Scott. This setup is just…wow!” she said, impressed.
“Shit! My tray." Scott scooted back to the kitchen. Alex and Michelle followed hurriedly. Scott grabbed his blue oven mitts, put one on, opened the stove, and reached in with both hands to pull the

tray. "Oh CHRIST! OUCH!" expressed Scott loudly waving his right hand. "I burned myself! Shit that hurts!" Alex moved to Scott, grabbed his hand, and kissed it. "Run it under cold water, there. Michelle and I will take care of this tray." "Thanks, baby," Scott returned. He removed his mitt with the worn hole where the heat snuck through and navigated to the sink to tend his wound. Alex and Michelle resolved the meatball tray without issue positioning them in the small, rounded platter Scott had set out.
"These smell so good! What's in them?" Michelle asked not touching them while putting foil over the top to keep them warm while they sit out.
"No idea. We got them from Irna at the store. I think some sausage, mixed with buffalo and some of her herbs. Wait till you taste the chicken and other stuff she prepared. Yum!" chimed Scott. He then added, while drying his lightly scorched fingers, "Can we move these food trays to the table, please? The door's gonna be ringing any moment, and I do not want to be running around like a crazy person when people arrive." Scott waved his fingers and hands in expression. He loved to 'queen out' when he could. Alex and Michelle each grabbed a tray. All one would hear for the next few minutes were '*pardon me*', '*excuse me*', and '*oops. Sorry*' as they navigated around each other placing the tray, little bread dishes, salt, pepper, butter, and condiments on the table from the kitchen counter. "Taskmaster, that one," muttered Alex, aloud.
"Seems like it," added Michelle smiling and smirking.
"Bitches. Both of you." Scott turned to look at them humored. "Let me get my whip, girls, and I'll show you what a master is," he winked.
"Oooohhh! Turn me on, daddy," teased Alex.
"You're messing with me…" sung Michelle in jest.
"Alex. Wine. Michelle. Coasters in the living room and family room in the back." He slapped his thigh barking orders with care and pointing needlessly.
"Done!" said Alex while Michelle bopped her head in the "Dream of Jeanie" fashion approving the direction and assignments.
"Bubbles anyone? I will get some for us! I'm parched!" shared Scott.
They were ready for the night. "Here we go," muttered Scott to himself.

Gabriel

Gabriel had arrived back at his 2400 Webster Street fourth-floor one-bedroom apartment. He was feeling a little jet-lagged from his Chicago flight and running his “replenishment” errands, as he termed them. He needed to stock up on shaving cream, hair gel, lube, condoms, and basic grocery items. He grabbed a Rolling Rock from the refrigerator he just filled and headed for the sofa to listen to his voicemail. He dreaded this given he spent two weeks in Chicago and was negligent in keeping them current during his trip. He plopped himself down onto his soft black leather sofa and fluffed one of the plush cream and black decorative pillows to place behind his head and upper shoulders to get comfortable. He picked up the CD remote from his glass and chrome coffee table, then pressed “Play” to enjoy his “The '80s top hits” disc. *“Oh Mickey, you're so fine...”* pumped out of the speakers in the room. He softened the volume, then pressed “Play” on his voicemail recorder for his messages.

Beep

“It's Shawn. I haven't heard from you in a while. I was wondering if you want to get together. Call me. 555-7431.”

Gabriel smirked trying to remember who “Shawn” was.

Beep

“Hi. It's Veronica. Thanks for letting me know about you-know-who. I am so pissed off at him. I don't even want to think about or say that asshole's name. I'll call you when you get back.”

"Good girl," he thought. “Don't settle for less than you deserve.”

Beep

"Hey, Gabe! Tim here. I was wondering if you knew where I could score some weed. Maybe we can get together…hang out…have a little fun…well…call me. You have my number."
"In your dreams bud. Getting stoned is all you think about. You're about as fun as a bag of hammers," muttered Gabriel as he rolled his eyes and took a swig of his beer.
Beep
"I got your number from a friend of mine…" began the message. The voice sounded nervous and unsure. "…I was wondering if…well…you know…um…shit. My number is 555-9954," and hung up leaving a brief dial tone.
"You could have left your name, dumbshit. How will I know who I am calling?" muttered Gabriel to the answering machine slightly irritated as if it would respond and took another swig of his beer. *"Oh, Mickey what a pity you don't understand"* played overhead in his apartment as he playfully bopped his head listening multitasking listening to his messages.
"Hi Gabe! Josh here! Anyway…can you cover for me Saturday after you get back? I finally got a date and would really appreciate it. It would help me out a lot. Let me know. Hope you had a great trip, man."
"That's cool," replied Gabriel aloud. He liked Josh. He was very fussy about who he dated, and it had been about eight months since he had broken up with his ex or seen anyone. "I'll call you tonight, bud," affirmed Gabriel aloud talking to himself.
Beep
"I've got something for you. Call me when you get back. You have my number, and you know who this is."
"Count on it," muttered Gabriel with a smile recognizing the owner of that deep voice. The voice aroused him.
Beep
"You shit! I can't believe you told Veronica! It was a party! I was drunk! It was none of your business! Wait until I tell her what really happened! I wanna kick your ass so bad right now!" Click…dial tone.
Gabriel chuckled. "After all of the lies you've told, you think she's gonna believe you?" he replied looking at the machine.
Beep
Hang up. Dial tone.
Beep

“Hi…I called earlier...” It was that nervous voice again. Gabriel looked over to the machine, and said, “This time leave your name,” he instructed.
“My name’s Michael. I’ve seen you out before, and was wondering if you would want to go out sometime? Oh…my number again is 555-9954.”
“Now that’s more like it. You sound nice. I’ll call later. Maybe tomorrow,” Gabriel whispered and took another swig of his beer. He was feeling a little tired. Several other messages from friends played. He had five callbacks to make, while the remaining he would follow up with while he is out at the clubs. He was seriously considering going to Alta Plaza, or ‘Ultra Plastic’ as locals would say, for a drink or two, just to mingle with his local “gang.”
Beep
“Hey. I heard you were back. I was thinking of going to a little party near your place. I was thinking maybe you might want to join me as a plus one. Some couple…um…Alex, I think and his boyfriend. It’s supposed to be nice. Anyway…let me know.” Gabriel smiled. Aarav. He was a house flipper. Aarav Khatri. A lover of cashmere sweaters from Neiman Marcus. He could never miss a sale. Gabriel was always trying to snag one to “borrow” when he stayed over at Aarav’s place in Berkeley. Aarav also usually had invites to parties and he occasionally was his plus one. He networked with purpose, and he knew how to work a network. Aarav always had contacts for just about anything. He also had a great laugh that would sometimes have a deep full sound to it. Gabriel was jealous of his hair because it was thick, black, and soft. They only had sex twice, but the passion was very short-lived. They had mutually decided they were better as ‘sisters’ than lovers. It was fun, but just not what either was looking for. They were great friends and never judged the other. Aarav liked his independence and kept his money to himself. He wasn’t cheap. He just wasn’t generous, either. Always a tough one to open his wallet and buy drinks, yet always around for a free drink and meal. He was someone, a friend could always count on when needed. He had a good heart. He sometimes wondered why or how they became good friends. He was thankful for their friendship, though. It was effortless.
Gabriel picked up the phone and dialed him.
“Hello? Aarav here.”
“Hey, queen. I’m back. I got your message,” said Gabriel.

“Welcome back, sister! Great! Oh…you were missed, queen. I could have used your help on this house I am trying to get ready to flip. Have time tomorrow? I need to finish some exterior painting. Pretty simple. I am just finishing the inside cleaning. Yuck! But hey, a girl’s gotta make a living,” shared Aarav.
“I might be able to swing tomorrow. Let me see how I feel. Right now, I'm a little jet-lagged, but tomorrow is another day,” Gabriel replied. “About tonight. I don’t think I am up to Alex and his boyfriend's Scott's party. I think I want to lay low. Was thinking of going to Ultra Plastic tonight just to say hi to a few people. You gonna be around?” Gabriel asked with a glint of hope. "I might change my mind later. We'll see."
“Sure! I am just finishing here. I’ll go home and shower then head into the city. Think I’ll BART in. I gotta make it an early evening tonight, though. It is only Tuesday, after all. And who the hell throws a party on a Tuesday night?! I mean really!” cited Aarav. “Can’t wait to see you and hear about your trip.”
“I know. Tuesday night soirees?! I agree. Must be a *couples’ thing,*” stated Gabriel sarcastically in agreement. “Anyway…great! I have a few stories, but nothing that will curl your toes. See you later. Maybe around seven-thirtyish?”
“Perfect. See you then,” Aarav replied and hung up.
Alex hung up and decided he needed to take a little nap before the evening ahead. He thought he would finish his messages later. He finished the rest of his beer, turned off the CD player, sprawled out on the sofa, closed his eyes, and crossed his arms over his chest. “Should be a nice little evening. Welcome home, Gabe” he said softly to himself, then dozed off.

Party of Mysteries

Bing-Bong chimed the doorbell.
"Coming!" yelled Scott from the kitchen towards the front entry. He pecked Alex on the cheek, looked at Michelle, and said, "Here we go! It begins" and moved quickly towards the door to greet their first arriving guests. Michelle and Alex each grabbed a few bottles of Chandon to place next to the champagne glasses.
"Right behind you, babe. We'll start filling the glasses" stated Alex as they followed Scott out from the kitchen.
"Don't forget to turn the garden lights on," ordered Scott. Alex looked at Michelle.
"I don't think anyone is going outside in this fog. It's cold out there" he added.
"Fog? That was fast" replied Michelle. They stopped at the glasses while Scott continued to the door. They both began fumbling with the foil and corks while Scott greeted the newcomers.
"Hey! Yay! So glad you were able to come tonight!" He turned his head and yelled back to Alex and Michelle, "Laura and Mer are here!" then turned and hugged the longtime lesbian couple. Laura was a dark blond, short-haired green-brown-eyed radio sales type. Meredith was a shoulder-length curly-haired brunette who managed restaurants. They were about the same height around five-foot-eight or nine with healthy curves. Alex at times stated they were a handsome couple.
"Hi sweetie! We were so glad to get your call about this little party. We always love to see you guys!" shared Meredith.
"Where is that handsome man of yours?" asked Laura as they both worked to remove their light jackets and scarves.

"Let me take those, and Alex is just over there in the dining room with his newly arrived sister, Michelle. Go say hi while I hang these in the armoire."
"Oh…here!" said Meredith as she handed Scott a wine bag that imprisoned a bottle.
"Thanks, Mer! That's so nice of you," he replied as he accepted the gift and placed it next to the wall near the armoire out of the path so as not to be kicked over. "Go. See Alex" he ordered with a smile waving them both on. Alex and Michelle greeted their guests as they neared them, with glasses of Chandon sparkling wine, smiles, and reserved excitement. As Laura and Meredith were introduced to Alex's sister, the doorbell rang again, and the procession of guests began in multiples. Scott continued with his warm welcoming greetings and salutations accompanied by hugs. He handled jackets, scarves, and pashminas with gentle care maneuvering their positions in the armoire. He carefully placed the bags and gifted bottles of wine along the wall in the entryway so they would not be kicked by the incoming traffic. A couple of flower bouquets and an orchid were among the gifts. He placed those atop the armoire, to load into vases after the arrivals were complete. He would later place the three gifts of flowers throughout the house for others to appreciate. The short salmon-colored rose arrangement on the end of the fireplace mantel. The tall mixed flower arrangement with swirly twigs and eucalyptus on the dining room table. The orchid would go in the guest room with Michelle.

The small party was underway with the murmur of many conversations mixed with the various musical genre assortment playing throughout the house. Songs from the '80s and '90s, including dance hits on a low volume just enough for their guests to occasionally comment, "*I love this song!*" and "*oh…who sang this?! I am trying to remember…*" among others. It was all in fun. Everyone enjoyed the food Alex and Scott would credit and praised Irna for coming to their aid. Scott took notice that the Chardonnay seemed to be the beverage of choice for the night and would occasionally slip out to replenish the bottles as they emptied. He would simply leave the new bottles on the dining room table for guests to help themselves. It was a lovely evening. Everyone noted the chill in the air from the fog that seemed to quickly roll into the city like a blanket encouraging residents to get warm and cozy in their homes.

Michelle felt a bit automated when answering the repetitive questions.
"So…you're visiting from Chicago?".
"Yes."
"How long are you visiting for?"
"A few weeks."
"What are you doing now?"
"Taking a break from Landscape architecture."
"Are you seeing anyone?"
"I was. Didn't work out."
Then… "Why so long since visiting?"
No response. Her mind was racing. *Think Michelle. Something vague, but true.* Finally, it hit her. '*Deflect*' she thought. "Not sure. I think life just got in the way. But I'm here now." Then she forced a smile and sipped her bubbles and countered with, "What are your favorite things about San Francisco? What do I need to see?" This led to a host of responses. Golden Gate Park, the windmills with caution about the cruising activity in the bushes there. China Town, Angel Island, Sausalito, Fort Point were other obvious suggestions.

Michelle paused and assessed the ambiance, guests, and interactions. She watched Scott and Alex stand together talking with their friends. They took turns stepping away to bringing a bottle of wine or Chandon to refill near-empty glasses. The other would remind them to eat while making suggestions. Laura and Mer would separate off and have individual chats with their friends, rejoin, then separate again. Talk radio industry conversation from Laura was usually her consistent topic. She loved ranting and comparing the different talk radio talent. She adored JB for whom Alex worked, repeatedly stating he was always the deep true voice of reason. Alex would naturally always agree with her. The next chain of events between Laura and Alex would be Bitsy and Ally chiming in since they all worked at the radio station. Jerry would share some plays he was working on directing and the classes he was teaching at ACT. Troy would periodically interject and sing a verse of whatever song was playing overhead drawing attention to himself. Scott always thought he had a flair for drag and loved watching him perform at Marlena's in Hayes Valley. He was exceptional with Whitney Houston's "One Moment in Time."

Michelle observed the dance of conversations and ballet of service throughout the party. She noticed Bitsy's partner, Fred, was a quiet man. He smiled. Listened. Nothing about which to boast. She thought he had somewhat of a commanding presence. He seemed wise to her. A man of few words, kind and thoughtful. Michelle spotted him a few times just reaching over and gently caressing Bitsy's back endearingly. It then hit her. This was a warm gathering of people who cared for each other. They engaged, respected each other's thoughts, laughed together, and enjoyed each other. She smiled deciding to take a quiet moment in the back garden just outside the door. Bitsy looked over and saw her stealing away and got up to follow her without Michelle realizing she was going to have some company. Just moments after she was outside to bask in the silence, she heard a voice behind her.

"Is this a party of one or can an old lady join you for a few minutes?" Michelle turned and gave Bitsy a warm smile.

"Sure. I just needed to take a moment. This is just lovely. I needed a night like this," whispered Michelle.

Bitsy opened her small hand-size purse hanging across her shoulder and procured a small joint. "For the record, I am not a stoner, but smoke now and then. I make them extra small because an old lady like me only needs a little puff or two to get a buzz on. Want to share?" She held it out to Michelle.

"Sure. It's been a while. What the hell. I'm in San Francisco after all."

Bitsy pulled out her mini-Bic lighter, took a hit from her petite joint, and handed it to Michelle. She took a hit. Coughed a few coughs. Took another small hit. Coughed twice. Took another small hit then handed it back to Bitsy who giggled at Michelle.

"I guess you needed that. Good for you," she said as she noticed Michelle's distant gaze. "You know. I'm a good listener if you ever need to talk. I sense there's something on your mind. No judgments here."

"Thanks. I appreciate that. I might take you up on that. Just not tonight."

"Any time. Here. Let me give you my card. Email or call me. Whatever. Happy to meet you somewhere, too if you want." Bitsy procured her business card and handed it to Michelle. "Can I ask you a question?"

"Sure," Michelle was feeling her buzz kicking in and enjoyed feeling light and a little hazy. She had to be careful.

"Why did you wait so long to visit here this time? I know you and Alex talk by phone and send each other send cards now and then…but Alex shared you used to be close." She wondered if she was pushing too hard, but Alex often mentioned Michelle to her whenever they talked. She knew he missed seeing her.
"Well…let's just say there's a story there. We all go through a shitty period in our lives. That's why I'm here. I need my brother."
"Ah. Again…I am a good listener. Maybe we can talk this week? Let me know. I'm just a kind, nosey old broad who likes to help others."
"Thanks. I'll consider that, Bitsy. I appreciate it. I should get back in there. Thanks for the hits." Michelle smiled and gestured Bitsy to the door ushering them back to the party. Bitsy patted Michelle on the arm and smiled warmly. "I can take a hint. Let's go," and proceeded in with Michelle following closely behind, picking up an opened bottle of Chandon on the way.
Bing Bong. Bing Bong.
Troy looked to Scott and Alex. "I'm closest, queens. Want me to get the door?" he asked loudly. Alex gave him a thumbs up so as not to interrupt the conversation they were having with Melissa. Troy opened the door greeting Aarav and Gabriel. "C'mon in! It's a party in here. You're a little late, but there's still some food and drink back there." Aarav looked at Troy appraising him from head to toe. "I've seen you. Marlena's, right?" he asked.
"Lady Alotta Balls or Ivanna Hump. Depends on the night. That's me!" Aarav laughed.
"I love your Whitney shows! Girl! Those gowns are trashy elegant, too! When will you be there next?" Troy looked at him with appreciation.
"Thursday through Saturday each week. You get to buy me a drink or two next time," Troy half-joked and winked.
"Sure!" replied Aarav laughingly.
"And who is this tall drink of water with you?" asked Troy as he shifted his eyes to his friend next to him.
"Gabriel."
"You wanna blow my horn?" teased Troy.
"Not into brass, but thanks for the offer," replied Gabriel.
"It wasn't an offer. Just stop looking at my crotch," Troy scolded then touched Gabriel's nose and blew a kiss. "Nice meeting you

both. Go circulate." He waved them off and turned to grab some food and wine. He was starving.
Aarav and Gabriel started their way into the room heading for the glasses hoping for a fun evening. Alex noticed the two and tapped Scott.
"Don't look now," he warned.
"Shit. What's he doing here? Did you invite him?" Alex whispered back to Scott unnerved.
"You kidding me? I don't have a death wish. He must have come with Aarav. What do we do?" Melissa looked at the couple.
"What's wrong?" Then looked over at the new arrivals. "Oh shit, I think?" She sensed it was not a welcoming moment and decided to let them handle it. "Got it. Go deal. I need a little more wine anyway." She got up and headed to the kitchen for her replenishment. Alex and Scott rose and headed over to greet their new guests.
Alex opened. "Hello there." Scott stood by his side.
"Hey!" Aarav smiled happily at Alex and Scott. "Sorry I ran late. I heard about this from someone. I thought you wouldn't mind. No excuse. I'm lame. I didn't feel like flying solo tonight, so I asked a friend of mine to join me. You guys know Gabriel." Michelle overheard the name and looked over her shoulder. Her eyes widened recognizing her shuttle partner. Her curiosity piqued. But, for some strange reason, she decided to hold back and continued her conversation with 'barbeque Mary' with her back to the group. Scott was fond of their lovely Polynesian friend. He had shared that one day when he was living with his ex, she had purchased a grill for her balcony. One day she decided to use it and the smoke would billow into his place, hence the reference "barbeque Mary".

Questions started running through Michelle's mind about the encounter going on. She wondered how they all knew each other. She caught herself pondering Gabriel's sexual preferences. She thought he was handsome, but there was something in her gut that whispered, '*don't do it*'. A red flag. She turned to Mary and asked about paralegal work. "Any tasty dirt you can share with me with your work? What kind of cases are you working on?" Mary smiled and started sharing info about a PG&E case that involved the groundwater without specifics. Michelle's mind wandered while listening.

Alex looked at Aarav. “In the spirit of being gracious, welcome. I am not one to create a scene,” he stated with a straight face and a tone that was friendly, yet stern. He looked at Gabriel. “Not sure why you’re here. It’s obvious we have a common friend. Regardless, don’t start shit in my home. Okay?” He raised his eyebrows. Gabriel smiled back. “Sure. Just here with Aarav. We’ll grab a bite, have some wine, then go on our merry way. Thanks for the warm welcome.” he responded with some sarcasm. Then nodded back to him and Scott. Scott returned the nod with a strained tense countenance. “Wine’s in the kitchen. You found the glasses. Oh…beware the meatballs. There is a peanut sauce on one of them that might have gotten on the others,” then walked back to the kitchen. Gabriel walked over to the table of food and glanced watching Scott walk away. Alex looked after Scott and decided to let him alone. He knew he was pissed off.
“I fucked up, didn’t I?’ stated Aarav to Alex.
“Yes.” He paused then added, “before you just bring someone with you, would you mind asking first? Especially, him? We don’t mind friends bringing friends. We just want to keep situations like this from happening. That’s all.”
“Sure. I’m really sorry. We’ll leave really soon. I didn’t mean to stir shit, you know.”
“Thanks, bitch. I don't believe you. I’d appreciate that, though,” said Alex with a frustrated look. Aarav was generally a good guy. He just screwed up on this one. He gets a pass, he thought to himself. Aarav motioned for a hug with Alex accepting a reciprocating. “Hey, friend. Now…can I get a drink?” They forced their smiles and proceeded to fill their glasses with bubbles.
Scott stepped outside to the garden for a moment. He felt uncomfortable with a pang of anger and looked up to the sky for answers. The fog took a brief break above with some stars twinkling down.
“Can I join you in a moment of truce?’ the voice behind him asked.
“Why did you come here? Every time I see you, I just remember all the shit,” Scott said keeping his back to Gabriel.
“I thought it would be okay. I thought ‘*you'* would be okay, by now.”
“I forgave you a long time ago, but that doesn’t mean I need to see, talk with, hang with, or anything else with you around. Whenever you are around, trouble follows.” He turned and looked at Gabriel.

He looked him straight in his eyes. “You cause me pain every time I see you. I think you’ll understand if I simply ask you, as a gentleman, to please leave. This was supposed to be a nice evening for Alex’s sisters’ arrival. Your presence here deflects from that. Please,” he stated with a blend of angst, torment, and confidence. His eyes did not waver from his stare.
“Got it. Sure. Sorry to have ruined your evening. But for the record, it took two,” Gabriel replied meaning he was culpable for the discomfort.
Scott just stared at him. "Fuck you."
“Good night”. Gabriel turned and walked away to retrieve Aarav. He knew he struck a nerve and he needed to leave.
Scott took a few minutes. Took a few deep breaths, then moved to join the party again. He regained his composure. As he walked back in, Alex was standing by the table of food. He nodded to Gabriel as he brushed past him. Aarav saw Gabriel and followed after him.
He lightly muttered to Alex “I think we’re going,” and opened his eyes wide and relaxed them. Alex smiled back.
"You can come back if you want. Alone. We can talk tomorrow. Or not.” He nodded to Aarav and watched the two men leave. Scott came up behind Alex and put his arm around him.
“Thanks for that. Sorry if I acted poorly,” he whispered. Alex kissed Scott on the cheek.
“No problem, baby. It’s you and me. Are you okay? Better now that he left. We can talk about it later if you want. It’s over." He paused noticing the anger on Scott's face. He needed him to refocus. "Let’s get to our guests."
"Love you, Schmoo,” said Scott. He kissed Alex on his cheek reciprocating the earlier gesture then smiled. He took a deep breath and moved to the group in the living room. The conversations were still going. Laughing. People having fun.
Michelle moved next to Scott. “What was that about?”
“Nothing. It’s all good now," replied Scott.
“Tomorrow you’ll tell me?” she asked inquisitively.
“Not much to share there. Another time. Let’s just have a nice evening, okay?”
“Okay. But you are going to tell me,” she smiled empathetically and gave Scott a small squeeze.
Scott smiled back. He held up his glass. “Cheers. Welcome to San Francisco.” They clinked their glasses sipped and pecked each other

on the lips as friends sometimes do. A moment of peace moved in and the party moved forward.

Clean up

Guests began filtering out around ten o'clock given they had to get up early to work the next morning. Alex, Scott, Michelle began cleaning up after saying the goodnights to their departing guests. Melissa, despite Scott and Alex verbalizing their objections, volunteered to help. Scott always appreciated her Italian persona of hospitality, warmth, and kindness. Her wavy light brown and blonde hair wisped along the sides of her face. Her joy was contagious always bringing smiles to faces wherever she was. He was also appreciative of how she mastered the speed of cleaning up in a kitchen.

"Hey, Melissa. How is that cute apartment of yours? I love your stories about where you live," asked Scott.

"It's great! I love my little apartment living at the top of this Victorian near Lafayette Park. It's just so perfect for me. I don't need much," she chimed back.

"Any good stories lately?" prodded Scott. Alex supported the question while Michelle watched and listened with curiosity.

"What's with this apartment?" she asked. Melissa began to spill a story.

"Oh…One of the tenants, Bette, is kinda nuts. I'll play some music, then next thing you know, she's banging on my door to turn it down. Now…I never have it higher than level 2 on volume. She must have dog ears! Then, if I don't turn it down, she wants to come in and talk. Last week, she came in wearing a dress. Sat in my pink beanbag chair…her skirt hikes up and she sits there…NO UNDERWEAR! Just showing me her vagina. Just out there for the world to see." Melissa motioned her hands around her groin. "I motioned to her dress and suggested she pull it down. She just looked at me and said 'it's nothing you haven't seen before. You have one too, you know'. Of course, I rolled my eyes at her. I told her I wasn't interested in her vagina staring me in the face. So I had to think about how to get her out of my apartment. I then told her that I was getting ready for work and had to leave in ten mins. Ya know...giving her the obvious hint. I felt so uncomfortable. Talking with her unshaved vagina staring at me. Blech! It's not something I wanted to see or talk with if you catch my drift." She laughed and continued chiming her story. Michelle joined her and was laughing in amazement. Scott and Alex were holding their stomachs with tears forming in their eyes. "She gets up. Farts something fierce. Then says she would see me later. Not even an apology! She just farts and leaves! Can you believe it?! First, I have to stare at her unshaven vagina, then she boldly farts!" she ended and shook her head.

Michelle asked in hysterics, "Why did you let her in?".

"I didn't have a choice. Once I opened the door, she just pushes her way in and makes herself comfortable. I think there's something wrong with her...you know..." She circled her ear with her index finger, crossed her eyes while sticking out her tongue to the side suggesting crazy. "Tales from the Victorian" she ended. "And with that...I am done cleaning! All set! I hate to say it, but I gotta run home. I need to make sure I get home before midnight, otherwise Mr. Wong will catch me and want an explanation of my late arrival. You'd think he was my dad," she said shaking her head.

"I look forward to more stories during my stay," said Michelle with a giggle. Sounds interesting.

"Oh...you ain't heard the half of it," added Alex. "She has some doozy stories. I wouldn't be surprised if it's an experiment." He chuckled. Melissa grabbed her jean jacket and wrapped her scarf around her neck.

"I hope they tell me if it is. The good thing...at least the rent is cheap." She added half-jokingly. She turned and hugged and kissed each of her hosts then waved good night and left through the door.

"She hilariously wonderful," Michelle commented. The couple agreed.

"What a night! I'm bushed. Mind if I head up and get ready and go to bed? See you in the morning?" asked Michelle.

"No problem. We will follow shortly. Did you have a nice time?" asked Alex.

“Lovely. Thank you for the nice welcome.” She hugged and kissed Scott and Alex. “Thanks for having me.” She turned and headed upstairs.
“Okay then,” said Scott. “That was good, yes?” he turned to Alex asking.
“Yes. Despite Gabriel showing up. Are you really, okay?” Alex asked with a hint of concern.
“Yeh. I’m fine. He always plays head games on people. He likes to get reactions.”
“But are you okay?” Alex asked again.
“Yes. Let’s go to bed. I’m tired. You must be too and we both have a day tomorrow,” Scott stated deflecting avoiding the conversation.
“Okay. We can talk more about it another time when you’re ready. I still have to talk with Michelle. I’ll check in with her tomorrow. Oh…and you did an amazing job.”
“Thanks, Schmoo.” Scott was looking forward to just being held by Alex. He knew sleep would come quickly once he was in his arms feeling his protective warmth.

A Bad Day

The alarm went off at eight AM.
Beep-beep-beep-Beep-Beep-BEep-BEep-BEep-BEEp-BEEp-BEEP-BEE…
Alex reached over and pounded the snooze button then rolled over and put his arm around Scott cuddling in close. Scott reached up and put his hand on Alex's forearm.
"MMmm. Morning, Schmoo," he whispered.
"SShhh" replied Alex quietly. It started again…
Beep-beep-beep-Beep-Beep-BEep-BEep…
Alex rolled over and pounded the alarm off. "Ugh."
Scott lazily rolled over and groggily muttered "up and at 'em. Let's do this. Sun is shining. You want to shower first, or should I?" he asked knowing the answer starting to move.
"You go. I need a few more minutes," muttered Alex.
"Okay. Done."

When Scott finished getting ready about thirty minutes later, he leaned over Alex. Kissed his ear and cheek. Then whispered, "C'mon, Schmoo. JB is waiting for you. I am going downstairs to make coffee. Love you." Alex stirred and stretched moving the covers off his nude body. He rolled onto his back and outstretched his arms and yawned waking up. He started moving to get out of bed.
"Mmmm. Coffee." And looked sweetly up at Scott who looked back with affection.
"I love how adorable you look in the morning. Your hair all tousled up and over an eye." Then leaned over a kissed him. "See you with coffee shortly. Go get ready." He turned and headed for the kitchen. Alex moved to his morning routine. He loved how Scott always

gave him his own time in the bathroom. They both thought morning routines were important and everyone should have their private bathroom time. He made the bed then headed for the bathroom. Usually, Scott did this, but he felt obligated to do it this morning given all Scott did for the party. The day had begun.

Scott entered the kitchen to find Michelle already at the breakfast nook table. She had made coffee, toasted bagels, brought out the melon-wrapped prosciutto leftover from the party, prepped the variety of fresh berries from the fridge all cleaned and ready to eat. She placed a few eggs next to the stove.

"Good morning" she whispered happily. "I am still two hours ahead of you and thought you would appreciate breakfast. You do eat breakfast, right?" She hoped they did.

"Not all the time. But today? Yes. Right now, I need coffee. Mind if I take a cup up for Alex quickly?" Scott asked with great appreciation.

"Phew! I did something right! Go for it," she replied with understanding. Scott poured coffee into the two large black mugs they had gotten from Pottery Barn. Both with cream. Alex was two heaping sugars. He grabbed Alex's cup and ran upstairs careful to not spill. "Be right back."

Scott returned smiling triumphantly. "He needed that. And I got a nice morning kiss for my valor. And now…Good morning to you, princess. How did you sleep?" Michelle looked out the window to the garden and said, "Like the dead. I love that bed. It was comfortable. I was also a little buzzed from Bitsy's joint, so that helped, too." Scott looked at her a little surprised.

"Really? Bitsy and you got stoned last night? She rarely does that. I think the last time she asked me was about two years ago. She must already like you." he jested. "She did that to me in the garden at one of our parties. I was a bit stressed over something goofy, but she sensed it. She's a great listener. A good friend." he added.

"Hm," replied Michelle with a small smile and a pondering gaze.

"So…what are you up to today? I have some things to do this morning before heading to the shop. Can I give you some directions? You feel like exploring? Oh…and did you see the tickets to the DeYoung we had in the bowl in your room? We're members and get complimentary tickets that we give to guests…if you're into going…they're there if you want to use them." Scott rambled unsure what Michelle was planning.

“I think I am going to wander around the neighborhood today. I’ll explore more later this week,” she replied.
“I think you’ll love the area. Just in case, you can catch the 22 Fillmore that runs to the Marina if you feel up to it. The Palace of Fine Arts is always really inspirational to walk around. I love that area. The Marina itself is kinda cool. It’s on a landfill, so the buildings tend to get a little rustled when there’s an earthquake, but it’s a great area. You can also check out Chestnut street. Great stores, small restaurants, and shops...Sorry. I’m rambling again. I just get excited.” Michelle looked at him with a grin.
“I’ll check it out. Don’t worry about me. Thanks for the bus tip, though. Where’s your shop?” she asked.
“It’s on Fillmore at Wilmot. If you step out of the house, turn left and walk down Sacramento to Fillmore, then turn right. It’s just a few blocks down. Scott’s Closet. Stop in, say hi to Troy and me.” He answered with a hint of hope.
“Great. I will,” she said with a mouthful of breakfast. Scott started eating, excited for the day. He then looked over at her, gulping his coffee wondering if she was going to say any more about the evening. He paused.
“What did you think of everyone last night?”
“I had fun. It was a bit unexpected, but everyone seems so kind. Genuine. Laura is a true salesperson. She always went right back to radio talk. She has strong opinions about the talk show hosts, that’s for sure.” She giggled.
“True,” said Scott affirmingly.
“Brandon and Troy are funny guys. Mer is really sweet. And…who was with her husband who was in the theater? I'm spacing I met them last time I quickly visited. Sorry. My heads a little cloudy this morning," she asked with curiosity.
“Oh…they’re not married. They have just been living together for a while. That’s Ally and Jerry. She is an Aussie sweetie. Accident-prone, for sure! I think one time she stapled her thumb to her desk. Another time, she fell off her heels and sprained her ankle. I have witnessed her walking into door frames a few times with some nasty face bruises resulting afterward. Poor thing. But a heart of platinum.” Scott replied smiling and shaking his head a little. Michelle’s eyes widened as he was describing Ally and let out a small giggle of disbelief with an endearing look.

"That's right. Ally! Wow. Well…I really like her. Jerry smiles a lot. Actor, teacher, and acting coach? Right?"
"Yes. He's a good guy. I think he was in the movie Scream, too. He's a good guy," answered Scott in-between bites.
"That's crazy. I will have to ask him about that next time I see him. I'd love to hear his stories about acting," she added finishing her breakfast. "Will we see that group of people again, soon?" she asked avoiding asking about Aarav and Gabriel. She thought it would be too much after one night. She'll dig for more later.
"Well. It depends on how long you are staying for…you never said," Scott hinted.
"A few weeks, if that's okay. I have some things I need to sort out. I didn't want to say anything, but I was dating this guy back home in Chicago, and I needed to get away for a bit," shared Michelle hoping he wouldn't ask too many questions. She took a chance.
"Oh. Sorry to hear that. What happened? Did he cheat on you…or you on him…?" he asked trying not to pry but was interested.
"No," She lied. "Nothing like that. It was me. It was just…well…something was off, so I broke it off, and came here." She wasn't ready to share more, yet. It was complicated.
"Okay. Got it. I won't pry," said Scott taking a hint. "You know…I am a good listener, too. Just in case…okay?" He put his hand on her upper arm near her shoulder.
"Thanks," she quietly replied with appreciation patting the back of his hand.

Loud heavy steps were resounding. Alex entered the kitchen.
"Good morning," he said as he filled his coffee cup then moved to sit and have a quick bite. "Sleep well?" he asked looking at Michelle.
"Yes. She slept well. Yes, she had a lovely time last night. Bitsy got her stoned. Laura showed her sales personality, the boys made her smile. She is going to stay for a few weeks and wander around today." Scott answered for her with a quick summary so she wouldn't have to repeat everything, then got up and pecked Alex on the cheek. Alex's eyes widened, but he surrendered shrugging his shoulders knowing he will learn more later.
"Fascinating how I ask over here, and the answer comes out over there…. just fascinating." Alex said jokingly as he nibbled on some fruit. "I would love to stay and chat, but I need to get down the street to see JB. I am already late, and I have a feeling he is already

tapping his foot waiting for me." He gulped down his coffee, popped two more blueberries in his mouth, and got up. He turned. "So, Michelle…I should be home around 7 tonight, after the program. You should listen in if you're interested. JB is the best when it comes to talking about political hot topics. Probably one of the more reasonable voices."

"Okay. I'll try," she responded in a noncommittal tone.

"We'll talk tonight, too? Yes?" Asked Alex while looking her in the eyes. Scott felt like he was starting to watch a tennis match watching them go back and forth.

"Yes," she replied, again in a noncommittal tone.

"Okay. Gotta run. See you both later. Have a good day, baby." He leaned over and kissed Scott.

"You too, Schmoo," replied Scott. "Text me."

"Muwah!" replied Alex as he grabbed his bag from the chair and scurried off out the door.

"He's a bit of a whirlwind, isn't he? He hasn't changed," stated Michelle.

"Yep," replied Scott. "Wouldn't have him any other way." then he changed the subject. "Okay…I am gonna do dishes, pick up a bit before heading out. You good?" he asked as he got up starting to grab dishes from the table and clean up.

"I'm good. Don't mind me. I'm going to head upstairs and get ready for the day. See you later." She got up, leaned over to Scott, and pecked him on the cheek. "Thanks for having me. It means a lot," she said softly with a hint of mystery.

"Anytime. Remember, I can listen whenever you are ready," Scott reinforced.

"Thanks." She turned, placed her coffee cup in the sink, and headed up to get ready for her day.

After Scott cleaned up the kitchen and combed the house cleaning up any remnants from the previous night's festivities, he straightened himself out then yelled upstairs, "I am off to the shop. See you later, Michelle! Hugs!!!" He paused.

"Hugs back!! See you later! Have a great day!" yelled Michelle back.

Scott grabbed his keys and headed out bouncing to the store.

Scott arrived at his store to find Troy dusting the calendars section.

"Hi, queen!" greeted Troy. Then flapped around his ostrich duster.

"Hi! How are you, girl?" asked Scott.

“Good. Dragging my ass, a bit. Brandon and I went a grabbed a drink at Alta Plaza last night before heading home. Not a good thing to do. Gabriel and Aarav were there. Quite the little scene last night both at your place and the bar” replied Troy with a wink. “Wanna talk about it?” he added.
“Not much to talk about,” replied Scott.
“Of course, you can!” pressed Troy. “It’s not every day that a bitch of an ex would have the balls to show up at his Ex's’ house thinking it was okay,” he commented back.
“I can’t believe he showed up. I knew he and Aarav were friends, but I thought better of him. Now I am not sure what to think,” said Scott with a hint of disbelief and frustration.
“Well…I think you guys handled it very well without causing a commotion. Alex wasn't having it. At least he didn’t throw him out the door. He’s quite the gentleman. Me? I would have simply said, ‘Bitch, OUT!’ and pointed him in the direction for him to walk. Know what I mean, girl?” shared Troy.
“I felt like it, but I just didn’t want to make a scene,” answered Scott. “It’s over. I don’t want to dwell on it,” he added.
“Okaaaay. I am still wondering some things about your relationship with him. You gonna share more sometime?” Troy prodded. He loved gossip and he cared about Scott.
“Sure! One cool night in front of a fire and a warm brandy…” replied Scott half jesting then added, “Another time. Just not at the moment. Thanks, sister.” He smiled warmly at Troy; thankful he had such a friend.
“Well, all right. By the way…Rich stopped by and dropped off a letter. It’s on your desk upstairs,” shared Troy as he moved to reorganize the sunglass display with his duster under his arm. “Oh, thanks. I wonder what that’s about?” muttered Scott as he moved to the upper work area and his desk to retrieve the envelope. He arrived at his desk and saw the goldenrod envelope. He picked it up, tore the top using a phallic handled letter opener Troy gave him to reveal the edge of the paper inside. He pulled it out and began to silently read. He stared at it, then dropped into his chair. “Well shit,” he said. And stared at it some more, thinking this was not a good day.
“Any good news?!” asked Troy loudly as he was climbing the stairs to be with his friend.
“The opposite. I need to talk with Alex tonight. Shit” replied Scott softly. ‘

What is it?" asked Troy.
"They are raising the rent," answered Scott.
"Oh shit. Sorry, girl," replied Troy sympathetically. "What does that mean, other than paying more money here?" he asked with curiosity.
"Not sure. I need to talk with Alex," Scott replied with uncertainty. He did not want to alarm Troy. "Okay, girl. Well…I am here until noonish then off to my other gig at Marlena's. You need me to stay?" Troy asked.
"Nah. You go whenever. Thanks. I'll know more after Alex and I talk." He looked up at Troy with a fake subtle happy grin trying to hide his despair. It was getting really expensive in the neighborhood. Four other businesses had moved out due to rent hikes. Fillamento up the street was fortunate to own their building. Peets Coffee was solid. Everyone drinks coffee and tea. His shop was kitschy knick-knacks, sunglasses, small business bath products, artwork, gift cards, stationery, and such. "Okay. Buck up! Let's get some things done and hope the day gets better," said Scott loudly forcing a smile. He had hoped Alex was having a better day than him.

*****

Alex arrived at JB's place at 2039 Sacramento Street with his keys in hand. It was an Edwardian-styled building right across the street from Lafayette Park. JB's first-floor flat was spacious with large bay windows facing the street. The overgrown trees in front obstructed most of the park view but allowed for plenty of light to highlight the brightly painted yellow walls with white trim living room area. There were wood floors throughout the three-bedroom flat. JB had a contemporary flair of decorative style with warm wood touches throughout. His wall of art always captured his visitor's attention. Alex consistently found appreciation in the art collection that inspired him to pursue his photography.

Alex noticed JB sitting in his dining room area with KGO radio playing in the background. He was working hard to read his Wall Street Journal. He enjoyed listening to his colleague's perspectives with him often exclaiming words when a caller into the program would express what he would refer to as 'thoughtless and baseless opinions'. A commonly used reference was "blow-hard!"
"Morning JB," greeted Alex.

“Good morning. You’re late,” greeted JB to Alex in his baritone voice.
“Sorry. I chatted with my sister for a few minutes this morning before heading over. I’ll get your breakfast started. Oatmeal? Eggs and bacon? Toast or English muffin?” offered Alex moving quickly to the kitchen. “Oatmeal and whole-wheat toast, please,” responded JB. Alex had the routine down to a ballet. First, the coffee was ground, put in the filter, then placed in the coffee maker. He then got the water for brewing poured from the glass pot into the restaurant-style maker. Once that was going, he would start the oatmeal and put out the sugar packs, flatware, and JB's napkin on the table in front of him. He would stir the oatmeal, then retrieve the bread from the refrigerator and pop four slices into the toaster, with two more on the side for himself. Then a glass of orange juice was poured and placed. “Here’s your juice JB,” shared Alex as he placed the glass to JB’s left on the table. “Do you have your insulin pen?’ he asked. JB reached for his orange juice and shakily raised it to his lips taking a sip. “Yes. It’s right here,” he replied, clumsily retrieving it from under his San Francisco Chronicle with his right hand feeling slightly interrupted from his reading. Alex smiled with endearment at JB. He had recently recovered from having his neck broken and head reset due to Ankylosing Spondylitis, an arthritic condition of the spine. He was a tall man who was moderately heavyset. Because of his condition, he could not move his head side to side or up down. If he had to look up, he would lean back. If he had to look to the side, he turned his body to see. This in addition to his arthritis, bursitis, left hip, and foot issue which caused a slight limp. His diabetes took the vision from his right eye. His left eye’s vision was fair. He had to wear very thick-lensed glasses to read. Alex always took double takes as they would magnify JB’s blue eyes to an animated size. He was inspired and fondly dubbed them ‘coke bottle' glasses. JB's eyes looked enormous through the lenses. Depending on the print size of the papers, books, or whatever he wanted to read, JB would pull out his magnifying glass. He loved reading and was a master of the English language. It was known throughout his listening audience. Some of them openly shared that as listeners, they learned to speak English listening to his programs. His thick salt and pepper hair was an envied feature stated openly by some of his many acquaintances. The characteristic that brought him fame was his deep clear baritone voice. It was definitely a voice for radio

and one that commanded attention. JB had a uniform. Khakis for work. He had a pair of black, brown, and oxblood leather casual shoes for work, all the same style. Tailored suits for events along with his large fashionable tie and cuff-link collections. He consistently donned one of his three outer jackets and carried what he would call 'the football" which was a beige canvas and brown leather-trimmed zipper briefcase. During breakfast this morning, he was getting worked up reacting to a radio program in progress. He was scheduled for the 11 am-3 pm shift with his program, soon to move to the 3 pm-7 pm slot. He was excited about that given it was the Bay Area commute time slot. "Alex…no dawdling. We need to get a move on and get to the office. I have plenty to read to prepare for the program. Oh…how was your party last night?"
"Good. Michelle seemed to have a good time," replied Alex as he placed JB's breakfast in front of him. "Breakfast served. Coffee coming up. By the way, Fred and Bitsy say hi, along with Ali and everyone. We had some good laughs."
"Did Laura and Mer show up?"
"Yes, they did. You know…Laura loves you. She ranked you top of the other hosts at the station," shared Alex.
"Of course, she did. She makes good ad money from my program," JB replied, chuckling. "She's sharp and knows her customers and business." Then asked, "So what's going on with your sister? Am I going to see her?"
"Of course! But let's give her a few days to get settled. Not sure how long she's staying, and I set no time for her. As you know, there are some things we need to catch up on, and some questions I hope she'll answer." replied Alex.
"Mmm-hmm," mumbled JB. "People will share things when they're ready. Don't rush her, or she'll run off. Based on what you've shared with me thus far, she seems to be a rather perplexing and enigmatic individual. Give her time," he advised.
"Okay. I'll try not to push it," Alex moved to change the topic. "Topics today?"
"I think we'll talk about the dot-com crash impact on the Bay area. Jim Fords' left the Republican party leaving the house to the Democrats. I am not sure the other, yet."
"I'll start checking to see what's trending when we get to the office," said Alex.

There was a knock at the door followed by the appearance of an envelope slid under the door.
Alex got up to retrieve it.
"What is it?" asked Gene.
"I don't know. An envelope was slid under the door. Want me to open it?" asked Alex as he retrieved the envelope.
"Sure," replied Gene with curiosity.
Alex opened the envelope. There was an official document. "Well, shit," said Alex handing the document to JB after reading it quickly.
"What?" asked Gene reaching for the envelope.
"Read for yourself," Alex replied tensely. "You always pay your rent on time. You've fixed the place up. Why didn't he offer it to you to purchase?! There doesn't seem to be much of a notice, other than the minimum, here."
"Actually, he did. I turned him down. He wanted seven hundred and fifty thousand," replied JB. "I told him no. I have too many other responsibilities. It's a bit much for this place, I think," he added as he read the document while Alex stared at it in frustration.
"I wish you would have told me," said Alex with a heavy sigh.
"Sorry. It would not have changed anything. I wouldn't want to buy the place, anyway," JB muttered with a hint of tension.
"Well…I guess we need to find you a new place to live. Since you didn't opt to buy the place, the owner is having his daughter move in. The good thing is, it looks like you'll probably get your deposit back, and he is not charging you rent next month."
"Well, shit," muttered JB, resigning to the reality beginning to set in.
"Okay then. I'll give him a call when we get to the office. Tommy coming today to clean the house?"
"No. He's coming tomorrow. I'll talk to Scott and see what we can find for you. We'll start looking for a place," replied Alex firmly and annoyed.
"Okay. We'll deal with it. Let's get going. I will run to the Salle de Bain before we leave," JB stated as he wiped his mouth finishing his breakfast and coffee. "Not sure about this day," he mumbled.
"Me either," replied Alex as he got up to take care of the dishes. "I'll put the papers together, too. About ten mins?" he asked JB as he began his organization ritual.
"Yep. My jacket is on the chair over there, yes?"
"Yes," Affirmed Alex.

Shortly after, they head out with Alex cautioning JB "Step. There are three more steps.... I'll get the car door.... watch your head..." as JB sunk into his passenger side seat in the Honda Accord nicknamed 'Ezzi' short for 'Esmerelda'. "And we're off."

*****

The radio program went superbly. Alex handled all the call routing with expertise. JB was a pro handling the irritable callers. He would always have his facts ready for those who attempted to dispute him. He was politically astute, and a lover of history. His ability to draw on facts from memory was inspirational and would draw awe and amazement from those who listened. They would fact-check him to find him correct. Rarely was he wrong. If he didn't know, he would state it, then research it heavily so he would learn more and add to his arsenal of knowledge.

Alex assisted JB back to his desk away from the studio informing him he had to make a few calls, including Scott. JB waved him off when he sat down. "Go make your calls. I need to check my emails anyway. Oh...we have a few errands to run on the way home."

"Thanks. Be right back," said Alex. He pulled out his phone and dialed Scott.

"Hey Schmoo!" answered Scott. "How'd the program go?"

"Great! I have some news though," answered Alex. "JB needs to move, so we need to find him a place."

"Shit," replied Scott. "Well...my rent went up. I don't think I can afford this spot anymore. Retail is down. I think I need to get a job," he added.

"Crap. Let's talk about it when I get home. Shitty day. You okay?"

"Yeah. I'm fine. Just uncertain. You?"

"I'm fine. Don't worry. We'll get through this. Love you. See you in a bit."

"Love you, Schmoo. Muwah!" Scott replied with affection.

"Oh! Before I forget..." added Alex loudly hoping to catch Scott before he hung up. "Have you seen Michelle?" he asked.

"Funny. No. She was supposed to stop in the store and never showed. I don't think we have anything to worry about. I am sure she is just walking around checking out Fillmore. I gave her directions on how to get to the Marina. She's a big girl. I am sure we'll hear all about it later."

"Okay. Hmmm. I'll see you later. Kisses," Alex said with a hint of uncertainty.
"Kisses back."
Then they both hung up.

Scott wandered back to the register. It was another slow day. Only about $400 in sales. Bath and lotions, some cards tourists bought, candle holder set, and small decorative kitschy gay-toys from the bins in the loft area that included the Magic Earring Ken Doll, which seemed to fly out the door during Pride month. It still didn't help his situation. He decided to close up early and head home. There wasn't much foot traffic today. He would stop to pick up some odds and ends for dinner on the way and moved to close everything up for the night. He hoped Michelle had a better day than he and Alex did.

Scott stopped by the grocery store on the way home. He picked up some chicken thighs for baking. He was in the mood for something simple. He passed by the deli counter and spied Irna.
"Hi Irna. How's your day going?" inquired Scott.
"Oh, fine, sweetie. How was the party last night? Did the food go over well?"
"Oh yes," replied Scott. "Your balls were a hit!" he giggled. She winked back at him. "Good. And how's that sister of Alex's? She get in okay? Michelle, right?" she asked.
"Yep. She arrived just fine. A little drama during the party, though, Nothing crazy. It all ended well," he answered.
"Good. Good. Am I going to meet here sometime?" she asked with a Cheshire cat smile.
"Yeh, Sure. I am sure she will come in sometime soon with either me or Alex. She's kinda off wandering on her own right now. I am hoping she'll be back when I get home. It's been a day," he shared.
"What happened?"
"Alex said JB has to move, and my rent went up at the store. I don't think I am going to be able to hold onto the place much longer." He was starting to feel down about it. "We'll figure it out."
"I know you will, sweetie. You're both smart. Everything always works out. Ya know?" Irna said assuredly and with a wise calm.
"I believe that, too," replied Scott.
Irna looked at Scott and pouted a smile with her rose-red lips. Her blonde wig, looking a little more tousled than usual fluttered a bit when the store's air conditioning came on. "Brrr!" she said. "Let's

move over here out from under the vent above." She motioned him over a few feet near the sliced deli meat section, next to the fancy cheese case. "I got a note from my niece the other day. She's going to come down in a few weeks to visit from Oregon. She has a little girl. Have I ever told you about her?" she asked Scott.
"Sorry. No. You never mentioned her. What's her name?"
"Rebecca. She was my sister's daughter. She, my sister, died a few years ago. Her daughter is about 6 now. Cutest little thing," she smiled with affection. "I want you and Alex to meet her. Okay?"
"Sure! We would love to," Scott replied with a subtle burst of delight.
"Maybe if Alex's sister is still around…she would see her, too," she said a bit reserved.
"We'll see. Not sure how long she's planning to stay. Speaking of which, I'm sorry. I need to pay for these breasts and get my ass home. Nothing like a hungry hubby coming home with no dinner ready," he said, glancing at his watch.
"You go, dear. Oh…I have a little something for you." She reached into her white smock. Looked around to make sure no one was watching them and placed a little joint in his shirt pocket. "For later. You boys go sit outside in your garden and chill out tonight. Don't worry. Things will work out." She patted him gently. "Go on now. See you later." She gave him a final squeezer on his shoulder, turned, and went back behind the counter to serve a brawny man staring at the sandwich menu options. Scott smiled back and went off to the express register. No one was in line, so he was quick to pay and was out the door.
Scott arrived home, grabbed the mail, and moved into the house. As he sorted through the mail, he spied a letter from their landlord, Phil. He opened the envelope and pulled the note out.
"Shit. Things do happen in threes." He decided to deal with it once he and Alex could be alone. "What a fucking day," he muttered to himself as he moved to the kitchen.
"Michelle?! You home?!?" he called out loudly up the stairs. No response. He called out again, just in case. Nothing. "Good. Let me get dinner together quickly. Simple tonight." He muttered to himself. He moved to the kitchen on a mission. He decided he would not say anything to Michelle about their situations until after he and Alex would talk and decide what they were going to do.

Changes, The Past and Present

A furious and eventful week had gone by for the trio. Michelle had not shared her situation yet. She was enjoying her exploration of San Francisco. Every evening at dinner, she regaled the couple with her adventures and asked questions about where to go next. She had visited Fort Point under the Golden Gate Bridge in the Presidio and walked around the grounds in the wonder of the military buildings and barracks. She wandered through Pacific Heights and found the Lyon Street steps, where at the top, was a gorgeous view of the bay, Palace of Fine Arts, Alcatraz, and what Scott and Alex dubbed the Sharon Stone house next to them. They thought it looked like the house in the movie "Basic Instinct" (which was actually on Vallejo Street), but they liked to poke fun. She had wandered through Golden Gate Park, enjoying Stow Lake, the stables, the Botanical gardens, the DeYoung Museum, and the buffalo. She even got a kick from catching a glimpse of the men cruising around the windmills near Ocean Beach. Her sightseeing reminded Alex and Scott of how amazing their city was. They chuckled when she mentioned the nature-lovers near the windmills. She attempted to coax out why that made them laugh a little, but they would only reply "just don't go in the bushes". She shrugged her shoulders yet remained intrigued.

They finished eating an early dinner, and Michelle gently stated, "Okay. I think I am about ready to start sharing some things with you." She looked at Alex. Then, she looked softly at Scott. "May I be so bold? Would you mind if Alex and I had a talk, just him and I?"

Scott looked at them both a little surprised by the request but knew this was coming. “No Problemo. I will make myself scarce. I have some things to do at the shop, anyway.” He stood up. “You have the dishes?” pointing to the table waving his finger around.
“Um…okay…I think we do,” replied Alex taken aback. He looked and Scott then Michelle then back to Scott with a surprised look on his face. “Thanks, love. Sorry about this. I had no idea.”
Scott leaned over and kissed his man “It’s cool. You need to do this.” He stood up straight and said, “Y’all better share with me when I get back…. Okay?”
Michelle replied “Yes. Sorry. Count on it. There are just some things…well…you know.”
“No. But thanks. Hugs. Talk it out! Love you.” He grabbed a jacket and headed out the door.
Michelle started the story. “I know this is a bit surprising. I just didn’t know how to do this, so I thought I should just do it with you and get it out.” She paused and took a deep breath.
“Okay.” Alex softly replied.
"Just don’t ask questions or say anything until I get this out, okay?” she asked nervously.
“Sure,” he replied with warm assurance. She started.
“Well…remember when we were in LA? Our roommate?”
“Yes,” Alex replied. “It was funny how you two seemed to hit it off and become fast friends.”
“Well…it was more than that. We hid from you that we dated a few times. Then, one day, I came home early from work to find him watching some strange porn. He was surprised by my arrival and quickly turned it off knowing he was caught doing something wrong…it was weird. I didn't see exactly what kind of porn it was. Anyway, next thing you know, we started talking. He really wanted to deflect being caught doing...you know..” she added nervously but kept going. Alex could only imagine. “Well. As we were talking, he had a wild look in his eyes…and just slowly moved closer to me asking me about my day. He moved in and around like a predator, thinking back on it." She stammered a little and looked up at the ceiling, then returned her gaze to Alex. “We were chit-chatting and then it got really weird.” She paused. Her voice was shaking a little. She took a few slow breaths, then looked at Alex with her eyes starting to tear up. “He moved in and started rubbing my arms with that weird look in his eyes. His gaze and mannerisms seemed to lock

me like I couldn't move. Next thing you know, we started kissing. At first, it was soft. Then it started getting a little rough. He started pressing on me and pulled me in really close…almost tight." She began to sound strained yet caught herself and continued. "Then he began to get more aggressive and forced me down onto the sofa reaching under my blouse. I said no, but he didn't care. He kept moving and forced open my top. I struggled, knocked over the lamp and a few other things off the coffee table. Next thing you know, I was stuck. He was on top of me holding both my hands over the arm of the sofa and slid down his sweatpants. He then raped me. When it was over, he looked at me and said, well that was fun wasn't it?" she paused, tears running lightly down her face. "He seemed to turn the whole thing into a rough consensual sex act, but it wasn't. I got angry and slapped him. Then ran into my room, crying. He threatened I better not tell you or anyone. He called me a whore and that I was asking for it. I sat on my bed, shocked…hurt…feeling disgraced and dirty…I didn't know what to do but knew I had to leave. While I threw my stuff together, I heard some rustling then the door slammed. When I came out with my bag, he was gone. I wrote a note to you and left. I am so very sorry." Tears were running down her face as she contained herself.

Alex stared at her with tears in his eyes. Empathy and anger mixed. He reached over and pulled her close to him.

"Go ahead. Let it out. You do not need to be sorry. I thought it was something I did. I am so sorry I was blind to what was happening." Tears were running down his cheeks, now. Michelle was fully sobbing. Releasing all of that secret and pain. She needed to hear this from her sweet brother. He held her tightly and whispered, "It is in the past. You are beautiful. I love you. I am always here for you. So is Scott." They held each other for about 20 minutes. She leaned back and looked at Alex. He got up and returned with a box of Kleenex. After they cleared their noses and wiped their faces, Alex looked at her and said, "You need to report this." He was doing everything to hold his anger inside. He was angry at the man who violated his sister. He wanted to kill him. He was angry with Michelle for not telling him. He felt helpless. He wanted to do something but had no power to do anything. He could only support his sister.

"I did. The problem is that his name was fake. He wasn't on the lease since we let him move in. They have a description, and we didn’t confirm his work, remember? He was so nice and charming…which his work wasn’t true, either. All the police have is a description. They have my info. I asked them not to see you about this. You didn’t know any more than I did, and I felt ashamed. They tried to push to speak with you, but I made it clear if they did, I would rescind my reporting of the incident. They obliged…reluctantly. Then I went to the bus station and went to Portland, Oregon.”

“Um…wow. What can I do?” asked Alex, holding her hand.

“Just be my supportive brother, okay?”

“Okay,” he replied with affirmation and warmth.

“And another thing…” she continued.

“What?” he looked at her.

“I became pregnant. I thought about having an abortion but ended up giving the baby for adoption. A little girl.”

“What the fuck?! You’re kidding, right?” Alex said surprised.

“No. I wasn’t ready to have a child, and I met this nice lady one day in the Portland State University commons. It was so serene on the campus...all the trees... Anyway, I was sitting there feeling depressed and pondering my options. She came up, introduced herself, and asked to sit down. Anyway, we became friends. She had a daughter who had recently been informed she could not have children. We became friends. She shared stories. We went to lunch. She helped me out a few times, just being kind. So next thing you know, I ended up giving her daughter my baby. I never met her. I didn’t want to. I just knew she would be fine. Then I went to Chicago to move forward with my life. I didn't look back. I couldn’t. It was too painful. I just knew she was in a good place.” She smiled reminiscently with contentment on her face.

“Aren’t you curious about her? Did you reach out to keep in touch? Do you want to? After all, that little girl is family…right?” Alex looked at her with empathy and a hint of consternation.

“No. She is their family. It’s alright, Alex. She would only remind me…and you…of a black moment in our life. She was a light at that moment. But there would still be the pain. She is so much better off there. Understand? And I don’t want you telling my story to anyone…that is…except to Scott. But I want to be there when you do, okay? I will tell our family when I am ready to. I just needed to tell you. Okay?” She looked at Alex with confidence and direction.

“Got it. It's your story. Not mine to tell. I need a drink. Want a vodka tonic or something? Gurl!” said Alex getting up not sure how to feel with the bombshells dropped on him. He also knew he had to honor Michelle’s wishes. It was her story and experience. He found it difficult to believe she kept it to herself these past years.
“Sure!” replied Michelle, feeling the weight of the world was lifted off her shoulders. “Let’s call Scott and tell him to come home.”
“Fine! The numbers by the phone. You call him while I fix our drinks and start dishes.... Oh...” Alex continued. “Any other secrets or skeletons to drag out before Scott gets back?”
“Not really. I’ll tell you about the guy in Chicago tomorrow.”
“Oh...can we just have it now? I don’t know if I can take it. I hope a better story than this last one...” he replied.
“It is better. Not sure about the happy ending, though. Just nothing like the last one.”
“Phew! Okay then.”
Michelle dialed the shop. “Scott? Come home. We’re done.... Yes, we cried.... No. No fighting.... Yes, we are having a drink now. Alex just started dishes.... And yes...we will share.... Okay.... See you in a few minutes.” And hung up.
“He’s on his way back. Can I help with the dishes?”
“Sure. Oh...just so you know, JB has to move. The owner of the building sold out. I found out our landlord is going to sell, too. The market is hot right now. So we will have to move and probably scale down a bit...and Scott’s shop rent went up, so he will close his shop and look for a job.”
“Oh, for fuck’s sake! When it rains it pours, doesn’t it? Are you guys okay?” Michelle asked concerned.
“We’re fine. JB wants to have dinner tomorrow night-his place, given he is going to move into a new time slot for his program...and he is dying to meet you. I have held off as long as I can. Scott and I have been looking at different places during lunchtimes. We think we found a house for him out in the Inner Richmond that he can rent. Good thing you’re around so you can help us move...maybe?”
“We’ll see,” replied Michelle. “What a trip! Is it always this dramatic...er...exciting here?”
Alex laughed. “No. We are generally pretty boring. Dinner parties with great people. Dining at restaurants meeting the chefs. Napa Valley trips. Mustard Festival. Sonoma Valley harvest wine auction. Sausalito Arts Festival. Trips! Recipes...We are pretty fortunate.

We are just having a moment," Alex replied smiling. "Even though we end up in the emergency room every holiday with JB, he always comes out more amazing than ever. A great soul, that one. We're in it all together."
"Helooooooo!" resounded through the entryway with a door slamming. Scott walked briskly in eager to see his man and his man's sister. "Dishes done yet? I can't wait for the spill!" said Scott walking over to Alex to hug him from behind. Then he looked at Michelle and hugged her. "Your eyes are puffy. You were crying," Scott said in an accusatory tone. "Let me grab a drink. We'll move to the living room. We will sit and share. Yes?"
"Yes," confirmed Alex finishing washing the dishes and rinsing the sink.
"We're ready. I think Alex and I need a refill first," added Michelle finishing drying the last of the flatware and returning the towel to the handle on the dishwasher. They all coordinated their drinks and moved to the living room. Scott turned on the stereo and played some CDs with a mixture of ballads low volume for background music.
"You are such a queen," said Alex. "Grab tissues. Sit down. There's a lot to share." Scott looked at the pair. He saw the seriousness in their eyes.
"Good thing I made this a double, then." He followed the directions and sat. "I'm listening." Alex began to share the story. Throughout the two sharing the tale, all three of them teared up. By the end, Scott moved next to Michelle and held her tight, both of them crying.
"No words," said Scott tearfully. "That is so fucked up and wrong. I am so sorry for your experience. Whatever I can do, please…just tell me. Don't even ask. And a little girl! Again…no words."
"Just your support and love. That's all I need. And please don't say anything to anyone. It's my story to share and I will share it with others when I'm ready. Okay?" requested Michelle.
"You got it, sweetie," Scott replied with promise. "Cross my bra – Hope to spy – Zip my lips – Until I die" and he held up his hand with his sign language 'I love you' gesture with his fingers crossed.
"And you have your dramas going on with your shop, JB needing to move, and you needing to find a place, too. I already get tired thinking about all of that!" declared Michelle.

“Oh. Alex told you,” he turned and looked at Alex who blew him a kiss of apology. “He-was-supposed-t-wait-so-we-could-tell-you-together,” he stated as he stared at Alex with his eyes widened intense with an accusation of betrayal.
“Sorry, Scott. I had to offset the drama. It was intense, as you can see. We needed to shift dramas,” Alex shared apologetically.
“Got it. Forgiven. I have a question. did you, or are you getting any kind of counseling for your ordeal?" asked Scott.
"In short, yes. After I moved to Chicago and landed my job, I sought counseling. It has been very helpful. I found I was not alone." answered Michelle.
"Are you still getting counseling? I don't know. Pardon my ignorance. I don't know how long you get counseling for something so horrible."
"I still have monthly sessions. I don't really feel like talking about that right now. Do you mind?" she asked.
" Sure. I'm sorry. I just feel so bad for what you experienced." Scott didn't let on about his past. He thought it a good idea to change topics. "Soooooo…should we have another drink and then go to bed? This was a heavy night, and I think it is fair to say we are all exhausted from this. And tomorrow, after all, is another day.”
“Yes. You guys go ahead. I’ll head up in a little bit. I think I just want to sit down here for a while. Is that okay? I’ll get the music,” asked Michelle softly.
“Sure. Love you. Sweet dreams. See you in the morning," said Alex. The three exchanged hugs and kisses and good nights, then Alex and Scott ascended the stairs to their rooms with their drinks in hand. Michelle moved to the garden. She sat down on a chair with the stars above and the fog slowly wisping in above. It would be perfect one moment, then a light chilly breeze. She thought about the lady, he daughter, her husband, and her little girl. She wondered for a moment how they were. She hoped they were happy. Her little girl would be almost 8 now. She sipped her drink smiling feeling light and thinking happy thoughts for them. She knew she made the right choice.
Alex and Scott sat in their room and to finish their drinks, recap their days and the evening before getting ready for bed. “What a fucking night,” said Scott.
“You said it,” affirmed Alex.

"And there is no way to catch the asshole? That fucking dirtbag? Really?" asked Scott.
"Not sure. The police have everything, according to Michelle. I am sure they will reach out if something comes up. It's been a while, but who knows. It's pretty fucked up. But the most important thing…Michelle is okay now. I just don't know what to make of the little girl. Wow. I'm an uncle, but I will never know her. At least, not at this moment. Who knows?" answered Alex thoughtfully.
"Well. Things always have a way of working out. Funny how that always happens, you know?" shared Scott.
"I never really thought about it. But you're right. They do. One way or another. By the way…how was your day?"
"It was okay. Slow," Then Scott paused for a moment remembering something. "This is gonna sound weird," he said with a curious tone.
"What?" asked Alex.
"I forgot to tell you about my chat with Irna the other day. I didn't think twice about it. But come to think of it…oh…I don't know." Scott shook his head as if trying to wave off an odd feeling.
"What? Go on," encouraged Alex. He knew that if Scott didn't get out of his mind what lingered, it would manifest into other things until it came out.
"We had a curious chat near the counter. She shared with me that she had a sister who passed away a few years ago. Her daughter, Rebecca, was coming down from Oregon to visit with her little girl, and she wanted us to meet her. She said the little girl was six. Funny, huh?" Scott looked at Alex with a look of wonder.
"Oh please. Just because her daughter is visiting from Oregon with a little girl doesn't mean anything. That's just a coincidence. Did she mention if Rebecca's husband was coming with her?"
"No, come to think of it. You're probably right. Just a coincidence. Funny the timing, though, right?"
"True. And that she shared that with you. Maybe after these past couple of years, she decided to finally befriend us. She's always been exceedingly kind to us. I've seen her with other people, but with us, she acts kind of mom-like. Sweet, you know?" Alex shared with warm reflection. "I know we both have moms…you know…"
"Hm," replied Scott. "You're right. Let's not overthink this. I'm tired." He finished his drink and placed the glass on a small table by the doors to the deck. "I'm gonna go brush." He leaned over and kissed Alex.

“You’re right. Go. Brush. <yawn>” said Alex. He reached over and turned on the alarm and turned on the music at low volume and sat back on the bed. A few mins later, Scott returned from the bathroom all refreshed for bed. Alex lazily got up, pecked Scott on the lips, and departed for the bathroom for his nightly ritual. “Don’t forget dinner at JBs tomorrow night” he groggily reminded Scott as he sauntered off.
“I won’t. Go get ready. I need to spoon with my honey-bunches-of-ohs.” And climbed under the covers and began to get comfortable. Alex returned a few minutes later. Climbed into bed with Scott, who already was asleep. He snuggled close to Scott while lifting Scott’s arm to place over him and snuggled his back to Scott’s chest. He could feel Scott’s breath lightly on his neck. He smiled. “I love you Smoo,” Alex whispered. Then reached over and turned the music and lights off. They fell into a deep sleep.

A Day of Surprises

It was a beautiful June 21st day with change in the air. The sun was shining with a clear brilliant blue sky of promise. The fog left early morning, and it was going to be about 69 degrees. Michelle awoke early and decided to go out for a walk. She felt like exploring more of San Francisco. Scott and Alex awoke to prep for their morning appointment with a landlord who personally reached out to JB at the radio station. She had a house on 11th Avenue that was a possibility for JB to rent, and they were going to check it out. Troy was at the store starting following directions to pack up return-to-vendors. Scott decided to take a break from retail after discussing it heavily with Alex. He needed a change. JB had introduced him to a few people with whom he would connect to start looking for a new job, but nothing was resonating with him. JB's program was moving to its new time slot next week after Gay Pride, so Alex's schedule was about to change. The scheduled dinner that evening was also bringing some news that JB wanted to share. He was also eager to meet Michelle. Alex had held off on it a bit because he felt they needed to reconnect first. For some strange reason, for everyone that day, everything seemed brighter than usual. It felt good. There was optimism in the air.

Alex and Scott were at the table eating their toast, fruit and having their coffee. "Did you call JB to remind him we were looking at a house for him this morning?" asked Scott.

"Yes. I did. I asked Brandon to take care of JB's breakfast this morning. He was very happy to do it. He enjoys his discussions with JB. He's also kind of a fan. He keeps joking about the way JB gets frustrated on the air calling people 'blowhards' and impressed how

he recites facts off the top of his head. He considers it kind of a treat for him," answered Alex a bit in jest.
"Cool. And how are you feeling after your talk with Michelle last night? Better?"
"Hm. Better. It feels like a haze is lifted. I know we have some other things to work through, but that was heavy. I also know it wasn't easy for her. I don't know how she held it in for so long. That's a whole other conversation and a lot to process. Regardless, I am glad she was able to talk with us about it."
"Me too," said Scott. "Okay. We have an appointment. Let's finish breakfast and go look at this place and cross our fingers. I think we can both agree that neither of us likes doing this, and the sooner we find a place for him, the better," added Scott commandingly.
"Ok. Oh…and how are you with your store? You alright?" asked Alex. "I know this was a tough decision for you. I also think you made the right choice for now. I just want to make sure you're good with it."
"I'm fine. Change is always scary. We just seem to have a lot thrown at us at once…but that's life…right? We just have to keep going," Scott replied while gathering the dishes and putting them in the dishwasher. "We might have to get a smaller place and be a bit frugal. I know you hate that. It just feels like we are taking a step backward, but I know two to three steps forward are forthcoming."
Alex picked up his coffee, stood up, and took the finishing swallow. "As long as we are together and we're happy. I'm always in your corner." He hugged Scott from behind and kissed his neck. "I love you, my little weirdo," he added. Scott turned around and kissed him back. "I have your back, too. I'm your biggest fan. Know that," and reciprocated the hug. "Now…let's go."
Alex laughed. "Okay. Let's go." Scott finished loading the dishwasher and they both walked to the door. They grabbed their sunglasses and keys and headed out. It was about a fifteen-minute drive to the Inner Richmond location.

They arrived at 738 11th Avenue. A mature Italian woman was standing on the stairs near the open front door, looking around, then at them as they pulled into the driveway. She smiled at them as they exited the car. "Good morning!" she warmly stated as she descended the stairs to approach them.
"Good morning! Maria Gelato?" asked Alex.

"Yes. That's me. Alex and Scott? JB is not with you?" she confirmed with an added inquiry.
"Sorry, no. We are scouting for him. He trusts us to decide for him. He is prepping for his program later today."
"Oh. I was so looking forward to meeting him. I listen to him all the time," she replied with less energy in her soft Italian accent.
"He will love hearing that. We are excited to look at the place. He may come and check it out for a final say," chimed Scott reaching to shake her hand.
"I hope you like. I will give him a better deal. I really enjoy his show on the radio. He is to me the most logical and sensible during these crazy times," replied Maria.
"From your lips to gods' ears," chuckled Scott.
Maria continued, "I love it when he says that a caller has...how you say it...'testicular fortitude'. Ha! He makes me laugh so much at those crazy people. Then I get mad and yell at the radio when someone says stupid things. It's crazy, you know. But a good program." She paused. "Come. Come. Let's look. I hope it's what he is looking for." Maria motioned to the couple.

Alex and Scott roamed through the house. They loved the wood floors, the fireplace. It had a nice size master bedroom with a room JB could use as an office in the back that overlooked the backyard and garden. They quietly commented with each other about the garage, the kitchen size and pantry seemed good sizes for JB's cooking. A fair-sized dining room for the dinner parties with an enclosed deck behind that would allow for some sizeable parties, JB liked to throw.
"It's gonna need painting and a little cleanup," stated Alex to Scott. "Do you have the tape measure with you, by chance?"
"Yep. Let's measure the spaces. It would be good to see if we can see if JB's furniture will fit." Scott looked over to Maria. "Mind if we take some measurements for furniture sizing?"
"Sure! And you can paint. Not a problem. Just so you paint it back if he ever moves. That's all I ask."
"Perfect. Thank you!" said Alex.
The duo measured away. "Alex looked towards Maria again. "How long before we have to give you an answer?"
"Two, no more than three days. I will tell you that if he wants it, it's his. I know who he is. Just first and last month's rent plus $1500 deposit. Okay?" replied Maria.

“Not a problem. Thanks so much. We'll move fast. I promise,” replied Alex.
Scott and Alex finished measuring the spaces and windows, taking notes, and writing quickly. An hour later, they hugged Maria and went on their way. They got into their car and drove off.
“I really like the place,” said Scott. It would take us about two weeks to get it ready for JB. That’s painting and packing and getting everything moved and in place. You think you can get him here in the next day or two?”
“I agree. After all the places we looked at, a house for him, especially at the price she is giving him...it’s a good deal. Some long hours to get him moved. You ready for it?” Asked Alex.
“Yep. Let’s do this and get him in there. You know we’ll have to diagram everything out for him and discuss so he can make the decision. I hope he likes it,” replied Scott.
Alex softly laughed. “You’re right. We’ll go back to his place and draw it up quickly for him. Can you spare another hour?”
“Sure. We have to find a place, too, you know. I wish we could take the place, but he needs to get settled quickly. We’ll find something, I’m sure.”
“One step at a time,” added Alex. He squeezed his partner’s hand. They headed back to JB’s place to share the news and draw up everything. They crossed their fingers hoping for a positive response from JB.

*****

Michelle slowly wandered through Golden Gate Park, taking in all the beauty. She walked around the Music Concourse for a bit and stopped to admire the Steinhart aquarium. There was much talk about the renovation that was being planned. It needed updating but was still beautiful. There was also a plan for the new DeYoung Museum renovation. There seemed to be quite a stir in the community about the proposed new architecture. By the signage on the buildings and people talking openly in the park, she knew the structures facing each other in the Golden Gate Park Music Concourse were getting ready to undergo a major transformation. She also loved the simplicity of the pollarded trees in the center area in front of the music stage. She admired how the construction of the past was solid and simple in design. They were lasting structures from early in the century yet held the sparkle and transparency that contemporary design offered. She meandered through the park then made her way through the different neighborhoods to Laurel village and grabbed a Peet's coffee and bagel. She sat and enjoyed the crowds walking around. Upon finishing her bagel and coffee, she kept going and made her way down California to Fillmore Street. The area drew her in. She loved wandering through Fillamento and the small local shops. She especially enjoyed meeting Mrs. Dewson at her hat shop. Scott had shared with her that she was the 'unofficial Mayor of Fillmore' and an absolute joy of a human being. She avoided Scott's shop because she simply felt the need to be alone. She would visit there another time. She felt lighter today after sharing her story with Alex and Scott. She wanted to take some time to enjoy the feeling. As she walked by the Elite Café, she couldn't help but feel like she was being watched. She looked around but didn't notice anyone. She also didn't seem to notice the gentleman peeking around from a booth inside, privately watching her. She kept walking, shrugging off the feeling, and decided to stop by the grocery store to pick up some fruit and a bottle of wine to take home.

*****

It was her first time in Molly Stones. She looked around and was surprised to see so many people grocery shopping in the early afternoon. She walked over to the fruit section and spied some nice grapes and gala apples. As she was searching for which bunch of grapes to purchase, she happened to glance up and over towards the deli counter. She noticed the woman behind the counter. She had blond hair...maybe a wig? There was something strangely familiar about her. She resumed and pulled a bunch of green grapes, then another bunch of purple grapes. After bagging them, she continued with her apple selection. She glanced back over towards the deli counter and looked at the woman behind the counter again. It was bothering her. She looked so much like her friend in Portland...but it couldn't be. She shook her head and decided to walk over to the counter and look at the cheese selection.

"Hi there," greeted the deli hostess.

"Hi. I was just looking at your cheese selection. I think I might go for some brie to go with my fruit for later. There seem to be a couple of different ones here," said Michelle.
"Well. I can help you with that. My name's Irna. Yours?" she inquired.
"Oh...Michelle. Nice to meet you," she replied a little hesitant.
"Well...I am not a cheese connoisseur, but I always like the softer versions of brie. It should be creamy. This one in the front should be just fine. I have some small rounds if you want," said Irna.
"Sure! That would be great," replied Michelle unintentionally staring.
Irna looked at her, smiling. She pushed up her blue-tinted glasses with her deep pink nails. "Great. I'll just grab that for you. While I do that, mind telling me why you keep staring at me?" she asked.
"Oh. Sorry. You just look like someone I knew. Your hair is different, but I can't shake the familiarity. Sorry," replied Michelle.
"Hm. Did you like this person?" asked Irna being forward.
"Very much. She was such a good person. We lost touch some years ago. You just remind me of her."
"Hm. Well. I think we all remind each other of people in our lives one way or another. I could say the same for you," said Irna, still smiling. "I'll take your brie to the register. Just over here. If you want, I can ring you up for your grapes and apples, too." She motioned Michelle over to the cash register.
"I guess that's true," stated Michelle with a hint of wonder.
"I haven't seen you here before. You live here? Or are you visiting?" asked Irna, making conversation.
"Oh. Visiting. My brother and his partner. They live close to here. Alex and Scott. They live just a few blocks away," she answered.
"Oh my, yes! I love those two. They are very special to me. You must be Alex's sister... Michelle. Yes?" she asked.
Michelle beamed with a small amount of nervousness. "Yes. My brother is Alex. We are catching up. It's been a while since I've seen him. It's a good visit. Overdue."
Irna looked at Michelle with a new understanding and with clarity. "It's very nice to meet you. Maybe we can grab a coffee or a glass of wine nearby sometime soon. You staying long?" she asked strategically.

"I don't know how long I am visiting for. I'll have to go back to Chicago at some point. I kept my condo there." She paused. "Why am I telling you this?" she chuckled at herself in embarrassment.
"Darling. Stop worrying about it. You're sharing with me, and I with you. We're people. Relax. Besides. We're almost family. I have been taking care of Alex and Scott, for a few years now. Just like their friend, JB. They're good people. Always socializing. Being friendly. And I love listening to Jefferson on KGO. The only rational man around. And now you're here." She smiled back at Michelle.
"$18.64"
"Michelle was startled. "Oh...yes. The fruit and cheese. Sorry." She opened her purse and grabbed a $20 bill from her wallet. "Here you go." Then added, "You wouldn't by chance..." she paused. "Never mind. It was nice meeting you. Maybe I'll see you again."
"How about tomorrow. Let's have a coffee. I like Starbucks dark roast. Want to grab one? It's always nice making new friends. Never hurts," said Irna being forward in her invitation.
Michelle pondered for a moment. "Sure. Coffee. Tomorrow. What time?"
"9:30?" suggested Irna.
"Sure! 9:30 it is." She paused. Then looked at Irna in the eyes. "This is so weird. I usually am not like this, but for some strange reason, I just feel compelled. Weird, right?"
"Oh, dear." Irna reached over and placed her hand atop Michelle's, giving it a few taps. "Life is weird. Let's just enjoy it." She raised her eyebrows and pushed up her glasses. "9:30? See you then?" She winked and walked away to wait on the man making attention-grabbing sounds.

Michelle walked away and headed out the door towards the house. She felt a little more alone time coming and knew Scott and Alex were out. This would give her a chance to have some lunch in the garden. She also wanted to nap before dinner and log on to the computer using the guest credentials, they gave her so she could access her emails. She hadn't checked them in a while and had a feeling there may be a backlog to clear. Her day was pretty much set.

*****

Scott and Alex arrived at JB's excited to share the news.

"Hey JB! We're here!" yelled Scott as they entered the flat. Alex noticed Brandon in the living room on the sofa reading.
"Thanks so much, Brandon. We appreciate you hanging with JB for a bit while we checked out this other place for him."
"No problem. He's easy to hang with. He's in the back in his office on the phone and computer. He had a lot of calls today," replied Brandon.
"I am not surprised. Thanks. You can head out. Anything happen while we were out? Is his diabetes, okay? Any issues?" asked Alex.
"Nope. Nothing. All good." Brandon rose and grabbed his jacket off the chair by the table. "I'll head out now. I have some things to do along with another client to take care of. Let me know if I can help more in any way."
"Sure! Thanks, again." Alex got the door for Brandon. Scott had already headed back to the office to see JB.
Alex entered the office where Pavarotti was playing in the background. JB always liked to have his music playing…usually vintage 40's to 70's music. Jazz, classical, blues, opera, Andrew Lloyd Weber. It was always different. He noticed that Scott was standing back in the doorway given JB was still on the phone.
"uh-huh," mumbled JB. "Sure. Sure." JB continued listening to his sister raving on about his other sister and her twenty-seven cats.
"Uh-huh. Well, if she didn't have so many goddamn cats, then there wouldn't be an issue would there?" Pause. "Uh-huh. Well…" he interrupted his sister. "I have to go. The boys just got back, and I need to get ready and head to work. I will send out a check tomorrow." Pause. "Okay. Talk tomorrow." He hung up the phone.
"Christ-sakes. Who in their right mind would have over twenty goddamn cats?! Now my sister wants a room added on for the cats, so they stop shedding, pissing, and shitting everywhere in her house. She must have thirty litter boxes. I think she's finally lost it!" Scott looked at JB and chuckled.
"And you're writing a check for her because…?" he asked with curiosity.
"Because she is my sister, and I can," responded JB.
"Go it," chuckled Scott. "Makes perfect sense." And shook his head.
"Hey JB," chimed Alex.
"Hi Alex. So how was the appointment? Did you check out the place?" asked JB.

"Yessir. It's a nice house. Not a flat and it has a backyard slash garden. A garage. Two-bedroom. A back office. Plenty of closet space. Scott and I will draw up a diagram for you. It also has a fireplace. It will need a paint job. We will also need to have the wood floors refinished. We can move fast on those things if you want it. She wants to know within two days," shared Alex.
"And she's a fan," added Scott.
"Good. Good. I will wait to see what you draw up. We'll have to paint this place back, too. All white."
"That's a lot of painting," said Scott.
"Let me see if we can get some quotes." Alex looked at Scott. "Let's see how this goes before we make decisions. Cool?"
"Cool," replied Scott.
Alex motioned to Scott. "Why don't you go grab the pad of large drawing paper in my room and see if we can draft up some floor plans for JB." He reached around JB and grabbed a ruler from his desktop that was in his pencil box. "Use this."
"Okay, bossy," Scott said in response to the orders. "I know when I'm being kicked out of a room," he said smiling. He knew that JB needed Alex to enter the checks he needed to send to his sister and enter into the QuickBooks accounting program. Alex usually did all the bookkeeping for JB, meaning that JB wanted checks sent out and Alex would do it for him. Together they would review the balances so JB always knew where he stood financially.
Alex smiled back. "Thanks, smoo." Scott smiled back, rolled his eyes, and winked. He was used to this routine.
"I'll be performing my architectural masterpiece on the dining room table. I'll have this done by morning so we can review it with JB. Don't take too long in here. Remember, you need to get to the station. I need to run to the store to see how the sale is going and start helping Troy with packing things up. " He paused noticing JB trying to read his computer screen despite the magnifier over it. He found it a little amusing when JB would take his right index finger and lift his right eye a little. He wondered if it really helped but refrained from saying anything. "Oh. Not that I think you did, but don't forget we're having dinner here tonight with Michelle joining us. Are we cooking or you guys picking up?"
Alex turned to JB. "What was the plan for dinner tonight, JB? Michelle is a bit nervous and excited to see you."

"Lorenzo will have takeout for us from his restaurant, North Beach. Pasta, meatballs on the side, fried chicken, prosciutto and melon, olives, small veal chops…and a few other items. I forget. He said we can pick them up on the way home after the program. He said not to worry." JB replied.
"I bet he'll include some of his chardonnay and a bottle of his Borello," Scott chimed.
JB grunted with humor. "And that would be a bad thing?" he chuckled.
"Nope!" said Alex.
"Okay then. I guess it's all settled. I will leave you to do your thing," Scott said waving his hand then turned and headed out to the dining room.
"Heinrich. Always making sure. Checklists on his brain. You can pick 'em," laughed JB to Alex.
"Thank goodness for that," whispered Alex back and tapped JB on the shoulder. "If you want me to do these checks for you, I need you to slide back so I can scoot in."
"Fine. I'll write up the envelopes on the side here. Here is the list of the amounts and checks to be entered. Let me know if I need to transfer some savings over to my checking. Any I need the mortgage check made to my sister. That should cover both of their houses for next month. And my brother's lawyer needs us to overnight his check." JB reached for the business card he had pulled out earlier. "Here is the address for it to be sent to. Can we drop that off to FedEx on the way?"
"We can use the station for pick up," replied Alex. "No problem. Looking at this, it might be a good idea to transfer about three grand to your checking."
"Fine. I'll stop by the credit union window at the station," JB stated with understanding. "We'll leave after this. We're cutting it a bit close."
"Sure."
Alex entered and printed the checks and performed the ledger entries for JB, reading everything off with the resulting balances. He was always impressed by how sharp JB was. He watched him calculate numbers in his mind. In the background, despite the music playing. When they finished, JB grabbed the pile of envelopes to put in the outside pocket of his "football" of a briefcase for mailing on

the way to work. Alex saved everything then powered down the computer. “Let’s go,” he said.
Alex returned to the dining room where Scott was standing back reviewing his work, with JB taking a trip to the bathroom.
“How’s it coming?” he asked.
“Good, I think. Take a look,” replied Scott, cautiously.
“Wow. You work fast. It looks like you finished the main floor and almost done with the second,” observed Alex impressed and put his arm around Scott’s waist and his chin on his shoulder looking at the two pieces of paper with markings.
“We need to get this done. It’s gonna take two weeks to paint both the places. Here and there. I would bet a week for the floors. Then that’s it. Moving in time. Right?” Scott stated seeking confirmation.
“Yep. That’s correct. We need JB to approve this by tomorrow. And you need to get to your store. We have a lot to do these next two months. And I don’t know what JB has up his sleeve for tonight. As I was working on his checks, he asked a few questions about our passports. Might want to check yours. I'll check mine later.”
“Crap. Let me check. I think it’s current. Good idea to check, though. But why? Did he say anything? We can’t just go off somewhere. We have to move; I need to find a job…good lord.” Scott stated with some edge.
Alex answered back “No stress until we know. I feel the same way, but it’s JB.” He paused. “Go to the store. Finish this later. Think you can make it back to set the table? JB will probably want to use the Jefferson china since my sisters’ coming. Let’s also use the Russian crystal. It will be fun.”
“She’ll get a kick out of that,” Scott said as he nudged Alex. “Love you. I will head out. You taking Ezzie?” Asked Scott referring to JB’s Honda Accord that Alex named ‘Esmerelda.’ “I'm parked behind it, so I should leave before you.”
“Yes. Go. See you later. Leave this as-is. Move it off the table later.” Alex leaned over and kissed Scott. He turned him to give him a full hug then kissed him again. “I love you.”
Scott looked back into Alex’s eyes. “Me too, you, Schmoo,” and kissed him back. “See you in a little bit. Should I try to check on your sister?” he asked.
“Nah. She’s a big girl. Maybe head to the house after the store and bring her with you when you come back.”

"Good idea. See you later." Scott picked up his keys and artifacts and headed out.
"C'mon, JB! Let's move!" yelled Alex.
"Coming!" replied JB gruffly. He donned his khaki jacket over his blue polo. Blew his nose. Made sure he had his insulin pouch. Checked his wallet. Triple verified all he needed to account for and headed towards the door. "Let's go!"

Out they went. Alex had to assist JB in sliding him into the car to make sure he didn't hit his head or get his foot caught in the door. He barely fit given his large frame and movement limitations. Once the door was closed, he was able to quickly dance to the driver's side and get their journey underway. Nothing was ever easy. Everything was always an adventurous and cumbersome chore.

The afternoon went fast. The radio program was smooth. JB was his articulate self, full of witticisms towards the callers. The sale at Scott's store was successful. Merchandise was flying out the door at 50-60% off original prices still providing nice margins that would hold him and Alex financially for a few months. Troy was in rare form with customers and knew the importance of this.

Michelle enjoyed her garden time with cheese and fruit. She had treated herself to a glass of Mondavi Cabernet with her quiet lunch that enhanced her need for a nap from which she had peacefully awaken to get ready for dinner. The bed was cozy. Her head was clear.

Everyone seemed to have a good afternoon.

*****

Scott entered their home feeling energized but wanted to take a quick shower to prep for dinner. He was excited for whatever news JB was going to share with them. He was also interested in hearing about Michelle's day. "Girl! You around?" he yelled.
"Up here. Finishing getting dressed for dinner. Come up!" she loudly answered back.
"Want a glass of wine?! White?!" yelled Scott back.
"Sure!" came the muffled feminine response.
Scott scrambled into the kitchen and pulled out an open bottle of Honig Sauvignon Blanc. He procured two glasses from the cabinet

and filled them leaving the bottle on the counter turned and headed up the stairs.
"You decent?" he asked through the partially open guest bedroom door.
"C'mon in. Yes," replied Michelle.
Scott entered and noticed Michelle had put on the outfit he and Alex gave her. "Lovely. A bit formal, but lovely," he stated admiringly handing her a glass of wine. "Sauvignon Blanc," he informed. "How was your day?" he asked.
"Nice. Interesting. Relaxing. I walked around a lot today. I bought lunch at the store nearby. Came back and ate it in the garden with a glass of wine. Then I decided I needed a nap before dinner," she responded thoughtfully.
"...and interesting, how?" asked Scott, intrigued and took a sip of wine.
"Oh…you caught that, eh?' she grinned. She took a sip of her wine. "Well. I don't know why, but I felt like I was being watched part of the time. It was a weird feeling I couldn't shake." She paused with a small hint of reflection then continued to prepare for dinner. "Then I went to that grocery store a few blocks away and noticed the lady…'*Irna*' behind the deli counter. She looked like someone I knew. Anyway, I went over, and we talked for a few minutes. She's really interesting. I like her. I don't know why. It just seemed like we had a connection…you know?"
Scott was focused on her hypnotized by her prepping and talking at the same time.
"Yep. When we met her, we had the same experience. She's always been very kind to us. Always going out of her way. She's a special one, that's for sure. I love her wigs. Did you notice her nails?" He smiled. Michelle giggled.
"Yes. Well-manicured. Her little accent kills me…and those big blue-tinted glasses!" she laughed a little while trying to add lip liner. "But we were talking and next thing you know, I am going to have coffee with her tomorrow. Weird, right?" she asked.
"Nope. It's San Francisco." He took another sip of wine and got up. "I remember when we met her at the store, we got to talking. I forget where she said she lived prior here. I know she lived in the Northeast for a time…*hence the accent*" he added trying to mimic her. "She has a cute two-bedroom apartment or condo on Bush Street. If memory serves, I think it's 2351 Bush. It was the upstairs

flat. We visited with her a few times there. She had us over for a glass of wine. She's kinda kooky but really sweet…so don't freak if she asks you over. It's close by. We found out a few other of her '*regulars*' have been over, too."
Michelle was gazing a Scott. "Hm. Good to know. If you trust her, I do too. Anyway…she seemed like she wanted to tell me something…but oh well. I'm just going with the flow right now. It feels good."
"Good for you, girl." He looked at his watch. "Shit. I would love to hear more, but I have to take a quick shower then we have got to head to JB's. Alex is there with him getting everything ready for dinner. You almost ready?"
"In about another fifteen minutes. Is that okay?"
"Perfect. See you downstairs. Cheers!" He reached over, tapped glasses then headed off to get ready. "There's more wine in the fridge if you want a little bit of a refresher!" he stated loudly back.
"Thanks!" she yelled back.
Twenty minutes later they met in the kitchen. Gulped their last drops of wine and headed out.
"Time for dinner! And good news! So I'm told," Scott happily expressed.
"News? What news?" asked Michelle with curiosity.
"We'll see. JB didn't say. He's going to tell us at dinner when we're all together."

Scott and Michelle walked briskly to JBs. Along the way, Michelle shared with Scott the sights she had seen. She was enjoying herself. Scott could tell there was something she was holding back but decided not to press on it yet. She needed to share whatever it was in her time. He didn't mind her being around. He took her in doses, though. She talked a lot. He would listen and add his grunts, verbal cues and inject occasional exclamations acknowledging he was listening. When his ears were tired, he would have an excuse ready to leave to complete an errand or task. Then they arrived.
"We're here! Ready, gurl?" Scott looked at Michelle.
"I'm ready. That wasn't far at all," said Michelle. "I like that there's a park here, too. This city has a lot of parks and open space. I like that."
They walked up the stairs to the door. Scott reached and the door was unlocked welcoming them to JBs abode.

"We're here!" yelled Scott.
"I am in the kitchen. JB will be out in a sec. He is in the S*alle de Bain*!" yelled Alex from the kitchen. Scott turned his gaze to Michelle.
"You can put your bag and wrap over in the corner there." He pointed to an antique wooden beach chair with a removable back that had a profile carved into it allowing the chair to be folded up. Take a look around. We are in the living room." He waved to the right. "Check out the walls of art" pointing to the sunshine yellow walls with artwork covering a large amount of the wall space all highlighted by the track-lights positioned on the ceiling. The hallway was red with various Gregorian chants beautifully hand-written and framed along with some other works. "Back there on the left is a half bath. Beyond that on the right is an office, and the two rooms in the back are bedrooms. Feel free to check them out. JB is not formal about his place," he advised.
"It's lovely," she said feeling a bit intimidated noticing the table dressed with a gorgeous Italian gold and brown colored embroidered tablecloth with large fruits and lemons. She wasn't sure about the beige china with the gold and navy-blue borders. The thick wine glasses were covered with detailed engravings. There were tall blue champagne flutes in the same style as the wine glasses. As she took all of it in, Scott had escaped to the kitchen. She decided to take a moment to peruse the artwork.

Scott snuck up behind Alex and wrapped his arms around his waist hugging him. "Hi hunk. How's my Schmoo?" He kissed his neck.
"Good. The food arrived right before you both walked in. Maybe five minutes ago. JB should be out in a minute. While we're waiting for him, I'm trying to get all this food into serving dishes. Wanna help?" asked Alex with purpose.
"Sure! Direct me," responded Scott. Alex turned around and kissed Scott.
"Thanks. Love you. Glad you are here. Perfect timing. Grab the wine, sparkling water, and bubbles. The bubbles are in the fridge door. Should be chilled. Go ahead and fill the glasses…please," he directed while resuming his food prep. Scott went to work. And while pouring the Domaine Carneros, he heard JB.
"Everyone finally here?!" exclaimed JB.

Alex, Scott, and Michelle all answered asynchronously, "We are here!" and "Yes!" and "Yep!". Scott added,
"I'm hungry, too!" inspiring Alex to smile and wink at him as he brought out the pasta and broccoli sides. JB chuckled.
"Of course, you are." He moved to his spot at the table and sat down. "Michelle? Why don't you sit here to my right? Alex will sit on my left and Heinrich will sit next to Alex," he directed.
"Sparkling poured?" he asked.
"Yessir. Just finished. Alex is bringing out the food. Sparkling water is also poured. You have your special glass ready and full with about half an inch space from the top," Scott replied referencing the simple short round water glass JB always used conflicting with the other elegant glassware. He found it challenging to drink from a champagne-styled glass since he lacked movement in his neck.
"Bubbles at one o'clock from your plate." Scott knew JB couldn't see that well and needed these references to avoid tipping over glasses. He motioned Michelle to the table to her seat. As he was pouring, she leaned over with a questioning look in her eye. Scott leaned into her ear whispering very lightly "You're in the hot seat. He's blind in his other eye. That way Alex can help with any issues he has navigating his food and utensils. This way he can see you when he talks with you. It's all good," he assured her. She pulled back, smiled, and nodded.
"We need a cheers," ordered JB.
"JB! I am still bringing out food. Can we wait a sec? Really!" Alex stated with a hint of exasperation then laughed. "Jesus Christ!" Scott and Michelle laughed lightly.
"Fine. We'll wait. How long? I don't want the sparkling to get warm," JB asked comically with a deep chuckle in his baritone voice.
"One minute. Let me just bring out these two dishes and the tomatoes with burrata. Then the sausages, prosciutto, and cheeses. Lorenzo seemed to have sent over all the food from his kitchen." Alex walked off and returned with the final dishes.
"What a dinner!" whispered Michelle in awe as she assessed the spread of food before her.
"Typical Lorenzo. Always generous, kind, and a pain in the ass. You know this means I will talk about it on the program Saturday, right Alex? But…you have to admit...the man has a heart of platinum," JB shared.

Alex responded as he sat down, “Way ahead of you. I have the menu with details. The notes and information will be ready for you before Saturday. We’re good.”
“Good. We all ready now?” asked JB reaching for his sparkling wine.
Directing his inquiry to JB, “What are we cheering?” asked Scott.
“To travel. I thought it would be a good time to head towards someplace warm. You and Alex had been stating a warm vacation would be nice, so I made arrangements,” responded JB building suspense while still holding his glass in the air. “Tahiti!” he stated with reserved excitement in his baritone voice. “Drink!” he instructed his dining companions.
Alex, Scott, and Michelle sipped their bubbles laced with surprise.
“Holy crap!” stated Alex after taking his sip.
“Jesus. You’re kidding, right? Tahiti? I mean...it’s nice and all, but I don’t think I can afford this right now the way things are. Not be a ‘Debbie-Downer.’ It’s just…well…things are a bit strained. You know I already feel weird about the dinners and events we go to,” stated Scott with humility. JB sat back and rolled his eyes.
“You know what, Scott? I do these things because…well…I can. I think it would be much nicer if you just let me do what I can do and just appreciate it and say thank you.” JB understood what Scott was saying. He and Scott had a few of these conversations before. “Stop being so proud and enjoy the gift of these things. I enjoy doing them. I take care of my family in Florida. I consider you my family here. So, let’s just go and have a wonderful time.”

Scott looked down at his glass of Domaine Carneros. Michelle watched the exchange as if watching a tennis match waiting for the next comment to drop. Alex looked at Scott wondering what he would say. Scott had passed on a trip before. “What can I pay for? As long as you let me pay for what I can. You are always too generous, and I never ever want you to feel like we are taking advantage of you. Ever.”
“We will figure that out throughout our trip. Okay? We good then?” asked JB.
“When is this trip?” asked Scott.
“September. Around Labor Day.”
“Okay then,” said Scott meekly and took a sip of his bubbles again.
“I am so excited!” added Alex. “Tahiti! We’ve never been!” he beamed.

“Alex. There is a small box on my desk. Would you mind bringing it in?”
“Sure, JB.” Alex scooted off quickly shortly returning having procured the requested package. “Here it is.”
“Open it,” directed JB sipping his sparkling.
“I am so excited to see this. I wish *I* could go!” whispered Michelle with excitement and envy.
Alex opened the box and pulled out two silver boxes. He opened them to find folios for a cruise. He handed one of the boxes to Scott.
“Cool! A cruise! On the Paul Gauguin! And it’s all-inclusive.” Alex stated while reading the itinerary.
“JB. This really is amazing,” whispered Scott. “Thank you.” He reached over and squeezed JB’s hand.
“You’re welcome. We will probably have to leave Tuesday the 4th right after Labor Day. That will give us a few days to acclimate to the time change. We board the 8th. Alex and I will work out flight arrangements. Given it’s a 7-day cruise, we can fly back the 16th and return the same day, I think,” suggested JB with a tone of resolution.
Alex looked at Scott. “We are gonna have to move fast for moving so we can be settled. That gives us 2-months to get our shit together. Think we can do it?”
“We have no choice. We have to do it. The only dreadful thing I can think of is that, as usual, we'll get very little sleep the next two months,” Scott responded with a laugh and rolled his eyes.
“Sleep is overrated,” added JB. “Life is too short. Let’s eat.”
Michelle was mesmerized by the dialogue. “You guys are crazy. You have an amazing trip planned. Barely time to move…and might I add, all of you are nuts. You’re just nuts.”
“Well. Life is sure not dull around us, that’s for sure,” said Alex.
“Here. Here,” added Scott. “Who needs a boring life?! One thing that JB is teaching me…it’s how to live. And for that, I thank you, JB. And you, too, Alex. You have changed my life into an adventure. You keep showing me what’s possible. Thank you for believing in me.” Scott raised his glass to Alex and JB then took a sip. JB sat back in his chair and smiled.
“We need to start eating, otherwise the food will get cold. Michelle. Would you hand me that platter of fried chicken?” Alex asked motioning to the platter.

“Sure,” replied Michelle. “These look so yummy.” She reached over lifted the platter and handed it to Alex.

The dinner progressed with talk of clothes needed for the trip, the house found for JB, JB asking about Michelle’s visit and soliciting her thoughts of the San Francisco sites. They ate as a family. Shared their days and laughed. Winks were exchanged when sarcasm was expressed. JB was the master of wit leveraging his command of the English language. Michelle was respectfully impressed by the group, their camaraderie, and togetherness. She marveled at the stories Alex and Scott shared taking JB to the hospital on most holidays. JB just shrugged the visits off simply as aspects of his life.

The end of dinner came. Scott and Alex took turns clearing the table, washing a few items, and putting most in the dishwasher. Scott left the room and returned with a large board.

“Hey JB. Just so you know, I drafted as best I could, the layout of the house. Wanna see?”

“Sure. After a few glasses of wine, you picked a good time to try to convince me,” submitted JB resigned to the fact that Scott and Alex were going to do everything to sway him to take the place as his next residence.

Scott held the board. “As you will see, I have cutouts of your larger furniture pieces to illustrate suggested placement. It has a fireplace, garage, a large back garden that I would love to work on if you want…an office space just off your bedroom and a nice sized guestroom, kitchen, and enclosed porch area.” Motioning to each area as he mentioned them. After reviewing the layout, lifting his eyebrow to enhance his vision, pushing up his thick black-framed glasses, some occasional grunting, he finally said,

“Okay then. Can I go to this place tomorrow?”

“Yessir!” yelled Alex from the kitchen. I will call her in the morning. She would love to meet you.

“Good. Let’s have a check ready, too. We'll do that in the morning, too. I trust you, boys. If you think it's a good deal, I am sure it is,” JB affirmed.

“You won’t regret it, sir,” stated Scott reassuringly. “I will have colors ready to suggest for you when we walk through.”

“Of course, you will.” snickered JB. “Always a planner, organizer, and task-master,” he chortled. Scott blushed.

“I know. Sorry.”

"No need. It's a redeeming quality." JB commented with a smile. "Okay. It's getting late. Tomorrow is a big day. Can you help me prep for bed, Alex?"
"Sure, JB," Alex replied then turned to Scott and Michelle. "See you at home? I won't be long."
"Sure!" replied Scott and walked over and kissed his man then hugged him. "Love you. See you at home."
"Night JB. It was a pleasure meeting and seeing you. Thank you for a lovely dinner," Michelle said softly to JB and rubbed his back. JB grabbed her hand and patted it.
"Nice to have met you, too. Come again. You're always welcome," JB responded with affection.
"Let's go, doll," said Scott grabbing their coats and heading for the door. "Sweet dreams. JB! Love you."
"Love you, too, Night. See you in the morning." Scott and Michelle were out the door and headed up the street making their way to the house.
"That was fun," said Michelle a tad winded from their briskly paced walk. "You guys always eat like that?"
"Oh, hell no! If we always ate like that, we'd be 100 pounds heavier. Thank God for the gym!" answered Scott.
"You know, I never asked. What does 'JB' stand for?" inquired Michelle.
"Jefferson Barrister. Can you believe it? He told me his mother and father always thought highly of Thomas Jefferson. He was raised in upstate New York. A town named Hornell."
"Interesting. His last name suits him. The way he speaks. That baritone voice. He's an impressive man. Is he gay?" she continued.
"Not for me to say. You need to ask him that," replied Scott, cryptically.
"Don't you know?"
"It's not for me to say. That's all. Nothing more. Nothing less. Nothing to read into. If he is gay, he will tell you. If he's heterosexual, he will tell you that. That's all. Anyway…about your day…"
"Got it. None of my business and you're changing the subject." Scott laughed. "Ah…we're home! And you have a coffee date in the morning. Right?"
Michelle nodded. "Yes. 9 am. I almost forgot given the excitement of the evening."

Scott produced the housekey and opened the door. "You want a glass of wine before we go to bed?"
"No thank you. Water would be good," she replied.
"Sure. Sit. I'll get it." After taking off his jacket and hanging it, he bounced off to the kitchen. "You excited to see her tomorrow?" he loudly asked as he made his way.
"Actually, I am. As I said earlier, I feel a weird connection," she answered. Scott returned with two glasses of water and sat down with her in the living room.
"I think you'll have a wonderful time. No stress," he assured her.
"I have another question for you. Not to change the subject or anything. Gabriel came to mind. What's his story?"
"Wow. You do change tracks fast. Not sure where that came from." responded Scott a bit perplexed.
"Not sure. He just popped into my head. Weird. But…what's his story? It seems like you all don't like each other," she stated sharing her perception based on the night of the party.
"That's another conversation. Too long a story for now. Maybe tomorrow night?" He gulped his water. "…and I am a bit tired. I think I am going to head upstairs. Long day ahead." He paused. "Not to cut you off or avoid the topic. It's just there is more to it than just a simple answer and I prefer Alex was around when we discuss him. Cool?" Scott said getting up.
"Sure. Fine. Tomorrow, then," Michelle replied amiably. She knew he was putting off telling the story. He might avoid it altogether. She just wondered why. "Good night. Thanks again for a lovely evening. It really was fun. I am so excited for your Tahiti trip!"
"Me too." Scott leaned in and hugged Michelle. "Sweet dreams," and headed up the stairs.

Michelle finished her water. Went to the kitchen and filled her glass and headed up to her room. "Hey, Scott." She yelled softly. "Do we need to stay up for Alex? Or unlock the door?"
"Nope. He will be here in about 20-30 mins. It's typical. JB just needs help getting ready for bed. Diabetes, dentures, contacts…blind…you know." He replied loudly. Then stepped into the hallway with a toothbrush in hand. "He needs his PJs put out and his clothes prepped for the next day so he can get started without Alex or Brandon. He will need Alex to also set up his TV with the news so JB catches up before bed. It's a ritual." he shared.

“Ah. I didn’t realize just how much assistance JB needed.” She began to understand.
“Alex is more a personal assistant slash executive producer slash budding photographer. I help whenever I can. JB usually needs Alex or me around. We're more like a small family unit. He refers to us as ‘his boys.’ It’s sweet. Maybe a little weird, but we're all good together.”
Michelle let out a little '*hm*'. “You're right. It’s sweet. Thanks for clarifying. Good night, Scott. And thanks. By the way...this time is helping me a lot.” She winked at him. Scott blew a kiss using his toothbrush.
“Good. I love you. You are always welcome. No matter how crazy you are. Night.” He winked back then returned to his room to finish his nightly routine. As he crawled in bed and turned on the tv, he heard the front door. He knew Alex was home. He heard him rustle in the kitchen and climb the stairs. Then he overheard some murmurings between Alex and Michelle with a faint muffled ‘good night’.
Alex entered the bedroom. “You awake?” directing the question to Scott. Scott looked at him with a smile and turned off the tv.
“Yep. And I smell that Kouros a mile away. Ugh. Do you think we can ever get JB to stop wearing it? Between that and his foot spray…” he giggled crunching his nose. Alex smiled back and moved in close to Scott.
“Nope. He will take Kouros to his grave.” Then leaned in and kissed Scott deeply. He pulled back. “Tahiti.”
“Gurl. I know. It’s a bit much. But wow. It’s exciting! We will need to hustle on moving. And we are going to have to have the floors redone in the house and paint before JB moves in. Not to mention what we will have to do when we get another place.” Scott’s mind started reeling.
“Look. It’s a lot. I know. But one thing is for certain. We always make everything work. Right?” Alex looked into Scott’s eyes.
“That’s what I usually tell you,” replied Scott.
“I know. You have no idea how loud I am screaming on the inside right now,” he laughed.
Scott looked back at Alex. “Yes. You’re right. We will make it through this. Yes. Things always work out the way they are supposed to. Not sure how or why. They just always do. Go shower, get ready for bed, and get that cute, soft ass of yours with that

perfect chest, beautiful smile, cute feet, and warm eyes to bed."
Scott moved close and kissed Alex.
"Okay. Be back." Alex undressed and headed into the bathroom. He took a quick shower, brushed his teeth, moisturized, and made his way to bed. Scott was already deeply asleep. He positioned himself snuggling up close then kissed Scott's ear. "I love you," he whispered. He reached over and turned off the lights.

The Visitors

Irna had just finished her second cup of coffee from her French-press Bodum when the phone rang. She reached over to her radio turning the volume down so the talk radio program wouldn't distract her. "Hello?" she answered with hesitancy hoping it wasn't another telemarketer. She was arming herself.

"Hello. Aunt Irna?" whispered the woman's voice.

"Rebecca?" Irna asked.

"Do you have another niece?" the woman responded with a small amount of humor.

"Well, no. It's just that you surprised me. Ever since your mother and I had our falling out, I had not heard from you until she passed. Then you sprung your surprises on me that included you coming to visit. So, pardon my wariness. I know you were planning on visiting. You just were not clear on the date. Are you on your way?" responded Irna with sensitivity blended with a hint of annoyance. She was excited to see her niece and grandniece.

"We are here. We just arrived and checked into a small hotel called The Queen Anne. It's on Sutter Street. We got a good deal on the rooms," she replied.

"Oh. I know that place. Lovely." Irna reached over to the small carved wooden box she was gifted from Scott. It had an Asian carving of an island with men in boats who looked like they were fishing and smoking. She procured one of her small joints from it. "Well. I'm glad you made it. I wish I had known. Am I going to see you today? I mean...what are you planning?" she asked as she moved the joint to her lips then ignited a match. She was a little nervous.

"I am a little tired, so I think we will take a nap before seeing you. Is that okay?" responded Rebecca with fatigue in her voice.
"Sure, hon. It's your trip. Whatever you want. I have to work today. My shift is from eleven until four. I can meet you after?"
"Four-fifteen, then?"
"That works. The store address is 2435 California at Steiner."
"I'll bring Ashley so you can meet her...if that's okay."
"That would be wonderful, dear," said Irna a little more excited. She calmed herself quickly. She continued in a more sober tone, "I am just wondering the impetus for the sudden surprise visit. I am always happy to see you. I am just wondering...well...you know. You never stated the reason when you let me know you were coming," she asked cautiously.
"I have some news, but I think it's better in person. I'll see you in a bit, okay?" Rebecca replied softly.
"Do I need to worry?" asked Irna.
"See you at 4:15." She abruptly hung up the phone.

Irna returned the phone to its cradle with a slightly worried look. She didn't know what to make of it. Took a large puff from her joint then mumbled to herself, "No sense in dwelling on it. I guess I'll find out soon enough. Damn that girl has drama in her as my sister did. I hate that. She didn't get that from me." And shook her head exhaling, then took another puff before extinguishing her joint. She felt her light buzz coming on. Just what she wanted. Rebecca reminded her so much of her sister in many ways. Both had dark hair. Both were big-hearted, sarcastic, smart fools with deep green eyes. Ever since the incident about six years ago, they had not spoken, but once. Both were painful times. Her sister was not the best at sharing her life openly. Only when there was drama, but even then, she tended to lash out at many around her. She was no exception. They were very close as children. They laughed and shared happy and joyous times. She hoped Rebecca wasn't totally like that.

Irna returned to her coffee with her memories still flowing. Then she noticed the time. It was near her coffee date with Michelle. Time to head to the store to meet her. She could use another cup. She was feeling a little tired, today. She decided she would muster up some motivation and get moving.

*****

At the Marriott hotel, a handsome Jamaican man hit the snooze button on his alarm. Then the phone rang. "Hello?" he grumbled sleepily.
"Good morning, Mr. Brown. This is your 8 am wake-up call," said the young female voice.
"Oh. Thanks so much." He hung up the phone, then turned over onto his back and rubbed his eyes. He reached for the remote and turned on the international news. Excerpts included Syria evacuating Beirut withdrawing about 6,000 troops. Compensation payouts were started being received for Nazi-Era Slave labor survivors. Factions clashing in Northern Ireland in Belfast and the Pope planning to visit Ukraine. He was wondering if he was going to hear from his office, despite him being on vacation. He had taken a month off given his boss told him he needed to take care of his personal life. He reached for the phone and ordered room service. "Can I get two eggs scrambled, plenty of bacon, potatoes, orange juice, a small pot of coffee, a side of vinegar, and a separate side of mayo, please?" He paused as the staff repeated his order back to him. "Yes. That's correct. See you in about a half-hour?" he asked. They confirmed. "Thank you." And hung up. He reached over and pulled his wallet and flipped to the pictures. There they were. He and his girlfriend of two years. "I will see you soon." He flopped his wallet back to the nightstand and got up to get ready to head to the shower and prepare for the day. He noticed the little pink ribbon had fallen from his wallet. They had to talk. He had spent about a week in San Francisco. He had wandered around Pacific Heights. He thought he caught a glimpse of her but wasn't sure. He was hoping he would see her soon. He was worried given her leaving suddenly. She left a simple note that stated she had to see her brother in San Francisco. She wanted space and a little time. He needed to be with her. What they went through was tough. Flying back and forth. Now she was pregnant. He had a feeling that talk would come soon and proceeded with his morning ritual.

*****

Michelle missed Scott and Alex for breakfast. They were up and out early and left a note:
"*Good morning, doll!*

Sorry, we missed you. Help yourself to breakfast. I had to get to the store to check the status of the merchandise with Scotty and start packing things up to prep for closure. Alex had to run to JB's and make arrangements for us to see the house together for JB's walk-through. And JB has some errands to run. He has a new program schedule starting next week, which means soon, Alex will be working earlier than his regular schedule. We'll share more later. Oh! Gay Pride is this weekend! We are going! So are you! It will be fun. Pride weekend! Get ready!
Good luck, today! See you tonight!
Muwah!
Love you-
Scott and Alex"

Michelle smiled. Put the note down then stopped in the half bath to check her hair. She assessed herself. Jeans, pink Henley from The Gap, her new Etnies Czars. She thought she looked cute. She kept her hair down and just a little makeup. She turned and grabbed her bag and house keys and headed out the door. She should make it to the store just in time to meet with Irna. When she arrived, she saw her standing by the coffee stand looking around. Red hair wig this time. A brightly colored flowered blouse and jeans. You couldn't miss her.

"Good morning Irna," greeted Michelle.

"Oh, good morning, sweetie. I just got my coffee. What can I get you? My treat," Irna offered smiling.

"Thank you. Coffee. Cream. Sugars, please," she replied.

"The cream and sugar are right over there at the end of the counter. If it's okay, it's such a beautiful day. Mind if we take our coffees to the park up a couple of blocks from here?" asked Irna.

"Sure. That would be nice. I haven't had a chance to visit there. Not sure why," replied Michelle nervously. Her nervousness surprised her.

"Here's your coffee," she said handing it to Michelle from the barista. "I'll pay for this while you dress it up." She handed the barista some money. "Keep the change. Thank you. You're so sweet," she stated to the server smiling. She turned to Michelle. "This way." She led the way similar from where Michelle walked. "As you probably know, just up a block from Sacramento on the left is Alta Plaza Park. It's lovely there," she directed and motioned. As they began walking, Irna asked about her evening and listened while

Michelle shared stories of the dinner, the food, and the upcoming trip. By the time they reached the park, Michelle had shared all the details without giving Irna a chance to respond. Irna just giggled and replied with *oh's* and *ah's* and *my my's.* She was able to squeeze in a '*is that so'* to make sure Michelle knew she was listening. They reached a bench on high overlooking the neighborhood toward the store. "Let's sit here. Is this okay?" asked Irna.
"Oh, sure," replied Michelle as they both sat.
"It sounds like you had a wonderful evening," said Irna.
"Yes. Sorry. I guess I kind of talked the whole way, didn't I?" replied Michelle.
"That's okay, dear. Here." Irna reached into her small black and red handbag and procured a small joint. "I'm having quite a morning, and this takes the edge off. I have a feeling this is going to be a thing in the future," she smiled and winked.
"I think it already is," replied Michelle.
"Oh. Here maybe. But not everywhere. People need to relax a little. They get so caught up in working and making money. They forget what's important. Don't you think?" asked Irna.
"I guess. You sure it's not too early for this?" asked Michelle.
"Oh heavens no." She gave Michelle a small Bic lighter. She took a puff and handed it back to Irna. Irna retrieved the small doobie and took a puff.
"So, what happened this morning. You stated you're having a morning."
"Oh. My niece called me. She is going to meet with me later. She has a bit of drama going on I think."
"Seems to be going around," replied Michelle.
"Why do you say that?" asked Irna. Michelle shared about how JB, Scott, and Alex all had to move, and that Scott had to close his shop given the rent increases. Then added, "…and then there's me." at the end.
"What do you mean by that?" Irna pried.
"Well. I kind of left Chicago in a flurry. I had to get away," said Michelle with a small buzz hitting her. She felt like she could just keep talking.
"Why did you leave? Are you running from something?"
"I don't want to bother you with this. I don't even know why I am telling you this. Weird." Michelle started questioning herself.

“Sometimes it’s just good to talk to someone outside of everything. Go ahead. Let it out. What’s the worst that can happen?” Irna gently pushed.
“Well…I have been seeing this guy. Dom. He travels back and forth from Canada. We’ve been seeing each other for the past three years. He stays with me a lot. Almost lives with me, you might say,” Michelle said looking up at the blue sky with small whisps of fog floating overhead against a very blue sky and a sunny day.
“What does he do? If you don’t mind me asking,” asked Irna.
“Government work. He doesn’t talk about it, and I don’t pry. I tried to ask a few times, but he said he can’t talk about it and we should be able to talk about other things other than work.”
“Interesting. I haven’t thought about it that way. Makes sense. Just as long as you can trust him and know he’s not lying,” said Irna. "Men do that. I know from experience."
“He’s not. I saw his government ID card. And he insists on paying for part of my rent and stuff. It’s nice. We're both a bit introverted. I’m busy. He’s busy. We’d spend weeks apart, then we’d be together a couple of weeks. We would talk at least once a day. We ‘*get*’ each other. You know what I mean?”
“I do. So, what happened,” asked Irna.
“I got pregnant and unexpectedly had a miscarriage when I was around seven weeks,” said Michelle as she started to tear up. “I haven’t told anyone about that. I felt like something was wrong with me. I’m thirty-two years old and I had a miscarriage.” She started lightly crying.
Irna reached over and held her hand. Through her light sobs, she continued. “I told him over the phone when I thought I was pregnant. I probably shouldn’t have said anything, but it was almost two months. I wanted to be careful. He came down for a short trip…you know…he was happy. Then he had to head back. Three days later, I miscarried. After a few days, I called him, but I couldn’t say anything. Instead, I decided to visit my brother. When I left, I wrote a note and left it on the counter. I knew he would come down if I said something, but I couldn’t see him. I needed to get away.” She started slowing her tears. Irna reached into her bag and gave Michelle a small pack of Kleenex.
Michelle blew her nose and wiped her tears from her cheeks. “Some memories surfaced. I knew it was time for me to see Alex. I needed

to." She took a deep breath and started to calm herself. Irna looked at her with sincere sympathy.
"Oh, you poor dear. Well…it's a good thing you came here. If anyone can help you through tough times, it's those two young men." She patted Michelle's hand. "Is there anything I can do, sweetie?"
"Just listening was good. But you seemed like you wanted to talk with me about something. You know…have coffee and…I don't know. And here I am doing all of the talking. Bearing my soul, and you haven't said much."
Irna looked at Michelle. "Let's just leave it for another time. Right now, you have enough going on. I am simply your friend. Here to listen," she winked with endearment.
"This trip has been strange. I feel like I am just dumping out my personal garbage everywhere. And everyone is just listening. Am I being selfish?" asked Michelle.
"We all go through moments like that. It's just your turn. Hopefully, you feel better at the end of it." Irna looked across the horizon at the buildings in their view. "How are you feeling?"
Michelle took a moment and reflected on herself. "Better. I'm feeling good." She paused. "Do you have children, Irna?"
"I had two miscarriages," she reflected avoiding the question. "After the second miscarriage, the doctor checked me over. He told me I wasn't able to have children." She paused, then added, "Did you know that 10 to 20 percent of all known pregnancies end in miscarriage?"
"No. I didn't," replied Michelle thoughtfully. "I'm sorry."
"Oh, don't be. They don't talk about miscarriages enough. Women already feel bad enough about things. They don't get paid like men. Treated differently than men. And feel bad when they can't have children. Fact is, it's not uncommon, and people need to stop making women feel bad. Our time will come." Irna looked up. "I believe our time will come. But enough of that. I have to get back to work. How about you and I have a glass of wine some night soon? My place."
"Sounds great. And…thank you Irna. This meant a lot. Thanks for listening to me. You're a good listener." Michelle squeezed Irna's hand, then forced a smile and continued. "Next time let's do something happy. Scott informed me in a note this morning that it's Gay Pride this weekend. Are you going?"

"Absolutely! I have my rainbow blouse. I will be marching with the PFLAG contingency in the parade," boasted Irna as she pulled out a piece of gum from her purse to mask her pot breath.
"You're marching in the parade?!" asked Michelle.
"Absolutely. I am in it. I don't watch things happen. I am part of what's happening….one way or another." She laughed. "I have to run. See you soon." She leaned over and kissed Michelle on the cheek.
"Thanks, again. See you later," and she waved Irna off.

Irna made her way back to the store. She wanted to share more about Rebecca's visit. She would try to do it before they ran into each other. "God damn that girl has issues. A sweetheart. Just dealt a deck of jokers." she mumbled to herself. Upon arriving at the store, the staff greeted her with smiles and the usual daily comments from coworkers. She saw a small crowd at the deli and knew it was going to be a busy day.

*****

Alex, JB, and Scott arrived at 738 11th Avenue to find the landlord by the stoop as the first time they previewed the house.
"She's here," shared Scott with a smile. Alex was always driving them around with JB on the passenger side and Scott in the back. He quickly got out of the car and headed over to greet Ms. Gelato.
"I love her name." declared JB. "*Gelato*. Couldn't be more Italian than that, can you?" he added with a hint of humor.
"Remember. She is also a fan," reminded Alex.
"Yes. I'll be on my best behavior," replied JB while unfastening his seatbelt.
"Hey JB. I'm gonna come around to help you out, okay? One sec" instructed Alex watching JB struggling with his seatbelt and the door. JB had unfastened his seatbelt but was struggling with the strap that seemed to be entangled with him. He was snugly fit in the car given the tightness of space due to his large frame and build.
"Okay," muttered JB frustrated. He hated the need for assistance but knew he had no choice. Alex quickly made his way outside, greeted Maria, and opened the door allowing JB to escape the confines of the Honda. JB pulled himself up and out then straightened his jacket. And stepped aside allowing Alex to secure the car. Alex placed his arm on JB and guided him to Maria.

“Maria. This is JB…er…Mr. Barrister. JB, this is Maria. She owns the house you are considering renting from her,” said Alex as he introduced the two. Maria’s eyes lit up. Her Italian accent was pronounced as she started speaking, excitedly.
“What a privilege to meet you, Mr. Barrister,” she said as she reached out. Alex subtly guided JB’s arm not giving way to his sight challenge to Maria.
“JB, please, Ms. Gelato,” replied JB.
“Maria, please. Oh… I always listen to your show on the radio. You are the only one who is so reasonable and rational. I also improve my English by listening to you. You are so well-spoken.”
JB smiled with appreciation of his fan’s comments. “Thank you very much,” smiled JB flashing his charm.
“I have so many questions,” she added. Maria started asking about some of the other talk radio hosts. She and JB bantered for about fifteen minutes chuckling, comparing notes and perspectives on some of the callers. “I always laugh when you say to some of the men that they have…how you say…teeny-tiny kahonies,” she giggled. “The angry caller last night when you called them a ‘blow hard’. Didn’t know what they were talking about.” She laughed more. JB chuckled with her. He nodded a little then shifted hoping Maria would get the hint of his impatience.
JB spoke up. “It was very kind of you to meet us at the last minute. I need to get things squared away. You know…” he paused. “they are moving me to the 3 pm time slot starting next week. It was going to be a little later, but they pushed it up. Just in case you had not heard,” he shared.
“Oh. That is perfect. I usually start cooking around that time so I can listen while I cook. Sometimes, though, I get frustrated with some of the people who call you on your show. I have to make sure I don’t wave my sauce spoons around.” She laughed again. “I will get sauce all over my kitchen walls if that happens,” she declared in her Italian accent and laughed a little more with some nervousness. She looked over at Alex and Scott and winked.
“Oh…I know you are probably really busy. I have many questions about the other hosts, but I don’t want to gossip too much.” She proceeded to ask JB about the other hosts. JB kept his comments professional. He loved to talk more about the callers than his fellow hosts and news anchors. He and Maria bantered and laughed lightly for about 15 minutes before she began to feel like she was keeping

him. “Why don’t you all go in and walk around. I will wait out here for you. You have first choice. I would be so honored,” said Maria.
“Thank you. Alex…let’s go in and look around,” JB instructed.
Scott jogged up the stop steps and into the entryway.
“There are eleven steps up JB,” whispered Alex knowing JB would count on his way up. “And a handrail on the left,” to which JB reached and grabbed hold and began his ascension towards the entry. “There is a low barrier in the doorway so as not to trip,” warned Alex softly. He didn’t want JB falling on his face and having to the hospital, again. Once they reached the top and stepped into the foyer, Alex started sharing about the house to aid JB in his navigation.

The three of them toured the house. The living room was to the left in the entryway with a stone fireplace and bay windows. JB scuffled along the carpeting on the main floor and commented that it needed to be removed. He had a feeling there were floors below it. As he commented, Scott noticed a loose corner of carpeting and checked it to confirming JB’s speculation. JB appreciated the enclosed outdoor space off the large dining room area that also had steps that led down to the overgrown garden. Continuing on, they moved to the kitchen. After the approved inspection, they navigated up the stairs to inspect the bedrooms, office, and bathroom. Alex remained close to JB’s side gently guiding him along the way and supporting his climb to ensure his stability so as not to fall backward. As they reviewed each of the rooms and closet spaces, JB would fill the moments with mumbles and grunts. Upon completion, they made their way down the stairs, back through the kitchen, and descended to the garden.
“We shouldn’t walk too much out there,” cited Alex. There are raised brick borders around multiple beds for plants and flowers. Given it’s overgrown, JB, I want to avoid you tripping over anything for now. Is that okay?” he asked sensitively.
“Sure. Sure,” replied JB. “Can we check out the garage?” he asked.
“Absolutely,” replied Alex as he motioned to Scott to run ahead and lip-synced for him to get the lights on to enhance JB’s viewing ability.
The trio walked around the garage noticing the need for a new washer and dryer and a bit more cleaning up. Scott commented about the shelves along the wall and the storage space in the back. JB appreciated the spaciousness of the garage and the additional

enclosed room that had a doorway to the garden and a window. "I think this is a good size place and well worth the rent. What do you boys think?" JB asked.
"I think it suits you," replied Scott. "That's why we recommended it."
"I agree. It's a nice size," added Alex.
"It does need work, so we will need to ask her just what we'll be able to do to adjust it to your style, JB," injected Scott.
"Let's go out and have a chat with her and see what she says," directed JB.
"We can go out the garage door," suggested Scott to Alex who nodded in agreement. Scott scurried over and opened the garage door to find the landlord still standing in her spot looking at her watch as he opened the door. She turned and smiled. "Well? What do you think?" she asked with a hint of hope.
"I like it," replied JB. "Just a couple of questions, first."
"Okay," Maria replied with interest.
"First, can we get rid of the carpeting on the main floor? I'd like to expose the wood floors. Easier for me. I also prefer them…like the upstairs. The bedrooms are wood-floored, but the office space is carpeted. That's okay. I can work with that. The main floor, though…." JB asked with directness.
"You are welcome to remove the carpeting and paint. It has to come out of your pocket though. I trust you. Just don't remodel. If you have a problem with plumbing, just let me know. Give me some quotes and I will approve as needed and reimburse you. I don't want to invade your privacy. Is that okay?" replied Maria.
"Perfect," replied JB. "Will we have to repaint if I move?" JB asked. "I mean, not that I plan on moving out, or anything. I just want to keep everything simple."
"I would have to repaint anyway, so no. Let me note the lease." She pulled it out and scribbled some lines and notes. She then initialed and dated her changes, then held out the document. "Take a look. If this is okay, just sign and I will get you a copy in the mail for your records."
"Can you give us a sec?" Alex asked as he assumed possession of the document.
"Sure!" she said. "I will go sit in my car while you review and discuss." She smiled and walked over to her mocha-colored Cadillac parked in front of the house. Alex read the notes she made and the

two-year lease conditions. "It's all pretty standard, JB. Want to sign now or sign later and give it back to her in a few days?" asked Alex. "I trust you," replied JB. "Let's just do this. I'll sign it and give her the check from my pocket," he replied impatiently. He didn't like to dawdle or procrastinate on his decisions. He was clear that leases were pretty standard. As long as the notes are there for the changes he wanted, he was ready. "I don't plan on moving again anytime soon, so two years is fine," he added. Alex guided JB to the terrazzo stoop where there was a wall with three flat levels along each side of the steps.

"Here's a pen JB," said Alex as he pulled one out from his jacket and smoothed out the agreement. JB grabbed the offered pen. Alex guided it to the line where JB affixed his signature.

"There we go. I'll just add the date for you," said Alex while writing. Scott motioned to Maria to return to them.

"All good?" she asked.

"All good," replied JB. "Here is the check for the first month and the deposit you had informed Alex." He procured the folded check from his jacket pocket and handed it to Maria.

"I am so excited! I can't wait to tell my friends! They are going to be so jealous! What an honor to have you live here!" Maria expressed with excitement. "I just want to hug you!" she added holding out her arms with hope. Alex grinned and tilted his head towards JB while looking at her indicating for her to do it. He knew it annoyed JB a little but would enjoy the attention and the joy.

"Oh!" she squealed and hugged JB, with JB suddenly looking surprised He chuckled trying to hide his hint of annoyance as he stiffened up during the encounter.

"Alright. Alright. Heh, heh, heh," he said. "Thank you for the good deal on the house and your flexibility."

"I am so excited to have you as my tenant! People are going to be so jealous!" she beamed. "Don't worry. I won't bother you. Call me anytime for anything," she continued. "Also, you can move in anytime. It's empty. A home isn't a home until it's lived in with warm hearts. I just know this is good. Yes?" she asked.

"Yes," JB agreed. "Okay. So, I will go now. Here are the keys. All yours. I will mail you a copy of the lease. Thank you so much!" She handed the keys to Alex. She could tell he was the one to handle everything. She then turned, returned to her car, and drove off.

"Well, that was easy," said Scott. "Want me to close everything and lock up?" he asked directing his question to Alex.
"Sure," replied Alex as he handed Scott the keys."
"Be back in a minute." He ran off into the house and secured the windows and interior doors. He came back out and locked the front door then moved to the garage door bringing it down and making sure it was locked. "All set."
"JB. Let's go," instructed Alex.

The trio returned to the car and drove off. Along the way, they discussed the colors of paint. They agreed all the ceilings and trim would be white. The living room and dining room were to be bright lemon yellow. Entryway and the wall up the stairs a cobalt blue. The front guest room would be a golden ginger wheat color with the master bedroom and office celadon. Scott shared he was excited to work on the garden after they returned from their trip. He reminded them that he had been mowing lawns and gardening since he was nine years old. He loved playing in the dirt and working with plants and flowers.
"I think we should take up the carpeting first and have the wood floors refinished. What do you think?" asked Alex to the group.
"I think that's a great idea," responded Scott. "We can't paint until the floors are done. We'll have to get the paint, brushes, and supplies quickly." Scott started thinking about the projects and timing. "I think we should hire painters that hang out across the street from Divisadero Touchless Car wash on Divisadero. You know…the guys that hang out behind the paint store on the corner of Oak Street. What do you think, Alex? I just worry about the timing. We still have to find our place, and JB's place needs to be packed up and everything."
"That's smart," Alex agreed. "JB. Would that be okay with you?" he asked.
"I trust you boys," answered JB.
"We'll make sure you get a good deal. I'm cheap….er…frugal," Scott chimed. "I will make sure you don't get ripped off."
"I know you'll watch that, Heinrich. You're like a watchdog. You're always questioning people's motives around me," chuckled JB to Scott who was sitting in the middle of the back seat. He would occasionally lean forward with his head poking between Alex and JB sitting in the front when he made some of his comments.

"I always worry. It drives me crazy how many checks for dinners you pick up. You always throw great dinner parties and parties. You are always giving...and always generous. I just worry people take advantage of you. That's all. I don't see much reciprocation going on," shared Scott with some heartfelt concern.
"Well..." murmured JB. "That's my choice. And remember. I do because I can. It's just money," he solidly expressed. "You only live once. Make the most of it. You know.... like that movie you like so much...what was it...?"
"Auntie Mame," answered Alex and Scott in unison.
"I know. Live. Live. Live. Life is a banquet and most poor suckers are starving to death," quoted Scott from the movie. "Are you always going to throw my words back at me?" he asked humorously.
"Every chance I can," replied JB. Alex looked in the rear-view mirror and winked at Scott as they looked out to notice they were on Sacramento Street. "Speaking of frugality, Alex, I think we should check in with the sales team." JB also instructed Alex they needed to get a washer, dryer, new dishwasher, and refrigerator. He wanted to touch base with the sales department at the radio station to find out the clients and ad buys to see if he could work a deal somehow.
"Hey. Sorry. Would you mind dropping me off at Fillmore? I need to pop down to the store," interrupted Scott.
"No problemo. A block away," answered Alex as he slowed as he approached the corner to let Scott out. "This, okay?" he asked as he came to a stop.
"Perfect. See you at home later?" asked Scott.
"Yep. Love you," said Alex.
"Love you too, Schmoo," replied Scott as he blew Alex a kiss. He leaned forward and pecked JB on the cheek. "You too, Mr. Barrister!" and departed the car.
"See you later, Scott," said JB. "Good luck today!" he exclaimed as he and Alex drove off to head to the station.

Scott made his way down Fillmore and noticed Gabriel heading towards him. "Shit," he muttered to himself. He knew he was too late to run across the street to avoid the encounter. Gabriel approached Scott.
"Hi there!" he said.
"Hi," responded Scott, curtly.

"Thanks for the interesting time the other night. Quite the little gathering," he said looking at Scott in his eyes.
"Nice of you to crash a party uninvited," replied Scott.
"I came with Aarav. He invited me as his plus one. So, technically, that's not really an accurate statement…is it" Gabriel stated coyly.
"Whatever."
"So…I heard your store is closing. Going out of business? I guess you *couldn't keep it up*?" Gabriel asked.
"Oh bitch, please. What business is it of yours?" Scott retorted. The tension was slowly rising, and he was holding it back with everything he had.
"Troy told me. I just saw him." Gabriel paused. "you know…I like this neighborhood. I am always interested in what's going on around here. Your little shop is part of the scene. You're also the fourth business closing this month. Guess you couldn't make that go…"
Scott looked into Gabriel's eyes becoming perturbed.
"So what. Okay. We're closing," said Scott.
"I just feel bad for you, that's all. You're the fourth business to leave the neighborhood. RH left last month. Just a bit of change. And who am I gonna harass, now?" said Gabriel with a hint of sarcasm.
"I am sure you'll find something. Look. I gotta run. Next time you see me, cross the street," Scott said annoyed.
"Nah. Besides. I like Alex's sister. I think she and I could hang sometime. What do you think?" asked Gabriel toying with Scott.
"Won't happen. She's already started to ask about you. And believe me, I've been nice up to now. I haven't told her anything. I'm trying to keep it civil," Scott began to seethe. "Let's be clear about something. You're a selfish shit. You only cause chaos and drama with anyone with who you interact. Just leave us alone. Got it? Stay away from her," he directed. His eyes were projecting strong anger.
"What's the deal. I'm not sure why you have such anger towards me all the time," stated Gabriel trying to move closer to Scott.
"Fuck you," answered Scott. Then it came out. "When we were together, the last 3 years was nothing but verbal abuse. You made me feel like shit. I couldn't do anything right. You tried to rape me twice during the month before I moved out. You cheated on me, endlessly. You tried to force me into three ways after I told you I didn't want that. And let's not forget the lies upon lies. Stay away from Michelle. Stay away from me. And get the fuck out of our lives. Am I making myself clear?" Scott stated everything with a

harsh calm in an assaulting tone he had never mustered before. Years of pent-up anger had come out. He would not scream. He would not draw attention. He needed Gabriel to know that he was not the meek guy he once thought he was anymore. He leaned in towards Gabriel. "Now…get the fuck out of my sight." Gabriel looked at Scott. He knew he meant it. He grinned back at him. "Sure you don't wanna fuck first?" Scott stepped back and slapped Gabriel across the face with his right hand. Gabriel's head turned back from the slap. He was stunned.

"Get the fuck out of my sight," Scott directed for a second time staring Gabriel in the eyes. People who were walking on the street within the block were looking at the two men. Some kept walking while a couple stopped to see what might happen next. They heard the slap.

"I'll leave for now," said Gabriel rubbing the side of his face.

"And stay away from Michelle," Scott added. Gabriel waved it off and walked away.

Scott took another deep breath. He felt exhausted yet stronger and then made his way to the store to find Troy smoking on the sidewalk.

"What the hell. What are you doing, Troy?" asked Scott surprised to see him smoking. "You know that's not good for you. And it wreaks!" Scott waved the smoke away as Troy was exhaling.

"I felt like I had sex, today. You know us HIV pos guys right now have a bit of a challenge getting laid. So we enjoy a good thing when it happens," Troy said as he waved his hand in the air and camped it up. "It has been a day, girl! You go on in! Stuff has been flying off the shelves with the sale, girl!" he continued. "If this keeps up, you won't have shit to pack up! Just sayin'. The 'return to vendors' you were thinking about…. I don't think there will be anything to return. And if my calculus is up to snuff, you, girl, still made a profit!" He flicked his cigarette into the street. "C'mon!" he motioned Scott into the store. "Come look, girl!" Scott followed Troy into the store. It looked like a third of the store was missing.

"What the hell?! Why wasn't it like this more often? Shit," Scott stated appraising the store. "Well…. I guess it's out with a bang!"

"Did I do good, girl? You gonna stop giving me shit, now?" teased Troy.

"Yes, you did good, queen. And no, I will not stop giving you shit, because I love you and want you around a long time. So, stop smoking. Got it?" answered Scott.
"Yes ma'am!" replied Troy and blew a kiss to Scott.
"And, if memory serves, didn't you get laid just the other day? I don't think you have much to bitch about in that area, either," said Scott in an accusatory tone.
"Laid? Yes. But it had been about three weeks, girl. People get freaked when I tell them I'm HIV positive. Like they're gonna catch it from me. I play safe. I try to educate them, but they still freak. So, I just keep trying. It's tough," replied Troy defensively. Scott moved in behind Troy and hugged him.
"Sorry, doll. Let me know how I can help, okay?" Scott said empathetically. "It sucks, I know. Just…" he stopped. "I love you, girl," he whispered.
"Thanks. Me too, you."
"Um…not to be brash and change the topic, but you told Gabriel about the store closing? I ran into him on the way here." And he squeezed Troy a little harder hinting at his frustration.
"Um. Girl. Notice the sign in the bottom corner of the window there? It's not a secret. I just didn't tell him why. I told him he would need to ask you," Troy answered as he pried loose from Scott then turned and made his way to the cash register to assume his post.
"Well. I told him, why. He is such an ass. I don't know why he cares about it. I just can't stand the guy," Scott stated irritably.
"Well. After being with a guy who verbally abused you and tried to rape you and tried to force things on you that you didn't like or want…. what's to like? I mean…he cheated. He lied. He made you feel like shit. Thank God you left that bitch and found Alex. Lucky queen," Troy said pointedly. "Let it go. Don't hang onto that crap," he added waving his hands.
"You're right. But every time I see him, those memories pop right up with the pain."
"I know, girl. Been there. Done that." Troy waved his hand in the air again and snapped his fingers. "Let it go. You have a good life now. Crazy. But a good life. Enjoy it." Troy advised.
"I'll try," Scott said resigning to the advice. "Okay. Now." Scott decided to change the mood of the room and conversation. "I do need to box up the small toys. I think I will donate them for a write-off. Thoughts?" he asked.

"Go for it, girl. Those aren't selling. Everything else is," confirmed Troy. And with that, they got to work.

Evening came quickly for the trio. Scott, Michelle, and Alex were all mentally drained from the day. Over dinner, Scott shared the events at the store and regaled them about Troy's accomplishments. He also shared about running into Gabriel but avoided any of the conversational details. Alex shared he found a flooring guy for JB's new place. 'Jimmy Hardwood Floor'. Scott and Michelle joked and asked if he sure it wasn't 'Jimmy's Hardwood Floors'? Alex reassured them he stated it correctly. He went a grabbed a phone book and showed them. He was going to meet the guy Monday after pride weekend. Scott suggested heading down to the paint store across the street from Divisadero Touchless Car Wash. He reminded Alex that there were always freelance painters hanging around looking for work. Alex agreed. Michelle was in awe of how fast Alex and Scott worked. They made a great team. She added to the conversation by sharing how she had a nice time with Irna and that they got mildly stoned. She did not share much about the conversation. Just that it was nice to make a new friend.

Scott realized they had not made plans for the weekend. "Crap. It's Wednesday night. Pride is Saturday and the parade is Sunday. We haven't made plans yet. Thoughts?" asked Scott. Michelle and Alex looked at each other.

"I have never been to Gay Pride, so I am at your mercy," shared Michelle.

"Never?" asked Alex and Scott surprised and in unison. Alex looked at Scott and waved his index finger to not say the 'pinch a poke' thing. Scott refrained.

"Girl! We'll have fun," said Scott. "We can go down to the Castro Saturday night and walk the streets. They are usually blocked off with food trucks on Market." He was getting excited.

"The drag queens and the costumes are really fun. So much 'camp' everywhere. We can go dancing at the Café…" Alex suggested.

"Well, I guess we should do all that. What time does the parade start?" inquired Michelle.

"10 am! The theme is 'Queerific' whatever that means. But hey. It's fun! We'll need to find a spot to hang and watch the parade on Market Street. Then we can decide when we want to walk to Civic

Center for the festivities." Scott kept adding on to the activities and agenda.
"It's a busy weekend. Fun. We usually drink beer as we walk around Civic Center. There are all of the booths to visit. I hope you like it," continued Alex.
Scott looked at Alex and then at Michelle. "We make a point of going every year. We try to be 'good gays'." Michelle giggled at the comment.
"Whatever you decide. I am sure it will be fun. Can't wait." She paused. "What's up for tomorrow and Friday?" she asked wondering how to plan her days. She was still exploring the city.
"I am going to be tied up at the store." Scott looked at Alex and raised his eyebrows. "I think Alex and I are going to do a little drive around for about two hours in the morning looking for apartments. We have to pick up the pink pages, too. Right?" He was seeking agreement from Alex given they found JB's new place. Now they needed to find a place….and quickly.
"Absolutely," stated Alex. "Tight time schedules. I think we should also start packing up the garage and donating what we can get rid of. We are two months out."
Michelle knew she was on her own until Gay Pride. "Okay then. If you need me to do anything, just list it out. Otherwise, I'm going to do a little more exploring of this city. I'm loving it."
"Is that okay?" asked Scott.
"Absolutely. I have plenty to do, and I have a new friend," she answered.
"Alright then," Alex stated. "Let's get this all cleaned up. I think I am going to turn in early. Scott?"
"Let's do it."

The three of them cleaned up the dinner dishes. Michelle took out the recycling for them. It was like a ballet. They kept chatting about Pride weekend. Scott sharing about how many beads he had so he would bring them out for them to share. He was determined to get a boa or two this year. They laughed about wearing the rainbow feathers but understood Scott had his sights set and joked with him about them. Both Scott and Alex surprised Michelle with another glimpse of their lives sharing they had never been in drag. They clarified that not every gay man dresses in drag. They may at some point. Their day just hasn't come yet. When they were finished cleaning up, Scott and Alex headed to their bedroom.

Michelle stayed behind to have a glass of wine in the garden again. She liked that ritual of hers. It gave her time to reflect on the day. She had more to share with the boys. She was trying to time it all out. She also thought more about Irna. She knew there was something more coming. Just when was the question.

The Past Bites

Rebecca and Ashley arrived at Irna's flat around 4:30. Rebecca knew she was late but didn't care. Ashley was being a 6-year-old. Fidgety, inquisitive. Wanting to run ahead pulling on her moth's arm. Rebecca was not in the mood today. She raised her hand to the door.

Knock knock.

She heard rustling then a muffled, "Coming!" from inside. The rustling of the door lock and chain indicated there was nervousness in there, too.

"Hello, Rebecca. Welcome. Come on in," stated Irna in her Jersey accent waving them in. "You must be Ashley," she said looking at the young black-haired, blue-eyed girl. She had a few freckles on her nose.

"Mommy says I had to be good. Can I have a cookie?" she asked smiling.

"Of course, you can. Er…if your mommy says it's okay. I pulled some chocolate chip cookies out just for you. Do you like chocolate chip?" asked Irna surveying Rebecca's and Ashley's faces for approval.

"Yum! My favorite! Mommy? I promise I'll be good," smiled Ashley up at her mom.

"Go ahead. Only two, Ashley. After you have one, another one after that, and that's it." She looked a little frazzled. "Sugar. Just what she needs," she muttered looking at Irna.

"I'm sorry dear. Maybe I should have waited. I have some tea or coffee ready. Would you like some? Any preference? If memory serves, you liked Earl Gray," offered Irna.

"Tea would be nice. Thanks. With lemon, if you have it," she answered as Irna trotted to the kitchen.
"Does Ashley like milk with her cookies?" she asked as she scuttled in the kitchen getting cups and the setup. "Please. Sit down there in the living room."
"A small glass. If you have a plastic cup, even better. She's a bit accident-prone," replied Rebecca. "Only two cookies, Ashley," directed Rebecca to her daughter sitting on the floor with her cookie. Ashley looked over at her. "Okay, mommy."
"I have a pad of drawing paper for when I doodle sometimes. And some crayons and colored pencils. Over there underneath the coffee table," shared Irna. "If you think that would be okay, you are welcome to give those to her to color with."
"That's okay. I have her coloring book and small crayon set here for her." She reached into her *magic bag* as Ashley called it. It always seemed to have everything she needed. Rebecca reached in and procured the book and box of crayons.
"Here you go, sweetie. Why don't you go color over there while your Aunt Irna and I talk, okay?" Rebecca looked at her daughter lovingly. Ashley got up and clumsily grabbed the supplies from her mom and returned to her spot finishing her first cookie. Irna handed her a plastic cup of milk, half full. Then retrieved a small tray with teacups, a small teapot, and some cut lemon wedges and sat on the sofa. Rebecca was close to her sitting on the comfortable lounger with pillows.
"So, now that we're a bit settled. How are you?" asked Irna.
"Things could be better. Look. I don't know what happened between you and my mom. I just know it left a rift. My husband dies in a car accident. I then lose my mom. You're not around and never reach out. I don't know what to think. What happened?" asked Rebecca directly. "You seemed to have abandoned me."
"Well…you sure don't waste time getting to the point, do you?" replied Irna as she prepared her cup of tea. "Help yourself, dear." She motioned to the tea, teapot, cup, and lemons. "I am not much into ceremony."
"Thanks." She reached out and poured herself a cup of tea, then squeezed a lemon into it. She had a slight tremble. "I need to understand what happened. I went through so much on my own. You used to come up and visit. You called us. Then when you stopped. I stopped. I thought you didn't care anymore. But now,

I…." she stopped herself. Took a sip of tea, then continued. "What happened?" she asked again. Irna looked at her with sympathy. She knew it was time to share with her.
"Your mother and I had an interesting relationship. We were very close at one time. But when we disagreed, she was hot-tempered. Boy, was she hot-tempered. Ever since we were little girls growing up. I remember the fights we would have over toys. If she didn't like the color of the dress I put on my dolls, she would desperately try to force me to change it so it would coordinate with hers. If I didn't, she threw a fit and wouldn't talk to me for a day. Sometimes two. Our parents would talk with us. Try to get us to reconcile. Sometimes it worked, sometimes not. And when she was mad, it was like I wasn't in the room. I guess you might say she was a bit of a narcissist then. It only got worse with age."
"I know she was tough sometimes… but still," interrupted Rebecca.
"Nope. She could be, not just difficult, but also mean." Irna paused. "Remember when you went you were accepted to Portland State? You were excited. But you had your hopes on NYU. Remember that?" asked Irna. She got up and approached her bookshelf with a few photo albums and full of different novels. She pulled the album next to the book "*The Crystal Bible*" and "*The Complete Works of William Shakespeare*".
"Yes. You had been visiting that week. I remember," Rebecca answered. Irna returned to her seat with the album and opened it. She flipped through two pages and pulled out an envelope.
"Did she tell you NYU accepted you?" She handed her the letter. Rebecca's eyes widened slightly. She hesitantly accepted the envelope from Irna.
"What? She didn't," whispered Rebecca a little wary of the news.
"She did. She told me after you had gone to bed happy you were going to Portland State. You were happy to have received an acceptance letter." Irna procured another envelope. "You were accepted to two other universities." I was so angry with Claire for hiding that from you. After you left to go tell your friends the next day about Portland State, Claire and I fought. She simply did not want you going away and wanted to keep you there. I thought that was wrong. She should have let you make your own decision. Instead...she made it for you." She handed Rebecca the second envelope. "I took these from your mother's drawer right before I left the next day. I thought you should know. Not in a mean or

vindictive way. Everything worked out. Things were not just what they seemed to you." Rebecca's eyes showed a hint of anger while tearing up a little.

"I don't get it. Why didn't she just tell me?" she asked in a quiet yet tense tone. She tried not to alert her daughter who was humming along while coloring her book. Little did she notice she was on her third cookie. "If she would have talked to me, maybe I would have decided to stay."

Irna looked at her full of empathy. "Your dad wasn't doing well. Did you know that? He had heart disease. She did not want to be left alone and didn't know how to talk with you about it. She forbade me to say anything about anything. If I did, she would make sure I would have nothing to do with you."

"I didn't know," Rebecca whispered still staring at the acceptance letters. "But things worked out at Portland State. At least I had a partial scholarship. My mom was able to pull together money that paid for my schooling so I could stay at home. I remember when I went to pay my tuition. It had been paid. So, I think she found ways to make it up to me. When I found that out, I ran home and hugged her thanking her and my dad. Otherwise, I would have had to get a job."

"Actually, dear. That was my doing. It was another part of the argument. If you look at the acceptance letters, NYU was giving you a full scholarship. The others were partial. I knew Claire couldn't afford it given the hospital bills for your father. My husband had passed a few years prior. He left me a nice sum from his insurance and some savings he had put aside. I called the school and paid it." She flipped another page of the book and pulled the document showing the payment receipt and handed it to her niece.

"What the…mom never said anything." She reviewed the receipt handed to her. "They were both so quiet about it when I arrived home thanking them. They just looked at each other and smiled. I thought they were being humble." She faltered in her comments. Her voice shaking a little. "Why didn't they say anything? And why are you telling me all this now?" She looked at Irna with tears in her eyes. She wasn't sure how to feel.

"Don't blame them. It's in the past. I am not showing you all this to be mean. I am just letting you know that I was always there, even when you didn't think I was. Claire did not want me around. She thought I interfered too much in her life, and yours." said Irna

solemnly. “Claire did let me know when the child came into the picture.” She looked over at her daughter. “I was surprised to get the call after a few years. Out of the blue. She was upset at first. She shared how you had received the news you couldn’t have children. Then a few days later, she had met a young lady who was pregnant. Well…” she reached over and filled her cup again with tea. “I think you can piece that story together. I would hear from her off and on and just listen. She did not want my opinion in any way. Irna added matter-of-factly and swished her hand horizontally. She put her teacup down and patted her chest lightly. “My heart hurt for you. But I was getting a little worried. Every time she called, it seemed like she was manipulating the girl. Then, sure enough…” Irna nodded. Rebecca looked at her in disbelief.
“You think my mom ‘wormed’ her way for me in that situation?” she looked over at Ashley. Then lowered her voice.
“Yes,” replied Irna. “Again, I don’t think she had any ill intent. She was thinking of you. She thought you needed it and she was going to do whatever it took. In many ways, she was wonderful. In others, not so much. There was a level of selfishness, too. She wanted grandkids. It probably wrecked her as much as it did you.”
“How would you know?” Rebecca asked somewhat accusatory and sternly. “You weren’t around. Yes, I know why, now…but still.”
“I was the recipient of the same news." She held back something. She almost continued her thought but decided to continue with that story. "I couldn’t have children, so I know exactly how it feels,” replied Irna. “I’m not sure I wouldn’t do what she did, but I argued with her about how she was handling it. I could tell.” This was upsetting Rebecca. She wanted to find out answers, but instead, she had more questions. Her emotions were getting the better of her. She rose from her seat.
“We need to leave. This is a bit much. Maybe it was a mistake to come. I needed to…” she caught herself. She took a breath. Stood up. “Ashley. Bring your things over. We need to leave.”
Irna looked at Rebecca. “Please don’t. We need to talk some more. And I didn’t have the pleasure of meeting with your darling daughter. Such dark hair. Lovely eyes.” She paused then stood up. “Please don’t leave yet. I’m sorry this was all so much. Maybe I shouldn’t have told you, but I thought you had a right to know.”
“My mind is just spinning right now. I am going back to the hotel. Give me a moment. You just dumped some heavy things on me that

I need to process. I just need to think through them, okay?" Tears were slowly running down her cheeks. Small tears. She kept wiping them away.
"Why are you crying, mommy?" asked Ashley observing her mom. Then she looked towards Irna. "Why did you make my mommy cry? That's not nice," Ashley said accusatorily.
"It's okay sweetie. Mommy just found out some things. They surprised me. We're going to go back to our hotel, okay? Say goodbye to Irna. You'll see her again," instructed Rebecca as she put away Ashley's coloring book and crayons and prepped them to go. She bent over and hugged her daughter. "Come on. Let's go." She led her daughter to the door.
"Will you call me later?" Irna asked, hoping for a positive response. "Please? I mean it when I say, I'm here for you. I always have been."
"I'll call you later. Just give me a moment, okay?" Rebecca said as she and her daughter left the flat. Irna watched them depart with sadness in her eyes. "Okay. I'll be here." She closed the door behind them and sat down for another cup of tea. Rebecca had taken the acceptance letters with her long with the receipt Irna showed her. She was confused. She didn't understand why Claire never said anything to her about this. She had more questions, but she had a feeling she would not find answers to all of them. But she hoped.

As Rebecca and Ashley walked back to the hotel in the San Francisco sun with the cool breeze, Ashley would sing and hum songs and skip in between some of her steps. She was holding her hand tightly, with little resistance from her little girl. She thought to herself how she was jealous of her. She didn't have to worry about paying bills, or politics, or family issues. Her daughter depended solely on her for support. Oh, the innocence. She wished sometimes she could stay that way. She wouldn't need to worry about family disputes, family lies, or family dramas. She was carefree. Cookies, milk, coloring books, a small circle of friends. Life for her daughter was simple.

When they arrived back at their hotel room, she asked Ashley if she was hungry for dinner. The front desk clerk at the hotel shared that there was a Johnny Rockets on Fillmore they could go to. When she told Ashley, she just lit up. "Can I have French fries?" she would ask.

"Absolutely, snoogie," she replied using her nickname of endearment. She was a snuggler with her mom. Whenever she would wake Rebecca up at night, she struggled with the word, '*snuggle*' and would pronounce it '*snoogie*' instead, hence the name.
"Yay! I get French fries! Can I have ice cream, too?" she asked meekly.
"How about a milkshake? That's a soft mushy ice cream that you can eat through a straw," Rebecca answered in a childlike tone. She was feeling better from the walk. She needed this time with her daughter.
"Yay! Okay! French fries and mickshake!" she said as she mispronounced the beverage. It brought a small smile to Rebecca's face.

Upon arrival to the 50's themed diner with black and white checkered floors, red vinyl booths with mini jukeboxes in each the scent of burgers was in the air. There was a white laminate counter with chrome trim where people could sit and eat, which included a view to watching the cook prepare the food. Rebecca looked around for seating options. She spied an available front booth by one of the windows. The young man behind the register informed her she could sit anywhere and that someone would be with her shortly. She and Ashley made their way with Ashley chanting, "French fries and mickshake! French fries and mickshake! Stwawberry!" she added.
"Snoogie…scooch in and sit. You okay?" Rebecca asked.
"I need to potty mommy," replied Ashley. A server arrived as she said that.
"Hi! Welcome to Johnny Rockets! Here are some menus. Can I get you something to drink?" asked the young Asian girl.
"Strawberry milkshake for my daughter and I would love an iced tea, please," replied Rebecca. "We're gonna run to the restroom. Can you point to where it is?"
"No problem. Through the door and all the way back on the left. I'll put this in, and your drinks should be out by the time you get back," replied the server as she dropped the menus, noted the drinks, and twirled off.
Rebecca and Ashley returned about fifteen minutes later to find their drinks in their places on the table. The place had become busier in those few minutes that passed. She was not alone in treating her daughter to dinner there that evening. There were a few other parents with their kids. She also noticed a Jamaican-looking

gentleman sitting at the counter on his phone. She always thought it was rude for someone to be speaking on their cell phone in a restaurant, but who was she to judge. She didn't mean to eavesdrop but couldn't help it. "No, I haven't talked with her yet... yes. I know. I have a couple of weeks to get my shit together. You don't have to remind me…sorry… I know…I will let you know once I see her…okay…and what about the issues in Syria…can I help... I know, I know. You want me to focus on this. I can't help worrying though…okay…okay…I'll call you…I promise. Thanks." And hung up. He was frustrated and dealing with something of a personal nature. But 'Syria'? She was curious but knew she had to mind her own business. The server arrived.
"Are you interested in anything to eat? Can I take your order?" she asked.
"Ashley would love some French fries…," said Rebecca.
"French fries!" interrupted Ashley and she struggled with her milkshake. She was trying desperately to suck the milkshake up. It generated a smile from the server. She leaned over pulling a long-handled spoon from her apron and handed it to her.
"Here. Use this. Stir up the milkshake just a little. Be careful. And then it will move the hard stuff around so you can taste it through the straw," and kindly winked at her as she demonstrated it showing how to use the spoon with caution and care. "Be careful not to spill it from the glass edges. And if you do really well, I will bring you a coloring mat with some crayons!" she smiled.
Rebecca watched the interaction. "That was very nice of you. Thank you," she said appreciatively.
"No problem" responded the server watching Ashley in her success. "Good job! You get a coloring mat and crayons!" then looked at Rebecca. "Can I bring you something to eat?"
Yes, please. A Johnny Rocket burger. Well done. Everything on it. Side of chili fries and a small salad." She paused. "Can I also get a glass of water?"
"Sure! Be right back."
After their exchange, Rebecca noticed the man who was on the phone earlier from the counter was looking at them and smiling. She felt a little creeped out.
"Can I help you?" she asked the man.

“Oh, sorry. I was just finishing eating and I noticed your daughter. She’s adorable. Not to be weird or anything. She just reminds me of someone. That’s all,” he answered.
“Do you usually stare at moms and their little girls? You’re kind of creeping me out a little,” she said looking at him surprised he spoke to her.
“Oh. Sorry. I’m not weird or anything. Just going through a strange time. Visiting here. That’s all. My name’s Dom. I’m staying at the Marriott. Crazy city.”
“Rebecca,” she answered suspiciously of the man. “Visiting, too.”
“I’m visiting from Quebec. Ottawa.” He remained seated with his eyes moving back and forth from Rebecca to Ashley and back to Rebecca. He was intrigued with the little girl's focus on stirring her milkshake and sucking on the straw for her reward. It made him smile.
“Chicago. Visiting my aunt.” She answered curtly with a lie then sipped her iced tea. She was from Portland. She grabbed a napkin from the dispenser and reached over to wipe the ice cream around Ashley’s mouth.
“Ah. Well, that explains the directness. Big city. Well…sorry to disturb you. Thanks for the smile, though. Have a nice evening.” He got up and walked out when his phone rang. A few moments later, the server dropped off two orders of fries. One for each of them Her burger and salad followed shortly after. They giggled at each other as they scarfed their food.
“Are we going to see Irna again?” asked Ashley. “Her cookies were good.”
“Yes. Mommy just needs to think about a few things tonight. I’ll call her tomorrow again,” replied Rebecca.
“I wish daddy was here,” she said as she stuffed her mouth with another fry.
“Me too, snoogie. Me too.”
“Do you think grandma is watching over us right now?” inquired the little girl.
“Yes. I know she is.”
“Who was that man talking to you?”
“I don’t know. He’s gone now, though,” replied Rebecca.
“He looks like my friend, Ronnie at home,” she said. “You think he knows him?”

"I am sure he doesn't, sweetie. Just because they look alike, doesn't mean they know each other," she giggled.
"Oh," Ashley replied then moved her focus back to her milkshake and fries.
They finished dinner and headed back to the hotel. Once back in their room, it felt like watching some tv and calling it an early evening. The two played around for about an hour with the pay-per-view Sesame street playing in the background before they both started yawning.
"I think we should go to bed early tonight. What do you think, snoogie?" asked Rebecca. "Let's go brush our teeth. Wanna sleep with mommy tonight?" she asked.
"Okay," replied Ashley yawning again. She and her daughter got up and she led her to the bathroom. They were in bed and asleep an hour later. Ashley was all snuggled in with her mom and her little unicorn stuffed animal she called 'Oonie".

The next day, they awoke refreshed. The two of them headed out and grabbed a small breakfast at a little bakery a few blocks away near Japan Town. While they sat and ate, Rebecca reviewed the acceptance letters and the payment receipt. She thought deeply about what Irna had shared. She defended her mom, but simply didn't agree with how she did things. She remembered her mom being a bit self-centered during her growing up. Her dad would periodically scold her when she put herself before them. She had overheard sometimes when they argued in the kitchen. She would hear the word 'selfish' being said. Despite the arguments, they loved each other. It wrecked their lives when he had his heart attack not long after she started college. Claire did not like Jeff, who later became her husband. Black hair, blue eyes. He wasn't overly handsome. Good-looking. Just not devastatingly so. He was smart and worked in a micro-brewery, the Blue Moon, on 23rd Avenue in NW Portland. He made good money with his craft beers. He was a bit nerdy and possessed an exceedingly kind heart. He loved helping people. He would always drop a five-dollar bill when he passed a homeless person. He held doors for old ladies. That was what struck her. His kindness was attractive. When she met him one night at the Blue Moon, he was giving an old homeless man a burger at the counter. He didn't charge him. When they met that night, he just smiled at her. They started dating. When she brought him home to meet her mom, all she could see was distrust in Claire's eyes. But she didn't care. He helped her study whenever he could. When she finished school, they were married. When they were having problems conceiving, he and she agreed to try in vitro. He remained supportive. Loving. He doted on her whenever she needed it. They occasionally argued, but nothing lasting. Then the kids. Then the tragedies.

She knew it was time to put things to rest. She and Ashley returned to the hotel, and she called
Irna. *Ring....ring....ring..."you've reached Irna. You know what to do and when to do it. Here it comes" ....beep.* "Hi Irna. Sorry for leaving the way I did yesterday. Can we meet again..."
"Hello? Rebecca?" was Irna's voice hastily interrupting the message being left. "Sorry, dear. I was in the bathroom getting ready for work. I'm glad you called," she said slightly out of breath, yet with warmth.
"Hi. Yes. Sorry for interrupting you," replied Rebecca.
"Oh no bother. You wouldn't know. It's not like you can see me through the phone now, can you? Or that you know my bowel schedule, or have ESP...if you believe in that sort of thing," said Irna hoping she didn't offend Rebecca again.
Rebecca smiled. "Well. I do but never mind that. I would like to see you again. I am going to be here through next Wednesday. Then I have to head back to Portland.
"Oh. Well, how about tomorrow. Today is my long shift at the store and Gay Pride is this weekend. I have to make up several trays for my clients for their Pride parties, and will be picking up stuff into Saturday morning." suggested Irna.
"Gay Pride? We have that in Portland. It's not that big, but I went twice. Is it this weekend here?" she asked.
"It's San Francisco!" replied Irna all excited. "Every day is Pride, but the big event is this weekend. I'm marching in the PFLAG contingent on Sunday and working the booth Saturday morning for a couple of hours. Want to join me?"
"Um. No. Thank you, though. I am not feeling up to being around big crowds. So tomorrow? What time?"
"How about the same time. Four-fifteenish?"
"Sure. See you then. Have a good day."
They hung up and went about their days. Irna was looking forward to seeing them again. She knew it wasn't easy. She could tell things

were kept from her and some airing of family laundry needed to be done.

More Family Laundry

The Friday had gone quickly. Gay pride was in full swing. Irna had finished all the trays and foodstuffs for her clients. They had been coming in picking up their orders. Anything left was in the walk-in fridge all bagged, boxed, labeled, and ready for pick up. She let one of her co-workers know before she left for the weekend. Irna marched and worked Pride every year. She loved it. This year had a different feeling to it. She knew it would all be okay, but there were things to go through. Things that needed to be seen all the way through.

"Okay then." She muttered to herself. She looked over to her counter team covering for her. "Have a great weekend. Wish me luck." She pointed to Jose'. "You. Watch your nuts this weekend. Last year you were kicked a couple of times for hitting on the wrong people. Got it?" she ordered with a smile. He nodded back in agreement noticeably embarrassed. "And you…" she pointed at her French counter partner, Charmaine. "Leave the gay boys alone. They're gay. They like boys. You aren't gonna change 'em," and laughed. "Try as you do!" Charmaine waved her off and laughed. "Wi. Wi. You go now. Have fun. See you Monday!" she replied in her French accent. Out the door, she went.

Irna was looking forward to seeing Rebecca and Ashley again. She rushed home in time to quickly shower and freshen up. She put on the tea, pulled down the Earl Grey, and sliced some lemons. She pulled some meatloaf she had the other day from the refrigerator and placed it in a baking dish, then into the oven to warm. She had brought some salad with her from the store, along with some fresh chocolate chip cookies. She had some pizza her neighbor brought her the other day. She thought that might be better for Ashley to eat

than meatloaf, wrapped it in aluminum foil, and placed it in the oven below the meatloaf. Just as she set everything up, there was a knock at the door. Irna yelled, "Coming!". She made her way to the door to welcome her guests for their second visit.
"Please. Come in. I have our tea ready…with lemon. I have a slice of pizza for Ashley if that's okay…*along with some chocolate chip cookies*." She sang winking towards Ashley. "I also have some meatloaf for us, if you want. Up to you. I just don't want you to go hungry…and it will be dinner time before we know it."
"Just tea for me. We had a big lunch. Ashley might like the pizza. I can't guarantee it." She paused and looked over to Ashley. "You want some pizza?" she asked while Ashley was grabbing her coloring book and crayons from her mom's magic bag.
"Pizza!" she nodded with a smile as she scurried to her spot to color. Irna set up the tea and snacks as everyone got settled. Once done, Irna sat and looked at Rebecca. "I'm sorry for dropping all of that on you yesterday," she said. "I didn't mean to upset you. I just thought you should know. I never abandoned you. I was just pushed away by my sister. We had a strange and stressful relationship."
"I thought a lot about what you shared. It all surprised me and just left me with more questions. I am not sure I will ever get all the answers I am looking for," said Rebecca in a soft voice. "When Jeff died in the accident, it wrecked me. My world was shattered. I had my mom and our friends. But never heard from you. Nothing." She looked at Irna.
"I was at the funeral," she whispered. "I saw the news. Horrible accident. That oil truck skidding…just horrible," said Irna shaking her head.
"You what? You were at the funeral? Why didn't you say anything? I mean…it would have meant the world," snapped Rebecca.
"Mommy? Are you okay?" asked Ashley from across the room looking at her mother. "Are you gonna cry again? I don't want you to cry," she added.
"Mommies okay, sweetie. Sorry. Just keep coloring. I'll be okay. We're just talking," she told her daughter unconvincingly.
"Okay," Ashley replied reluctantly returning to her coloring glancing suspiciously back and forth between Irna and her mom. Rebecca looked back at Irna.
"Well?" she asked softly with determination expecting an answer.

“I couldn’t. Claire did not want me around. I hid from her, too. The last thing I wanted to do was to bring any attention to myself during that horrible time. You all had enough going on. She and I were still not speaking. If I had shown myself, she would have caused a scene…” she paused. “I just couldn’t do that to you.” Irna then got up and pulled the photo album down again. Returned to her seat. She opened the book and flipped a couple of pages. She lifted the document out and handed it to Rebecca. It was the card from the service. Rebecca looked down at it and put a hand to her face.
“I don’t know that I will ever really understand your relationship,” whispered Rebecca. "I feel like we were both robbed." Irna looked at her then reached out and put her hand on her knee.
“We have plenty of time to make that up, now. And I would love to get to know my grandniece over there.” She looked over towards Ashley and smiled. Ashley looked up and waved to them, smiling.
“Coloring my oonicorns!” she yelled.
“She is always so excited, isn’t she?” asked Irna. “Anyway, we have time now.”
“Actually, Aunt Irna. That is why I am here.” Rebecca’s tone changed again. This time, it was hesitant with a slightly ominous inflection.
“What do you mean?” asked Irna shifting her focus back to Rebecca and taking a sip of tea then putting her cup down.
“I wanted to find out why you weren’t around. Why you didn’t visit, or call. I needed to know. Things are hard, right now,” stammered Rebecca.
“Why? What happened?” asked Irna. “Everything is fixable, sweetie.” She tried to change the mood that was creeping up.
“Not this, aunt.”
“What?”
“I have pancreatic cancer. Advanced stages.” Rebecca started tearing up.
“What? What do the doctors say? Can we get another opinion? We have great doctors here...” Irna started rattling off. Rebecca interrupted her.
“I have been through all of that. I have seen specialists. I've had some chemo. But it did not work. I have a few months. Ashley and I have been talking about me going on my trip.” She looked over at Ashley coloring away eating a chocolate chip cookie she seemed to

sneak off the counter. She looked up and over towards Irna and Rebecca. She picked up her coloring book and scrambled over. "Look! Oonie is colored! I used lots of colors. The way you like, mommy." Said Ashley holding out her book with the sloppily colored unicorn.
"Beautiful, sweetie," stated Rebecca admiring the artwork. Irna looked at Rebecca. She was fighting back the tears.
"What can I do?" she asked in a cracked and raspy voice. "Please," and she put her hand on Rebecca's knee, again.
"I just need you to be there. I would love it if you got to know Ashley. Spend some time with her while I visit. I have to get back. It would be great if you came to visit." Rebecca said trying to lighten up. "It's time to get things right, you know?" she said petting her daughter then looking at Irna with teary eyes. "I will need my aunt," she added.
"Okay. When would you like me to come up? Do you need me to travel back with you?" she asked.
"No. Not immediately. In about a month. I need to do some things when I get back. I have some friends helping me," replied Rebecca.
"What about Ashley?" Irna asked concerned. Ashley looked over at her hearing her name.
"Mommy is sad, again," said the young girl. "But I will keep coloring oonies for her. They make her smile. Right mommy?"
"Right, snoogie. Go color another one for me, okay?" asked Rebecca.
"Okay!" smiled Ashely, and she returned to her spot and began coloring again.
"There are some friends of mine. I have made arrangements for them and Ashley. I wanted you to know. I think it would be a good idea when you visit that you meet them. They are really wonderful. Ashley loves them. It's all arranged," replied Rebecca.
"How long have you known?"
"Not long enough. I should have paid attention to the signs. We all missed it. No one is to blame. It just is. It sucks," she replied tearing up. "Look." She paused to compose herself. Irna passed over the tissues and they both grabbed one and blew their noses causing Ashley to look over at them again.
"You okay, mommy?" she asked.
"Yes, snoogie. Keep coloring. We're okay," she replied.

“Look,” she resumed her sentence. “Let’s just move forward and stop hashing all this over. The important thing is that I want to make the most of what I have left. That means repairing our relationship. Making sure you and Ashley have one. And making sure she is taken care of. If I accomplish that, then I will be happy. Okay?” She looked Irna in the eyes. She was searching for the affirmation she needed that her message was being heard.
“Okay then,” said Irna resigned to the news and giving into her niece. “Okay. I will do as you wish. I will come up in about a month.” she repeated her instructions. “I will meet the couple. I will develop a relationship with my niece.” She thought of something. “But I have a couple of conditions, too.” Her face brightened. Rebecca looked at her not knowing what to expect.
“What?” she asked.
“You and Ashley march with me in the Gay Pride parade on Sunday,” she commanded. “I know you have not been *in* a parade before. It’s high time you were.”
“I think that might be a bit much for me, Irna,” said Rebecca. “I tend to get tired,” she added.
“Well, then you sneak out and leave the group early. It will be fun. Okay?” Irna countered.
“Okay. Why not. But know that I hate large crowds.”
“Well…get over it for the day,” Irna said with some sternness.
“What’s the other condition?” Rebecca asked.
“You meet my family here. Scott and Alex. They are special to me. And Alex’s sister, Michelle. She’s visiting right now, and I think you would like them.”
“Okay. That would be nice to meet some of your friends.”
“I’ll set it up. Probably Monday or Tuesday before you leave. Okay?”
“Okay then. Anything else?”
“Nope. Just take care of yourself so you are around longer than you plan.” She winked at her. “Can I hug you, now?” she asked.
Rebecca got up from her seat. Irna rose to her feet using the sofa arm to push up. She leaned over and they embraced each other. It was a deep, warm and long embrace. Ashley looked over and then decided to join. She hopped over and wrapped her arms around the women’s legs.
“Yay! Hugs! I love you!” said Ashley with no direction of her comment. “I love you!” she said again smiling.

“I love you, too, snoogie,” said her mom.
“Me too,” added Irna.

After a few minutes. They all separated. Ashley went a grabbed another cookie. Her mom just shrugged her shoulders and waved it off. Irna poured another cup of tea for them. They started talking about other things. They needed to just talk and share about things in their lives. Irna shared about her work at the store and how she met Scott and Alex. She shared about some of her friends and her reading group. She liked going to church and alternated between attending Glide Memorial and the Metropolitan Community Center. She wasn’t gay, but only supported churches that were all-inclusive. Rebecca was a Christian, but she did not believe in organized religion. She thought it hypocritical and greedy. She believed wars were started on religion and hated violence. She shared about her love of gardening, playing with Ashley, and spending time with her close friends. She had only a handful, but they were always there for each other. Being an only child, she was more introverted. She shared her love of reading. As time went by, Irna had fed the three of them. They were all suddenly engaged with each other.

It was almost nine pm when they realized the time. They were all exhausted. So much was out and being shared. They agreed the visiting session was ending. Irna and Rebecca arranged for some playtime in Alta Plaza Park before they left. Irna would bring a bottle of wine and some food for them. They would make time to discuss the Sunday marching and plan. As Rebecca and her daughter were preparing to leave, there seemed to be still something missing. Irna couldn’t put her finger on it. And she looked at Ashley, who kept smiling at them both. She would figure it out. For now, she would focus on the moment with her niece and grandniece. They bid their goodbyes until Saturday in the park.

“Oh my,” whispered Irna talking to herself. She looked around and cleaned up after her guests. She knew would sleep well. As she cleaned and straightened her place, her heart was sad with the news. She lightly cried as she cleaned up. She understood, though. She looked at the picture on the shelves of her and Rebecca, and when she was a teenager waiting for her acceptance letters, and the one next to it with her and Rebecca at a carnival when she was a little girl. She would deal with her grief as it came. She reminded herself to talk with Alex and Scott. That must not slip by and she wrote herself a note before heading to bed.

Pride Weekend

Michelle was standing with Alex and Scott around Market Street and Montgomery for the Pride parade on a beautiful Sunday morning. She had been experiencing a whirlwind weekend. It was her first Gay Pride…and in San Francisco, where it all began. She had learned that Gay Pride originated in 1970 to commemorate the Stonewall riots that occurred June 28, 1969. It was the pivotal moment in LGBTQ history when the New York police raided the Stonewall Inn, a club in Greenwich Village. One of the offices struck a lesbian over the head and forced her into a van. The LGBTQ citizens were tired of the constant harassment, abuse, physical attacks, and discrimination they experienced. Many were often kicked out of their homes and disowned by their families. The first Gay Pride parade consisted of 20 to 30 people and grew over the years as people began to educate themselves and learn that homosexuality wasn't a choice. It is part of being human. It was also documented and illustrated in many cultures throughout history. For Michelle to see the amount of support amongst the crowds overwhelmed her at times. The diversity of people. The creativity of costumes and make-up. She felt fortunate to have had a brief conversation with a 'Sister of Perpetual Indulgence' Saturday night in the Castro and learned that it was an 'Order". Their focus as a charity is to use drag and religious imagery to call attention to sexual intolerance. She watched people eat and drink in the streets. The dancing was everywhere. It was such a celebration. Scott and Alex were commonly holding hands. The three of them wore their rainbow beads and the feather boas that Scott bought from a carted street vendor selling pride accessories on the walk down to where they stood, now.

The parade started with the ‘Dykes on Bikes’. A coalition of lesbians on motorcycles wearing everything from basic clothes, leather gear, topless and nude. Many had fellow lesbians, girlfriends, partners, or whatever riding what she heard referenced as ‘bitch’. That meant behind the driver. She saw a Sister of Perpetual indulgence in an orange jumpsuit and a ‘flying nuns' hat’. The Gold’s Gym float with a cast of diverse fit passengers baring what they could just short of nudity. Another float from the Wild Side West. A popular lesbian bar in the Bernal Heights neighborhood. So many groups like Leather Pride, PFLAG (Parents and Friends of Lesbian and Gays,) Pacific Islander Pride, Porn studios representation like Falcon. Political figures rode in cars showing their support of the community. The Eagle, a leather bar South of Market had a float with shirtless, fit, hairy men wearing assless leather chaps and house music blaring through the crows. A few lipstick lesbian groups holding hands and yelling “women power!” with signs highlighting their career positions like lawyers, accountants, business owners, realtors, to name a few highlighting that their presence was in almost every facet of the Bay Area society. Bisexuals also made their participation known through their organizational factions. It was a cavalcade of over 250 contingents. A few groups of buff-gym types walking on stilts wearing angel wings strutted their way through the crowds inspiring whistling and catcalling. The boys, Alex and Scott, just yelled, hugged, and kissed each other. It was a moment she would never forget.

Around one pm, they decided to make their way to the civic center where the post-parade festivities were taking place. They snaked their way through the crowds. About thirty minutes later, they hit the entrance. Again, Michelle was overwhelmed. She observed a sea of people. Booths lined the streets around the center. Music was playing everywhere. People lounging on the grass in the sun wherever they could find a spot. Smoke and aromas from food vendors blended with pot and fragrances filled the air. ‘Stand Against Hate’ flashed at the main stage in between the theme ‘Queerific’. They were announcing the upcoming B-52s performance. The San Francisco Gay Men’s Chorus was gearing up to perform. There was a group of men with angel wings walking around. Her senses were being flooded. So much going on everywhere. Booths selling their goods from Rainbow bow ties, candles, mineral and quartz, sunglasses, jewelry, artwork, vintage

San Francisco photographs…just about anything and everything was available for purchase. All this including dildos, cock rings, lube, and other fetish equipment and toys. Various LGBTQ fundraising organizations were also out soliciting volunteers and donations. Academy of Friends, The Quilt, LGBTQ Legal Services, San Francisco Suicide Prevention Crisis Line, Gay Adoption, Same-Sex Marriage…you name it, it had representation. Music and dancing of all styles were also represented. Techno, disco, square dancing…you name it. There was a section that was gated and secure from sight, but one knew the activities were of a sexual nature just by the ambiance and signage. A Leather Daddies booth was next to it if that was any indication of the fetish. The boys just toured Michelle around. She kept taking it all in. They took turns grabbing Miller lite and other beers whenever they ran low. It all depended on what was available wherever they were. They all agreed to avoid the Smirnoff drinks. They were not out to get plastered. Just inebriated enough to maintain a nice buzz. They all agreed to get to the main stage after walking around, in time to catch the B-52s.

It was around four-thirty, and they were getting tired. They all had been sun-kissed and were still buzzed from the beer they had consumed throughout the day. Scott looked over to Michelle. "You ready to head back? My dogs are barking, and my brain hurts from all the noise," and laughed. She nodded in agreement. He looked at Alex. "Schmoo? You ready?" Alex looked at him. Kissed him.
"Yes. Let's go. We need to check on JB, too. I promised we would stop by. Wanna grab a cab?"
Scott nodded. "Great idea. Let's do it.". They strategically made their way to the edge of Hayes Valley and hailed a taxi. Off they went to JB's. They were serenely quiet the entire ride.
"Wow," whispered Michelle as if sharing a secret. That was an experience I will never forget. Thank you, guys." Then she smiled and followed with an unintentional smirk. Alex and Scott smiled at each other and giggled.
"Glad you had fun," whispered Alex, back and snuggled into Scott putting his head on his shoulder.

Never A Dull Moment

The trio entered JB's flat where Alex heard the TV blaring from the master bedroom.
"Be right back. I'm gonna check on JB. There's some water in the fridge." Alex hinted as he bee-lined his way to the noise. Scott and Michelle headed into the kitchen to hydrate and took turns excusing themselves to the half-bath to relieve themselves of the beer they had enjoyed throughout the day.
"You decent?" asked Alex outside the bedroom door directed towards JB.
"I am. Just watching a documentary on Benjamin Franklin. You boys have an enjoyable time with Michelle?" JB asked.
"We did. We are not very hungry. But more importantly…. did you eat?" Alex asked concerned.
"I did. I fixed myself a spam sandwich with pickles on the side. I had my Ruffles chips. I was good. I have some leftovers in the fridge for dinner."
"Okay. Just making sure. Do you have your insulin pen nearby?" Alex asked probing to make sure JB was prepared in case of a crash. He had experienced a few of them with JB. He hated seeing him go through such misery when they hit.
"I do. It's right there on the bed. I just got off the phone with Mags. I will need your help getting some checks off tomorrow." JB stated then winced.
"No Problem. What's wrong?" Alex asked concerned. Then he heard Scott.
"Yo! JB! Somehow, it would be amazing if we figured out how you could join us when we go to Pride. You were on our minds when we

were down there." Said Scott as he perched his chin on Alex's shoulder peeking over at JB. JB winced again.
"What's wrong?" asked Scott, concerned.
"Hi JB! What's going on?" Michelle piped in behind Scott.
"I am feeling some chest pains," stated JB.
"I will call 9-1-1," said Alex.
"No. No." He winced. "I'll be fine," grunted JB as he took a deep breath.
"Nope. 9-1-1. I can't drive you, JB. We have been drinking beer. You need assistance and need to get in to see Andy. I'll give him a call." Alex stepped over to JB's office and called Dr. Rosen. He had a special phone number for emergencies. There was a prompt answer. He explained what was going on and was quickly off the phone.
"Dr. Rosen said for me to call 9-1-1 and he will see you at the hospital." Then Alex dialed and provided the information. Afterward, he hung up his cell phone. "They are on their way."
Scott was on the bed holding JB's hand. JB kept muttering "Christ it hurts." Scott would reply "So sorry, JB. You're going to be fine. Hang on."
"What can I do?" asked Michelle feeling helpless.
"Watch for the ambulance from the Livingroom. Please. When they get here, let them in and guide them back here," Alex directed.
"Okay."
"I'll do it," said Scott as he rose from the bed and rushed to the spot. As he neared the door, he heard the siren and decided to just open the door to help speed things up. Moments later, they were at the door. Firemen, paramedics, and an ambulance. Scott guided them to the back where they were met by Alex and they began to interview JB. Within fifteen minutes, they had him on a gurney and were on the way to the Sutter Health Emergency room in Pacific Heights.
Alex looked at Michelle. "Why don't you head to the house. We'll call you once we know what's going on. We've been through this before."
She looked at him, worried. "You sure? I can go with you." Scott gazed empathically at Michelle.
"No. Really. We have gone through this many times before. Hopefully, it's nothing. Cross our fingers. Lord knows how much he doesn't deserve this."

"Alex is right. Go on back to the house. We'll lock up here and follow up with you once we get an update. We'll just stand around a lot, waiting." Scott added.
"Okay. I hope everything is okay. Tell him I'm praying for him, please."
"Of course. Let's get going, Scott," instructed Alex.
The trio departed and went on their way. Alex was able to grab a taxi a half-block away off Gough Street for him and Scott. Within minutes they were in the Emergency Room and Alex was talking with the doctor on call reviewing JB's medical history with both him and JB. Scott sat next to JB listening intently. They were both asked to step out of the area while they ran an EKG and taking blood for tests. Shortly after, Dr. Rosen appeared.
"Hi Alex. Hi Scott. How are you?" he asked.
"As well as can be expected," Alex replied solemnly. "We just don't get why these episodes happen as they do. It's so strange. And always sudden without warning," he continued.
"That's just Jefferson for you. I am checking out the blood work to make sure there are no cardiac issues. He has so many conditions, so his symptoms can be confusing. We just need to make sure we take all the precautionary steps. I think he will be fine. I'll know more a little later. Probably within the hour. Okay?" Dr. Rosen was always calming when he shared JB's condition. He had saved JB's life a couple of times now. He was completely trusted and one of the top cardiologists in the country. "I'll see you in a little bit," and he stepped out. About 10 minutes later, a handsome brown-haired, scruffy six-foot-one male nurse with wire-framed glasses stepped out from behind the curtain where JB was laying.
"Is he okay?" asked Scott.
"He is loaded up on some meds. His sugar was a little off, so we gave him a little insulin. He has an IV running. The EKG was done, and we will get that promptly to Dr. Rosen. Don't worry. He has pretty much declared we let him know of every step of care we take and any symptoms. He's in good hands. You can go sit with him if you want," he stated in a friendly tone then smiled compassionately.
"Thanks. Your name?" asked Scott.
"Jake," answered the nurse.
"Thanks, Jake," added Alex.
Alex and Scott sat with JB for about ninety minutes chit-chatting about the day. Scott would tease him a little.

"Just can't let us have a fun holiday, can you? You have to make it about yourself again and attract the drama," he toyed.
JB cleared his throat. "Blowhard." JB grinned. "You're just jealous you can't command the attention I do," he joked. Then added in a more solemn tone, "Actually, I hate these trips. Sorry to put you through all this again."
"Oh, stop. It's not your fault. You just need to feel better and get home. This does not suit you." Alex added reassuringly. "It's okay. We're here for you. We're not going anywhere."
"You don't have to stay here. Go home. I'll be all right." JB said half-heartedly.
"No way. We love you. Not going anywhere until we know you're okay and coming home," declared Scott. He held JB's hand. A few moments later, Dr. Rosen appeared.
"Okay. Here's the update. It doesn't appear to be cardiac, but I think it would be a good idea we keep him overnight for observation. He can go home in the morning. If everything is good, he can leave by around 8 am."
"Thank you. Do you know what happened? What was it?" asked Alex.
"It seems to be gastrointestinal. Sometimes these can feel like a heart attack. He'll be fine. He may have a touch of acid reflux. We'll watch it. I'll prescribe something for him. But just to make sure, we'll watch him tonight. Okay?" Dr. Rosen seemed relieved, but still cautious about the news he was delivering. JB grunted.
"Thanks, Andy. Although I think it's unnecessary that I stay," he paused. "Boys. You go. Alex. I'll see you first thing in the morning. You'll take me home. Okay?" he ordered half questioningly.
"Will do, JB. Glad you are okay. Thanks again, Dr. Rosen. We appreciate it," answered Alex. Scott leaned over and pecked JB on the cheek.
"Good night, sir. Glad you're okay. See you tomorrow. By the way…. your nurse, Jake. He's hot," he joked. Alex scoffed.
"He's right, JB. The nurse is hot. I wouldn't kick him out of bed," and giggled. "C'mon, Scott. Let's go. G'night JB. See you in the morning." They turned and left. Both of them glanced over for another peek at the nurse.
"Woof!" whispered Scott quietly. Alex reached over and pulled Scott close for a tight side hug and kissed his cheek.
"I love you," he said aloud.

"I love you back," responded Scott. "Walk or cab it home?" asked Scott.
"Cab it. There's one right there. Michelle will be pacing. Trust me. I'll call her to let her know we are on our way home," said Alex as he pulled out his Motorola.

Michelle was sitting on the stoop of the house with a Heineken waiting for some news. She had the front door open in case the phone rang and her Nokia cell phone to her side. She noticed people straggling to their apartments, drunk. Obviously from their time at Pride by the way they were dressed...or not. She giggled to herself, but then felt bad given the circumstances.
"Why haven't they called?" she muttered to herself. She kept watching the time. It had been over two hours. Then her phone rang.
"Hello? Alex?" she answered.
"Yep. We are on our way home. JB is fine. See you in a few minutes. We'll share all the details when we see you," he said soothing her.
"Oh, thank God. Thank you, See you shortly. I'm on the stoop." She hung up. A few minutes later, the cab pulled up with Scott and Alex jumping out.
"Hey, girl! Get enough drama for the day?" Scott teased loudly trying to lighten her mood quickly.
"Oh, shut up. I was so worried," she said. "What was it. Heart attack?"
"We worry every time," said Alex. "It's almost like clockwork. I think we are in the hospital about every holiday. Just about, mind you. The good news is that he's okay. They are keeping him overnight for observation. It was gastrointestinal…something associated with acid reflux, they think. I can pick him up in the morning," answered Alex as they both stood on the stairs looking up at Michelle.
"Let's go in. I need to take a quick shower and put some moisturizer on my face. I saw my face in a mirror at the hospital. It's turning beet red! Gurl!" shared Scott as he began mounting the stairs.
"Me too," added Alex. Then we can grab a beer….AND SOME WATER…hint-hint." Alex added in agreement directing the comment towards Scott. Scott turned and gave his partner a thumbs up affirming the proposed actions. "Got it, Schmoo," he said.
"Ooof!" expressed Michelle as she grabbed her phone and stood up to navigate her way back into the house. "I guess I'm third in the

shower…" she whispered, resigning to the planned activities. "I am exhausted. What a day. My first Pride. An Emergency Room. What's next?" as she made her way into the house following her hosts.

Back at the hospital, an ambulance pulled up with a police car behind it. The first responders quickly pulled the man out on the gurney and wheeled him into the Emergency room where they whisked him into a curtained section. "What do we have here?" asked the male nurse to the ambulance team.

"The guy's name is Gabriel Vegas. He's been beaten up pretty badly. He keeps fading in and out of consciousness. He may have a concussion, a couple of ribs broken. His BP is 90 over 110. Pulse is weak but steady. He seems to have been drinking and we can smell the pot on his breath." stated one of the EMTs factually. The nurse took the documented information from the other paramedic and started reviewing it. A young doctor of Indian descent entered.

"Let me see that," she directed reaching out for the documents. After scanning, she directed the nurse. "Get him to x-ray. Let's see if he has any broken bones. My guess is that he may have a few broken or fractured ribs and most likely a concussion." She looked over at the police officer who was standing by. "Do you know what happened here?" she asked.

"We saw him getting beaten up. Two guys were on him about a block from the civic center events down one of the alleys. We just happen to be driving by and my partner, Jim, here noticed it. He wasn't robbed. The backup we called in was able to apprehend the attackers when they attempted to run away. They cut them off at the opposite end of the alley around the corner. We were lucky. My guess is that it was a hate crime, but we'll know more in a bit. We just want to make sure that he's gonna be okay. Any information you can give us so we can get a statement from him would be appreciated," stated the stalky officer. His five-foot-ten-inch frame seemed to tower over the five-foot-two physician.

"We are going to have to run a few tests and get some x-rays. We'll know more after that. It'll be about an hour or two before we have all the details. You're welcome to wait or come back later. He's unconscious right now, so I don't think he is going to be of much help to you at the moment," replied the doctor in her calming matter-of-fact tone. She was concerned, but her gut told her he would make it.

“We’ll come back. Here’s my number just in case he comes around. Would you mind letting us know? We need to get a statement from him as to what happened,” asked the officer. “My name is Mark. I just don’t want a *Matthew Sheppard* situation on our hands here, if you know what I mean.” There was a sincere and concerning look in his eyes as he handed the doctor his card. The doctor accepted the card.
“Thank you, officer Doh. I’ll have Jake here give you a call.” She looked over at Jake who was finishing taking blood for testing from Gabriel’s arm. “Jake. Would you mind calling Officer Doh when Gabriel comes around after we are done with the tests when he awakens?” directed the doctor in her perfect English.
“Of course, doctor,” replied Jake. He was moving swiftly to get the work at hand completed. He had a few other patients to tend to. Tiffany was a socialite and a regular. She had married well and lived in a house a few doors down from the Gettys on Broadway Street. She kept thinking she had brain cancer when her real issue was migraines. Another was a couple who had gotten drunk at the events and accidentally dropped their beer bottles and somehow managed to fall in the glass resulting in cuts and small pieces that needed to be removed from their arms and butts. Neither was wearing undergarments except for the gold lame’ short shorts and matching rainbow tops. Suddenly, an orderly appeared.
“You have a patient I need to get to radiology for some x-rays?” he asked looking around.
“Yes. Here. Gabriel Vegas. Here’s the info,” stated Jake.
“Got it. I’ll have him back to you within the hour,” replied the orderly. Gabriel groaned, “*asshole*” he whispered angrily, half-opened his eyes, then was out again. They all glanced at each other wondering if there would be more. Nothing. They then resumed. The officers left; the doctor continued her rounds as Gabriel was wheeled off to radiology.

Monday Monday

Scott and Alex awoke Monday morning feeling groggy due to the Pride festivities and the additional couple of beers they had with Michelle in the garden afterward. Scott looked over at the Bose clock radio finding they had luxuriously overslept. It was just after 8 am and they usually started their days around seven. He nudged Alex gently.

"Good morning, Schmoo." Then leaned over and kissed his cheek given Alex was on his side with his back towards him. Alex grunted.

"Good morning, Schmoo," he sang lightly. Alex was not a morning person. Just opposite him. He scooched closer to Alex and kissed his cheek again. "Time to get up," he sang softly into his ear. Alex grunted again.

"No," he whispered. "Just a few more minutes." Scott smiled and nudged him again.

"It's after eight, Schmoo," said Scott hugging him. Alex rolled over. His bed-head hair all floppy and disheveled. Scott thought Alex was so handsome. Especially in the morning. He had so much scruff. He was always amazed at how fast his facial hair grew. Even after he shaved, a few hours later, he would quickly don a five o'clock shadow. He leaned over Alex and kissed his lips. "Morning, Schmoo," he whispered again. Alex slowly opened his eyes with a small grin.

"Good morning," he whispered. He pulled Scott's head down again and they began kissing. Softly at first. Then passionately. They slowly rolled back and forth taking turns laying atop each other.

"Well, this is a good start to a Monday," whispered Scott friskily. All Alex would say is "*Mmmmm*" and pull Scott back to him for more kissing then guiding him to his neck. The morning passion continued until they both climaxed after half an hour of appreciating each other's bodies.

"You go first," directed Scott indicating who was going to start their bathroom routine.

"You sure?" whispered Alex.

"Yep. You need to get to JBs. Then head over to the house to meet with Jimmy about the flooring project. I'll say one thing. He sure didn't waste any time, did he?" commented Scott about the flooring company owner.

"That's true. But we need to move fast. JB has to be settled before we go on our trip in September. That's going to come fast," replied Alex as he got out of bed heading towards the master bathroom. "We have to find a place, too."

"I know. Ugh. The timing sucks," said Scott as he wiped semen off his abdomen with the hand towel, he pulled from the nightstand drawer.

"How is the store coming along? Getting everything packed up, okay?" Alex asked from the bathroom.

"It's coming along. We will have everything packed up and ready to either store or donate by the end of the week," he answered back.

"I'll stop in today to do some packing up. Then I'll head down to see if any of the day-laborers are interested in a paint job. Before running to the East Bay." Scott tossed the towel in the laundry bag by their closet and arose from the comfort of their bed and comforter. He quickly made the bed then moved into the bathroom where Alex had finished brushing his teeth and was preparing to enter the shower.

"Why are you heading to the East Bay?" asked Alex.

"Meeting with Sabrina. We're going to have coffee in Alameda. I hadn't spoken with her since the party. I won't be long," replied Scott.

"Oh. Cool. Hug her for me," Alex requested.

"Will do," Came the muffled sound from Scott's mouth as he brushed his teeth. Afterward, he left back to the bedroom to give Alex his bathroom time in seclusion. They both valued their bathroom alone-time. He grabbed his robe from the closet and headed to the kitchen to make coffee for them. He had noticed Michelle's bedroom door was still closed and assumed she was still asleep. As he prepared the coffee and put out the continental breakfast, the phone rang.

“Hello?” he answered.
“Good morning dear,” said the female voice.
“Irna?” Scott asked.
“Yes. Scott?” the voice replied.
“Yeppers. Good morning. To what do I owe the pleasure? You hardly ever call,” Scott stated inquisitively.
“Oh, I know. Sorry, dear. How was your Pride weekend?” she asked.
“No biggie. Fun! It was Michelle’s first Pride. I think she’s still recovering.” He giggled. “We missed seeing you in the parade. Weren’t you marching?” Scott asked.
“Oh yes. I was in the PFLAG contingency. My niece and her daughter marched with me part of the way before they left exhausted. There were so many people! I think it gets bigger every year. I just hope the corporate world doesn’t take over,” said Irna.
“That’s cool that your niece was with you. Did she have a good time? Was it her first Gay pride?” Scott inquired.
“Oh, I think she saw one or two small parades in her life. It was the first time she was in one.” She paused. “It was such a beautiful day. It always is,” she added.
“True. I also don’t mind the corporations participating. It helps the visibility of the LGBT community. The more mainstream, the better for everyone. You know?” said Scott.
“I hope you’re right, sweetie. Anyway…the reason for my call is that I would love for you, Alex, and Michelle to meet my niece and her daughter.” Irna continued. “I was thinking dinner at my place tomorrow night. Would you be up for that?” she asked.
“I think so. One sec.” Scott put down the receiver and ran upstairs to their bathroom. “Alex. Irna is on the phone and is inviting us to her place for dinner tomorrow night. We don’t have any plans, right?” Scott asked.
“Nope. Sure. Why?” asked Alex.
“I’ll tell you shortly,” replied Scott as he turned and ran back to the phone in the kitchen. He picked up the receiver. “Sorry for the pause, there, Irna. I just checked with Alex.” He breathed a little heavy from running up and down the stairs. “We are good to go. Tomorrow night. What time?”
“How about 6:30, dear?” she asked.
“Great. Want us to bring anything?”
“How about two bottles of wine. A nice white and red?”

"You got it. Bubbles?" he asked.
"Does a bear shit in the woods?" she replied. "Never ask a lady if she wants sparkling wine or Champagne. Just know that the answer is always yes," she answered with humor. Scott giggled again.
"Yes ma'am. Got it. Anything else?"
"See you tomorrow night." She hung up.
"Wait. You didn't tell me …their names." And he heard the dial tone. She had hung up. "Damn. Oh well," he muttered. He hung up the phone.

The coffee was brewing, and the aroma was filtering throughout the house. "We're gonna have to start packing up the house too." He looked around whispering to himself. He shook his head and went back upstairs to the bathroom finding Alex with shaving foam on his face getting ready to shave.
"Mind if I talk with you while you shave?" asked Scott to his soul mate.
"Sure," Alex replied warming his razor with the blade in the hot slow running water.
"Irna is having us to dinner to meet her niece and her niece's daughter. She requested we bring her a bottle of bubbles, a bottle of white, and a bottle of red wine. You. Me. Michelle," recapped Scott. "Her place. Around 6:30."
"Okay. Should be fun," said Alex as he ran his razor down his cheeks clearing away the foam.
"Don't you think it's weird?" asked Scott.
"Nope. We've been there before. Granted a while ago. But she has had us over before. Don't read into it, Scott," said Alex moving quickly to shave realizing the time. "Michelle up, yet?"
"No. Doors' still closed," answered Scott. "I wonder how much longer she's staying?"
"We should ask. Not that we're kicking her out. It does seem that she's been here a while. She will have to leave before we move. We have a lot to do," said Alex. "I'm not worried. She has just been going through a lot. We are here to help her. She'll leave when she's ready. Let's not focus on that, okay?"
"Okay. Sorry. The timing of all this moving and the store sucks, you know? Now I have to get a job. At least we have money enough to move and that will last us a few months. Probably six or seven if we work it right," said Scott a little tensely. "I don't want you to worry, Schmoo. Never."

“We’ll make it no matter what. As long as we’re together. I believe in us. I believe in you, Smoo,” said Alex finishing his shaving and rinsing his face with water. “So. What do you think about when we should start packing up? Where do you want to start?”
“Well. We don’t have much in the garage. Just wine, Christmas, and a few miscellaneous items. You think JB will let us store some stuff in his new garage if we need to?” Scott asked. Alex was rinsing his hands and pulling out the gel for his hair. Scott was always envious of Alex’s hair. It was effortless.
“I think JB wouldn’t mind at all. But you didn’t answer my question.”
“Ah. Living room. Kitchen non-essentials, office non-essentials, guestroom, non-essentials in our room and the dining room. The bathroom should be last and set up first. Same with our bedroom and closets…however they will look…. wherever we land. What do you think?” he asked.
“Sounds good. We’ll have to pick up boxes this week. Let’s talk more later. I need to get running and you need to get showered. See you downstairs.” And with that, Alex leaned over, and kissed Scott then disappeared into the bedroom to get dressed for the day. Scott began his morning routine. He really wanted to get planning. He was nervous about all of the changes going on at once.
Within forty minutes, both Scott and Alex were in the kitchen having coffee and planning out their moving strategy. Scott usually took the lead on planning and Alex went along with it all and would simply reinforce Scott’s suggestions. As Alex was talking about the artwork packing up, Michelle slowly wandered into the room.
“Good morning, boys. Any coffee left for me?” she asked groggily. “I think I have a bit of a hangover. But I have to say, well worth it. Thanks for the fun yesterday,” she said as she pulled down an Alcatraz-themed coffee mug from the cabinet. Scott and Alex looked at her smiling.
“Good morning. Glad you had fun. Sorry for your hangover. Just in case, there’s Tylenol or Advil in the medicine cabinet. In the upstairs bathroom. Help yourself,” shared Alex.
“Irna has invited us for dinner tomorrow night. Her place. 6:30. She wants us to meet her niece and her grandniece. You up to it?” asked Scott. Michelle began pouring her coffee and yawned. She rubbed the side of her head mussing her hair a little more and then adjusted the white terrycloth Fairmont robe that was given to Scott from their

friend, Lina who was the Public Relations representative for the San Jose property. She had given both Alex and Scott matching robes with their names embroidered on them. She sipped her coffee and looked at the male couple with her bloodshot eyes.
"Sure. Sounds great. I hate you two. How can you look so fresh after yesterday? And adorable! I mean, really!" she said as if they performed a criminal act. They just chuckled.
"Practice," Scott replied.
"What were you guys talking about packing? What's up with that?" she asked as she took another gulp of coffee. Alex reminded her.
"Remember? Our landlord is selling the house. We have to move. And we need to move before we go on our trip. Between JB moving and us needing to, there is a lot to do. So just be prepared for us to be a bit messy and crazy right now. We would love any help you can give. Scott has thought of a pretty solid plan for us to get ready, so we are not in a last-minute jam, scrambling."
"Ah. Yes. I spaced on that. Sorry. Sure. I'll help if you want me to. Just let me know what you want me to do." She picked up a croissant and began to pull it apart then sloppily stuffed a piece into her mouth then took another gulp of coffee. "I feel like crap. I'll be fine. Just give me an hour."
"You can take all the time you need. We are outta here," said Alex. "I need to go see JB then head over to his new place to meet with the flooring guy."
"And I need to get to the store to pack up the remnants with Troy so we can close up by the end of the week. I also have to meet a friend of mine, Sabrina Spenser over in Alameda. Across the bridge. I think you met her at the party. She was with her boyfriend," added Scott amending his scheduled activities with his own.
"Sabrina?" Michelle asked raising an eyebrow.
"She was the Latina. Cute. A little loud. Funny. Her boyfriend wants to be a coach for a girls' soccer team. Ring any bells?" replied Scott to his hungover guest.
"Ah. Yes. I remember. I like her. Alameda?" She said as she took another gulp of coffee and then getting up to get some more.
"Yes. So, you get to go do whatever it is you want to do, today without any interruptions from us," Scott said feeling a little sympathetic to Michelle. "Why don't you take your coffee back to your room and lay down a little longer. I am sure after a little more

rest, some Tylenol, and a shower, you will feel so much better. Poor thing," he suggested.
"That's a good idea," she replied. And she headed back up to her room.
"Poor thing. What a mess," Alex said half-jokingly. "Kind of reminds me of the Monday after our first Gay Pride." He nudged Scott.
"True," replied Scott then looked at his watch. "Shit. It's getting late. You better get running. I have a boatload of stuff to do," he added and got up from the table. He rinsed his cup and placed it in the dishwasher. "Off I go. I will walk down to the store then come back and get my car then head to see Sabrina." He walked over and kissed Alex. "Say hi to JB. Call me about the floors. I'll stop by the paint store to see about painters, too. Love you!"
"Love you, too. Say hi to Sabrina!" Alex yelled as Scott grabbed his stuff and headed out the door. "Busy day," he mumbled to himself. He rose and echoed Scott's activities then yelled up to his sister. "I'm leaving! Feel Better! Have a lovely day! Love you!" and headed out the door with his bag, car keys, and jacket in hand.

After seeing JB, Alex arrived at 738 11th Avenue to meet with Jimmy Hardwood Floor. The name always made him laugh. He wondered why there was no 's' at the end for the plural version. Jimmy showed up about five minutes after his arrival. After they greeted each other, Alex guided Jimmy into the house. They walked through the main level, then up the stairs to the bedrooms.
"You no want the stairs done?" asked Jimmy. He had moved from China about eight years ago. It was something he shared with Alex when they first met. He was a kind man standing five-foot-four, slightly balding wearing his overalls. His modesty and warmth were evident in his facial expressions.
"No. Not the stairs. The two bedrooms, the landing, and the entryway, living room and dining room." Alex replied slowly. He wanted to make sure he didn't take Jimmy's English skills for granted.
"I take carpet up from downstairs. Then remove nails, sand then stain. I will need to put down three coats of verathane. I could have all house done by Thursday. You can move in Friday. We start today. Now if you want. My guys close by," declared Jimmy.
"How much?" asked Alex wanting to confirm the price. "I will need to make a quick call." Jimmy pulled out a small pad and pen from

his chest pockets. He started scribbling some numbers and ripped the piece of paper off the small pad and handed it to Alex.
"Really? And move-in ready by Friday?" he asked to confirm.
"Yes sir," Jimmy replied.
"One moment." Alex pulled out his cell phone and called JB. He shared the news. He paused. Then walked away to get out of earshot. "I think it's a great price. And they will have it done so you can start moving in your things by next Friday. But we still have to paint. I think it might be better if we get the floors done, then have it painted. Then you move in. What do you think?" he asked his boss and friend. A few moments later, he hung up and returned to Jimmy.
"Deal. Let's do this. Do we need to sign anything?" asked Alex.
"One moment. I get the quote on the paper for you to sign." He left and returned a few minutes later with a document that was in triplicate. He handed the document to Alex. "Just sign and date here." He pointed the pen to the lines. Alex reviewed the document and the newly added quote.
"Perfect," he said and signed the form. Jimmy pulled off the yellow copy leaving the pink and white forms attached and intact.
"Thank you. You pay us when we finished. Okay?" directed Jimmy.
"Yessir," replied Alex with a little bow. "Thank you so much! Here is a set of keys for you so you can come and go as needed. "You'll make sure the stain color is similar to the way it is now?" He asked.
"No problem. We match easy," replied Jimmy as he pulled out his phone to call his crew.
"Okay. I will go then. You will take care of the carpet and all that? You take to the dump?"
"We take care of it. You no worry," he replied, then jumped to Chinese to speak with the crew member on the other end of the phone.
"Okay. Bye then! See you later," said Alex as he started to leave. Jimmy simply waved at him then turned so as not to be interrupted. He was focused on his new job.

Alex stepped outside and saw a carboard sign being placed in a window in the small apartment building across the street. It was sloppily written in black marker. The phone number was written in red marker. "For Rent now. Call 415 751-9890." Alex couldn't believe it. Apartments were hard to get right now. The occupancy rate in San Francisco was at an all-time high and apartments were in demand. He and Scott had heard stories where renter candidates were offering higher than quoted rents and even plane tickets for trips to get the apartments. Anything that would put them at the top of the list. "What the hell." He bee-lined to the horrible goldenrod painted building at 735 11th Avenue. The front door was open, and he hiked up the stairs and saw the apartment door opened. He took a chance and walked in to find a short Asian man in the front room that seemed to be the living space.

"Hi! My name is Alex. We are getting the house across the street ready for our friend to move into in the next couple of weeks. We, meaning my partner Scott and I, are looking for an apartment and I just saw your sign," he said to the man. The man looked at him and smiled.

"My name is Lou. I own the building. Rent is twenty-one hundred dollars a month. One thousand dollars deposit. If you want it, you have fifteen minutes to tell me." He wasted no time. He knew the market was tight.

"One sec. Let me call my partner Scott," replied Alex as he pulled out his cell phone. Ring. Ring. Ring. Ring.

"Hello?" answered Scott.

"Scott. Alex. Can you talk for a sec?" he asked.

"Yes. Just getting in the car. I am running so behind. I need to get my butt over to Alameda," replied Scott as he started his car.

"You won't believe this. There is an apartment across the street from JB that just came up. Second-floor apartment. In the front-facing JB's house. Wood floors. I am walking through it now. It looks like gas heat. A cute kitchen. Wood floors. One bedroom and a small room off the living room area with French doors between the bedroom, the living room, and the small room. Twenty-one hundred dollars a month and a thousand deposit. He gave me fifteen minutes to decide." Alex rushed to give Scott what details he could in such a short time as he was walking around the place. Lou was watching him pace through the rooms.

"Do you like it?" asked Scott.

"Yes. But I don't want to decide without you looking at it," replied Alex.

"I trust you. You know how hard it is to get a place in the city. If you like it, then do it. And…it's across the street from JB. That would make it easy for you. It's a good area, and it's next to the park. I say go for it," Scott stated in a supporting tone. "Write a

check. Nice job, Schmoo! Love you. We'll work out the details later. No stress. Okay?"
"I just want you to be happy," replied Alex.
"As long as I'm with you, I am happy, my love. See you later. Have a good day. So exciting!" affirmed Scott.
"Love you. See you later. Drive carefully," and they hung up. Alex turned to Lou. "You have a deal. I have my checkbook. Can I give you the check now?" he asked.
"I will get the lease from my truck. Great," said Lou as he removed the sign from the window. "You can do whatever you want to the place. I don't bother you. Just pay your rent on time. That's all I want. If something breaks or needs to be fixed, let me know. I will tell you to either hire someone and you can reduce it off your rent, or I will come to fix it myself. Okay? I usually don't like to come over, so hopefully, you find cheap ways to get things fixed if needed."
"Got it," Alex confirmed to Lou.
"Anything you do to make the place look nice; you pay for. I do not reimburse that. Okay? Like painting. You pay for that yourselves." Lou wanted to make sure Alex knew that he was a hands-off landlord. Some would say 'slumlord' but really, he simply didn't want to be bothered.
"Okay," said Alex.
"The last people that lived here bought a house. My tenants usually stay a long time. I am so happy I could help them to be able to save and buy a house," Lou added. "I'll be right back." He headed down to his truck parked in the driveway. "Oh. Only street parking. No storage."
"No problem," said Alex. He was just relieved to have found a place. The location was perfect. It might be a little small, but JB would be across the street and they both worked a lot. He couldn't wait to share the news with JB and show Scott the place. He anticipated Scott would want to work on it before moving in. A few minutes later, Lou returned with the lease and keys to the apartment. "You sign here. You have check?" he asked as he handed the document and a pen for Alex's signature.
"Yes. One sec," Alex answered pulling out his checkbook. He wrote out the check and handed it to Lou. Then signed the lease. "Can I add my partner's Scott's name to the lease?"

“Sure. He don’t need to sign. One signature is good enough,” replied Lou. “Here are the keys. Mailbox key is this one. Mailbox is downstairs. I will add names tomorrow. Okay?” He indicated the keys as he spoke of them. “This key is deadbolt for door. The other gold-colored one is building front door. Okay? You make copies if you need them. You pay for them, though.”
“Of course,” smiled Alex. He got the gist. "Thanks so much."
“You can move in anytime. I won’t charge you if you move in early.”
“Thanks. This is great,” Alex stated assessing the empty apartment. He noticed the glass on the French doors was painted over. The wood floors were a little scruffy. The kitchen could probably use a coat of paint. “Will you be cleaning it before we move in?”
“You get it as is. I’m leaving now. Nice to have you as a tenant. You have nice neighbors. They have lived here a long time.” With that, he turned to leave. “My address is on the lease. Just drop check off there. First of each month!” he yelled as he left through the apartment’s front door.
“Well, that’s that,” muttered Alex to himself. He felt good about this move. He looked around again, then left and locked the door behind him.

*****

Michelle had managed to get out of bed, shower, and prep for the day pondering how she was going to spend it. It was after 11 am and she knew she needed to start considering reconnecting with the world outside of the San Francisco bubble she seemed to enter. She dreaded checking her email given she had some clients she had put off. She also was thinking about changing her career path. She had a degree in education and thought about teaching or training. When she explored landscape architecture, she thought it would be more rewarding, but was finding that either many clients already had their minds set on certain plants and concepts, or she was not very good at selling her ideas. Either way, it left her feeling unfulfilled. She wanted to do something that benefitted people and their lives. Being a landscape architect wasn’t doing that. Yes, planting trees and plants were benefitting the environment. It just seemed to lack the creative aspect she needed. “Well, shit,” she muttered to herself. “I better just do it and get it over with. If I clear my emails, at least I’ll know the worst part is over." She continued talking to herself as she headed to the computer. She logged on and into her yahoo email account. She was surprised at the number of spams she received. "Delete. Delete. Delete. Delete," she muttered as she selected the emails to trash. Over the past week, she noticed she had eleven emails from clients. It was no surprise to find that eight had found someone else for their projects. Two were sending their final payments for the projects she had recently finished before her trip to visit Alex. Then there was one who wanted to speak with her about a project for her upon return. It was for an urban garden project that was cleared and permitted. It was for a series of 5 rooftop gardens working closely with Mayor Richard Daley's office. She emailed she was interested in working with them and that she would be returning in a couple of weeks. When she sent off the email response, they were quick to reply while she was deleting other spam. She smiled when the response was favorable. They would forward the project details within the next few days with their budget. The sooner she replied to them after reviewing the proposal, the better. They were on a timeline. After replying her acknowledgment, she finished clearing her email. She was relieved it wasn't as bad as she thought it would be. She had been saving, so financially, she was fine. She just needed to be frugal with her spending.

She signed off the computer. "Okay. I need to get out of here," she said aloud. "A burger. That sounds good." She kept talking to herself. "I think I'll hit that little restaurant next to the grocery store…I think it's called 'Curbside'." With that, she grabbed her purse, her housekeys copies, and a wrap and head out for a lunch to cure her hangover.

Michelle arrived at Curbside Café at 2417 California around the corner from the Molly Stones. It was a French-themed restaurant with a rustic feel to it. It was lined with about four outside tables. Large windows were facing the street. All the tables were covered with white tablecloths, a little red glass protecting a lit candle inside. The usual salt and pepper shakers were off to the side of the candles and pressed red cotton napkins with "CC" embroidered with white thread on the napkin corner. It was a small café where they staffed a single server and bus person. The server, wearing her red-checkered apron over her white short-sleeved blouse, casually arrived at her table with the menu. "Welcome to Curbside," she said. "Our specials are written on the blackboard there. The pork loin is delicious with a brown bacon gravy served with roasted rosemary potatoes and a side salad. Can I get you something to drink?" she asked as she dropped the menu then flipped her chestnut brown ponytail off her shoulder.

"Could I get some sparkling water and an iced tea?" asked Michelle as she perused the menu looking for a hamburger option.

"Sure!" said the server as she smiled through her red lipstick-covered lips. Her makeup was light and simple. She wore jeans that covered her large hips. Michelle noticed as she walked away to procure her beverages, she was wearing simple brown leather flat loafers. '*Effortless*' she thought to herself. Upon her return, the server asked "Have you decided? Or do you need a little more time?"

"The pork loin sounds delicious. I think I'll need to come back to have that for dinner," she stated thoughtfully so as not to offend for the suggestion. "I think I would prefer the hamburger with frites and a side of the butter lettuce salad." She looked up as she handed the menu back. The extra strength Tylenol was kicking in.

"Great. How do you want your burger?"

"Medium, please," Michelle replied.

"On the way." She finished her notes on her order pad and strolled off to the kitchen.

Michelle began sipping her sparkling water. The carbonation was great for removing the pastiness she felt in her mouth. As she took a long sip from the glass, she noticed someone walking by the window as if coming from the store. It was a man she thought looked familiar. Then she whispered to herself, "No. It couldn't be." She tried to get a closer look before he escaped her view. Then thought to herself again about the ebony-skinned man. "Nah. I am seeing things. He wouldn't be here." And shook her head and then changed the focus of her view and reviewed the artwork and antique artifacts on the walls in the empty restaurant. She thought to herself again. *What if that was him? No. couldn't be. It kind of looked like him. If it was him, why didn't he reach out? He could have emailed or called.* She then concluded that it couldn't have been him and shook her head again trying to push it out of her mind. After almost fifteen minutes, her food arrived.

After Michelle had scarfed down her savory lunch (she didn't realize how hungry she was), she went for a walk heading to

Fillmore street. After getting a cup of Peet's Coffee, she decided to walk towards the water down to the Marina. She felt all too familiar with the shops on Fillmore street and needed a fresh view and area to discover. She passed the Alta Plaza bar, which seemed to be unusually busy for a Monday. It was a beautiful day, and they had the windows open. People seemed to be in great spirits. Couples of all types, sitting in the windows. Three drag queens in the window appeared to be having a rather spirited conversation about each other's outfits and wigs. Michelle just smiled and forged forward. Between her lunch and the fresh air, she was feeling much better compared to when she first awoke. She trekked on and hit Broadway street, then turned left. She passed the different mansions of the highly leveraged. She was struck by the sizes of the homes and the amount of renovation going on. When she hit 2578 Broadway, the chateau-styled brick home caught her attention. "That's beautiful" she whispered to herself as she paused for a few minutes to admire the structure. As she neared Scott Street, there was a marked difference. The homes became larger. For some unknown reason, she felt these homes were old San Francisco family money dwellings. It might not have been the case, but as she looked at them, their beauty was simple, elegant, and strong. Some of the homes seemed like really old money. Especially when she stopped to assess 2801 Broadway. An old brick mansion with narrow multi-paned windows. She speculated if the interiors were updated, or if the family there simply maintained it, except for the electricity and furnishings. She tried peeking through the windows, but curtains were drawn hiding the homes' contents from view. Her favorite house was the brick mansion set back at 2907 Broadway. Large windows enabled one to see through the home, revealing a view of the bay that anyone would be jealous to have. As she moved to the end of Broadway that intersected at Lyon Street on the edge of The Presidio, she stood at the top of the exceptionally long stairs that appeared to stretch down to the water. There was a light gray contemporary styled mansion to the right of her view that looked like the home in the movie, "Basic Instinct". She was awestruck. A complete view of the inner San Francisco Bay spread before her. The Palace of Fine Arts, which was originally built for the 1915 Panama-Pacific exhibition where art deco was introduced, stood out capturing the eyes and attention of everyone who stood here. Taxis were arriving and departing dropping off and picking up tourists. It

was a popular spot. Those into fitness would jog up and down the numerous stairs for their cardio resulting in heavy sweat-drenched bodies and wet hair from their workouts. She spent about five minutes taking it all in. As she was ready to head back towards the house, she turned, and there he was. “What the fuck?!” she muttered aloud looking at the man who was approaching her. She wasn’t ready for this. She turned and saw a San Francisco cab sitting at the corner and ran to it.
“Wait! Don’t run!” the man yelled after her. “We need to talk! Please!”
Michelle did not stop and jumped into the cab without giving him a chance and directed the cab to take her back to the Sacramento Street haven where she had been hiding from the world. She did not even look back. She was angry.

Michelle had arrived back at the house just after four PM. She had spent the day walking around. She now knew why she felt like she was being followed. She poured herself a glass of Sauvignon Blanc she found in the refrigerator and went to sit in the garden. She needed to think some things through and calm down from her encounter. She hoped Alex and Scott were having better days.

Another Story Night

Scott had a nice time visiting with Sabrina in Alameda. They always had a great time together. He would listen to her talk about her family drama. She thought the world of all of them, despite how crazy she thought they were. They were all so busy in each other's lives. She was looking for a job, as was he. He had shared with her about his store closing and that he was interested in pursuing some type of role in Customer Service. She expressed that she had a connection with who might be hiring and that she would check with them before saying anything. She thought he would be good in training, too. He always explained things clearly and was high energy. Something lacking in some of the trainers she had known.

After an hour, they both had to get on their merry ways and vowed they would connect later in the week. She had to get back to her mom to take her to a doctor's appointment. She was sad to hear about their house but looking forward to where he and Alex might land. Scott was always amazed at how quickly they could catch up. She was like the sister he never had. They had a unique closeness that he believed would last their lives. After spending five minutes saying their goodbyes, Scott jumped into his car and made it to the store in record time. Traffic was generally light into the city from Alameda around eleven-thirty AM.

He arrived at the store to find Troy finishing a sale and a few boxes with bubble wrap strewn around the main floor. They had experienced a moderate day of sales merchandise, but still had much to pack up. Scoot knew that Mondays were low foot traffic and not the best sale days.

"How are things going?" Scott asked his friend. Troy dramatically turned his head, moved his glasses to the tip of his nose then back up to his eyes then swirled his right arm, and snapped his fingers.
"Bitch. I am good. I got laid. I came. I sold and I packed some shit." The elderly matronly dressed customer with whom he just finished was at the doorway, stopped. She turned and looked at him. Her scarf fluttered around her shoulders with the soft breeze. Her silver hair barely fluttered. Her black oversize round sunglasses faced Troy as she muttered loudly through her rose-colored lips, "Really? Do you have to use such language?" and shook her head and walked away. Troy pursed his lips in response.
"As I was saying…" and turned his attention back to Scott after being interrupted.
"Sorry I wasn't here longer this morning. I had to see Sabrina. How have sales been?" he asked.
"Slow. Steady. But I have been packing up some shit for the return-to-vendors you wanted to get out for delivery. Don't you want to hear about me getting laid?" asked Troy.
"Not really. Except…were you safe?" He eyed Troy suspiciously.
"Gurl, yes! And he was cute, too! Built like a brick shithouse. Redhead. Blue eyes that looked right through me. Hairy chest and a light beard. He was poz, too, so we both knew what to do *if you catch my drift*." he sang back to Scott. "I think I want to wear white on our wedding day," he teased.
"Um…okay," replied Scott. Have you seen him before?"
"No. What does that matter?" countered Troy matter-of-factly.
"So, you picked up a guy. Go back to his place. Fuck. Then you're married?" Scott laughed. "It doesn't work that way."
Troy snapped his fingers at Scott. "We'll see, bitch." he laughed. "We'll see."
"And I think scarlet red would be more your speed with a red sash and a ruby red tiara. Just sayin'," chortled Scott.
"Red ain't my color. Makes me look pale. Anyway…maybe not white. Maybe…" he paused. "Maybe Champagne with some rhinestones for some glitz," he delightfully teased. Scott giggled.
"Alright. Alright. You get married to this guy; we'll see how we can have a shindig for you somehow," Scott joked. "What's his name?"
"I-don't-know, Mary. I should say, I don't remember. He wrote it down with his number. It's on my refrigerator," replied Troy as he headed towards a box he was filling with stationery and envelopes.

“I think it was Harold or Mark, or something.” He waved his left hand in the air as if to make light of the question. Scott just shook his head and laughed. “Enough about me. Let’s get this shit done, now.” continued Troy.
“Okay. Okay. Cool,” chuckled Scott in reply. “Change the subject. I get it.” He moved towards another large box to fill on the upstairs area landing.
Scott and Troy had finished preparing about a third of the return to vendor packages for credit when Scott realized it was almost six pm.
“Hey. It’s time to close up. I gotta get home,” said Scott looking at his watch when the phone rang. “I’ll get it,” Scott muttered and headed towards the landline in the upper workspace area.
“Hello? Scott’s Closet” he answered.
“Hey Scott, It’s Aarav. Sorry to bother you.”
“Oh. Hey. What’s up?” asked Scott moving to a neutral tone.
“Look. I know we are not on the best of terms, but I have some news.”
“We are not on bad terms, Aarav,” replied Scott. “We just don’t hang out and you hang a lot with Gabriel. I don’t like Gabriel. Hence our relationship. Pretty simple really.”
“I know. I know. But look. You know Gabriel doesn’t have a lot of friends. He kinda holds himself at bay a bit. But you still know him, and you still talk… right?” Aarav was sounding a little bothered.
“As little as possible. We did have a little altercation last week. So, I would think we might not be talking much for a while,” shared Scott feeling perturbed.
“You know what? That’s between you two. The point is you still have a connection. Look." Aarav paused. "I just need to come out with it. He’s in the hospital. They are releasing him tomorrow. He was beaten up.” He paused again taking a breath. He was bothered by this situation. “I thought you should know.” Scott was silent. He did not know how to react.
“What?” Scott muttered back.
“Gabriel was attacked at Pride on Sunday. He was beaten up pretty badly. The police found him being beaten up in an alley by two guys. They were able to catch them. One was Veronica’s boyfriend or something. I guess Gabriel let it slip in his typical ‘*Gabriel style*’ that the guy was bisexual. She was unaware and was so pissed off that she kicked him out. She didn't like that secret being kept from her. And she must've thought that if he fooled around with Gabriel,

who else might he have cheated on her with. Anyway, the other guy was a skinhead. From what I understand, they're not clear how they are connected, yet. Anyway, the hospital has been keeping him for observation and is going to release him tomorrow. I am trying to get him to tell me himself what happened over the phone, but…I don't know. I'm just going by what the nurse and the police said," He rambled to Scott. "I just thought you should know."
"First. I am sorry he was beaten up. No one deserves that. What the fuck?! I'm shocked, but not shocked, but shocked...I mean…He's a prick who goes out of his way to hurt or annoy people, so it's either that someone has finally caught him at his shit, or it's a hate crime. Who knows? Probably a little of both. Either way, it's wrong and horrible. Shit…" Scott paused and looked over at Troy who was staring at Scott eavesdropping in on the conversation. Troy's eyes were wide-open and intent on Scott. "One second, Aarav." Scott put his hand over the receiver to help mute his voice.
"Gabriel is in the hospital. He was beaten up. They are releasing him tomorrow. The police don't know if it's a hate crime or something else, yet." Troy stared at Scott. His jaw dropped. He didn't say a word and just stared, then almost inaudibly mouthed "What the fuck!" Scott nodded in agreement.
"Sorry. I'm back," Scott spoke to Aarav.
Aarav spoke. "I did not know what else to do. The police called me because they found my card in his wallet. They told me what they knew and asked me a few questions. I am going to go down to the police station to see if I know the guys. Gabriel is at Sutter Health on Sacramento near Webster. Maybe you can go by there?"
"Shit. We were just there. JB was admitted last night and left this morning. We must have just missed Gabriel being admitted. Shit." Scott paused.
"I know. It sucks. But you are closest to him. I mean… I slapped the guy last week. We had words. So, I have a funny feeling I am not the one he would really want to see right now. Okay?" shared Scott. "I don't wish anyone any ill towards him. Shit. This sucks. Just let me know. I think that would be the best path to take for the moment, okay?"
"Okay. I get it. I'll let you know more once I hear. Mind if I call you on your cell?" resigned Aarav. "I just don't know who else to turn to, right now." He knew Scott was right. He was Gabriel's only real friend at this point. He knew him for quite a while when he lived in

San Francisco last time before moving back with Scott. He thought Scott was it for Gabriel but noticed the warning signs after they had been together a few months. He had hoped, for Gabriel's sake, that they would last. It just wasn't in the cards. "Thanks for talking with me. Talk soon." With that, Aarav hung up.

Scott hung up the phone both relieved and concerned at the same time. He was feeling conflicted. Troy looked at Scott. "You okay?"
"Yeh. I'm okay. A bit shook. I don't like the guy but, shit. No one deserves that. Do you think I should go see him? I don't want to be cruel or mean. I mean…I…" he stammered.
"Girl. You have a strange and bad past with that guy. You have every right to feel like you do. Just remember, though. He's still a human being. A shitty one. Human, nonetheless. If you don't want to see him. Don't. If you want to find out what happened…and make sure he's okay…go. It's that simple. You don't need to get drawn into his life, queen. Just sayin'."
"You're right. I need to call Alex," said Scott as he dialed Alex's cell. It rang twice.
"Hey Scott!" answered Alex. "How are you, Smoo?"
"Hi, baby. Hey. Something weird just happened." Scott proceeded to share the account of events with Alex reiterating the call with Aarav. Alex quietly listened.
"Go. Make sure he's okay, then just leave him alone. I get it. You're a better person than he is, so remember that. I'll see you at home afterward, okay? Want pizza or a burrito?"
"Burrito. Carne Asada. Chips." replied Scott. "Thank you, Schmoo. I'll head over now and see you within the hour." He blew a kiss into the phone then hung up. Scott turned to Troy.
"I'm heading over now. Wanna go with me?" he asked.
"Sure! Let's go," replied Troy. "Anything to get me outta here."
They quickly spot-checked their messes then left after locking up heading over to the hospital to arrive twenty minutes later. They checked in with information and were navigated to Gabriel's room. They had to check in with the nurse's station.

The heavy-set brunette nurse was standing at the station with her bright blue smock and white pants. "Yes. You're on the list. The police have you and Aarav listed." She looked at both Scott and Troy. "He can go in. You need to wait out here," she directed Troy.
"Yes ma'am," he replied sarcastically rolling his eyes. The nurse looked at him annoyed, then raised her eyebrows. "Okay. Okay."

Troy added in a more friendly tone then took one of the seats opposite the station. "I'll be right here, girl," he said to Scott.
"Be right back." Scott turned and headed into the room. He was shocked to see Gabriel. He had two black eyes. His right eye was swollen shut. His left eye was partially swollen, but the bruising was nasty. His lower right lip had a cut and was purple at the corner. He had some facial scratches and a wrap-around his head covering his forehead. An IV was giving him fluids. He stirred and moved his head towards Scott. He opened his left eye slowly and stared at him.
"What are you doing here?" he asked softly with a slightly irritated tone.
"Aarav called me. He told me you were here," Scott replied. He remained neutral given their recent encounter.
"Great. Isn't that just peachy?" replied Gabriel.
"Look," said Scott. "I don't wish violence or ill on anyone. What happened?"
"Why do you care?"
"Like I said. No one should ever get beaten up. I don't care what the reason. Violence is never the answer. So, what happened?" he replied.
"I fell down," said Gabriel sarcastically. "A busted face and a few broken ribs and a concussion. A helluva fall, okay?" and turned his head away shifting his gaze to the wall. Scott huffed. His frustration was mounting.
"Look. I hope you are okay. I know I am not the one you want to talk to about this. I didn't really want to come at first, but you are a person. I don't want to exchange Christmas cards or even keep talking with you. But, dammit, Gabriel. The police want to know if it's a hate crime or something else. Regardless, it's something that needs to be reported. You're in the hospital for Christ sake."
"I'm going home tomorrow," replied Gabriel solemnly. "I'll be fine."
"C'mon, man. What happened? You need to tell someone," asked Scott.
"Fine. I'll join a fucking support group." Gabriel paused then turned his head towards Scott again. "I will say this, then I want you to leave. Got it?"
"Fine. Okay. If that's what you want," answered Scott.
"I knew one of the guys. It was Veronica's boyfriend. The guy I blew before my trip that I just got back from. We fucked around

once. The other guy, I never saw him before. Some *skinhead* with tats running down an arm. That's it. Happy?" He had anger in his eyes.
"Shit. Sorry. Was it a revenge thing, you think? Or what?" asked Scott.
"I said that was all I was going to say. So, leave, okay? That's all I want to say right now. Fuck! Go!" Gabriel said loudly. The nurse entered.
"I think you should leave. He's getting worked up," she instructed Scott. "I'll follow you out."
"If you need something, Gabe. Just let me know, okay? Sorry, this happened to you. It shouldn't have." Scott tried to be understanding and turned to leave.
"Just fucking leave. I don't need anything from you," muttered Gabriel angrily. His pride would not allow him to give in to his weakness. He didn't want sympathy from anyone. Especially Scott.
When the nurse and Scott reached the nurses' station, he commented softly, "Thanks for letting me see him. I hope he's going to be okay. No one should ever go through this. It sucks."
"Sure. He'll recover. Poor guy." Then she turned and went back to tend to Gabriel.

Troy and Scott walked back to the store together. Troy kept silent while Scott shared what Gabriel said to him. He just listened to Scott ramble about how strange a situation this was. Now was not the time to give advice. Upon reaching the store, Scott turned to Troy.
"I have to get home. My car is parked around the block there. Stupid, I know. I was just being lazy instead of parking it at home. Anyway, want a ride to somewhere or anything?"
"Ah. Thanks. I'm gonna grab a drink up the block there. See you tomorrow?" asked Troy.
"Sure. See you in the morning," he replied. They hugged.
Troy whispered. "You did a good thing. At least you tried, queen. Don't change, okay?"
"Thanks. Okay." Scott pulled away and looked at his friend. "Thanks for listening to me ramble on the way back. And for reminding me to stay human." He winked at Troy.
"What's a sister for?" smiled Troy. He gave Scott a little wave, then turned and sashayed his way to Alta Plaza for a little nibble a drink. Scott watched for a second, smiling. Then he turned. "I need to get my ass home!" he muttered aloud to himself and rushed to his car.

Moments later, he was parked in the driveway and walking through the front door.
"Hey! I'm Home!" he yelled as he removed his jacket and dropped his keys on the entryway table. He noticed Alex and Michelle were sitting and just starting to eat. They each had a can of Dos Equis beer off to the sides of their plates of burritos and fresh tortilla chips from Gordo Taqueria on Geary Boulevard. "That looks good!" he added as he looked at the plates. Both Alex and Michelle looked at Scott. Michelle had just taken a large bite of her burrito.
"Hi, Scott. Welcome home. Sit down. Let me get your plate for you." Alex rose, went to Scott and pecked him on the cheek then turned moving quickly to the kitchen to retrieve Scott's burrito. "Be right back. Beer?" he asked from the kitchen.
"Sure! Yes, please, Schmoo." Scott sat in his usual place at the table. "How was your day?" he asked Michelle trying to gulp down her food.
"It started nice. Outside the hangover, I mean. But I had lunch at The Curbside. Then went walking," she replied covering her mouth with some remnants of her food still lingering. She was trying desperately not to allow any to escape. "With all of the walking I've been doing, I think I've lost five pounds!" she said a bit giddy.
"I love that place. We haven't been there in a while. Did you like it?" he asked.
"It was so good. I just had a burger and fries. I'd love to go there again, though," she answered. She took a sip of her beer. "mm. This beer is good, too," she said with praise. "Sorry. How is your friend, Gabriel?" she asked. Alex returned with Scott's plate and beer.
"Here you go, love," and rubbed the top of Scott's back then sat.
"Yes. How is Gabriel? What happened?" Scott quickly shared the story with them while they listened intently and eating their burritos.
"Good lord," replied Alex. "I just hope he's okay." Michelle looked at both him and Scott.
"Isn't he a friend of yours? I mean…he was here at the party. I guess I am confused. It's horrible news. Is that all you have to say, though?" she asked. Scott looked at her. He understood her reacting slightly confounded. She didn't know the whole story.
"Gabriel and I used to be a couple. For just a few years. They started nice, but quickly went South," shared Scott. Michelle looked at him and then Alex then back to Scott.
"What?" she asked. "When was this?"

"Right before Alex and I met. Gabriel and I met at Saks Fifth Avenue. He and I had a thing and became a couple. After about two years or so, he started to abuse me. It was verbal at first, then there were the games. It got to a point where I couldn't take it. I gave him a month's notice before moving out. During that time, he tried to rape me twice. Let's just say we did not part on good terms. When I left, I met Alex. My life has never been the same since." Scott wanted to keep the story short. The details always just made him angry, and he felt he had moved on.
"Wow. Now I get it," said Michelle with a sense of understanding.
"He also cheated on me a lot. I had gotten tested for HIV for a few years after that once I found out. It was not a good scene. Anyway, that's all in the past. Everything worked out the way it's supposed to…and for the better." He reached over for Alex's hand. Alex reciprocated and squeezed back then blew a kiss to Scott and smiled warmly. "So, although no one deserves what happened to him. It sucks and it was wrong. And yes, I feel bad for him. I hope he presses charges, and they are punished for what they did. I don't think I will be hanging around him anytime soon, though. I'll try to help however I can, from a distance. When I saw him, I noticed he was beaten up pretty badly. The nurse said he'll recover. My guess is that he'll probably need some counseling. But, that's up to him. Hopefully, Aarav can help him with that." He paused and took a bite of his burrito and a sip of beer. Michelle and Alex nodded in agreement, supporting Scott. Then Alex spoke up.
"So, not to change the subject, but we need some other news. Some good news…I am happy to share that we have a new apartment!" Alex smiled.
"Oh, yes! Yay! How was it? You obviously liked it! " exclaimed Scott adjusting to the mood change. Michelle looked at Alex.
"You what? How? What? Where?" she asked surprised.
"Well…I met with Jimmy from Jimmy Hardwood Floor to review JB's house and the project. We walked through the house and he was getting ready to strip the floors by the time I left. He said the floors would be done and ready for us to walk on by the end of the week, by the way." He looked at Scott with the news because he knew how Scott would start planning the painting. He continued. "As I was leaving, I noticed a 'For Rent' sign in a small apartment building across the street from the house. I walked over to check it out. It's cute. Needs some work, but it's kind of perfect for where we are at

in life right now. And it's across the street from JB," he beamed. "That way, we can be there if anything happens to JB and help him out."
"I can't believe you found a place so fast and so convenient. That is so weird. Wonderful. Yet weird. Congratulations!" expressed Michelle. "If you're happy. I'm happy." She looked at Scott. "And you haven't seen the place?"
"I trust Alex. Correct. I haven't seen the place. I am sure it will probably need a little work before we move in. Will we have to put much in storage from the house?" he asked Alex.
"Just the guest room furniture and probably some of our bedroom furniture. We might not be able to hang all of our artwork, though. It is smaller, so we also might need to scale down some of our clothes. I think JB will let us use his garage to store some things, so I am not too worried about that. And, we'll have to park your car in JB's garage, or we can switch for the driveway. There's no parking…except street parking." replied Alex with a little hesitancy hoping the terms weren't too much for Scott.
"It is what it is. At least we have a place. It's close to JB. I get to garden, too! Not worried. It's a moment. We will get through this and see what happens," said Scott. He took a deep breath and exhaled, then took a large sip of beer. "A lot of things going on at once. Keeps life interesting, we have to admit."
"True," said both Alex and Michelle just off from each other in their timing. "Also…" Alex added. "I went back and saw Jimmy and is also redoing the wood floors in the apartment. He gave us a deal. Only a thousand bucks. We can move in pretty quickly and paint afterward. What do you think?"
"If it's not that big, we can probably paint it in two days. Just a guess based on what you told me. We can do it this weekend if, possible. Why not hire movers for JB. We'll just pack and move the fragile stuff like the two chandeliers, the crystal, and his bathroom with all of his meds. The movers can deal with the rest," suggested Scott. Alex raised his eyebrows contemplating the thoughts.
"Then…" Scott continued, "I will check with the painters we use and see if they can paint the house this weekend and after JB's stuff is moved out, they can then paint the flat?" Alex thought about it. He then suddenly had an idea.
"I have a better thought. We both know that JB will not get his deposit back. Landlords do just about anything to keep it. So why

not just let the building owner who's selling the place clean and paint it? He has to anyway to prep it for sale. I think it would be a waste of time and money. And it's not all that much money in JB's eyes. Only two thousand, of which he might get five-hundred dollars of it. He already had to get the wiring redone in it. And that cost him some money." Scott and Michelle were listening intently as they were eating.
"That's not a bad idea, Alex," said Scott pondering the suggestion. "Talk to JB about it. See if he's open to it. You're talented at talking with people and partnering with them. You're also a super kind guy…which is just one of the many reasons why I love you so much." He looked over at Michelle. "We need more like him," and winked at her. She smiled back.
"I have some stories that may change your mind," she said in jest back to Scott. "I'll share some, one night over a bottle or two of wine," she joked and finished her burrito.
"How about you call the building owner and remind him of all the work JB did and that he will have to paint anyway. Maybe he'll give JB a break?" suggested Scott.
"Hm. Maybe," answered Alex. "I'll give him a call tomorrow. The worst he can say is 'no," and he shrugged his shoulders. "And you're right. I'll talk with JB, too, and share the plan. I think we can all be moved and settled by mid-July."
"Cool. This is exciting!" said Scott happily. "Oh. Shit. We got caught up in all of our drama, we didn't even ask you," Scott looked at Michelle. "You said you went for lunch at Curbside Café. Then what?" he asked.
"You went to Curbside? We love that place. We should go together." Alex said smiling and began working on the final portion of his burrito. "Oh. I'm empty," he said as he lifted his beer bottle and looked over to Scott.
"I'll get us another round. You want another one?" seeking a response from Michelle.
"Sure. I'm done with mine, too."
"Anyway…what else did you do today?" he asked as he left to retrieve a few more beers for them. Alex watched Michelle's face move into neutral. She seemed to be reflecting on something not so pleasant.
"I went walking. I ended up walking down Broadway. The houses on that street are amazing," she commented reminiscently. Then

paused. "I walked to the end. You know. Where those steps are. You can see the whole bay. Palace of Fine Arts, Alcatraz…it was beautiful."
"Oh!" Scott returned and plunked down the beers for each of them and sat down. "Did you see that large brick mansion…kind of Chateau looking just before you get to the end?" he asked excitedly.
"Yes. I love that house. The trees were pruned like large cones on each side of the lawn before the entryway," she answered.
"…and you can see through the house to the bay. I love those large windows. I would *LOVE* to live there. It's my favorite on that street," he injected.
"It is a beautiful mansion," she agreed in a lighter tone. Alex sensed something else happened.
"…and?" Alex asked, prodding her to continue.
"Well. I didn't tell you this yet. But…well…while I was in Chicago, I met this guy. His name is Dom. Short for Dominic," she said looking down at her plate with a small mound of chips left. Alex and Scott remained silent looking at her waiting for her story. They could tell there was more. They looked at each other. Scott raised his eyebrows with the *"I told you there was more to the visit"* look. Alex seemed to have read his mind and subtly nodded and they both moved their gazes back to Michelle awaiting her story. "I met him when I was working at a government building. I was redoing the trees. They had to be swapped out due to them being diseased. Anyway, we dated for a bit. I think we were falling in love." She paused and took a breath and looked at her audience at the table. Scott and Alex were waiting.
"…And?" Scott waved his hands for more encouraging her to continue her story.
"And we saw each other a lot. His job takes him back and forth between Ottawa, sometimes abroad, and to Chicago. He even pays part of my rent because he always stays with me…or has been the last two years." She took another breath. Alex reached over and grabbed her hand.
"What's wrong with that? You found a guy that has a job. Who you really like and possibly love? He seems there for you. So, what's wrong?" he asked her. She took another deep breath and exhaled. Then took a sip of her Dos Equis. She decided to just let it out.
"I became pregnant." She paused. Then added, "and I miscarried before coming here." And some tears streamed down her cheeks.

"Shit. Does he know? Are you okay?" asked Alex and Scott separately.
"I told him I thought I was pregnant, but I haven't told him about the miscarriage." She was softly crying. She was sad thinking about her lost child and put a hand on her belly. "I didn't know how to tell him. He was so happy. So, I wrote a note saying I was coming to visit you and left it on the table and came here." She looked at Scott and Alex wondering what they were thinking. Would they be supportive of her? She wasn't sure.
"First, we love you. You know that," said Alex reassuring her.
"Absolutely. That's so sad. But it's not uncommon," added Scott. "A lot of women have miscarriages. I bet there are some statistics about that that we could lookup. You didn't do anything wrong."
"No. You didn't do anything wrong," Alex said in agreement reiterating Scott's statement. "What can we do?" he asked of his sister.
"Nothing. Just being here. Again...listening as I dump my world on you. I just needed some support," she replied.
"Well, shit, girl. You, babies, and men. You sure do have the drama in your life," said Scott trying to lighten the mood. She chuckled and wiped her teary eyes. Scott got up and returned with a box of tissues. He looked over at Alex.
"You gonna be okay, now?" Alex asked. "Is that it?"
"Yah. Like you went on a walk that led to you thinking about your miscarriage and coming here. What are we missing with this? Was there someone with a baby at the steps that brought this up?" asked Scott. She looked at him then back to Alex.
"Remember I was telling you the other week that I felt like I was being watched?" she looked at Scott who took a moment to think back and remembered and nodded. "Well. When I was having lunch, I saw this man walk by the window. I didn't get a good look at him, but he looked familiar. I shrugged it off and went for my walk *afterward*." Scott and Alex were then now getting the picture and where this was going. She continued. "Anyway, so I was walking and reached the stairs. I was looking at the view. Then, when I turned, I saw the man coming towards me. It was him. *Dom*. He followed me here, or to there...I don't know. He was just there!" She looked at her plate. Picked up a chip and ate it then took a sip of her beer.

"And did you talk with him?" asked Alex. Scott was hanging on for the finale of the story.
"No. I saw him. Turned and got into a cab to get back here. I wasn't ready to see him. I know I have to. I just need a little more time. He freaked me out being there. I just turned and there he was. Jesus!"
"I think the sooner you tell him, the better. I think he'll surprise you," suggested Alex. "Don't write him off, yet. Talk with him." Scott nodded.
"Absolutely. Talk with him. Running away doesn't make it any easier. You're just prolonging the pain. Not that I'm a woman who has gone through what you went through. But if I were you, I would talk with him. *Gurl.*" He reached out and patted her hand. "I have to excuse myself to pee." He got up, leaned over, and pecked Michelle then ran off to the bathroom.
"You're both right. I will." Said Michelle. Alex rubbed her shoulder with his free hand then released his hold of her hand and took a sip of beer.
"I know it's not easy. I don't know what you're going through. I just think that you both would feel and be so much better if you just talked. Okay? Stop running away from things," Alex advised thoughtfully. "Any other drama we need to be aware of?" She lightened up just as Scott returned and sat down.
"What'd I miss?" he asked.
"Nothing," replied Alex. "I just suggested she stop running away from things and asked if there was any other drama we needed to know."
"Oh good." He shifted his gaze back to Michelle. "Any other drama? Do I need to get the popcorn?" he joked.
"I did finally check my email this morning before heading out the door today." Alex and Scott looked at her wondering if she was going to drop another bomb on them.
"And? What now?" asked Scott slightly animated. "Don't tell me that the hunk of your past is reaching out to you and asking for a date, now, and that he is now a she." Alex and Michelle rolled their eyes and shook their heads at Scott
"Well? Please say it was good news." Alex followed.
"I just got another contract when I get back. But I am thinking it might be my last one. I think I want to be a teacher. What do you think?" she asked. Alex simply smiled.

“If that’s what you want to do, you should do it. What’s this contract?” he asked.
“It’s part of an urban garden project. The city has been focused on rooftop gardens and I will be working with the Mayor’s office. I am excited about it, but I need a change, too. I think I want to work with kids,” she shared.
“Cool,” said Scott. “But you said in a few weeks. When are you planning to go back?” he asked, probing. “Not that I want you to leave or anything. It’s just we are getting used to you being around.”
“I think in a week or two…if that’s okay,” she replied. "I don't want to wear out my welcome."
“As we said when you arrived, you are welcome to stay as long as you need. We may need your help moving, though. The next couple of weeks are going to be a bit crazy,” said Alex as he got up to clear the table.
“I hate moving, and you know I suck at packing. I am only good at supervising, but I'll stay out of your way. Okay?” she teased half-joking half-serious.
“Got it,” said Alex. "No help from Michelle," he whispered and sighed. “Smoo! Grab the rest of the dishes and refresh our beers, please?”
“Yessir, Schmoo,” replied Scott to his orders. “I think with all the drama, we need a night of nothing more except maybe some boring shows. Let's watch some mindless tv. It’s Monday night, so we have Ally McBeal, West Wing, The Amazing Race, and I forget what else…any takers?” he suggested aloud. "We tired of talking, yet? I don't think my brain can handle much more." They began joking and playing rock-paper-scissors over which tv shows to watch and grabbed their beers.

After tv, they all went to bed. The evening of stories was revealing. They all felt closer than ever with the events the past few weeks. They bid each other goodnight, and Scott and Alex went into their room to prepare for bed.
“You know what, Schmoo?” said Scott to Alex. “I love you. Your sister has some demons, but I think we exorcised them during this visit.” He moved in close and hugged his partner.
“I love you, too. I agree. Let’s just hope the drama is done. We have too much going on for anyone.” He kissed Scott back. “Changing the subject...do you think you can set up the painters in the next day

or two? The sooner we move, the better. We have a lot of packing to do."

"No problemo," replied Scott. The store will be done by the end of this week. The painters, I am sure we can get done by the end of next week. Maybe sooner. So, we'll be good. Don't forget to call JB's building owner about the deposit."

"I won't" replied Alex. Now…how about you and I have some fun before we go to bed." With that, he kissed Scott deeply, driving him to the bed.

"Oh…okay," giggled Scott. "I see where this is going." Michelle was in the bathroom brushing her teeth when she heard the rustling and smiled.

"Good night, boys," she whispered after she rinsed her mouth with her bottle of Scope and went to her room to sleep. She was looking forward to the dinner party at Irna's tomorrow night.

...But It's Only Tuesday

Scott and Alex had to rush this morning given the tasks and events of the day. Alex had to head over to JB's early to make breakfast and make a few phone calls to prep for the upcoming Dining Around program. Scott needed to hire painters and stop by to view the apartment Alex had rented so he could prepare himself for what they needed to do. They were up and out of the house after quick check-ins with Michelle to make sure she was okay despite her boyfriend having followed her to San Francisco and shocked her with his presence at the Broadway steps. They also had to get packing the residences so they could move and finish with the store closing. They were exhausted thinking about everything on their to-do's, but it all had to get done. As Scott said, "Life just keeps going." After kissing each other and sharing well wishes for the day, they were heading out the door when the phone rang. Scott answered.

"Bob's mortuary. You stab 'em. We slab 'em," he joked wondering the response hoping it was a solicitation. He loved driving them nuts.

"Oh…I'm sorry. I must have the wrong number," replied the woman's voice.

"Irna? Is that you? Scott here." He giggled. "Sorry about that. I sometimes joke answering the phone," he added apologetically.

"Oh. Good. You might want to consider something a little different. It's a bit morbid for the morning, don't you think?" she commented half-joking showing her sense of humor wasn't lost.

"Yes. Sorry. I'll try something new next time. How are you, Irna?" he asked. Alex looked at Scott wondering what was up. He couldn't get out of the garage since Scott's car was in the driveway blocking

him from heading to JBs. He gave Scott the signals to look at the time and widening his eyes encouraging him to hurry. “We were just on our way out the door. A crazy day ahead. What’s up?”
“Sorry to disturb you. I am just confirming that you all will be joining me at my place for dinner. Just a reminder in case something might have come up before I get cooking. I am only working half a day today. Are the three of you still attending?” she asked.
“OH…yes. We almost forgot. Thanks for reminding us about dinner tonight,” he replied looking at both Alex and Michelle to remind them, too. “What time should we come over? Can we bring anything?” he asked.
“How about seven? Just to remind you, my niece, Rebecca, and her daughter Ashley will be here, too.”
“Seven? Great. And what can we bring?” reiterated Scott while bouncing glances back and forth between Alex and Michelle. Alex was tapping his watch. Scott just shrugged his shoulders feeling powerless.
“Well. I am making Poulet Roti from Julia Child’s cookbook. So how about bringing some Rose’ or, as it says in the book…a Bordeaux-Medoc. I think that’s a red wine, maybe?” she answered.
“Sure. Rose’ or Medoc. Got it,” he committed. “Just a reminder that Alex is allergic to shellfish and doesn’t eat food with a high…”
“I know. High in iron. I’ve paid attention, dear. See you at seven. Don’t be late. I think people who arrive late are a bit gauche.” She hung up. Scott hung up the phone and looked at Alex. “You’ll get the wine?” he asked. "You know it better than me."
“Sure," replied Alex. “We have to go. JB is gonna be antsy if I am late. *You know him.*”
“Okay. Okay,” said Scott. “Bye Michelle! Be back here by half-past six so we can all head over together for dinner. Okay?” waved Scott.
“Bye boys! Have a good day. See you later. Good luck, today!” said Michelle as she watched them scurry out the door slamming it behind them. “Jesus. *Queens*.” She smiled while shaking her head and sipped her coffee enjoying the solace. She would debate her day. She also needed to plan her trip back to Chicago. She headed over and logged onto the computer to review the calendar and started searching flights. She was thinking July 9th or 10th, whichever was cheaper.

*****

Alex arrived at JB's flat to find him just getting ready to sit at the table. "Running behind again, I see," commented JB in his baritone voice displaying a little impatience.
"Sorry. Irna called just as we were heading out the door. Held us up for a few. I'll get coffee and your breakfast going," said Alex dropping his jacket and bag on the chair then head into the kitchen. The radio was on with the KGO news playing in the background. Bloomberg was quoted having said, "*I chose to marry somebody of the opposite sex, but I don't think it's the government's business to tell anybody who they should marry, who they can marry.*" As noted in the New York Post. It was hitting the mainstream news outlets.
"What do you feel like for breakfast? Oatmeal? Cottage cheese and a fruit cup?" asked Alex.
"Some bacon and three eggs cooked in bacon fat," JB quickly answered.
"Really? You just got back from the hospital after a possible heart issue and you want eggs cooked in bacon fat? And it's only Tuesday. Usually, you have that on the weekends. Not only is that a bit careless given your health, but it's also gross," commented Alex back being a little surprised, given recent events.
"My life. My breakfast. You only live once. Oh. And two pieces of toast, too, please," replied JB simply.
"Got it. Butter with a little bread," he chuckled as he began making the coffee. "I can't believe that there are people, so hell-bent against gay marriage. What do two people who love each other and want to get married have to do with their lives? It's not like they live with them. Just because they want to commit to each other. I don't get it. It doesn't hurt anyone," said Alex shaking his head. "And they throw that it's against God and the bible. Not in the ten commandments. Jesus never said anything about it. Ugh! It infuriates me!"
"That's religion for you. What is not widespread is that the true original textual meaning is that men should not lie with boys. Pedophilia is a disgusting sickness. But the religious right, for some strange reason, believes that homosexuality in general tears at the heart of our society and family values. It doesn't, but they believe it does. It's an interesting argument. I think I'll add that to the topics list for the program this afternoon. That should light up the switchboard," JB explained.

"Oh." JB changed the topic. "I got a call this morning. The Sonoma Valley Harvest Wine Auction Labor Day weekend. We are invited to come to stay. How about you reach out to William there? They said we would be hosted at MacArthur Place and that he would be expecting your call."
"That's great! That's such a fun weekend, too. And right before we head out for our trip!" Alex was scurrying around the kitchen multi-tasking. Pulling out the bacon, putting it in the pan. Then JB grunted.
"Did the papers come?" he askedNoonYes. I put them on the table. One sec." He turned on the gas to cook the bacon. Then filled a glass with orange juice and then head over, placed it by JB warning him of the glass position, separated the papers, and organized them for JB to review while he completed breakfast preparations. "Don't forget to take your pills I set out last night."
"Thank you, Alex," JB responded with slight irritation. "What's Scott up to today?" JB asked.
"He went to go look at the apartment. I found one across the street from you! I forgot to tell you. It was a fluke that it came up, but I looked at it. Called Scott and he said to just take it if I liked it, so I did. You know how fast places are going these days," shared Alex. "He is also going to check out the floors. I think the stain is drying and they are supposed to put down the first coats of verathane this afternoon. I was able to get Jimmy to do the apartment, too."
"That's good news. I like that you'll be across the street," muttered JB. Congratulations on that quick find. Very serendipitous." He was focused on reading about the Taliban and Bin Laden threats. "The world is moving in precarious positions. Yesterday when I raised the Taliban topic, I seem to have attracted callers who prevaricated by asking other questions working to point blame to something else. I find it is a highly developed skill among those of Middle Eastern descent. Fascinating."
"Scott's going to hire painters for your place, by the way. Any budget in mind that he needs to prepare for?" Alex tried to get JB's attention focused on the upcoming moving preparations. He noticed he was intently captured in the politics of the day.
"Two-thousand. Not that I am not excited or interested in your new place to live or moving. There just seems to be much going on in the world. I trust you, boys." He kept reading. Then he put the paper down. "Okay. Article completed. Great. Across the street, you said."

“Yes. We might need to use a small area in your garage to store some things. Would that be okay? We don’t have much, but our place is small.”
“Sure. What about packing up here? When is that going to start.?” JB asked. Alex poured some coffee, put in two blue packets of Equal, and placed it by JB.
“Coffee sir. To your right. And I have already started doing some packing. Scott and I will take down the chandeliers and track lighting this week. The artwork won’t take long to wrap. Then we’ll pack up the crystal. We’ll move that over first. Then I’ll pack up your clothes and bathroom and get that settled, along with your bed. The rest we will move and settle as we can. How does that sound?” Alex continued to work on the breakfast. Bacon was finishing up with the aroma wafting throughout the flat. Eggs were cracked in the bowl ready for the bacon grease bath. He tossed the bacon onto a plate with a paper napkin to absorb the oily remnants then poured the three eggs into the pool of grease. The sizzling was loud with occasional spurts and pops. He salt-and-peppered the eggs and spooned the bacon grease over the tops.
“Are you and Scott planning on doing all of the packing and moving? If so, I have a feeling it will take longer than you think,” said JB loudly over the kitchen activity noise.
“Actually…” Alex spoke loudly while tending the eggs. “I was thinking we could hire a company like Student Movers. We simply provide the packing material and they come in. Pack it all up and bring it to the location. Like your new place. They’re really, as Scott would say, *cost-effective*. I’ve heard good things about them,” replied Alex. “I can reach out to them and get a quote sometime tomorrow if that’s okay with you.”
“Do it,” ordered JB. “Between working, me moving, you moving, painting, and our schedules…I don’t think we can afford to not find other ways that will help get all of this done. When do you think we can have me moved in by?” he asked.
“I think we can all be moved by July 8th. Our floors will be done before the weekend. If Scott can get the painters signed on, they can start painting your place this weekend and should be done before mid-week next week. That way, we can have the movers have your stuff moved by Saturday. Then, get settled and figure out what’s next. What do you think?”

"Seems aggressive but doable. What about your place? Are going to be ready? Do you need help? Are you going to have them move you, too?"
"We don't have as much stuff as you, so ours should be a little easier. We are going to donate the guest bedroom stuff and just keep our master bed and the Duncan fife nightstand and dresser. We'll probably have to store some of the artwork and the wine fridge in your garage, along with a few of the wine racks. Would that be okay?" Alex said as he served JB his breakfast. "Breakfast is served, JB."
"Mm. I know I usually wait until the weekends to have this, but I was in the mood for it today," he said smelling his eggs and bacon. He reached over and added a little more salt as Alex brought over the toast and butter. JB always liked to generously butter his toast. "Sounds like a plan. If you need any money, let me know," he offered.
"We'll be fine. Thanks, though, JB." Mind if I head into your office, use the computer, and make some calls? I'll give William and Roy a call about the wine auction weekend. I know we'll see them before, but maybe we can plan something with them sooner?"
"Sure. I'll be there after I finish eating and catching up on the news," JB answered. Off Alex went to make the calls, answer emails, and research for the upcoming program.

*****

Scott arrived at the 738 11th Avenue address to find Jimmy there checking out the stain on the floors. "Hi! You must be Jimmy? I'm Scott. Alex is my partner." He said introducing himself. Jimmy looked over at him. "Oh good. You're here. You and I walk through, okay? I want to make sure it all looks good before we put on verathane." he said. "Do I need to wait for Alex?" he asked with his heavy Asian accent.
"No. I can deal with it. Can we look at the apartment, too?" Scott asked.
"Yes. Sure. Let's go." Jimmy waved Scott in and they performed the walk-through at the house. Scott complimented Jimmy on his teams' work a few times.

"These look brand new! You work fast. Nice job, sir," Scott said praising the wood-tone colors and consistency. "So, you'll verathane today? Then what?"
"We will put down three or four coats verathane. Today. Tomorrow, and last one Thursday. You can then walk on Saturday. Not before. Okay?" Jimmy replied.
"Got it. These look really great. Can we look across the street now?" he asked. Jimmy stepped outside and motioned to the man in his truck. He jumped out and ran over. They spoke Mandarin to each other followed by the man pulling out his cell phone calling someone else. By the time Jimmy and Scott had crossed the street, another truck with a few men pulled up jumping out with supplies to tend to the job at hand. Scott was impressed. Jimmy and his team did not waste any time.

Scott pulled out a key and unlocked the apartment door. Jimmy seemed to have his key copy ready just in case, then put it away once the door was opened. Scott walked in and marveled at the recently stained wood floors. He walked down the hallway picturing the track lighting for the ceiling. There was a little nook on the left wall that used to be where a phone sat and for opening the front door of the building. He wandered straight into the living room and noticed both sets of French doors. One for an office/closet and another that led into the bedroom. He loved it was a front apartment with large windows facing JB's place. Jimmy was behind him following and listening for any hints of dissatisfaction. Scott was picturing the linen cream on the walls with white trim and a white ceiling. He stepped into the bedroom and thought *light lavender*. There was a door that opened into the kitchen and a door that opened into the hallway. The kitchen was old, with glass doors on the antique painted wood cabinets. The sink had dark brown wood-grained vinyl pressboard cabinet below it and was cheap. He thought to himself, "*Nothing that black and white linoleum tiles, some white paint, and porcelain tile for the countertops won't bring back this little kitchen to add some flair to it.*" He turned and looked at Jimmy. "This is great! Same timing for the verathane here, too?" he asked.
"Yes. It will be ready for you to walk on Saturday."
"Perfect! Thank you so much! Really nice job, sir. Thank you!" He gave a small bow to Jimmy. "I'll just leave since it seems you have a set of keys. Is that okay?" he asked.

"Yes. That's good. See you here Friday afternoon. Okay? You bring check," Jimmy replied.
"Yes. We'll bring your check, Friday! Awesome! Oh. One other question. I need to bring painters by to look at the place before they paint. Any chance you can do the house upstairs first and given me an hour or two before going too fast? Or they can verathane the apartment first, then the house. They may need to look around there quickly." He was nervous he was asking too much.
"Let me see what we can do. But don't take too long. We need to get this done," he answered tensely.
"Yessir. If I am not back in two hours, do what you need to do. Okay?" Scott looked for approval. Jimmy nodded, annoyed, and waved Scott out of the apartment.

Scott bounced out of the apartment with a full vision of what they can do with the apartment. It would do for now. He was surprised that he didn't see the neighbors, but they were probably working. He got into his car to head down to the paint store across the street from the Divisadero Touchless Car Wash. There was a little congestion on his drive, but he was feeling impatient. He was on a mission and everything always seemed to move slower when he was set to get something done.

Scott arrived at the paint store and saw a few painters standing around. He called them over and had a brief conversation with Jose' and Miguel sharing about the house that needed to be painted quickly. He added he would provide all the paint. They would simply need to do the painting and protect the floors. They seemed to nod, slightly annoyed given this is what they have been doing for many years. After some basic negotiation, Scott gave two men the address. They would meet there in thirty mins. Off he went. It seemed while driving back, the men in the truck were following him. When they arrived and both parked. Jimmy and his crew were still there. The men were in front eating on the stoop. Scott stood outside his car and the men stepped out of their double-parked truck joining him.
"Mind if we go in really quick?" asked Scott directing his question to Jimmy. Jimmy nodded.
"Hurry," he answered impatiently. Scott waved his Hispanic partners into the house. He pointed to the different moldings and trim stating "*white semi-gloss*". He pointed to the ceiling and said, "*flat white*". Then he pointed to the walls and stated the colors. One

of the painters had a small pad of paper, a pen and was taking notes. The half bath off the kitchen would be painted white like the pantry. The kitchen would be painted a taupe color. Including the ceiling. They walked upstairs. Reviewed the rooms. Then walked back outside past the stoop.
"What do you think?" asked Scott.
"fifteen hundred," one of the painters answered.
"One thousand," countered Scott. After some back and forth, they agreed on one thousand two hundred dollars. They would start painting Saturday. They would be done by the end of the day Wednesday. They shook hands. One of the men provided Scott his card.
"Here's my card. I have a few other men who will be here to help, so we should finish pretty quickly." He smiled.
"You speak perfect English, Jose'. Why didn't you say so?" asked Scott feeling a little stupid. He felt bad. "Shit."
"Don't worry. I didn't want you to feel bad." He winked at him.
"For that, we'll give you thirteen hundred. Sorry I assumed you didn't speak English. I'm embarrassed."
"Don't be. You're nicer than most. And…thanks. See you Saturday," he said then turned to his buddy and they got in their truck and took off.
"It's all yours, Jimmy. Thanks so much for your patience," said Scott. Jimmy nodded then directed his team in Mandarin to get to work. Scott looked at his watch.
"Shit. It's almost noon. I have to get my ass to the store." He changed his focus. He couldn't wait to talk with Alex tonight at dinner. When he got into his car, his cell phone rang. It was Aarav.
"Hey, Aarav. How are you? How's Gabriel?" he asked.
"Hey, Scott. I'm good. I got Gabriel all settled in his place. He just fell asleep. I think it's the drugs they gave him for his pain," he answered. "Have the police called you at all?" he asked.
Scott replied, "No. Not sure why they would. I wasn't there. I don't really know Veronica or the guy. Did you get any more info from Gabriel?" he asked.
"Actually yes. He never saw the skinhead guy before. I did get a call from the police, though. Seems like the skinhead has some connections to some neo-Nazi group in the Sacramento area. He isn't talking, but the police are checking out Veronica's boyfriend. I just hope that Gabriel presses charges. Anyway, sorry to bother you.

I just wanted to check in with you and give you a heads up in case they do call you…the police, I mean."
"Thanks. I appreciate it. Good luck with Gabriel. Let me know if anything comes up, or if I can help," replied Scott.
"Thanks. I'm sure it'll be fine. I'll give you a heads up if something comes up. Bye now." Aarav hung up.

Scott took a deep breath. He thought to himself how he felt bad for Gabriel. A little for Aarav, but that was his issue to deal with. He was also feeling a bit conflicted. Gabriel always took chances and was always fucking around. He tended to follow his dick most of the time without care or concern. Not that he deserved what happened to him. Maybe this might change some of his actions a bit. Then he caught himself. "Why am I going on about this? Good lord. Good luck, Gabriel. Good health and I just hope it all works out for you," he said aloud in the car. Then shrugged it off and headed home. He would head to the store from there and then freshen up before they all head to Irna's for dinner. As he headed home, he realized he was looking forward to the evening ahead.

*****

Michelle was up and finished her breakfast. Dominic, who she referred to as '*Dom*', was on her mind. Seeing him the other day surprised her. And not in a good way. She wished he had called her or something before just appearing without notice. Her first thought was that it was a little creepy. Her second thought was that she kind of understood. She did only leave a note that she needed to get away and was going to see her brother Alex in San Francisco. She had talked about him with Dom several times. She had talked with him about how she needed to reconnect with Alex but never shared the why's and Dom never asked for explanations. He always told her she would tell him if she felt he needed to know. She appreciated that about him. He was '*easy.*' He didn't probe too much. He enjoyed watching rugby on television. He also preferred to be the 'man of the house' and considered her his 'little lady.' Although he seemed a bit misogynistic, it didn't bother her. They had dated in high school. After they graduated, they amicably went their separate ways. She was off to college and he was accepted in a government role that would help pay for his college tuition. Years went by then, unexpectedly and serendipitously, they ran into each other in

Chicago at a coffee shop. They saw each other and it was like they picked up right where they left off. They dated and one thing led to another. He kind of moved in. Now and then, he would bring flowers. One bouquet had a beautiful Cartier love bracelet in it. Another had a silver Tiffany heart pendant and necklace wrapped around the stems. He would surprise her with some nice wine. He bought a small grill for her condo deck and would try to be the grill master (at least he thought he was in his mind). She didn't mind him disappearing for a few weeks at a time for work. When he returned, they were effortlessly together again. Who knew that after a few bottles of Chardonnay celebrating his recent success on a work trip and a raise that the one time they didn't use protection that she would quickly become pregnant? She didn't say anything until she thought she was sure. It was unplanned. When she nervously shared the news, he was so happy. She was cautious about everything she ate and drank. Then she miscarried. She didn't know how to tell him, so she simply left. She was feeling helpless and depressed. She needed some distraction. Memories were surfacing and they were painful.

As Michelle reflected on the moments that led her to Alex and Scott in San Francisco, she opened her phone and pulled up Dom's contact information. She tapped the call option. Then hung up right before the ring. "Shit. Should I?" she muttered to herself. She looked at the number again and pressed to call. "Here goes nothing," she whispered, drew a deep breath, and exhaled.

Ring. Ring. Ring. Ring.

Just as she was getting ready to hang up a click sounded.

"Hello? Michelle?" asked the male voice.

"h-h—hi." she stammered. She was nervous. She felt a little angry. She paused.

He spoke softly. "I'm glad you called. I wasn't sure if you would."

"Yeh. Sorry. I know I should have called sooner," she said lightly and carefully.

"I'm sorry that I startled you the other day. Showing up like that. It's just…I tried calling you. I left you messages, but no answer. I didn't know what was going on. I just had to see you." He tried desperately to hold back his frustration. He was confused and seeking to understand what happened. "You just left…" he stopped. "I flew back to Chicago and to find the note you left. That's all I had."

"I know. I ignored the messages. I didn't listen to them. I just needed to get away." She rubbed her forehead and played with her hair, fidgeting. "
"You shared some great news. I tried to get to you sooner, but I was stuck on an assignment. I was so happy when you shared the news. When I got to the airport, I…" he started to get excited, then caught himself.
Michelle interrupted. "I know. I was excited, too. Look…"
He jumped in. "Can we meet and talk? Doing this over the phone just doesn't seem to be…well… you know." He paused. Nothing.
"Shell? Can I see you?" he sheepishly asked.
"We should talk. You're right," she resigned. He was right. It would be more appropriate to talk face-to-face than over the phone.
"I am on Fillmore at Peet's Coffee, right now," he stated.
"Um…what? No. How do you know where I'm at, anyway?" she asked surprised and starting to get angry. She thought to herself, *'does he not know boundaries at all?'*
"At our place…I mean *your place*; you kept your address book on top of the fridge. You mentioned that Alex was living in San Francisco, so I looked in your book. It was all there. Your note said you were going to San Francisco to see your brother. So…"
"So, you looked or snooped in my book. That's just rich," she chided softly in a sarcastic tone.
"Probably not the best thing to do, huh?" he asked apologetically.
"No. But, I understand. I'm not totally innocent in this. But I needed to do some things and I needed to see my brother. There were some…" she stopped again. She was catching herself. "Look. How about we meet tomorrow. We can meet for lunch, or go for a walk? If we have lunch, we can meet at Vivande on Fillmore Street, since you seem to be becoming acquainted with the area? Or another place called Curbside Café, next to the grocery store on California off Fillmore. What do you think?" she asked.
"What about breakfast?" he kindly asked. "Or is lunch or a walk my only options?"
"I am going to dinner with Scott and Alex at a friend of theirs. So, lunch would be better." She took a soft breath. "I know I'm being a bit selfish, here. It's just that there are some things to discuss, and I need to make sure I am in the frame of mind to talk about them. Mornings are not the best for me on that. Okay? I'm really not trying to be difficult," she said, hoping he would understand. She

attempted a joke as a tear trickled down her cheek. "You know I don't function until I have had a cup or two of coffee in the morning anyway, so I think you can understand," she attempted a light titter and twisted her hair a little tighter while biting her bottom lip awaiting his response. She could hear the pause and deep breath through the phone.
"Fine. Lunch. Vivande. eleven?" he asked.
"Noon?" she countered.
"Eleven-thirty?" he suggested a little more firmly.
"Okay, then. Eleven-thirty. Tomorrow. Vivande." She took a breath. "Thank you for understanding."
"The problem is, I don't. Hopefully, when we talk, I will afterward. I just need to know. Did I do something wrong, here? It kinda feels like you're blaming me for something, and I don't know what," he cited seeking some kind of answer so he could mentally prepare for their meeting.
"No. You didn't do anything. We'll talk tomorrow, okay? We'll go from there," she replied trying to relieve him of any unnecessary guilt that she might have seemed to imply or that he might be feeling.
"Okay. And this dinner tonight…" he started to ask. She interrupted.
"Tomorrow. 11:30. See you then, okay? I'll tell you all about dinner."
"Okay. See you tomorrow." He almost said he loved her but held back. He wasn't sure where he stood and would wait until they met. They both paused, then he whispered, "Bye," and hung up.
Michelle pulled her phone from her ear and looked down at it for a few moments.
"Tomorrow," she whispered and wiped a second tear from her cheek. Then said to herself aloud, "I am tired of crying. I need to be around people and get a smile, goddamn it." She rose from her comfy spot in the living room and headed to grab her purse and jacket. It was time to get out of the house. She decided the head down to Union Street. There were always people around and shops to check out. It was gray outside. It was one of those Mark Twain quote days. "*The coldest winter I ever spent was a summer in San Francisco,*" kind of days. She would grab a pair of gloves at one of the stores. As she stepped outside, the cool breeze hit her face and the chill in the air startled her. She shuttered and then forced her march towards her Union Street goal. She was determined not to sit

around the house feeling sorry for herself. It was time to pick herself up and move on. Off she went.

The Calm Before Dinner

Michelle had walked around Union Street and landed at Café de Paris at 2032 Union Street for a late lunch. She had the L'Entrecote, as was recommended by Alexander. He was a charming Persian gentleman. He was in his young 50's, with salt and pepper curly hair. His smile was almost as bright as his heart. She loved the energy he projected. While she waited for her order, he brought over a glass of champagne.

"No one sits in my restaurant without having a welcoming glass of champagne. Cheers." He smiled and walked off as a few others entered for their dining experience. He seemed to know them by name as he hugged them welcoming their return. A few moments later, a butter lettuce salad was delivered. She loved the simplicity of the salad with its tangy vinaigrette dressing with a sprinkle of walnuts. As she finished, the sliced steak dish with a buttery green sauce generously drizzled over it was gently placed before her with a separate plate of shoestring fries and extra green sauce. Her window seat provided her street entertainment of passers-by while French music played giving the ambiance of a Parisian Brasserie. After she ate, paid her check, and bid her goodbye to the owner, she stepped outside into the chilly weather and hailed a cab to Fillmore and Sacramento. She was too full to walk and decided she would check out Scott's store. She regretted having not gone sooner.

When Michelle arrived at 'Scott's Closet', it was almost three o'clock. She noticed boxes around the store and the closing sale sign in the windows. When she walked in, she observed Troy lip-syncing and performing to Gloria Gaynor's "I Will Survive" playing loudly throughout the store. His back was to her and he held a large coffee table book of artworks in one hand and a small stream of bubble

wrap being waved around in his other hand. It immediately brought a smile to her face.
"Hey! Michelle!" Scott yelled from the upstairs landing. "Yay! What are you doing here?!". He rushed down the stairs as Troy turned and pursed his lips feeling interrupted during his flawless maneuvering to what he considered one of his theme songs in life. Then dropped the book in the box with the bubble wrap and walked over to register to turn down the music.
"Sorry for interrupting. I walked around Union Street. Had a late lunch at this cute French restaurant then cabbed it here. I thought I would stop by. Sorry for not coming sooner," she answered.
"Did you eat at Café de Paris, by chance?" he asked.
"Yes. You know it?"
"Absolutely! Alexander and Ladan are lovely, lovely people. JB, Alex, and I love to have the L'Entrecote. Some bubbles and maybe a Cosmo or two. It's one of our favorite places," said Scott smiling. "Shit! We should have taken you there sooner. We have been so caught up keeping you to ourselves," he added apologetically.
"Girl! You guys haven't taken me there," injected Troy as he strolled back to complete his packing of the final smattering of books from the book table.
"Yes, we have. We took you there about three months ago. You got so drunk, you and Alexander were singing duets…or I should say, attempting to sing duets. You didn't even know the words to some of the songs. We had to get you to sit down," Scott reported back.
"Oh. That was there? Didn't I pay?" asked Troy.
"Um. No queen. Alexander and Ladan treated the food in preparation for being scheduled on the Dining program with JB. Alex and I bought drinks. You acted like you were in a drag show," chuckled Scott. Michelle was amused by the back-and-forth between them.
"Oh. Well, shit. I guess I forgot about that," said Troy shrugging it off returning to his book packing to send back to the vendor.
"Well. You were pretty ripped. I wouldn't be surprised if you blacked out based on how much you were drinking that night. Did you also forget that we took you there for your birthday, too?" Scott laughed.
"Girl. Please. Stop embarrassing me in front of our guest," he snapped his fingers twice. "I'm gonna finish packing these books, okay bitch? Then I am going to head to the stock room to finish the

books there. Okay, bitch?" he teased. He loved calling Scott "bitch". Especially in front of female customers. He never understood why they liked to hit on him. It was his way of making sure they knew he was gay.
"I brought the books out already. Why don't you pack the elaborate decorative flower candles to return over on the landing display?" suggested Scott.
"Sure, girl. Pride gets packed last. I'll do it on Thursday. Okay?" replied Troy rolling his eyes.
"Sure. Thanks, girl," answered Scott. Then looked back towards Michelle. "Sorry about that."
Michelle just smiled. She needed the laugh. She thought it was fun to watch them banter like two old ladies. "No problem. Can I help?"
"Sure. If you want. We have a couple of hours left before we need to head out and get ready for dinner with Irna. I'm looking forward to seeing her." said Scott. "How was your day, otherwise?"
"Good, thanks for asking. I walked around the Marina. This morning, I did call Dom. I felt I had to after he saw me the other day. He freaked me out a little."
"Um. Yeh! Did you tell him where you were? I mean, did he let you know he was coming? Anything?" asked Scott. "I know I would have been freaked out if someone traveled across the country spying on me and not giving me fair warning. Just sayin'," he added.
Michelle motioned to the stack of gift cards pointing at herself and then to the boxes of cards with a box positioned adjacent to them ready for packing.
"Want me to pack those up while we chat?" she asked. Scott nodded and motioned her over to the area while he packed up the erotic and colorful glassware. He thought they would be fun to sell but was wrong.
"Sure," he answered.
"Well… the truth is, he did call. He left several voice messages, but I just didn't answer him or listen to them." She was multi-tasking packing and talking. "So, it wasn't his fault. I did leave on a whim, after all, leaving just a note. He simply put two-and-two together and figured out where I was. I mean, I did say in the note that I was visiting Alex. He just looked through my address book and found Alex's…I mean *your* address."

"Okay…but he followed you and surprised you at the steps. I get the flying out and shit. But following you around? *Stalking*?" he said with his voice inflecting as he packed the glassware.
"I know. Yes. A bit creepy. You're right. But…" she paused. "I am going to have lunch with him tomorrow at Vivande. We are going to talk. I will ask him about that, believe me," she confirmed with Scott.
"Vivande?" Scott asked surprised. "You know that's where Alex and I had our first date. I love that place."
"Oh. Good. I gave him a choice between the park, Curbside, or Vivande. He chose Vivande. We're meeting at eleven-thirty."
"Good time. It starts getting busy around one. You'll probably be the first ones there. Try to get seated in the front corner by the window. And the pasta carbonara is total yum! Especially with a glass of Pinot Grigio, or a rose'," suggested Scott with a light level of excitement.
"Noted," replied Michelle. "Thanks for the tip. So, if you don't mind, I would like to change the topic. You and Alex had your first date there? Alex never really shared how you met."
"Oh, God! That story again?!" said Troy loudly from above.
"Shut up, queen!" yelled Scott back. "I love our story!"
"I know! Everyone knows!" Troy yelled back in a humorously sarcastic tone while shaking his head.
"Tell me," instructed Michelle.

Scott proceeded with the story while the three packed. They all bantered over the next few hours ending the day with most of the store packed for return to vendors. They organized two large sale tables and displays in preparation for the next two days. Scott shared aloud that his goal was to pack up the remainder of the store and empty it by the end of the day on Friday. That would give him and Alex time to focus on moving both them and JB. He was stressed but focused on getting it all done. It was a lot at once. As the time approached close to five, the store phone rang. Scott answered to find it was Alex calling to check on him.
"Hey, Scott. I am going to be leaving from the station here in about thirty minutes. Jon has JB rocking tonight!"
"He's a great producer for JB's hot topics show. Smart. He was a good find for JB," said Scott openly sharing his opinion. "And he's a nice guy."
"True. You almost done at the store?" asked Alex.

"Yes. We'll finish up here in a few mins then head back home to freshen up. Michelle's here. Wanna talk with her?" offered Scott.
"She's there? Cool. No. That's alright. I'll see you both when I get home and you can fill me in on your days before we head to Irna's. Quick question. Did you get to the places today?" he asked.
"Yes. Love the floors. Love the places. Jimmy is doing a great job! I also was able to get painters for JB's place. They are going to start Saturday. Jimmy said that would be okay." He took a breath then added, "I *really* like the apartment. Good place for us to regroup. Maybe we can pop by Busvan for Bargains on Clement Street after we paint and get somewhat settled. What do you think?" asked Scott.
"Sure. Let's get all this other shit done first, okay?" Alex laughed. "We are dealing with a lot, and shopping is not really on my list of priorities at the moment."
"Who are you and what have you done with my boyfriend?" joked Scott. "I get it. Focus, Scott. Focus."
Alex chuckled on the other end of the line. "Glad you like the apartment. I know it needs a little work, but…"
"Baby. It's all good. Love it. Great spot. You're amazing. Good choice. Love you," Scott said interrupting working to let Alex know everything was just fine. "See you at home. Muwah!" he blew a kiss into the phone.
"Love you. See you soon. Have a glass of Sauvignon Blanc ready." And with that, Alex hung up.
"Okay, team! Let's clean up this mess," he instructed them. "We need to get outta here." He looked over at Michelle. "We have a dinner to get ready for."
The trio cleaned up their messes and they were out the door promptly at five-thirty.

*****

Alex walked into the house to find his glass of Sauvignon Blanc on the dining room table with a heart drawn on a small piece of paper just under the glass base with the letter "*S +A*" scribbled inside it. He heard the music from the AT&T Stormy Weather CD playing throughout the house. Paula Cole's version of "You've Changed" was floating in the atmosphere. Alex thought it was a perfect bluesy sound he found calming as he climbed the stairs to

find Michelle and Scott in each of their respective bedrooms getting ready for dinner.
“Hi honey! I’m home” he sang as he walked into the bedroom then took a sip of his wine. Scott ducked his head out from the master bath. He had a little toothpaste foam around his mouth.
“Hi Schmoo! One sec,” then disappeared for a few moments. Alex heard Scott gargling and spit. Suddenly Scott came scurrying over, shirtless. Even though they had not worked out for about a week, he looked good. Scott hugged and kissed his lover.
“Hi,” he said softly. “How was your day?” asked Scott.
“Fine.” He kissed Scott back tasting the remnants of the Cool Mint blue Listerine. He kissed him again. “How was yours?” he asked.
“Good. As I told you on the phone, I went and saw the places to meet Jimmy the floor guy, see the floors, and then set up the painters for JB’s house.” He released Alex from his embrace and grabbed his glass of wine and took a sip making a small face. “You know…wine and mouthwash don’t mix. Yech!” He took another sip indicating improvement then continued. “I do really like the apartment. It's cute. You’re right. It’s incredibly convenient to be across the street from JB. It’s a decent size. Not huge, but good for now. We can easily spruce up the kitchen and just paint it white. We can get those linoleum adhesive squares and do a black and white tiled floor. We would definitely have to paint the sink cabinet. That fake wood look just doesn’t do it for me, ya know?” He rattled off a little more while Alex sat relaxing on the edge of the bed smiling at him and listening to Scott’s ideas. He was just relieved he liked the apartment. “The paint job will be easy for us to do. We’ll deal with the paint on the glass of the French doors later. Who does that?” he guffawed and took another sip of wine. Then stopped and looked at Alex. “Oh my God. I’m so sorry. I was just blathering on. I got carried away. I’m so sorry.” He sat down next to Alex. “Anyway, before I shut up, I was incredibly lucky and got these painter guys. Jose’ has a few guys on his crew and they will paint JB’s place for $1300. I think that means we come in under what JB budgeted us for, which takes care of the movers, too.”
“That’s amazing!” said Alex. “I am just glad you like the apartment. I have to admit I was a little worried. However you want to decorate it, we will. We gonna look at paint this weekend, then?” he asked.
“Saturday morning. First thing. Creative paints over on Geary. Should be easy. I think it would only take us three days to paint, so

we should be ready to move in by next Tuesday or Wednesday. We can do carloads, or…" he paused.
"Or what?" asked Alex.
"One Big Man. One Big Truck?" I called them and the guy said he could move the big stuff and some of the heavy boxes if we have them packed for about $300. I figured $400 because they always underestimate. Then add $50 for a tip. It would save us the headache of carrying things up those damn stairs." He looked at Alex giving him a look of hopefulness.
"I think we can do that," he replied. "It's gonna be a fuck of a weekend, though."
"I know. I know. Ugh. Too much," replied Scott. "Good thing is, we get solid workouts that make up for us not making the gym," teased Scott. Then he changed to a more sweet tone. "Thank you, Schmoo. You are my angel, you know that?"
"I love you, too Scott," said Alex.
"And how about your day? Everything go okay?" Scott asked switching topics and getting up to put on a fresh black t-shirt. He assessed his khakis in the mirror and approved them. No wrinkles or marks from the day.
"My day was good. I am almost done booking the Dining program. I'll just have to put together the show sheet and confirm the guests and then double confirm and send reminders for the in-studio conversations. JB insisted on his eggs in bacon fat breakfast this morning. I swear I don't know how he doesn't fall over from all the cholesterol he consumes. The amount of butter he puts on his toast alone is not for the faint of heart." Alex and Scott giggled.
"Well. All I can say is that he is simply JB, and he lives the way he wants to live. Bless his heart. Stubborn kook. Kind and brilliant. Drives me nuts, but I love him," added Scott. "And bacon-grease eggs on a Tuesday? He usually doesn't have those until the weekend. Doesn't he usually have cottage cheese and a fruit cup with some oatmeal?" Scott inquired.
"Exactly. But I believe the hospital trip inspired this one."
"Hm. Well. As I said. That's JB for ya," said Scott shaking his head then turning and pulling out a black Donna Karan dress shirt.
"Oh. And we are going to participate in the Sonoma Wine Auction this year. They called JB and I had to talk with William about rooms at MacArthur Place. We are all set," Alex said surprising Scott with the news.

"No shit?" asked Scott eyes wide open.
"No shit," replied Alex. "Now, we can talk more about that tomorrow. I need to get ready, and we need to get scooting soon so we're not late. You know how Irna is. We'll be gauche if we're late."
Scott laughed.
"You said, gauche," he teased. "Okay. Go brush and do your thing. I'm just gonna spritz some Pasha cologne on. Do I look okay?" asked Scott.
"You look very handsome. I will wear my dark Navy shirt, so we are not both wearing black," he said as they both maneuvered around each other focused on their separate preparation goals.
"How's Michelle?" he asked.
"She's good. I'll let her tell you about her day downstairs. See you there," replied Scott as he picked up his near-empty wine glass and headed down the stairs.

Michelle was touching up her makeup after putting on the black outfit she was given by Scott and Alex when she arrived. She really liked it. Her black hair had a little more body given the moisture in the air. The fog seemed to do that to it giving it more body. As she was putting on her lip liner, the song "Good Guy" being sung by Trisha Yearwood was playing. "*She stares into the mirror behind the bar…As is somebody owes her an explanation…All out of chances and still empty-handed…Now she doesn't even try…But she could have held on…She should have held on…to a good guy…*"
She thought about Dom. She put on her Tiffany pendant and her Cartier Love bracelet. She was feeling sentimental. She took a sip of wine. "*there used to be laughter…behind those eyes…Sometimes you see a glimmer…and you will find her…Lost in the music…A song from a time gone by…*". She wasn't sure why the words struck her. They just did.
She stood up and assessed herself in the mirror. She felt good mixed with a little uneasiness. She hoped for a nice dinner with Irna. She stood up holding her glass of wine, picked up her small black leather purse, and made her way downstairs. She hadn't noticed Alex had come home.

Scott was in the kitchen pouring himself a half glass of wine when Michelle came in beside him. As he finished pouring, he looked at her with his eyes appraising her from head-to-toe-to-head again. "Love the hair. Love the makeup. Love the shoes. Love the

look," he said and leaned over and pecked her on the cheek. "You look wonderful." Michelle lightly blushed and smiled.
"Thanks, Scott."
"You're quite welcome. Cheers." He lifted his glass towards her. She touched her glass to his then turned and walked into the living room landing in the comfy chair. Scott flowed her after returning the half-full bottle of wine to the fridge.
"Alex should be down in a few minutes. He is quick about getting ready. Are you okay? You look a bit solemn," he asked as Billie Holiday sang "I Wished On The Moon".
"I'm fine. It just seems life threw some things at me. These past two months have been hard. You know? And coming here seeing you and Alex, I think, was one of the best things I could have done. It's helped me figure some things out." She put her hand on her heart when she said that and looked at Scott. "I know I've been here a while. I also know you guys are going through some crazy stuff, yourselves." She paused and took a sip of wine. "So, I mean it when I say, thank you. Today was something I needed, too. You and Troy were the perfect people for me to hang out with. Thanks for letting me help today."
"Thanks for helping. It was nice you came to the store this afternoon," Scott empathetically replied. "And you visiting us has been nice. We loved having you. I think the visit helped Alex in some ways, too. You both had some things to work out and you letting him in as you have…it's changed something in him. He has a…" Scott took a moment and looked around the ceiling as if searching for an answer or a word, then looked back at Michelle and continued. "…a calm. You know? It's like he had this slight edge, or something was bothering him a little, but he never really said anything because he didn't understand. Now he does and he seems like there's a peace that's entered his life. So, I thank you as much as you thank us. Okay? We love you. We're always here for you. No matter what." Michelle smiled back at him and raised her glass initiating a virtual silent cheer. They nodded at each other and took sips of their wine.
"I'm looking forward to dinner," said Michelle. "I like Irna. She's really sweet and interesting. Kind of like an oracle or something." she teased.
"I would love to get her and Bitsy together. Remember her from the party? And her guy, Fred?" said Scott.

"Oh yeh. I can see that," she nodded. "Have you heard from her since the party?"
"Yes. She's called twice. She's trying to get us to commit to seeing her around July 4th. I told her we would see, given we all have to move. She understood. We'll see her. We just need to figure out timing," replied Scott.
"That's great," said Michelle.
"Coming down! It's after six-thirty! We should probably get a move on." said Alex loudly as he descended the stairs with his empty wine glass. "You both ready to go or are you gonna sit on your asses and make us late?" he asked sarcastically while chuckling. "C'mon!"
"Yessir!" said Scott as he rose from the sofa and Michelle from her chair. They moved quickly to the kitchen to drop off their glasses next to the sink then followed Alex to the entryway where they gathered their jackets, keys, and belongings. "Shit. Alex. Rose'? Medoc? Bubbles?"
"Shit. Yes. It's on the dining room table I dropped it off there when I got home," he said running over to collect the bottles of wine. "I got six bottles, just in case. Three Pouilly Fume'. I couldn't find a decent rose'. Two Medoc and a bottle of Domaine Carneros Sparkling. The fume' is chilled, so we don't have to worry about that." He returned with the wine carrier. "Off we go!"

The trio left the house and walked briskly to Irna's. She was about a fifteen-to-twenty-minute walk, so they figured they would arrive just on time. Along the way, Alex and Michelle caught up to her day. He enjoyed hearing about the escapades at the store. Alex shared an idea with Scott about maybe posting some sales signs at Marlena's and in the Castro. That might take care of his Pride merchandise and erotic glassware collection. They all chatted about their ideas to help Scott generate some final lucrative sales before closing for good during their journey until they arrived at Irna's building.
"Here we are," said Scott. "We all ready?"
"Ready," answered Alex and Michelle half-hazard.
Scott pressed the button to ring the buzzer.

Dinner & Ghosts from The Past

The trio arrived at Irna's door to find it ajar with her yelling *'Come on in! I'm in the kitchen!'*. They stepped in finding Irna at the oven with her head ducked down assessing the status of her cuisine. "Shit. It better not dry out." They heard her mutter loudly. She rose and turned to see them brandishing her pink polka-dot oven mitts. She removed them and tossed them on the counter. Her charming, flowered apron had spots that illustrated its heavy use. She donned the blonde wig this evening with bright pink lipstick, a rose blush, and hot pink manicured nails. She wore a lightweight gray turtleneck sweater with charcoal gray slacks and hot pink patent leather low heels that showed off her hot pink painted toes.
"You look great, Irna!" said Scott admiringly and went over to hug her.
"Don't mess my hair, dear. Nice to see you, too," she said as they hugged. She stepped back and looked at the three of her guests. "Come in! Hang your coats in the closet over there. Did you bring the wine?" she asked as she directed them around her quaint flat.
"We did," replied Alex. "I have a bottle of Bubbles, three bottles of Pouilly Fume, and two bottles of bubbles. I couldn't find a nice rose'. I hope that's okay," he expressed as he placed the carrier on the kitchen counter.
"Oh, that's just fine, dear. Would you mind opening the bubbles and pouring us all a glass? The glasses are over there in that cabinet. The different colored Bohemian cut crystal ones. Let's use the nice ones. I found them at the outdoor antique bazaar over in Alameda last

year." She motioned to one of the cabinets in the kitchen right side of the sink.
"Sure. I'll just hand my jacket quickly and do that," Alex said following his orders.
"Want some help, Schmoo?" asked Scott.
"Sure. Why don't you open the bottle while I get the glasses?" suggested Alex. Irna scooted around them and navigated to Michelle.
"Hi, Michelle. Nice to see you again. Why don't we go sit in the living room while they get our drinks ready?" She patted Michelle on the upper arm. They took a few steps over into the living room with Michelle landing on the sofa and Irna in a comfy chair.
"It's nice to see you, too. Did you have fun marching at Pride? I'm sorry we didn't see you," asked Michelle.
"It was so much fun. How about you? It was your first, right?"
"Yes. It was a lot to take in. So many people! I have never seen anything like it. I had to look twice when I saw some men walking around, literally naked...NAKED!" she flushed thinking about it. "Some were just naked and there were others who had a small piece of gold lame' draped over their...you know...," and she waved her hand over her crotch area.
"It's called a penis, dear," said Irna. Michelle laughed. "We're adults. You can say that, now." Michelle was also blushing.
"I know. I know. I think it's the Catholic in me," she tried to excuse her sexual conservatism in her speech a bit. Irna just looked at her not buying it.
"I say bullshit, but okay. Whatever you say. I know better," said Irna as she winked at her friend.
Scott and Alex approached the seated ladies. "Here come the bubbles!" they said as they handed them their glasses. "Cheers!" he said reaching his glass to Irna. They all cited the word and touched glasses. Scott and Alex had a routine as guests at dinner parties where they touched the tops of their glasses, then the glass bases then the tops again. Then they would kiss and turn to the group. They always saved their routine for the last before sipping.
"Thanks for having us over for dinner, Irna," said Alex as he moved to the bookcase in the room.
"My pleasure, Alex. It's been a while, hasn't it?" she said taking a second sip from her champagne glass.

“It has.” He reviewed the shelved books. “Hey, Irna. I didn’t notice this before, but it looks like you have many history and math books. What’s with the math books?” he asked.
“Oh. I used to teach at NYU and Portland State before moving to San Francisco,” she answered.
“Teach?” asked Alex. Michelle looked at Irna slightly surprised by the response.
“Yes. Teach. I taught Algebra, Calculus, and Trigonometry.”
“What? When?” he asked surprised. Scott and Michelle were silent and shocked by the news. This was completely unexpected.
“I graduated from MIT. I had my Bachelor of Science in Mathematics then went to Stanford where I finished my Ph.D. I got a job teaching at NYU, then another at Portland State. Eventually, a position opened at Stanford. San Francisco was a change for me.”
“Wow!” said Scott. “Not meaning to discount you or anything, but wow! I would never have thought you were a mathematician. Or a math professor! It just doesn’t seem like you. I mean…by your personality.” Irna chuckled.
“And how should my personality be as a math professor, dear?” she joked and waved her free hand. “Oh, no need to be sorry, Scott. A lot of people don’t see women in these roles. They should. But enough of that,” she said wanting to change the subject, and took a large drink from her glass nearly finishing it. “Are we all empty now? We might need some white wine,” she suggested.
“Okay,” said Alex. “But before that, why did you leave that and come to San Francisco?” he asked.
“A combination of things, really. The man I was in a relationship with got a new job, and my sister and I had a falling out. It was over something stupid. It was a while ago. I thought it would be better if I put some distance between us. You know…family drama and dynamics. That’s all. I wanted a change, anyway. I got tired of the rain. Go Ducks!” she laughed and got up to set up wine glasses for the Pouilly Fume’.
Michelle watched her then asked. “Your sister? In Portland?” Her voice was softened and concerned.
“Yes. She didn’t like the man I was with. I met him at Portland State. He and I refused to get married since gay people couldn’t get married. So, we simply lived together. I still thought of him as my husband, though. She thought that to be depraved,” she responded.

“Wait a minute.” interrupted Scott. “I am fascinated that you were a professor at NYU, Stanford, and Portland State, and now you work at the deli counter at Molly Stones?”
“Well, actually, I came down and worked at Stanford for a bit. I worked on a student tutoring program. Then Fred passed. He was a Biology professor. That took the wind from my sails and I didn’t feel like teaching or tutoring anymore. I didn’t want to be on a campus, either. Too many memories. So I saw this job and took it.” As she shared the information, she pulled down the glasses, opened up a bottle of wine, and began pouring their glasses.
“You never shared that before. I would love to hear more,” said Scott feeling like he was learning a whole other side of Irna. Before, she was always just taking care of them with their dinner parties. Giving them extra treats. Sometimes some pot brownies. Showing entertaining eccentricities in her personality and clothes that always made people feel both welcome and special whenever she was around. Now there was even more depth and soul than he expected. He couldn’t put into words how he was feeling about this incredible woman and human being.
“Another time. Tonight, we are having dinner and you are going to meet my niece and my grandniece. They are just really late,” she said as she looked at her watch and the kitchen clock. She brought over the wine glasses and gathered the champagne flutes returning them to the kitchen counter next to the sink.
“Your niece and grandniece?” asked Michelle.
“Oh shit. Sorry, Michelle. My fault” said Scott. “When Irna asked us for dinner, she shared she wanted us to meet her niece and grandniece. They were down for a short visit. My bad. I should have said something.”
“Oh, it should not be a big deal,” injected Alex. “We’re all here together having dinner with Irna and we are lucky to be able to meet part of her family,” said Alex as he focused on Irna. “Can I help with anything in the kitchen, Irna?”
“Not yet, Alex. Thank you.” She then turned her gaze to Michelle. “Yes. My niece and grandniece. My niece’s husband recently died in a car accident. She has been on her own and has had a bit of bad luck in her life. It’s her story to tell, not mine. So, I’ll let her share what she wants. Let’s see how dinner goes.” Irna had a curious look in her gaze as she informed Michelle.

Michelle looked back at her. Nervous about the response to her next question. "What about your sister? Is she still alive?"
"No. Sadly she passed not too long ago. Cheers, everyone," she raised her glass. They all responded in kind, and she turned. "I need to check my Poulet Roti to make sure It doesn't overcook," she said as she headed towards the kitchen.
"Poulet Roti?" asked Alex.
"Julia Child's way of saying 'roast chicken'. It's just chicken rubbed with butter and salt. I like to include pepper and a little poultry seasoning. I make a little sauce on the side with a little carrot, onion, butter, and bouillon broth. We'll have some steamed haricot verts with a little bacon and some mashed potatoes. Sound good?" she asked.
"Yay! Um…what are 'haricot verts'?" asked Scott. Michelle was getting frustrated. She wanted to find out about the sister and the niece. This seemed all too coincidental.
"Thin small French green beans, dear. Just a fancy way of saying green beans," she laughed.
Michelle interrupted the banter and asked a little more loudly. "What was your sister's name?"
The buzzer sounded. "Alex? Since you're closest would you mind buzzing them in? Lord, she's late," said Irna. "Claire. My sister's name was Claire." Michelle sat there frozen. She took a big gulp of wine.
"Alex. I think I should leave. I think I need to leave and leave now," she said panicked as she looked at Alex. He noticed a very tense look in her eyes. Irna walked over quickly to Michelle and patted her shoulder.
"It will be fine. Please don't leave." There was a knock at the door with giggles coming from behind the door. *'Calm down'* was heard muffled through the door. Alex moved and opened the door. There they stood. Rebecca and Ashley. Irna moved quickly to welcome her guests. Michelle rushed off towards the rear of the flat with Scott following behind her. Rebecca didn't notice who the woman was passing as she was looking at Alex as Irna was unintentionally blocking her view of the room.
"Sorry, I'm late. Ashley was doing some water-coloring in the room and spilled the water all over the table and onto her clothes. I had to change her."

“Oh, that’s okay, Rebecca. This is my dear friend Alex,” said Irna brushing off the excuse and beginning the introductions. “My other two guests ran off…maybe to the bathroom or something. I’ll go check on them. Come in, please. Alex. Would you mind getting my niece a glass of wine? You do drink, Rebecca?”
“A glass of wine would be lovely. Is there any juice for Ashley?” asked Rebecca.
“Sure. Apple juice okay? It’s in the fridge.”
“Perfect,” she replied and smiled. She would try to be civil given there were guests.
“Alex. I hate to impose. Would you mind? I need to go check on Scott and our other guest,” asked Irna. Alex was a little confused but nodded to acknowledge the request. He seemed lost in what was happening but happy to accommodate.
“Nice to meet you, Rebecca,” said Alex and looked down at the little girl. “And you, too, Ashley,” he smiled as she moved behind her mother acting shy and hugging her leg.
“Oh, you’re not so shy. C’mon.” they moved into the living room and started getting settled. She pulled out the unicorn coloring book. “Here. Go color,” she said as she procured the crayons. Alex took her jacket then returned with a glass of wine while Irna trotted to the back of the flat. “Oh, I was kind of looking forward to this. You live here in San Francisco?” she asked looking at Alex. Alex quickly adapted to the situation and kept the conversation light.
“Yes. I live here with my partner, Scott.”
“And what do you do?” she asked. They began to banter. Alex had the sense this was time to distract from what might be going on in another room.

*****

Irna walked to the back of the flat to find Michelle and Scott in her bedroom sitting next to each other on her bed. Michelle was stiff with her hands gripping the edge of the mattress protected by a thick cozy red plush covered comforter. Scott was asking her what was wrong with no response from Michelle.
“Scott. Would you mind going and sitting with Alex and Rebecca while Michelle and I talked for a few minutes? Helping with the distraction would be helpful,” Irna asked softly while looking sympathetically at Michelle.

"You sure? I could stay if you want," he replied looking at Michelle then at Irna.
"Actually, I think Irna, and I need to talk for a moment," said Michelle softly with a hint of anger. She then looked up at Irna with a look of earnest in her eyes.
"Okay. Let me know if you need me to come back." He looked questioningly at both Irna and Michelle. He wasn't sure what happened. After he left the room, closing the door behind him, Michelle composed herself.
"Did you know?" she asked.
"Yes," she replied.
"You knew and didn't say anything to me?" Michelle was starting to become angry.
"First. Rebecca's visit was a surprise. It was very last minute. She said she was coming down and then she was here. The timing is, nothing short of, enigmatically suspicious. But here we are."
"But why didn't you say anything about this before…instead of springing this on me?!" she asked searching for some responsible explanation.
"I tried to tell you the other day in the park. But then you had your story. I just thought it was too much at the time. She doesn't know you're here either. So, I am not only going to hear it from you. I am going to hear it from her, too." Irna paused. "Look. Let's just go with it. I may be an old lady, but I know when life is sending me a message. Right now, life seems to be telling you to stop running. I think it's a hint, don't you?" she paused. Michelle was just staring at her. All the feelings she had in the past were surfacing again. She was tired of the hurt. "I'm truly sorry, Michelle. This was not meant to hurt you in any way. Rebecca is leaving San Francisco tomorrow or the day after to head back to Portland. This is the only other chance that I think I have to see her. Please. Let's see where tonight goes. I know it's difficult."
"Don't you know how much pain this is bringing up? What I went through?" Michelle asked.
"I can only imagine. I am so deeply sorry. Please don't leave. I know Rebecca has some things to share, too. It's going to be hard for her as well. You are not alone in this. You have family around you," she said. Michelle rolled her eyes and took a breath.
"Fuck." She took a breath. "Fuck." She repeated the word. "Fuck."

"I got it, dear. Is there another word you can use?" she sat down and grabbed her hand. "I know this is difficult."
"Well, in England they say '*bugger*'. I could say '*shit*' but I guess as a Canadian I could say *merde*. It's not as releasing in my mind, but okay. Merde!" she said. Then she followed up. "Nope. I'll stick with 'shit' or 'fuck' for the moment, thank you." Then another "Fuck." Escaped her mouth.
"Okay then," said Irna resigned to Michelle's rightful frustration and vulgarity. "Shall we go back out and see how this all plays out? I know this isn't the best time to talk about seating at the table, but, given the situation, we should plan, okay?" Irna asked softly with Michelle reluctantly nodding her agreement. "Why don't you sit by Alex? I'll have Rebecca sit to your right. Okay?"
"Fuck," said Michelle. Irna did not comment further on Michelle's continued use of her chosen explicative. After all, she couldn't blame her. She patted her arm again as they both rose from the bed with Irna leading them out of the room.

*****

When they arrived back to the living area, Rebecca, Scott, and Alex were chatting away about San Francisco listening to where Rebecca and her daughter ate and sharing some of the different sites she should try to see during her visit.
"We're back," said Irna. "Rebecca. This is Michelle. Michelle. Rebecca. I believe you two may know each other." Irna nervously took a sip of her wine. Rebecca looked at Michelle dumbstruck.
"H-h-h-hi." escaped Rebecca's lips.
"Hi," replied Michelle. She looked a little scared. Then looked around at her audience. Rebecca did the same thing.
"Is this some kind of sick joke?" asked Rebecca.
"No, Rebecca. It is just life throwing us some strange curveball. I never would have seen this coming. It just did," answered Irna.
"Would someone please explain what's going on here?" asked Alex.
"Yes, please," added Scott. He looked around at everyone's faces. He felt like it was one of those moments that happened in a soap opera. Each of them exchanged glances at each other. He used to laugh at the scene in "Soapdish" with Sally Field, Kevin Klein, Robert Downey Jr, Whoopi Goldberg, and a host of other famous

stars in the campy movie. The problem was that he didn't feel like laughing. Rebecca turned and focused on Michelle.
"Well, this is gonna be fun, isn't it?" she said and then gulped down her wine finishing her glass. "Can I have another glass, please?" she asked sardonically. Scott rose from his seat.
"Sure. I am getting a feeling we are all going to need another refill." And retrieved two bottles and began filling each of the glasses.
"Before we get to stories, mind if we all sit at the table? Alex. Would you mind helping me dish up the servings?" asked Irna. "That way, we can all talk while we eat."
"Really? You think I'm hungry, now?" asked Rebecca with a note of scorn.
"You? How do you think I feel?" said Michelle directing her comment towards Rebecca. "This is not just you having feelings about this."
"Mommy? Why is everyone being so mean?" came the little voice from the corner behind the table. They all became silent as Ashley rose from her corner with her coloring book and navigated her way to Rebecca's lap. They all stared at her having forgotten she was in the room. She had hidden in a corner behind the dining table to color. She had dark hair and blue eyes like Michelle's.
"Hi sweetheart. Sorry. Thanks for being so good while you were coloring." Rebecca hugged her daughter and kissed her head. "Scott, Michelle…this is my daughter, Ashley. Alex met her as we arrived. Ashley? Please say hi to Scott and Michelle."
"Hi," Ashley said sweetly to her audience. Then asked, "Please be nice to my mommy. Don't be mean, okay?" Michelle just stared at the little girl. Her heart was pounding. She looked at Rebecca asking the question with her gaze.
"We'll talk about it during dinner," Rebecca said softly directing her comment to Michelle. "Sweetie. Where's your juice?" she asked her daughter.
"By my coloring book. I finished another Oonie. I'm hungry though, mommy. Are we gonna eat?" she asked. Irna looked at her and answered her question.
"Yes, sweetheart. I have some macaroni and cheese for you with little hot dogs in it. Is that okay?" she asked Ashely.
"Yay! Macroonie cheese!" she replied.
"I set up a little spot over here for you at the table. Why don't you come sit? We are all going to eat now, okay?"

"Hokay. Come on mommy," said Ashley jumping from her mom's lap then grabbing her hand. Rebecca rose carefully with her glass of wine and looked at the faces around the room staring at her daughter and her.
"Coming, sweetheart. Coming," she said following her daughter.
"Let's all sit. Alex?" Irna waved Alex to the kitchen and the two of them got to work plating the food.
"I feel so stupid," said Scott. "We didn't even notice the table settings. We just came in, sat, started talking, and…bam! I need to be more observant." He said rolling his eyes while whispering to Michelle. She looked at him dumbfounded. "That's what you have to say? Really?"
"Okay, girl. I need to hear the stories, so you all are gonna spill, right? What's going on? I don't know what to think right now. My mind is reeling. You're acting strange," he whispered to Michelle as he took another sip of wine and found his place at the table. As he and Michelle sat down, Michelle motioned to Scott to move so that she would be positioned as Irna suggested earlier to her.

Alex and Irna moved like a ballet dancing their way around each other. Irna directing Alex on what utensils to use for doling out each of the culinary portions. She opted to put the cheese and Crudites' on the table so her guests could help themselves during dinner instead of before, given the direction of the evening. She improvised. She was feeling uncertain. It could either end early and badly or it would be an emotionally draining late night. She hoped it wouldn't drag on too long. It was difficult to say at this point. Alex and she moved quickly. There was a sense of urgency to get dinner served. The table was uncomfortably social. Rebecca was tending to her daughter while Michelle was trying desperately not to stare too long at either of them. She tried to make small talk before everyone was seated.
"When did you arrive in San Francisco?" asked Michelle.
"Last week. It was a last-minute decision to come down," replied Rebecca.
"Are you having a nice visit with Irna?"
"Let's just say it's been…educational. In some ways nice. In other ways, interesting," Rebecca replied with intentional vagueness. She didn't know just how much the others in this room knew about Irna and their family.

"I think all families are like that to some respect," said Scott. "My family is completely dysfunctional."
"Why's that?" asked Rebecca bluntly as she handed Ashley her favorite table toy to fidget with while dinner was in the process of being served. Ashley wasn't really interested in grownup talk. It bored her. She typically found other ways to entertain herself.
"Well…first, I'm an Air Force brat…er…military brat. My father was in the Air Force. We moved every 6-months to three or four years. When my dad married my natural mom, Ruthie, she had two sons from a prior marriage. After she and my dad were married, along came my brother Rick and me. My half-brothers are estranged from us. One, Doug, wants nothing to do with us. He's married with two kids, I guess my niece and nephew, so my stepmom says. I've never met them. My other half-brother, Matt is married with two daughters. I've met them once or twice. My brother Rick is in the Navy. He's a CB or something like that. I never hear from him. Except once when I came out. I guess my parents let him know and he came running back to see me to ask me if I was gay. You know. I guess he was there to confirm what I shared with my parents. I told him yes. And never really heard from him again. When he checked out of my life, he checked out. The only time I ever hear of anything is from my dad and my stepmom, who he married after my natural mom died, that is when I call them." As he was sharing his story, Dinner was being delivered and placed in front of them.
"Your stepmom?" asked Rebecca.
"Yes. My dad married her about a year or so after my natural mom died who passed when I was about a year and a half. She pretty much raised me. I guess she couldn't have kids. Want to know what's even more strange?" Scott asked. "Outside of none of us kids talking with each other…outside of me always calling my parents just about every Sunday."
"What's that?" she asked. Michelle was listening to Scott's story, a bit in awe.
"My last name. I found out that my dad's mom was married about four times. And the third marriage was to this guy Ed Rupert. I guess he was pretty fucked up. I'm still getting bits and pieces. But when my grandma registered my dad into school, she registered him using the name Rupert. When he graduated, he joined the Air Force. They told him his last name wasn't Rupert but Sawaya. He went home to find his mom talking with this man. Come to find out, the

man was Nicholas Sawaya, his natural father. The other guy, Ed never adopted him. Nicolas, I guess, according to my dad, tried to push him to keep the name Sawaya. He refused and legally had his name changed to Rupert to avoid the hassle of going back and having his school transcripts redone. He thought it was too much of a hassle. I'm sure there's more to it, but I think you get the gist. Again, I'm still finding out more stories as we speak. My dad doesn't reveal much about the family."

"You weren't kidding," said Rebecca. "I wonder if Alex has stories like that."

"Oh, we do," said Michelle.

"I'm not sure I follow," said Rebecca looking mystified at Michelle's comment.

"He's my brother," she said. Rebecca looked at Michelle with a subtle 'a-ha' look in her eyes. She was having dinner with Michelle, her brother Alex and his partner Scott and her aunt with whom she is trying to reconcile some things. It was all coming together now. As she said this, Alex and Irna joined the table with Irna dropping a healthy portion of Kraft Macaroni & Cheese with cut-up hot dogs embedded in the bowl.

"MMmmmm!" expressed Ashley. Alex noticed she was running low on juice and took care to refill her glass.

"Yes. That's my sister. Yes. All families have some level of dysfunction. Yes. This is my love and my partner, Scott," cited Alex as if he read Rebecca's thoughts.

"So how did you meet my aunt?" asked Rebecca to Scott and Alex. Scott and Alex looked at each other then back to Rebecca.

"A couple of years ago. At the deli counter," said Scott. "Alex and I were picking up some things for JB. He was having a couple of people over. Alex was going to put together a fruit and veggie dish. So, when we were at the store, we noticed the new deli counter, and there she was. We talked with her for a few minutes and ordered a couple of trays. She said she would put them together quickly and to just wait." Alex picked up from Scott's comments.

"That was the start. Then as we kept going back, we spoke more…next thing you know…I think we became friends," he continued.

"Interesting. Did you ever speak of your family with her?" Rebecca asked as if she were sleuthing or alluding to something slightly nefarious.

“Yes,” said Alex. “Why? What’s the big deal. People become friends over different encounters all the time.”
“It’s just so weird that here we all are sitting having dinner together,” she said.
“Why do you seem so hard, right now? I mean…you are being rather curt. I guess I’m not understanding the attitude,” asked Alex.
“Look. I don’t know you. I just met you. You don’t know me. But I feel like I don’t have time to mince words. We seem to be thrown into this situation and the only way is to either avoid it or just let it all out.” She took a bite of her chicken and a large sip of wine. Everyone looked at her hypnotized by the change in demeanor.
“You don’t have to say anything, Rebecca,” said Irna. “Not like this.”
“You know, Aunt Irna? Maybe this is how it all really needs to be said,” she replied scathingly. She looked at her audience who seemed frozen.
“I have terminal cancer. Pancreatic cancer. It was caught too late. My husband died in a car accident. This trip was for me to find out why my aunt deserted me. Only for me to find out other things that weren’t shared. So, some ‘bombs’ are being dropped on me right now, and I am not sure just how much more I can take. And now you're all here.” Then she fixed her gaze on Michelle. Michelle was in shock. This woman was going through nothing less than hell. She felt for her. Then looked at her daughter.
“I need to speak with you alone,” she said directing her comment to Michelle. “Aunt Irna. May Michelle and I go speak in the back room, please?” Michelle looked at her.
“You can say anything out here. Since you seem to be getting everything out in the open,” she said softly.
“Sure, dear. Go ahead. We’ll watch Ashley,” answered Irna. Ashley looked up at her with her mouth covered in cheese sauce.
“Daddy’s with the angels. Mommy says he looks over us,” she said with her mouth full. Rebecca looked at her daughter with warmth.
“Snoogie. You stay here and finish your dinner. Mommy will be right back, okay?”
“Ho-kay,” she replied. Then Rebecca switched her gaze back to Michelle.
“I need to talk with you for a moment.” She rose and grabbed Michelle’s hand. Michelle got up and followed after her. Rebecca walked to the back room returning Michelle to Irna’s bedroom.

She closed the door. “I know what you’re thinking,” she said.
“Is that my daughter? Ashley?” Michelle asked. “Oh my God. I never thought I would see her. She looks nothing like the man who raped me. I don’t know what or how to feel, right now. Angry? Happy? Relieved she is doing so well? Is she smart? Does she have friends? What are you going to do? Have you made plans?” Michelle started rattling off questions. Her mind was running a million miles a second. Her daughter. She looked at Rebecca who sat down on the edge of the bed watching her with sadness in her eyes. A tear streamed down her left cheek. Then another down her right cheek. She blinked and tears ran down both cheeks. Michelle paused having realized her ramblings.
“Oh. I’m so sorry. You just shared news about your cancer. Here I am asking about Ashley. That is so callous of me. I am so sorry.” Rebecca looked at her then down at the floor as Michelle sat down next to her on the bed.
“She’s not your daughter,” said Rebecca.
“Wha-a-at? She looks like me. She has my eyes. My hair. Of course, she’s my daughter. I mean your daughter, but I gave her to you because of Claire. Claire convinced me that would be the best thing for her,” said Michelle. “You know that’s true.” Rebecca lifted a thick silver locket that was resting on her chest held by a lovely silver chain around her neck. She removed the heavy locket from her and opened it.
“The picture on the left was my husband. The picture on the right is Ashley.” She showed Michelle. She noticed he had black hair and blue eyes. Then pressed a dainty clamp in the middle on the right. A section lifted. She flipped it revealing another baby picture and a tiny lock of hair tied with a very petit pink ribbon in the pocket.
“This was Mary. She was the baby you shared with me.” Michelle stared at the picture and small lock of hair. She pulled it out and smelled it. She caught a hint. “She died of crib death when she was almost 3-months.” Michelle starred at the picture holding the lock of hair to her nose as tears started forming in her eyes. She looked back at Rebecca and her teary eyes. “I’m so sorry. I didn’t know how to reach you. You made it clear you didn’t want to know anything about her given the circumstances.” She added softly.
Michelle quietly commented, “I thought you couldn’t have children. That’s what Claire said.”

"The doctor was wrong. I found out I was over 2-months pregnant after you had left. It was a fluke. And a blessing." Rebecca reached over and put her arm around Michelle. "If you want, you can keep the picture and the lock of hair," she heartfully offered.
"No," replied Michelle. "You were her mother," she said with a broken heart. "I gave her to you. I…" she clutched the picture and hair to her heart. "Where is she, now?"
"She's buried in a cemetery outside of Portland. I can send you the location if you want to ever visit her," offered Rebecca.
"I would very much like that. Thank you," she replied. "Mind if we sit here a few more minutes?" she asked.
"Fuck them. We can stay in here all night if we want," replied Rebecca. "But I think I would like some more wine." she tried to carefully change the mood.
"It must have been very hard for you. I can't imagine all you have been going through. Or even what you are going through, now," said Michelle.
"It was very hard. But…I am extremely fortunate to have found love from a man who I adored. I have the sweetest little girl. I have wonderful friends. Yes. Life is running short for me, which really pisses me off. It is what it is, so I am trying to make peace where I need to," Rebecca responded.
"What about Ashley? What's going to happen to her?"
Rebecca looked at Michelle then down at the floor. "I have some wonderful friends. A lesbian couple who has always been there for me. Ashley just thinks the world of them. They are going to raise her. The paperwork is almost done. I wanted to make sure Irna knew. That was part of my trip."
"Well. If there is ever anything I can do, please…let me know."
"Sure. Make sure to give me your information, okay?"
"Ok." Michelle paused and wiped away the tears. She had to stop crying and pull herself together. She could cry more later. "May I be so bold as to ask one more thing?"
"Sure," Rebecca looked Michelle in the eyes.
"Can I come up to Portland before going back to Chicago? I would love to see you, meet your friends and visit Mary." Michelle was hoping she wasn't over-stepping.
"Sure. You are welcome anytime," she answered. They stood up and embraced each other. The hug seemed to last an hour, but it was only a few long moments. They understood each other. When they

separated, Rebecca asked Michelle, "You ready to go back out there?"
"Yes," replied Michelle. "Let's do this." She replaced the lock of hair and closed the locket. She gently placed the necklace around Rebecca's neck and softly positioned the locket back in its resting place on her chest. They hugged again then left the room to return to their dinner.

*****

After Rebecca and Michelle left the table, Alex and Scott looked towards Irna searching for answers. They were unclear about the events of the evening.
"What's going on?" asked Scott.
"What do you mean, dear?" replied Irna as she took a bite of her chicken then followed with a sip of wine. Alex looked at her.
"You know what he means. What's going on?" Alex reiterated.
"How would Rebecca and Michelle know each other?"
"How much do you know about Michelle and her past?" Irna asked. Alex stared at her. She was quizzing him. He wasn't sure why. He had a feeling, but there was uncertainty. "Let me just state that my sister, Claire, was a manipulative bitch. I loved her. She was my sister. So I can say that."
"Oka-a-a-y," said Alex unclear where this was going.
"As I shared, we lived in Portland. She met your sister in Portland. Rebecca lives in Portland. So, they all knew each other." Irna took another bite of chicken with some mashed potatoes, then took a sip of water. Alex's eyes widened. He elbowed Scott and looked at him. They both suddenly understood remembering Michelle's tale.
"O-o-o-ohhhh," they both said in unison. Alex and Scott both took large drinks of their wine, then looked at Ashley. Irna noticed the behavior. She now knew that Michelle had shared her story with them. She knew she didn't need to say anymore. "Shit," said Alex.
"Watch your language around the young one," Irna said softly chastising Alex for the use of an explicative.
"Sorry," said Alex apologetically. He switched his gaze to Ashley who was happily enjoying her macaroni and cheese. "How is your dinner, Ashley?" he asked.
"It's weally good! I wike the hot dogth!" she said with her mouthful. Her face was slowly being covered with the cheese sauce. She

clumsily reached over, picking up her glass, and shakily brought it to her mouth taking a sip. She replaced it while licking her lips. Scott just watched her, then picked up his napkin.
"Hey, Ashley. One second, sweetheart." He reached over and wiped her mouth removing the sauce remnants from her face. "There you go," he said, feeling accomplished. He took a few bites of his food. He was hungry. Alex was periodically looking back towards Irna's room. They all seemed to be waiting for something.
"She told you, didn't she?" asked Irna.
"Yes," said Alex.
"Good. Hopefully, they can clear things up a bit," she added.
"Did you know about her cancer?" asked Alex.
"I just found out about it the other day. We have been estranged. My sister made sure of that, but I think this visit will change a few things," she replied.
"What about…you know?" he gestured towards Ashely with a nod.
"Arrangements have been made. That's all taken care of. That, I am sure is one of the topics being mentioned back there."
"Just like that?" asked Alex.
"It's between them. We'll see," replied Irna.
"Don't you have a say?" asked Scott.
"Scott. I'm an old lady. So, no. I don't have a say. And I think it's the right thing to do. She made a good decision," she replied.
"But...," Alex looked at her. She simply raised her finger and waved it.
"Let's wait to see what happens. Okay?" she stated cutting him off. He nodded.

The three ate and drank making small talk about the meal. Scott got up and refilled their wine and water glasses. Alex got up and refilled Ashley's juice glass and dropped the last bits of macaroni and cheese into her bowl to finish. They waited until finally, they returned to the table. They looked like they had been crying, but there were subtle smiles. Alex looked at Michelle.
"You okay?" she asked.
"I'm okay," she answered. Irna looked over at Rebecca asking the same question with her eyes. Rebecca softly smiled back to reassure Irna everything was under control. She softly nodded showing understanding.
"I'm hungry. My food is cold, though," observed Rebecca.

"Oh. Sorry, Rebecca. There's more in the oven staying warm. Alex?" Irna gave him the look requesting his assistance. He rose and retrieved her plate.
"I'll take care of that. One sec," and scurried off to the kitchen and refreshed her plate with warm food returning it to her moments later.
"Thank you, Alex," said Rebecca, appreciatively.
"You're welcome," he said.
"Okay." chimed Scott. "So, what happened back there? Are you going to share?" he asked. Michelle looked at both him and Alex.
"I'll tell you when we get home. Let's just have dinner and enjoy the moment," she replied and looked at Rebecca for solidarity. She didn't want to relive the moment right away. She felt at peace. She needed to cry more, but for now, they needed to simply be with each other.
"She's right. Let's just have dinner and enjoy each other's company for a bit," Rebecca stated in agreement. Irna slowly ate feeling the calm that hit the group. Alex and Scott would learn from Michelle, later.
Rebecca looked at Irna. She smiled. Irna did not know everything yet. She did not know about what happened with Mary. She would tell her later, as well. She would work on finalizing some things for which she needed closure. She decided at that moment she would stay another day to reconcile. It was important, and time was short. She learned much from Irna and was now beginning to understand why things turned out the way they did.

The rest of the evening was finishing dinner, learning about Irna as a mathematician, and hearing about Rebecca's husband before he died. Ashley brought delight to the conversations with her welcomed childish interruptions. She showed off her artistic talents sharing her unicorn coloring book with completed pages of rainbow manes, tails, horns, and other magical ingredients captured in the illustrations. The group carried on until around eleven-thirty after Scott and Irna loaded her dishwasher and cleaned the kitchen. Rebecca and Michelle seemed to have developed a newfound bond and exchanged contact information and phone numbers. They all parted ways with hugs. It was a night to remember. A night when the ghosts of the past seemed to be put to rest. As Michelle, Scott, and Alex rode in the cab home, Michelle knew she would have a deep sleep. She had only one more ghost to face tomorrow.

The three arrived home and once in the house, Scott hung his jacket and brushed ahead into the kitchen.
"Water or wine anyone?" he asked as he opened the refrigerator.
"Water, please," answered Alex.
"Water for me, too," replied Michelle. Scott filled three water glasses and returned to the living room where Alex and Michelle sat.
"Here you go," Scott said as he handed them each their glasses then sat down on the sofa next to Alex. "So, what happened?" he asked.
"Yes. What happened with Rebecca?" asked Alex.
"I can't explain it. Let's just say we have an unusual bond," she replied.
"What about Ashley?" asked Alex. He needed to know what was going to happen to her. Michelle had a calm on her face. There was a sad peacefulness that seemed like a veil over her countenance.
"Rebecca has made arrangements for her," she answered.
"yes, but…" Alex tried to continue. She interrupted.
"Alex. Ashley is going to be well taken care of. That is what we all need to know. Okay? Please?" she replied. She did not want to say anymore right now. She did not want to cry anymore in front of them. She was 'good' inside.
"Okay. Fine. But promise me you will tell us a bit more before you leave?" he asked.
"I will. I'm going to bed. You should too. It's been a long night," she said getting up. "Good night." Then leaned over and pecked Alex and Scott on the heads and made her way upstairs to her room. Alex and Scott just watched her. They cared for her.
"Must have been some conversation they had, huh?" commented Scott to Alex.
"Absolutely." Replied Alex in agreement. "I hope she tells us what happened soon."
"She will. So much drama! I can't wait for things to calm down," said Scott. "let's go to bed. I'm tired," he said.
'You got it, Pontiac," replied Alex. And they rose from the sofa, picked up the glasses and dropped them off in the kitchen then head upstairs to their room.
"What a fucking day," said Scott.
"I concur," said Alex.

.

Hump Days Are Meant To Persevere

Michelle had slept throughout the night to awaken just after nine am, finding the house empty. Alex and Scott had already left for their days, and she was scheduled to have lunch with Dom at Vivande's. She was feeling groggy, emotionally drained, but lighter. She felt as if a fog was lifting from her consciousness of which she did not realize was there before. She was a little nervous about her lunch, but not scared. "Ugh." She grunted as she pushed herself from the warm and cozy bed. She was tempted to just call and cancel her lunch date but couldn't. It was something she knew she needed to do. She pushed herself from the bed and prepared for the day.

Michelle decided on something simple. A pair of jeans, her recently purchased sneakers, and a black blouse. She looked out her bedroom to see it was partly cloudy. The trees in the neighborhood seemed to be waving a little, indicating a breeze. She touched the window to feel the chill. "Brrrr," she whispered. "I'll never understand why it's so warm or hot everywhere else but freezing here." She muttered to herself. She pulled a linen scarf from her bag and headed downstairs to the kitchen. "I hope they left me some coffee." When she arrived at the kitchen, she saw some boxes laid out with packing paper, bubble wrap, and tape. "I guess they are going to start packing soon." She said aloud and then smiled when she noticed the carafe with a little note in front of the coffee cup left for her.

"Sorry to have left so early this morning. We thought it best not to wake you. Apologies for the mess. We have to start packing, soon to get ready for our move.
If you want, come by the store. Good luck with your lunch with Dom.
We love you.
S & A xoxo"

The note brought a smile to her face. "Thanks for not pushing me, guys," she said staring at the note. They did not reference the dinner topics or request her to tell them anything. They just allowed her to work through things in her own time. She put the note down and poured herself some coffee and organized a bowl with yogurt, grapes, strawberries, and some blueberries from the fridge.

Her cell phone vibrated. It was a series of three texts from Dom.
"Looking 4ward to seeing u."
"I'll probably be early."
"Just in case you want to meet earlier."

She texted back, "see you at 11:30". She was not going to arrive earlier. She wanted to ease into the day. She proceeded with her breakfast. After finishing eating, she cleaned her dishes, refilled her coffee then went into the garden. She wondered if Scott and Alex would miss this place. She felt bad that they had so much going on. She also felt a little guilty that she had put them through so much during her visit. She would find a way to repay them for their kindness. They wouldn't expect it, but it was something she wanted to do. After sitting a while in the garden with the chill in the air, she looked at her watch noticing the time had flown. It was time to go. She dropped off her mug in the sink and scurried to the foyer where she put on her jacket and grabbed her purse. Out she flew mumbling to herself, "Let's do this."

Michelle arrived on time to find Dominic standing in front of the restaurant. She wasn't sure if she should hug him given how she left their last encounter and their phone call.

"Hi," she said with a light smile and a glint of hope in her eyes.

"Hi," he replied. He had a look of uncertainty. He didn't know what to expect. "You look great," he said, complimenting her. "Should we just go in? They just unlocked the doors." He moved towards the door and opened it for her.

"Thanks. Sure," she replied and brushed past him entering the restaurant. Anthony rushed to greet them. He was in his usual outfit.

White pressed button-down oxford shirt with black slacks and black shoes. He added a black unbuttoned vest to his repertoire for the day.
"Welcome! Welcome!" he said. "You here for lunch so early?" she asked smiling.
"Yes sir," replied Dom. "Michelle" he motioned to her on his right, "picked the place. She said it was really good."
"She's smart," he said then pointed to his head. "Smart woman." He turned his gaze to her then back to Dom. "I like smart beautiful women. You better watch out. I might steal her from you." He winked jokingly then laughed.
"Oh…you stop it, you old fool! Leave them alone!" yelled Giselle from behind the counter. She came rushing out. Michelle and Dom were smiling. It seemed like a little show. "Don't mind him He's just being a foolish Italian." She smiled warmly and pinched her husband's side then kissed him. She looked at her husband, fondly. "Go sit them already. I'll get the Prosecco," she ordered and scuttled off.
"Would it be possible to get the front window seat in the corner there?" she asked, remembering the suggestion from Scott…. or was it, Alex? She forgot but just shook it off.
"Sure. Sure," replied Anthony as he pulled the menus then guided them to their table. "I'll get your water. Flat or sparkling?" he asked.
"Flat," they both replied in unison as they situated themselves.
Giselle was quick to arrive with their glasses of Prosecco. "Our specials today are Pasta Carbonaro and pan-fried sole with some Italian roasted potatoes and steamed broccoli dressed with a lemon sauce." She paused. "You think about it. "Would you like some wine? It's listed there on the back of the menu," she asked.
"We'll look it over. Thanks so much," replied Dom. She smiled and walked off. Anthony then returned and dropped off the water glasses and a small decanter they could use to refill it on their own. After a few moments reviewing the menu, Anthony returned and took their orders. Michelle decided on the Pasta Carbonara with a small side salad and a glass of Pinot Grigio. Dominic ordered angel hair pasta with meat sauce. He opted for an iced tea.
"What's with the wine offering everywhere you eat, here? Every time I go to any restaurant, they give you a wine list and menu when you sit down…then they offer you flat or sparkling water? Why not

just give water and leave it at that?" He shook his head then looked out the window then back at her and smiled.
"Well," she said. "Alex shared with me that JB, the man he works for, is a radio host who talks about political hot topics during the week and reviews food, wine, and travel on Saturdays. He's learned that this area attracts a large number of chefs given its proximity to the wine regions of Napa and Sonoma. It's also an agricultural region and state. They love their cuisine here. It's really interesting," she answered. "I had no idea, either until my visit." She finished her Prosecco and then took a sip of water. Anthony returned and dropped off Dom's iced tea and collected their empty Prosecco glasses.
"And what's 'Prosecco'? Isn't it champagne?" he asked. "Tastes like it." She giggled.
"It's Italian sparkling wine. Alex told me that Champagne only comes from the Champagne region in France. There's this big hullabaloo about Champagne versus Sparkling wine," she smirked while playing with her glass. She didn't realize how much she was learning during her visit.
"Hm," grunted Dominic. "Anyway…how are you?" he asked with sincerity. She was about to answer then paused. Their food was being delivered. Once they were finally alone without any more disturbances, she felt as if she could finally talk.
"I know I left without telling you much. I just needed to get away. There were a lot of things that were going on in my mind," she said as she started eating and tasting her food. She was hungry and started getting a little nervous.
"Like what? You're pregnant. And which I should remind you that you should not be drinking," he said looking at her. '*Oh, shit*' she thought to herself. She realized her mistake. "I mean…I guess you could have one glass of something light…like that Prosecco, but now a glass of wine? You have a baby inside. *Our baby,*" he whispered leaning in towards her. She knew she couldn't work up to it. She just had to tell him. Then the words came out.
"I miscarried," she said. "Shortly before my trip, I miscarried. I was alone. You had visited and then you were off on assignment and couldn't get back. I didn't know how to tell you. And I didn't want to tell you over the phone." She watched his face and could see the light in his eyes just fade before her.

"What?" he asked softly. "You mean…" He stopped and then sat back in his chair. He looked her in the eyes and then looked out the window then at his food then down to his lap.
"I'm sorry. It was so hard. I was hurt and getting depressed. I had to get away." she said. Then she took a sip of her wine. Then a tear rolled down her right cheek, then another down her left. He looked up at her and saw her tears. He had a forlorn look on his face. She never saw him so sad. "So you're not pregnant?" he asked.
"I was. And now I'm not. I saw my doctor. It just happened. There was nothing that caused it. It just happened. I'm so sorry." She moved her left hand and reached for his.
"I wish you would have told me." He reached into his pocket and pulled out his wallet. There was a little pocket under the credit cards. He pulled out a small folded up elastic pink ribbon that had a tiny little flower on it. He placed it in her hand and then held it with the ribbon in-between their touch. "I was walking in the airport after you shared the news. I was so happy. I saw this. I know we didn't know if it was a girl or boy, but when I saw this ribbon, it just felt like I needed to buy it. I guess I kind of hoped for a little girl," he said quietly. "Are you okay? I mean…are you really okay?" he asked. She pulled her hand from his and held the ribbon and stared at it with affection, massaging it with her fingers.
"Yes. I'm better, now. This trip was something I needed. It helped me through it," she replied.
"Do you still love me?" he asked warmly.
"Yes," she replied.
"Can we try again?" he asked. "You know…you don't have to answer that now. I'm sorry." He caught himself. She looked up at him from the ribbon.
"Yes," she said. "Not right away though. Give me another month or two. Okay?" she answered. He took a deep breath and exhaled. "I do love you. I'm sorry."
"You have nothing to be sorry about. I just wish you would have told me sooner, that's all. I would have moved mountains to get to you. I'm sorry for not being there. I can't imagine what you went through. And you were alone…" He paused. He held back his frustration. It was not her fault. "I'm sad. We'll get through this. Then we'll try again," he forced a small smile. Michelle could see the hurt was still there. He had every right to feel as he did. She didn't blame him. "Now I understand. So…now what?" he asked.

"How long is this trip? I need to tell my boss when I can get back, but he did give me a little time…"
"Well," she said. "I have a new contract that starts in a few weeks. I do need to do something first before going back."
"What's that?" he asked.
"I need to go up to Portland…Oregon," she replied.
"Why do you need to go to Portland? And for how long?" he asked.
"I have a friend that I knew before I met you. She is here visiting her aunt. It was a surprise running into her. Anyway…she is going through some things and I offered to help her with something. Just for a few days. Maybe a week. I'm not sure. But I'll head back. I should be home in about two to three weeks at most," she answered. She did not think he needed to know everything about the past that didn't concern him. She also did not feel like reliving the experience at the moment. She wanted to move forward.
"Two to three weeks?" he asked.
"Well, yes. Maybe. Alex and Scott have to move. JB, the guy Alex works for, has to move and Scott's closing his store…which is across the street and up about half a block. I think I should stick around a few more days and help them out before leaving. They have been so gracious and kind. Wanna go see his store?" she asked.
"Nah. It's closing. So, what's there to see? It seems like a lot of drama going on with everyone here. I think I'll just head back to my hotel and do some work. Why not you do the things you need to do. And we can see each other later. Do you want to have dinner tonight?" he asked.
"You sure?"
"Yes. I'm sure," he answered.
"Okay then. Dinner tonight. I'll come to your hotel around seven. Is that okay?"
"Seven it is. The Marriott Marquis."
"Great." They both smiled at each other. She reached back out and squeezed his hand. She felt better. They both knew where they stood. They would be together soon.

Dominic and Michelle spent the rest of their lunch commenting on the food and other topics attempting to catch up on lost time. After Dominic had another iced tea and ordered Michelle another glass of Pinot Grigio, Michelle shared some of the things she had seen, and about her new friend Irna including how she took care of Scott and Alex for their dinner parties. He enjoyed listening to

Michelle share her stories about Gay Pride and just shook his head laughing as she regaled him with the escapades of men wearing feather boas and the lesbian cyclists. She seemed so excited about life again. Something he hadn't seen in a while. When she shared her thought about becoming a teacher, he became excited. He had a friend with whom he could connect her to teach at a Catholic school in Ottawa. He wouldn't push it, though. He started thinking about the possibilities and was happy about her new contract. At the end of their lunch, they looked around to notice the restaurant was full and they had been there for over two hours. It was time to go. They rose from the table after having paid the check. They walked out of the front of the restaurant and deeply hugged. Before separating, they kissed.

"Too long since we kissed," she said.

"Yes. Maybe we can kiss some more tonight?" he commented and smiled at her.

"We'll see," she said with a hint of flirtation. "See you later." She turned to make her way to the store.

"See you at seven!" he said loudly, then hailed a cab to make his way back to the hotel.

*****

Scott and Troy were unexpectedly busy at the store thanks to Troy's stop on the Castro Tuesday night. He used his gay telegraphing skills to spread the word about Scott's shop closing sale. When Michelle arrived at his store, there were drag queens, two Sisters of Perpetual Indulgence, several 'Daddies', and a handful of Dykes rummaging through the sale items. The Pride section was thinning out quickly. Scott looked up and noticed Michelle scanning the room.

"Hey, girl! Welcome back!" he yelled from the upper landing. The Sisters looked around then turned to catch Michelle behind them.

"I'm Sister Chanel and I approve your outfit," she said waving her hand up and down, then turned and resumed her shopping. Michelle smiled. She made her way through the crowd and up to Scott. As she neared him, the phone rang. He raised his fingers to Michelle to hold off a moment.

"I got it, Troy!" he yelled down.

"Good! Cuz I'm busy, Ho!" and he refocused his attention on the two beefy Daddies in front of him holding 4 bottles of lube while he was gathering the penis stemmed rainbow rimmed martini glasses.
"Hello? Scott's Closet! I'm Scott and I'm out!" he answered.
"Hey, Scott. Aarav. I tried to call you on your other phone. You got a sec?" he asked.
"Sure. What's up?" he changed his tone to one of a more serious nature.
"Did you ever hear from the police?" he asked.
"No. But as I said before, I don't hang out much with Gabriel nor do I know many of the people he hangs out with…other than you. So, I don't think I would have been any help. Why? Is he okay?" Scott asked concerned.
"That's why I'm calling. They found out some information. As you know, the guy he fucked around with really screwed up his relationship with Veronica," said Aarav reiterating some of what was shared previously.
"yeh. So?" replied Scott.
"Well, get this. The guy goes to some bar on Pride day. Meets this skinhead and I guess he started spouting off about Gabe. But didn't say anything about what his part in it was. He hid the fact that he was bi in his story. The police found out that the skinhead is part of some hate group in the Sacramento area. They came into town to '*express their beliefs*'. So, when they were heading to get more beers at a bar near Pride, they crossed paths with Gabe. The skinhead was on a mission. Gabe got caught in a wrong-place-wrong-time situation."
"Shit! No kidding," said Scott in disbelief.
"The reason I'm calling is that what happened to Gabe was a combination of revenge and a hate crime. Both guys are being charged. I and a few other friends were able to get Gabe to press charges. But I wanted you to know. Just be careful around Civic Center and when you guys go out in the Castro, okay? Hate crimes have been going up. I asked about it and the police said that the California Department of Justice said that if this keeps up, the trend is like a twenty percent rise in the past six years. Gay men seem to be more targeted. Just be careful, okay?"
"Yeh. You're a ray of sunshine. Thanks for the info, Aarav. We will. Gabe okay?" asked Scott.

"He's recovering It'll be a few weeks before he's going out and to the gym. He'll be fine."
"Okay. Thanks. Wish him a speedy recovery from us, okay?"
"Will do. Talk soon." And with that, Aarav hung up. Scott slowly returned the phone to its cradle.
"Shit," he muttered.
"What was that?" inquired Michelle. Is everything okay?
"Yes. That was Aarav. He was giving me an update about Gabe."
"What about him?" she asked. "Is he okay?"
"Yes. He'll recover. But the beating he took was both revenge and a hate crime. Some skinhead from the Sacramento area who is part of some group that hates gay people. Aarav was just giving us a heads up to be careful when we go out." He paused. "And I was having a good day, too!" he said.
"Let's focus on the good stuff. You have a crowd down there with a flirtatious clerk who may have a date tonight," she said observing Troy writing down some information on a piece of paper and handing it to the daddies. She laughed lightly through her words.
Scott looked down and smiled broadly.
"He is such a slut, sometimes," he said endearingly. "If this keeps up today, I won't have too much more to pack."
"Well then let's see how we can make that happen," chimed Michelle.
"Okay," said Scott in agreement. "Wait a minute. How did lunch go?" he asked.
"Better than I thought. We're having dinner tonight at his hotel. Do you mind me skipping out tonight?" she asked.
"Not at all. Good for you, girl. Was he okay with the news?"
"He's hurt of course. We both have some healing to do, but I think we'll be fine," she said trying to reassure herself. "He wants to try again."
"Do you think that's a good idea? I mean…I don't know... just asking."
"I told him to give it a little time, but yes. I would like to try again. We just need to get through this first. We'll see," she answered.
"Anyway, I am going to see him tonight. We'll talk more."
"You coming home afterward?" asked Scott teasingly.
"Maybe," she sang mystically and grinned. Scott nudged her. She nudged him back.

"Okay. I'll stop playing mother hen, now. You gonna help me close this place and sell some shit?" he asked.
"Absolutely!" she replied happy that they changed the subject.
They both joined the crowd and engaged with the potential customers handling some of the items with consideration. Michelle was drawn to the man flinging around his rainbow boa holding a beige porcelain bowl with what appeared to have a ring of men around the edges. She at first thought they were in a Conga line. When she looked closer with her customer, it was much different than she thought causing her to snicker.

Moving Forward

Scott and Alex were hanging the contemporary Russian art prints down JB's freshly painted staircase. They had finished the "wall-of-art" as JB called it in the dining room and had also hung the glass chandelier. Alex kept commenting that the light fixture was 'noisy' given all the clear and blue glass loosely hanging bobbles kept clacking with each other. JB's place was coming together quickly. They still had to organize the garage spaces. JB was sitting in his new office space listening to his Mob Music CD and talking with his sister in Florida while they finished with the artwork placement.
"I can't believe it's already July 8th, can you?" Scott asked Alex.
"Nope. Just think. In two months, we will be in Tahiti! September 4th, 2001, we leave and will be in a warm tropical location. I can't wait!" Alex replied.
"Me either. It's been a month, hasn't it?"
"It has. I spoke with Irna the other day. She and Rebecca are starting to talk more. Rebecca still doesn't want her to come up yet. I think it's bothering her."
"I bet. She never really did share everything that went on between them. What do you think?" asked Scott.
"I think she will tell us when she is ready. One thing I know is to be patient with people. They'll share when they're ready," he answered.
"Well. You know me I lack patience. It is not one of my finer qualities." joked Scott. Alex just looked at him and raised an eyebrow and nodded in agreement.
"You? Patient?" he laughed.
"Okay. Okay. I am working on it." Then he changed the subject.
"Did you hear from your sister since she left for Portland? I spoke

with her the other day. She is planning on heading back to Chicago on the 10th. Dom is going to meet her there."
"Yes. She and I talked. She met the couple, Trisha and Elise, who is going to care for Ashley. She really likes them. They are going to keep in touch. I guess they live in 'Beaverton'." he answered. "She and Rebecca seem to have a nice friendship." He struggled with one of the pictures. "Hold the bottom of the picture for a sec, would please?" he asked so he could position the hook behind it.
"Thanks…Anyway. After talking with Elise, she made up her mind that the contract she has in Chicago will be her last one and she is going to make a career change and become a teacher. She thinks grade school."
"Wow. Good for her! You think she'll come back to see us again?"
"We'll see. I just hope it's less drama. I think we've had our share this past month, don't you?" said Alex as he secured the hook.
"Agreed. But JB is our drama every day. I mean, c'mon. he was in the hospital again the evening of July 4th. Same thing as last time. I swear, it's something else and not his heart," said Scott.
"The doctors will figure it out. I'm just glad he was off-air and was able to take the long weekend. I have a feeling the station will play his reading of the Declaration of Independence every July 4th. It always gets high ratings."
"And his '*best of*s'…except for the Dining Program yesterday. You guys worked your butts off getting that program together. Here we were moving and getting settled and you're dealing with cancellation calls and rescheduling calls…let's just 'impressive'. You're amazing, Schmoo," said Scott.
"Thanks, Smoo," said Alex. "Okay…the wall's done. What do you think?" he said standing back assessing their work."
"Looks great," said Scott. "I have to say…I like our new place. It's smaller. It was easy to get settled. We have a few things we need to buy, but generally, it's set. It came out nice. I do want to pick up some floor and ceramic tiling this next weekend, though, okay?" he asked.
"Sure!" Alex replied and looked at his watch. "Okay. It's half-past one. What's next?" he asked.
"I think we need to take a break and get out of the house. How about we go for a walk on the beach…down by the Cliff House?" he asked.
"Okay. Let's check in with JB," suggested Alex.

"Cool."
Alex and Scott put the tools away then visited JB in his office space, just off his bedroom. He had just gotten off the phone with his sister and getting ready to call his other one to whom he referenced as '*lard ass*'.
"How 's the family?" asked Alex. JB turned from his desk and looked up at the couple.
"Good. Good. They need more money. You and I will need to go to the bank tomorrow. I will write up some checks today if you wouldn't mind updating QuickBooks with the information."
"No problem," replied Alex.
"Baby sister's just moaning about all the cats 'lard ass' has. And she thinks a house is coming up and the end of their block that might be good for her kids as they go to college. Who knows?" he complained. "It's always something with them. She also wants to go up to Hornell and visit her friend's next weekend. I guess she and Will are arguing again."
"Sorry to hear," said Alex limiting his comments and response.
"How's the artwork project coming along?" JB asked.
"All done. Scott and I are going to go for a walk on the beach. Do you mind? Would you be okay for a little bit?" he asked.
"Oh. Sure. You guys have been hard at it. Nice job on all of the work you've been doing," JB said complimenting them. Scott smiled.
"I'm glad to do it," said Scott. "It's fun. I can't wait to hit that garden of yours." JB chuckled at the comment.
"Heinrich…you're like a taskmaster and an energizer bunny in one. I swear, we are going to get you that riding-crop to slap against your leg one day," JB joked. "How's the job front coming?"
"Sabrina and I were talking the other day. She knows someone who knows someone at this company called Pitney Bowes. They might have an opening coming up for a Trainer to cover their Northern California territory. We'll see. In the meantime, this gives me time to get that garden of yours in shape so you can have the housewarming party you wanted," replied Scott.
"Good. How is Sabrina, anyway?" asked JB.
"She's good. She wishes Chris would get off his ass and marry her, already. They've been together a while. I don't get why he doesn't. I feel bad for her. But I guess he is also talking about girls' soccer.

She doesn't know what to make of it all. I don't blame her. It's frustrating," he replied.
"Well…next time you talk with her, say hi for me, would you?" said JB.
"Sure!" Scott replied. Alex gave Scott a look hinting they need to go if they were going to go for their walk. Scott took the hint and started backing up.
"What do you want to do for dinner tonight?" asked Alex.
"I think I am going to have a can of Spam and some potato chips. Can you make sure my Diet Coke is in the front on the second shelf in the fridge?" JB asked.
"How about I put it out on the counter next to your glass and you can just add ice to it? I'll set up your plate, too, and put the chips out. Would that work?
"Perfect," replied JB. "You guys go have fun. See you in the morning, Alex. Thanks for all of your work. I'll look at it when I go downstairs after I talk with 'lard ass'."
"See you. We'll check in with you when we get back before going home across the street," said Alex. "Love you!"
"Love you!" added Scott.
"Love you, too, boys," he replied.

Alex and Scott left the house and stepped into the sunshine. It was almost seventy degrees and the chilly ocean breeze made it feel much cooler. The sky was a crisp clear blue above. After they got in the car, they made their way to Geary Boulevard via Cabrillo to 18th. As they made their way to the ocean, they could see the heavy fog bank sitting out on the ocean. It was clear now, but the fog would come in later and cover the city like a blanket before the evening would set in.
"It's beautiful, today. Thanks for doing this, Schmoo," said Scott.
"It was a good idea," replied Alex. "You have been busting your butt helping get JB settled. You pretty much got our place set up…which looks great, by the way."
"We both painted and did all we could, Schmoo. Teamwork," said Scott. He reached over and grabbed Alex's right hand and held it. Then he reached up and pulled back the inside sunroof cover to allow the sun to shine in the car. Alex opened the sunroof to cool off the hot interior.

They rode in silence with a "Queer As Folk" music CD playing. Scott would do his little car-dancing while Alex would roll his eyes and call him crazy. Scott would just chuckle. Make his weird face with a goofy half-smile. His mouth was open and he waved his hands and arms. After about five minutes into it, Scott stopped and put his left hand on Alex's leg until they reached their destination fifteen minutes later. There were plenty of parking spaces along the Ocean Beach waterfront. After they parked, they took off their shoes, placed them in the trunk, then headed directly to the sandy beach about 18 feet away from their parking spot. The breeze was consistently blowing their freshly cut hair. They had gone to see Cesar at Rick's Barbershop on Geary and 18th early Friday morning, as they did every four to five weeks.

"It's really beautiful down here. Windy, but beautiful," said Scott.

"It is," said Alex.

"You okay, Schmoo? You got quiet." Scott asked and moved to the left of Alex and grabbed his hand. He really enjoyed walking and holding hands with his soulmate.

"I'm fine. I was just thinking. About Irna and her niece, Rebecca. And everything that Michelle has gone through. I feel for them. I know it all turned out okay, but I just feel a little sad for them, you know?"

"You have such a big heart, Schmoo. I mean…I get it. I feel a little sad for all they went through, too." He paused and looked up at the sky as they turned and started walking parallel to the water towards the Cliff House. The bright sun caused him to squint his eyes then he looked back down at the sand. "Did I tell you I spoke with Irna on the phone when I was cleaning up the store before doing the final lock? She called me unexpectedly."

"No. What'd she say?"

"She just really appreciated us coming for dinner and would like to do it again, soon. She said that she and Rebecca had cleared up a few things and that she would share them with us sometime. I told her we would be happy to listen anytime..." then he smiled and nudged Alex with a light comment, joking, "You know me. I love listening to people's stories." But then she said something a little odd that just hit me…"

"What was that?" asked Alex.

"The way she referred to Rebecca. She said Rebecca was very special to her."

"Hm. Don't try to read that much into it," Alex suggested.

"Anyway, they have a few months to finish working everything out.

I am sure they will. I just think it's exciting that I have a niece up in Portland. I am still waiting for Michelle to tell us what happened in the bedroom between her and Rebecca. Every time I have asked, she just smiles and says, 'it's a woman thing'. Then she says she'll tell me sometime. I also asked if I could go visit Ashley. She told me to give her a few years to get through what she needs to. She is about to go through a very difficult time and needs her stability right now and not to worry. Can you imagine? Not seeing my niece? But I have to trust her."
"I get what she's saying. I mean, think about it. She's about to lose her mom. She already lost her dad. Now she's going to be raised by a whole other couple. I am guessing that her dad was an only child, otherwise, you would think his side of the family would be coming around." commented Scott.
"That's a good point, Smoo. I didn't catch that," said Alex appreciating his lover's insight.
"But you know what?" asked Scott.
"What?" said Alex.
"If it wasn't for you, your sister would not have come to visit. And if she didn't visit, she wouldn't have met Irna who was connected to the person who cared for her child. You're always there to help others, baby. Especially all that you do for JB. You literally changed my whole life exposing me to things I never probably would have experienced. You're amazingly supportive, kind, smart, and handsome. And you have a perfect chest, and you have sugar lips," said Scott complimenting his partner. "We need to turn around. We are getting close to the end here." They walked to perform a 180 reversing their direction still hand-in-hand. "Scott looked down and ahead of them reviewing their tracks in the sand. "You know what else?" he asked.
"What, Smoo?"
"It's not true. Angels do leave footprints." He pulled Alex close to him and they kissed. "You're my angel," he whispered.
"You're mine," said Alex. They kissed again and hugged deeply for a few minutes before continuing their walk.
"I love you."
"I love you, too, Smoo. Tahiti. Two months! September 6th we'll be in Tahiti and on September 8th we board the Paul Gauguin!"

"It will be a great trip! Neither of us has been there, before. So exciting! Gym time has to double up and we need to get new swimsuits," said Scott getting excited.
"I am working on some things to help make it special. Some listeners will be joining the cruise. JB is now going to host a group, and tickets are already selling," Alex said with enthusiasm.
"A dream trip, huh, Schmoo?"
"Yep. Get ready," said Alex.
"We are so fortunate," said Scott.
"Yes, we are," said Alex in agreement as they kept walking along the beach letting the water splash on the feet. "Yes, we are," he whispered.

LGBTQ Resources

GLAAD.ORG
ITGETSBETTER.ORG
GLSEN.ORG
THETREVORPROJECT.ORG
COVENANTHOUSE.ORG
NCFR.ORG

About the Author

Robert Moon is a Talent Development professional who lives in many directions. Robert's early years were spent as a "military brat", living in different places and his continued travels and exposure to five continents with a vast array of cultures fuels his extrovert personality. His travels are far from over. Robert and his husband, Joel, take advantage of the San Francisco Bay Area's scene that include charity auctions, Wine Country functions, and cultural experiences. When home, they enjoy hosting dinner parties…co-hosted by their adorable Morkie, Lola.

Made in the USA
Middletown, DE
20 June 2021